THEME MUSIC

T. MARIE VANDELLY

THEME MUSIC

DUTTON

DUTTON

An imprint of Penguin Random House LLC
penguinrandomhouse.com

LIBRARY OF CONGRESS CATALOGING-IN-PUBLICATION DATA
Names: Vandelly, T. Marie., author
Title: Theme music / T. Marie Vandelly.
Description: New York : Dutton, [2019] |
Identifiers: LCCN 2018048002 (print) | LCCN 2018058062 (ebook) |
ISBN 9781524744717 (ebook) | ISBN 9781524744700 (hc)
Subjects: LCSH: Psychological fiction.
Classification: LCC PS3622.A5876 (ebook) |
LCC PS3622.A5876 T48 2019 (print) | DDC 813/.6—dc23
LC record available at https://lccn.loc.gov/2018048002

Printed in the United States of America
1   3   5   7   9   10   8   6   4   2

Book design by Francesca Belanger

For my mother

THEME MUSIC

PROLOGUE

When I was still in diapers, yet to be stripped of my innocence and tooth hopeful, my father excused himself from the breakfast table, made a casual exit out the back door, crossed to a fabricated shed hunkered in a bone-dry cradle of honeysuckle in the far back corner of our lot, fetched an axe, and dragged a muddy rut back across the dormant lawn. He reentered the kitchen, extra warm and cozy thanks to a turkey in the oven, looked upon the bewildered faces of his adoring family, and butchered them all. Well, not all, of course. I lived. Though I do believe I died a little that day.

The reason he did it is almost as mysterious as why I was spared. Perhaps I was too young to be hated so utterly. Being only eighteen months, I couldn't have pissed anyone off that royally. Maybe my father couldn't bring himself to kill his baby girl. Maybe he came to his senses as he yanked the blade of the axe out of my brother's back, my mother's chest, the kitchen counter, the linoleum flooring, the refrigerator door, any one of the four walls . . . In my younger, darkest days, I believed that I had been spared to live a never-ending life of torment, one last act of cruelty before my father took a butcher knife from the kitchen drawer and dragged it across his throat.

Not that this was told to me as a bedtime story. It wasn't all "chop, chop, chop went the mean ol' giant," lullaby, and good night. Most of the grislier details were saved until I was old enough to handle it, when I could distinguish right from wrong, fact from fiction, the living from the dead, supposedly when I was in the third grade.

It was suggested that my mother took the brunt of the attack while trying to save her four children. Her blood tasted the worst, though I only imagined her blood in my mouth. Crime scene photographs showed that a dark fluid had puddled on the tray of my high chair, Froot Loops floating about like tiny life preservers. I pray I wasn't so dim to have continued to eat, but the annihilation of an entire family might have taken a while, so I may have gotten hungry. Try as I believe she did, my mother could not have stopped him. Her hands were cracked open to the wrists like scallop shells. Maybe she tried to catch the axe as it took a swing at one of her sons. Maybe she had been begging for our lives with clasped hands when the blade cut through to her chest. Whichever is true, Debbie Wheeler died from a great hurt to her heart.

Another theory is that my eldest brother might have been the first to die. Being fifteen, Josh stood the best chance of fending off the attack. *Let's take care of this little problem straight off* was what Billy Wheeler probably thought as he gripped the hilt to get as much force behind his swing as possible.

Next, only because it seems chronologically sound, would have been my eight-year-old brother Eddie. As an expert dodgeball player, Eddie would have known that a moving target would be harder to hit. Or perhaps terror held him perfectly still while his head was lopped off. It was found in the corner next to a ten-pound bag of potatoes our mother had bought for Thanksgiving dinner. How it got there is anyone's guess.

You would have thought my father would have gotten into the swing of things by then, but it still took a dozen or so hacks to bring down his four-year-old son. They found Michael under the table, holding on to our mother's foot with the only hand he had left.

I was found by a neighbor boy, Rory, a friend of Josh's who had stopped by to collect him for the annual Thanksgiving Day tag football game down at the high school. When no one answered his repeated knocks, he let himself in. He told the police that the music struck him first. Not the blood, not the savagery, not Eddie's severed head in the corner, but the heartrending desperation pouring from the speakers in the living room. He covered his ears before it even occurred to him to cover his eyes.

I

The Wheeler family home was for sale. I couldn't believe it. For all my preoccupation over what had transpired in that house, it had never once occurred to me to pay it a visit, or that it might still be standing. In fact, most of my thoughts about the house, and what occurred there, were just those, thoughts. As with most all disturbing nightmares, I banished these horrors to a cerebral purgatory that was unreachable by mere curiosity. On the few occasions I summoned the nerve to type that dreadful address into my search bar, something always stopped me. Like searching the internet for some soft-core porn, you might get more than you bargained for.

The house wasn't much different from the listings it was pinched between: white aluminum siding with charcoal-colored shingles, double mulled windows, and a three-step concrete stoop, a blacktop driveway with a two-car garage . . . Same as a hundred others I had scrolled past. But this particular nondescript house glared just a little brighter than the rest in the Zillow template it was set in. Enough to stop my scrolling finger dead.

6211 Catharpin Road, Franconia, VA.

Yep. That was my old address. The one Aunt Celia had in her address book with a line drawn through it. My old phone number had been in there, too, inked out but still legible. When I was younger and still lived with my aunt, I had dialed the number a thousand times, but always hung up after the first ring, afraid of what might answer.

A slight chill ran down my spine as I leaned closer to study the business-card-sized photograph.

I always imagined the house in a collapse of dusty lumber, the spine of a chimney jutting out among the rubble like a fractured bone. A KEEP OUT warning stabbed in the front lawn, not a RE/MAX signpost. Though it was no more than a thirty- to forty-minute drive away, being on the other side of the beltway, it might as well have been in Beirut. I had asked Aunt Celia to take me once, and she had specifically said that there was nothing to see, which to me meant the house was gone.

But it wasn't gone. She just didn't want me to know it was there. Like everything about my family, Aunt Celia thought I couldn't handle the gory details, when in reality, she was the one with the weak stomach. She had paced the room to tell me how my family died, one hand over her mouth, one covering her eyes, and bemoaning my need to know every step of the way. I just wanted to finish my homework assignment before *Futurama* started. The "My Family Tree" template had been preprinted on yellow construction paper. All I had to do was write in the names. I knew my family was dead, so that hadn't been news to me, but that didn't mean I couldn't complete the assignment. I also knew from my cousin, Leah, that their deaths were "really gross," but Leah thought everything was gross. Up until then, I thought it was just a car-crash type of gross. I wasn't prepared for Aunt Celia to cut down my family tree with an axe. As I touched my pencil to the leaf marked "Father," Aunt Celia snatched up my assignment, wrote a note to my teacher, and stapled it shut. By the time I thought of a few hundred thousand questions to ask her, the Q&A part of our conversation about my family had closed, and remained closed for the duration of my childhood.

That included the house.

The shutters and front door were a different color than they once were. I wasn't sure if I liked the cottage red. They were hunter green in the one exterior snapshot I possessed. I wondered where that picture had gotten to—probably dumped in a box somewhere along with all the rest. When I was growing up, Aunt Celia doled out family

photos like they were part of my allowance, reluctantly and not without a heavy sigh. Though Aunt Celia claimed each picture was the
last she had, there always seemed to be one more hidden away somewhere. Most of the pictures were taken inside the house around
the holidays, but one group shot was taken on the front stoop of the
house I was currently scrutinizing online. I could almost see the
shadow of us sitting on the front steps. Michael sulking under his ball
cap, my mother burping me over her shoulder, Josh and Eddie ham-
ming it up with fierce grins; the blur of my father as he slid into frame
just before time ran out.

I hovered the cursor over the View tab, afraid to click. I felt a bit
like a child who'd found a gun in a shoebox under her parents' bed.
Now I had found it, I might as well touch it. Now I'd touched it, I
might as well pick it up. Now I'd picked it up, I might as well point it
at my face. The lure of such accessible danger was irresistible. Something deep inside that wanted you to slip your finger around the trigger and pull. Not because you wanted to harm to yourself, but just
that you suddenly could.

I clicked the tab.

"This lovely three-bedroom home is spacious and full of upgrades," the ad proclaimed. I scanned a vaunt of features and convey-
ances that sounded impressive, but were really just the basic
necessities of life: water heater, heat pump, washer and dryer, refrigerator, garbage disposal, dishwasher . . . "Just minutes from the metro,
this trendy neighborhood offers convenient shopping and local
restaurants."

Yeah, I thought, if you considered Hardee's, Wawa, and Food Lion
trendy. I had vague knowledge about the area. Nothing worth the
trip across town, except the DMV and an outdoor concert arena. My
boyfriend, Garrett, and I had seen Kid Rock there last summer, but
most of the shows were outrageously expensive, unless you wanted
to sit in a drunk pile on the lawn, which I did not.

At the very bottom of the page, in lettering too small to read without cranking the zoom level up to 200 percent, was the caveat emptor:

"Stigmatized Property."

Though this sounded innately bad, even if you didn't know exactly what had stigmatized the property to begin with, a list of potential side effects of what exposure to said stigma may cause should have been included: *Confusion, nausea, blurred vision, a sudden and inexplicable desire to murder your family, headache, suicidal thoughts, irregular heartbeat, psychosis, dry mouth, bleeding from—well—everywhere, and, in some rare cases, decapitation has been reported. Do not use drugs or alcohol while inhabiting this property.*

Having built up an immunity to all of the above, I picked up the phone to dial the agent. Garrett wouldn't mind. He didn't think we could afford to buy anything worthwhile, and wanted me to stick to rentals, but this one was just a hair outside our guesstimated price range. I could always get a second waitressing job to make up the difference. Anyway, a quick look-see couldn't hurt. I didn't tell the agent who I was, only that I was house hunting and wanted to take a quick peek. Would I like to see it today? Why, yes, I would. Three o'clock? Marvelous. Did I need directions?

As a matter of fact, I did.

I WAS ELEVEN when my cousin, Leah, asked me to kill her. I think about that day from time to time, but like what happened to my family, I never allow myself to dwell on much beyond the fact that death had occurred. I remember the terror I felt, the overwhelming guilt, but not her face. I couldn't stand to look at it. But as I stared into my shot of whiskey, killing time at a local bar and gathering nerve until my appointment with the real estate agent, my mind bloomed forth Leah's face like a ray of sun on the single rose I had laid on her headstone. The rose had endured rain, wind, and leaf blowers for twenty-seven days. Then it was gone. As I scurried around tombstones in search of it, Aunt Celia, tear-streaked and shivering in a thin sweater, insisted I stop. "It's gone, Dixie! Just forget about it!" I knew she meant Leah. And I did forget, easy as that. Ice cream sundaes had done the trick.

I hoped alcohol might, too.

I fought the memory even as I searched for it, squinting around the back of my brain until my eyes adjusted to the shifting, murky light of denial. I saw Leah clearly, cruelly. How the skeleton under her skin had yanked down her eyeballs to find passage through her face. How her bleached fingers gripped the fold of the bedspread like the edge of an icy cliff. How the pillowcase, folded around her bald head, was just as sick and gray as she was. Slid deep into the cavity of her mattress, she blinked up at me. A grim smile slid forth freakishly large teeth. There was a calm to her normally scared batty eyes that frightened me more than anything.

"I'm so sick, Dix," she had whispered.

"You'll get better," I said, averting my eyes as an anemic tongue slipped out to wet her lips. Rather than openly grimace, I looked to the storm outside the window. A sludgy leaf hit the glass. It left a murky handprint as it fluttered away.

"Not this time," she said, then smiled brightly to horribly add, "I'm dead meat."

She was. I could smell it on her breath.

"But you have that new doctor," I tried. Aunt Celia had talked about Leah's new doctor like he was Christ risen: "A miracle worker. The answer to all our prayers. I tell you, he's a godsend."

"He can't help me." Leah confirmed this with a cough. "No one can. I heard them talking about it. I'm going to die no matter what they do."

"You got better before when you didn't think you would," I offered.

"I don't want to get better! I'll just get sick again. I can't take it anymore!"

Her thin fingers clamped a shackle around my wrist. So strong I cried out. I was just about to point out the strength she still had when she wrenched my cheek into the side of her pillow. The stitched corner was like an elbow to my eye.

"You have to help me, Dixie. Please."

"What can I do?"

"Hold the pillow over my face," she said equably, as if she had asked me to hold her cup of tea, or her hair as she threw up. A regular request when she still had hair to hold, or the stomach to keep down a sip of tea.

"But you won't be able to breathe."

"That's what I mean."

I snatched my hand back, rubbing the sting of the sweaty bracelet from my wrist.

"Please, Dixie," she begged as I backed away. "No one else will do it."

"I won't do it, either."

"But you have to."

I shook my head.

"Couldn't you just try?" She pushed onto her elbows, then fell promptly back. "If it doesn't work, I won't ask you again. I promise."

I turned for the door. "I'm getting Aunt Celia."

"No, don't." She sighed, defeated. She curled a finger to motion me back. "Forget it. I didn't think you would do it, anyway."

I stepped back to the bed. "Do you want to watch TV?"

She yanked my shirt so hard my shoulder popped through the collar. I tried to pull it back into place before my nipple was exposed, but before I could, she dragged me to my knees at the side of her bed.

"You don't get it, Dixie." Her face had superheated to an angry boil, except her lips, which were as white and thin as ice. "You don't know what it's like to be this sick. You don't know what it's like to just lie here waiting to die. I pray for more pain sometimes because I know it means I'm getting close. I thought last night was it. I hurt so bad I knew I would die. But then I woke up and felt a little better. But

I'm not better! I'm just not dead. I don't want to be in pain anymore. Dying's all I can do. You have to do this for me, Dixie. You can do it. I know you can. You have it in you."

I looked back at the door. "But I'll get in trouble."

"You won't get in trouble," she said, eyes bugging with optimism. "I promise. She won't even know what happened. I'll just be dead. It's going to happen anyway, so why not now?" When I looked down to consider this, she smoothed my shirt back into place. "This is nice. Is it new?"

I shook my head.

"I don't remember it." She drew a finger across the whiskers of my Happy Bunny T-shirt. "I don't want to be in pain anymore, Dix. I can't take it. You don't want me to be in pain, do you?"

"No . . ."

"Then you'll do it?" She brightened. "You'll kill me?"

"But it's a sin. You said my dad would burn in hell for doing it. I don't want to go to hell."

She rolled her eyes. "This is totally different. It's only a sin if you kill someone who doesn't want to die." She rattled off a string of ugly coughs. I hoped she had coughed herself unconscious, but she opened her eyes to nod weakly. "I'd do it myself, but I'm too weak. If you think about it, you're just helping me commit suicide. Doctors do it all the time. It's just not legal in Virginia. It will be soon. Just not soon enough for me."

"Ask your dad to do it the next time he's here?" I suggested. "He'd do it. I heard him tell Aunt Celia that it was wrong trying to keep you alive this way."

She shook her head. "He just wants her to stop spending money on doctors. Ford's a cheap-ass. And a coward. He couldn't even change my bandage without puking. Besides, who knows when he'll be back again? He never showed up last week and he promised. He's a total jerk."

Though ragging on Ford had always been one of my favorite pastimes, and I could usually get a laugh out of Leah by doing so—which she really needed at that moment—I didn't. I had just learned that Ford, too, had lost his entire family in a tragedy when he was a kid. Calling him names didn't seem like fun anymore. I had always been curious about the scar on Ford's face, a tight purple stain that ran up the side of his neck to a melted ear, but I never had the nerve to ask. When he caught me staring at it as we strolled the aisles of a liquor store one day when he was supposed to be babysitting me—Aunt Celia had to take Leah to a doctor's appointment, and in a rare coincidence, Ford was home and had nothing better to do—he said he got it pressing against a burning door to save his little sister, who was trapped inside. When I told him that he was lucky to have proof of what had happened to his family, he said that I had a scar, too, but that mine was more like shadow, a "bruised aura" that followed me around me like a dark cloud. "I see it on you all the time," he said as he flipped a bottle of whiskey in his hand like a juggling pin. I found this remarkable. I thought I carried my suffering on the inside, like a distended can of peaches. He admitted that he was glad to have the scar. It reminded him never to forget, or to forgive. "Letting someone you love die in pain like that when you had a chance to stop it . . ." He had shaken his head. "It's the worst feeling in the world."

I looked back at the door, cracked wide enough to let a head poke in. Dishes clacked in the kitchen. The garbage disposal started, stopped.

"What if Aunt Celia comes in when I'm doing it?" I said.

"She won't. She thinks I'm asleep. But I didn't take my pill." She uncurled her left hand to reveal a half-disintegrated white tablet. She wiped it into the bedspread. "Go shut the door all the way. But be quiet. Don't slam it."

After closing the door extra slow and gentle, I returned to her bedside. She slipped her fingers into my hand. They were as cold and sharp as keys.

"Count to a hundred before you go get my mom." She coughed

up a glistening red spit bubble. "My body will fight for air, but don't get scared. It won't last long, just a couple of seconds." The bubble popped and stamped a red star on her chin. "It's perfectly normal." The *P* in "perfectly" launched something wet onto my lip. "No matter what happens"—*a blood bubble!*—"don't stop"—*on my lip!*—"and remember"—*AH, GOD!*—"to put the pillow back under my head when you're done."

I wiped my lip with the back of my hand as she released it.

"Do it just like I said, and everything will be fine."

She gave me a nod and I pulled the pillow out from under her head. She crossed her hands over her chest in a death pose.

As I held the pillow to my stomach, warm and damp from her fevered neck, praying that Aunt Celia would walk in at any moment, a form gathered from the pleated shadows of the bedspread and stood beside me.

"Well, go on," it said.

I shook my head.

"You can do it, Dixie."

When I closed my eyes to cry, the pillow was snatched from my hands.

"Oh, give that to me."

The sounds were horrible, a scuffling of muffled cries that left me exhausted. When I opened my eyes again, Leah was limp in a tangle of sheets, her hand in a stiff claw atop the pillow over her face.

The bartender turned. "Ready to go another round?" he asked, nodding at my empty glass.

I shook my head, slapped a ten on the bar, and left.

A WALL OF wilting camellia bushes separated 6209 from 6211 Catharpin Road. I held my breath as I inched the car forward, choking the steering wheel with both hands. The need to pee was sudden and painful and urgent. This was it: the residence of all my fears.

The location of all my nightmares. The abode that housed every torturous—

It was a lot smaller than I expected.

In fact, it was quite charming.

Since there wasn't one, no bats were swirling from its chimney. Nor was there a black storm cloud gathered over it, sunny day notwithstanding. No swamp gas rose from the lawn, and blood was not oozing from the windows or boiling up from under the foundation. There wasn't a single dead animal nailed to the front door. In fact, there wasn't anything scary about it.

What a gyp.

The agent, Suanne Arnold, was waiting for me on the sidewalk. Tall, blonde, and irksome, she waved me forward when I hesitated to turn into the driveway. I'd hoped to have a private moment to mourn the site of my family's massacre. Maybe pick a flower and set it on the welcome mat. But as soon as I exited the car I was up to my knees in curb appeal. Suanne pointed out the new cement driveway as we strolled up the recently overlaid sidewalk.

Though the house was in good repair and appeared welcoming, I knew it was rotten to the core. No matter how many fresh coats of paint it received, evil lay at its center. The apple the witch offered looked tasty. That was the trick. She wanted you to take a bite, to watch you die as you savored the taste. Whatever demon had staked its claim here, it was too clever to blemish the guise it hid behind. It wanted you to feel welcome, to move in, to put your feet up, to let down your guard.

A wink of sun caught the gleaming white exterior. So pretty. My shiny red apple. *Eat, my sweet.* I took a step back before the spell could take hold.

To stall for time, I asked Suanne if there were any noisy neighbors and wondered aloud if the gutters had been recently cleaned. I speculated on the presence of radon gas in some of the older neighborhoods, and challenged the need for a homeowners association altogether. Suanne responded with optimistic noncommittals as she worked the lockbox. With a *click*, the key fell into her hand, and as easy as that, she unlocked the door to the scene of the crime.

I lingered in the doorway as she strode across the wall-to-wall carpeting of the empty living room. When she realized she was giving herself the guided tour, she turned and motioned me inside.

"Come on." She patted her hip like I was a timid stray. "It's okay."

I leaned my chin over the threshold. It was definitely colder inside. And moist. Like a damp cellar. I stepped back and rubbed a chill from my throat.

"I don't think it's right for me . . ." I said, leaving off the last few words of my objection: *to disturb the dead.*

"What?" She gave me a bright, mannered smile as she gamboled back to fetch me. "You haven't even seen the best part yet. The kitchen!"

When I let out a caustic laugh, she scrunched her nose to pretend she got the joke. She took me by the elbow and pulled me gently off my braced heels, then kicked the door closed as I stumbled onto the carpet.

"This is the living room." She waved a hand to conduct my imagination. "Isn't it just perfect for a relaxing evening at home or entertaining guests? Cable television is already installed, so you just have to call and activate it." She walked over to two thin doors that were to the right of the front door as you entered. "Here's the powder room." She held the door open until she realized I was not going to travel five feet to get a look at a commode, then closed it to quickly open and close the next. "Coat closet. As I was saying before, all the rooms have a fresh coat of paint and . . ."

Her voice faded as I stared into the kitchen through the cut-out entryway. The hardwood floor was warm and freshly polished, gleaming sunlight from a picture window over the sink. The old linoleum had probably been ripped up by some professional aftermath company.

"Do you want to see the rest of the downstairs or start upstairs and work our way back down?" Suanne asked.

I headed toward the kitchen.

She brushed by to enter first, threw out her arms ta-da style, and almost caught me in the face. "Isn't it just fabulous? It's been completely remodeled. All new appliances." She swung a finger at an opening on the left wall at the end of the counter. "The formal dining room is through there. It's a bit narrow, but there's plenty of light. It would make a great home office. I prefer to eat in the kitchen, myself, but that's just me."

There was no table or chairs, so my mother's and Josh's bodies were propped midair in my mind. I looked down: Michael under the table. I pivoted slightly to see my father spread-eagled and facedown on the floor, butcher knife clenched loosely in his hand. I refused to think of Eddie, so I looked at my feet. Certainly the spill of blood from five bodies would have reached far beyond where I was standing. The sole of my shoe felt tacky as I raised it. Probably just residue from Murphy Oil Soap, but still . . .

"Oh, isn't the floor sensational?" Suanne expounded. "Real bamboo. Tough as nails. There's three coats of polyurethane so cleanup will be a breeze."

I almost said that you could never get blood up entirely, but instead I walked over to the back door. The chain lock was hanging loose. I slid it into place.

"Oh, don't lock it before you've seen the backyard," Suanne said, moving beside me. She slid the chain off the lock and then inverted the turn latch on the knob to the open position. "It's got a huge backyard." She eased me back as she opened the door. "Nearly a quarter of an acre. It grades away from the home, so if it rains you won't find a drop of water on the patio."

Suanne was good at putting a positive slant on things. The patio looked like it had been pitched up during an earthquake. I smiled at her because she was smiling at me.

"Where's the shed?" I asked.

"Did it say it had a shed?" Her head vibrated slightly as she thought of a way to spin this negative into a positive. "I'm sorry, it doesn't. But I know a great company with really affordable prices. We could have one put up before you move in."

I turned to go back into the house. She followed me saying, "If that's really an issue for you, I could see if the owners might come down in the price to make up the difference. They're very flexible."

I crossed the living room and headed up the stairs.

"The master bedroom is really something," she said, overtaking me on the right to get up the stairs ahead of me.

We poked our heads into the first room we came to. I wasn't sure which brother it had belonged to, so I assigned it to Josh. Or perhaps all three boys shared one room and I had the next one down the hall on the left. A nursery all to myself. Maybe Josh and Eddie bunked together and I shared the room with Michael.

"Linen closet," Suanne said as she opened a door on a larger-than-closet-sized room with three walls of ceiling-high shelves. "Look how big it is. You can set up an ironing board and still have room to walk around." She glanced at my frumpy attire, then pointed to the wall in the hallway. "There's an outlet right here. Makes vacuuming a cinch."

We stopped midway down the hall to look in on a full bath. I imagined myself as a teenager, fighting for sink space with Michael. Josh and Eddie would have been out of the house by then, Eddie off at college and Josh likely living on his own. After a quick nod at the tub, we moved farther down the hall.

"Here's another bedroom, or office, if you prefer."

Though the room was of equal size and the same neutral color as the one before, there was a dirty-sock quality to the air that suggested young boys had once occupied the space. It couldn't have been Eddie's or Michael's scent I was detecting after all this time, but the aroma definitely belonged to some sort of holy terror. I pressed a hand to my nose as I backed into the hall.

Suanne made a curious sound as we approached the door to what I expected would be the master bedroom.

"I could have sworn this was open when we came up the stairs." She looked at me for confirmation, and I shrugged to say I hadn't paid it much attention. She waved away her concern and took hold of the knob. "It must have just looked open." She twisted the knob and bounced off the door as she stepped forward. She gave an embarrassed laugh, jiggling the handle. "It sticks a bit with the new paint job." She gave it another twist, harder, a bit desperate. "Once it dries, you shouldn't have any problem. Jeez, it's really stuck."

"Here let me try." She pressed against the wall to allow me to take a shot at it. The knob turned smooth as silk in my hand. The door fell easily inward. Suanne gave a discomfited grin when I looked sideways at her.

"I guess you've got the touch," she said as she followed me inside. She turned and closed the door, and opened it again without issue. "Huh. Seems all right now. I'll get my handyman to come take a look at it, just in case." She ran her hand along the door frame and shrugged. "Oh! Get a load of this." She flicked a wall switch to activate the recessed lighting in the ceiling. She patted her hands together to generate some enthusiasm. I nodded that I was impressed. She waved at the en suite door. "There's a brand-new soaking tub and a walk-in shower."

"Why are the owners selling?" I asked, staring up at a ceiling fan. Grimy dust pellets clung to the edges of the blades. Suanne flipped a switch and it started rotating.

"Oh, I think he got transferred with his work or something," she said. "They just hated to give it up. They really put a lot of money into it."

"What's the stigma?" I asked as I walked over and peeked in on the bath. When she failed to respond, I turned to look for my answer. Her lip quivered as she tried to maintain her smile.

"Wh-what's that, now?" she stammered.

"The ad said it was a stigmatized property. What's the stigma?"

"Oh, that." She waved a hand to shoo away any concern. "That happened a long time ago. I don't even know why I need to include that. There've been two owners since who haven't had a second of worry. But in the spirit of full disclosure, I do need to tell you that a murder did take place here."

I tried to look surprised. "What, like a home invasion?"

"No," she said quickly. "This neighborhood is very safe. Hardly any crime at all." Which meant there was some. "No. This was more of a domestic violence type of thing."

"Oh," I said. "You mean like some guy killed his wife or something?"

"His entire family, actually." When I offered no reaction other than a blink, she continued: "The father had some sort of mental breakdown. He killed his wife and three sons."

"Oh, my god. When did this happen?"

"Oh, this was back in the late eighties or early nineties, I think." She folded her arms around her as the ceiling fan gained speed. "Only the little girl survived. I don't know if you're old enough to remember Baby Blue."

I feigned confusion to repeat, "Baby Blue?"

"That's what they called the little girl who survived. I think that song was playing when they found her or something. It's by . . ." She closed her eyes to remember, then shook her head. "Oh, shoot. I can't remember. They played it at the end of *Breaking Bad*. Did you watch that?"

Garrett and I had only watched the first three seasons, so I shook my head.

"Oh, you know who I'm talking about. They do that other song, um . . . Not Golden Earring."

"Badfinger?" I offered.

"That's it." She rolled her eyes with relief. "Thank you! That would have driven me crazy all day long. Oh! 'Day After Day.' That's the other song I was trying to think of." She turned and opened a door next to the bathroom. "The closet is a bit modest, but there's plenty of wall space for an armoire, if you need it."

Back in the kitchen, I turned on the faucet to rinse my hands in cold water. My palms felt hot and sticky, like I had touched some corrosive epoxy that had left a residue on my skin. Maybe some varnish had transferred to my hand when I held on to the handrail as we went up the stairs. It had felt a bit tacky. The doorknob to the master bedroom was a little hot when I touched it, but I just thought Suanne had warmed it up for me. Whatever it was, it wasn't coming off. My palms stuck together as I rubbed them under the icy stream. I looked around for a bar of soap; even an old can of Ajax under the sink would have been a welcome sight. A good real estate agent should have stocked the house with liquid soap and hand towels, though I suspected Suanne wanted to keep soap scum in the stainless steel sink to an absolute minimum.

As I scrubbed my hands like a neurotic germaphobe, Suanne busied herself by opening cabinets and drawers, pointing out excellent craftsmanship as it was encountered. "All the lower cabinets have sliding shelves for easy access. The lazy Susan's real wood, not one of those cheap plastic thingies. This counter was made from an entire sheet of granite. No seams." She checked to make sure the fridge was cold, said that it was. Freezer, too. "The ice maker has a sensor so you never need to turn it on or off. The washer and dryer are over here." I heard her slide open an accordion door near the entryway, and then struggle to reclose it. "Most everything is still under warranty, except for the hot water heater, but I'm having that replaced next week."

As she came to my side, a boy ran through the tree line at the back of the yard. He was young, maybe eight or nine, wearing a heavy red sweater. Overkill for the warm fall day.

"Did you see that?" I said, pressing my nose to the window as the boy vanished behind a sturdy tree. For as fast as he had been moving, he had stopped on a dime.

As she joined my nose at the window, she turned off the faucet. "I don't see anything."

"There's a boy out in the yard." I tapped the glass with a wet finger that left a mark. "He ran behind that tree over there."

She squinted into the sun. "Oh, it's probably just a neighbor's kid. There're a lot of families on this block. The schools are some of the best in the county." She used her sleeve to wipe my poke from the window. "Don't worry. I'm sure they won't play in the yard once you move in. Kids are drawn to a vacant house like mice to a restaurant. Some teenagers broke into one of my properties a few years back and threw a huge party. Keg and all. Filled the pool with shaving cream! It cost a small fortune to clean it all up. Little bastards."

I continued to look for the boy, and began to wonder if I had actually seen him in the first place. Either he was still hiding behind the tree or he had scurried up it. I checked the branches for a glimpse of his red sweater.

Suanne jangled her keys. "If you're not interested in this one," she said, "I have a lovely split-level in Reston I can show you. It's a little bigger, but the price is comparable to those with a basement. We can head over there now, if you have time."

I dried my hands on the front of my shirt as I turned. "I like this one," I said. "It feels like home already."

2

I didn't want to pervert Garrett's opinion of the house before he had a chance to see it, so I kept its history to myself. The house was a giant step up from the tiny apartment we had lived in for the last two years. It originally was used as a flophouse by him and his three roommates, but once he cashed a steady paycheck as a water treatment specialist, Garrett turned it into a bachelor pad. But the frat house decor remained glued to the walls and floor with god knows what. I did my best to introduce a woman's touch, as Garrett skillfully put it to entice me to move in, but my eye for interior design was nearly as blind as his. I tore down the beer wench and concert posters, slapped up an Ansel Adams calendar, and proclaimed the apartment transformed.

As we entered the house on Catharpin Road, Garrett hitched his pants and nodded around with a shrewd expression. He wore the same face to the Mazda dealership where he bought his car, and often donned it for staff Christmas parties at the restaurant where I worked. During the tour of the first floor, he kept his opinion under lock and key, one which Suanne worked furiously to pick open. But I could tell he liked it. He was impressed with the upgrades and absolutely loved the backyard. He pointed out a water stain on the ceiling in the living room, but didn't seem overly concerned about it. He played with the thermostat after commenting on a chill, then gave a satisfied nod as heat rattled through the vents.

We left Suanne in the kitchen to explore the upstairs and to speak privately. He chose what I had come to believe was Josh's room for his home office, which I took as a good sign. As we stepped into the hall, he tripped headfirst into the wall.

"Garrett!" I caught his arm to steady him as he stumbled back. "Are you okay?"

He chuckled sheepishly as he rubbed his forehead. "Yeah. I don't know what happened. My toe must have snagged a seam in the carpeting."

We looked back at the seamless pile. "I think you're a klutz," I said. I ran my finger over a half-moon dent in the wall. "Oh, look! You broke the house. Now we have to buy it."

"The wall can be fixed," he said. "My head's another story."

He watched his step as he swayed off toward the closed door of the master bedroom. I was pretty sure it had been open when we came up the stairs. Like Suanne, Garrett struggled to open it, but I was granted access with barely a turn of the knob. I patted my hands like Suanne had as I flicked on the recessed lighting.

"Pretty cool, huh?" I said, hitting the switch to start the fan.

He nodded and headed into the bathroom. "It's awesome, Dix. But I don't think we can afford it." His voice echoed as he poked his head in the shower. "We'll have to put down one hell of a down payment."

"We've been saving like misers," I said, entering the bathroom and turning toward the mirror. "If not to buy a house, then what are we saving for?" I fluffed my hair and checked my limited makeup. Movement over my right shoulder turned me in a quick spin. The tub was empty, as was the window over it. I turned back to find Garrett standing in the doorway to my left. I looked over my shoulder and back again to say, "We should have plenty for a down payment, don't you think?"

I could have kicked myself for not accepting the offer to do that TV interview when I turned seventeen. Ten thousand dollars to tell my story, "Baby Blue: Fifteen Years Later," would have come in handy. Aunt Celia had talked me out of it. "I didn't keep you a secret all this time just to have you go on TV for the whole world to see." Sending me to private schools where kids didn't know me or my brothers didn't stop me from blabbing about what happened to my family, but I did appreciate that any rumors were started at my discretion. Even though the interview never happened, it did give me a chance to see Rory Sellers again, the neighbor boy who found me the day of the murders, who had also been contacted about doing a segment for the show.

Rory became a fixture around Aunt Celia's after the murders. Aunt Celia said he hovered over me like an angel fresh out of heaven. He bought me gifts and took me to the park. Sometimes he just came by to stare at me. He didn't come around much when Ford was home, which was more frequent once Leah died, but he came for nearly every Thanksgiving dinner. Aunt Celia thought the memory of what happened that horrible Thanksgiving could be drowned in a vat of gravy, buried under a heaping spoonful of mashed potatoes. That Rory would be there made how pitifully small our family had become a little less noticeable. Leah had such a crush on Rory. He visited her once before she died, but she refused to see him. "Do you think I'd let a guy like that see me like this?" She slapped her bald head so hard the handprint lasted for a week. Being only ten, I didn't see what all the fuss was about, but when I saw Rory with my seventeen-year-old eyes, I got it, and I got it hard. Shoulder-length dark hair and blue eyes, broad shoulders and tight jeans, Rory slunk like a tiger when he walked. I fell in love with him instantly and eternally. Not only was he the most beautiful man I had ever seen in person, he also was my brother Josh, if Josh had made it to manhood. He was Eddie, if Eddie still had a head. What Michael could have become one day. True, I might have gotten my affection for him a bit confused. I wouldn't go as far as to say that I stalked him, but I definitely overstepped the bounds of our quasi-sibling relationship. So what if I stabbed my tongue in his mouth when he gave me a good-night peck on the lips. And yes, I did grab his crotch when he took me to the movies, but that was no reason to refuse to see me for months on end. He left me no choice but to follow him home from work, jimmy his back window, and slip into his bed as he slept. The hours we spent talking that night were worth it, even if he was yelling most of the time. He still checked in with me now and then, but after his girlfriend fell down the steps and broke her neck, we kind of lost touch. I should call him and tell him about the house . . .

"Dixie?" Garrett laid his hand on my shoulder. "Didn't you hear me?"

"Sorry." I tucked my hair behind my ear and turned from the mirror. "What did you say?"

"I asked if you knew if a home inspection had been done."

"I'm not sure," I said, feeling a little unsteady. I couldn't catch a breath around my racing heart. My hands were hot and sticky again. I wiped them on the front of my shirt to work up a deep breath. "I'll have to ask Suanne. Is it hot in here?"

At six foot three, Garrett had to bend down to find my five-foot-four eyes. "Are you okay?"

"Sure," I said with a quick blink, then poked him in the shoulder. "So you like the house, right?"

He bobbed his head as he righted himself. "Sure. I love it. It's a great location. I could walk to work if I had to. The backyard's got plenty of room for my boat."

"You don't have a boat." I laughed.

"No, but when I get one, I'll have a place to keep it."

I clasped my sticky hands to my heart. "So we're buying it?"

He shrugged. "I guess it couldn't hurt to find out if we qualify. If we get approved, then I don't see why not." I hugged him tight around the waist. He kissed me on the top of my head and said, "Since we're buying it, do you want to christen it real quick?"

I gave him a look. "Suanne's probably downstairs listening."

He picked me up and sat me on the sink. "Then you better be quiet."

I let him smother my guilty conscience in kisses. There was plenty of time to tell him the truth about the house. What was the point in saying anything until we found out if we were even qualified to buy it? Once we knew for sure we could afford it, I would tell him. Definitely before we moved in. Right after we got settled.

Surely before he bought a boat.

HAVING GROWN UP in the Midwest, Garrett had never heard of the Wheeler Massacre until I told him about it. Given that he was only four years old at the time, and that they didn't preempt morning cartoons to report on the mass murder of a family in Virginia, especially in Wisconsin, he knew nothing at all about my family. Not that living in Virginia would have changed that, regardless of his age on Thanksgiving Day in 1992. A new president had been elected earlier that November, and the only family worthy of the news cycle was the First Family. For as tragic as Baby Blue's story was, Chelsea Clinton captured America's attention. She ruled the tabloids until JonBenét stole the crown a few years later. No one could compete with her, until Caylee Anthony, of course. After what happened to them, Baby Blue seemed almost lucky.

Maybe if I had died, Garrett would have heard of me. Or maybe not. I would have just been one of the unfortunate Wheeler children. My story would have been *our* story, and what happened in that house wouldn't have troubled Garrett for a second. Unfortunately, I did live, and fell in love with a man who I had seen knock on wood to thwart bad luck, so I expected moving into a stigmatized property, especially *my* stigmatized property, might trouble him greatly.

With a few white lies and a little subterfuge, Garrett might never find out we were living in a house of horrors. Aunt Celia, however, was another story. She had been to dozens of barbeques and Christmas Day brunches at that address. Not to mention more kids' birthday parties than any one person should be forced to attend. She had eaten all but one of my mother's Thanksgiving dinners in the dining room I planned to make my home gym. She knew the house too well to be fooled by a new paint job and a few strategically placed potted plants. As did Ford, Aunt Celia's husband, Leah's father, and one-time friend and brother-in-law to my father. Though I didn't imagine Ford tagged along to many events, much to the joy of everyone, including himself, he had been there enough to know the address in question.

As I saw it, I only had three options to buy back my birthright, or, in this case, "deathright," without Garrett getting wise: (1) Fake a fight and never speak to either one of them again—a breeze to accomplish with Ford, but not so easy to pull off with Aunt Celia. (2) Buy their silence—Ford would do it for a six-pack, but Aunt Celia couldn't be bought for any amount. (3) Come clean and beg them not to tell Garrett about the house. No option was perfect, but begging their silence might work if I kept Garrett a safe distance from them until we were moved in. Once that happened, he'd be in too deep to get out.

I stopped by to speak with Aunt Celia on my way home from work. My manager wasn't happy that I wanted to take a few weeks off to move, but being one of the only two servers old enough to actually serve alcohol at O'Toole's Bar and Grill, I had a bit of leverage. He reluctantly agreed when I threatened to quit.

Aunt Celia was in the kitchen doing dishes when I arrived. Ford was in the basement trying to unjam a weed whacker. Muffled profanity rose through the floor and infused our conversation with an angry tension I did not need. Three quarrels ensued before I even broached the subject of buying the house. When I finally came out with it, Aunt Celia looked at me like I had told her I was having the bodies of my family exhumed to stuff and hang over her mantel.

"Why on earth would you want to do that?" she said, hand to her heart.

"Why not?"

"Because it's sick, Dixie, that's why not."

"Why is anything concerning my family sick? Maybe a lifetime of suppression and denial is what's sick, Aunt Celia. You ever think of that?"

"I try not to think about it at all," she said.

"I know it seems strange," I offered as I opened the refrigerator door. I scanned the shelves and came out with a beer. "But the house is perfect for us, Aunt Celia. It's exactly what we were looking for."

She turned back to the sink in a huff. "Well, you'll never find me over for dinner, I can tell you that much."

"Oh, come on."

She whipped a glare at me. "No, you come on, Dixie. After what happened in that house? Would you really want to fall asleep under that roof? Raise your children there?"

I threw my hands in the air. "Who said anything about having children?" This was something else I would need to come clean about . . . eventually. Garrett wanted a houseful of kids. Lucky for us, twins ran in his family! My uncommunicated stance on this subject was pretty simple: No way, no how. Wheeler children got snuffed out faster than baby moths at a bonfire. I was the anomaly or, more precisely, the freak of nature as far as Wheeler kids were concerned. Perhaps tragedy skipped a generation and the next batch of Wheelers might enjoy the tedium of old age. After all, Aunt Celia was still alive. Uncle Davis died of a heart attack, but since he was sixty-two and a raging alcoholic, no one besides his wife, Charlene, would ever suggest that he was taken too soon. My father snuffed himself out, so he hardly counts as a predictor—for untimely deaths, anyway. The only way to find out if tragedy did skip a generation was the hard way, and I wasn't about to subject my children to that sort of test.

"Even if you don't have kids, Dixie, it's not right. Just thinking about stepping one foot in that house gives me the creeps. I can't believe Garrett agreed to this."

I looked at my feet.

"Oh." She raised her chin to look down on me. "You haven't told him, have you?" When I shrugged, she stomped her foot. "Oh, Dixie, how could you!"

"I didn't want to scare him off. After we've get settled in, I'll tell him."

"Oh, don't be a fool!"

"*What?*" Ford yelled up through the floor, misinterpreting the insult for his name.

I hid a smile as Aunt Celia screamed "Nothing!" at the floor.

Heavy feet started a slow trudge up the wooden staircase.

"Garrett wouldn't have agreed to buy it if I told him," I reasoned.

"Of course he wouldn't. It's absolute madness!"

"What's madness?" Ford asked as the door opened.

Being a mechanic, Ford always looked like an exhaust pipe had just coughed on him. Today, however, it appeared as though a lawn mower had hacked up on him instead of his Corvette. The ball of clear weed whacker wire in his hands was stained the same perennial shade of green as his skin, jeans, blue work shirt, and Aunt Celia's front yard. The scar on the left side of his face, which usually stood out as bright and fresh as the slap Leah had laid upon the top of her bald head, looked tarnished beneath the speckled patina, as though his cheek had finally begun to rust out.

It was hard not to stare at Ford's scar. Though I had spent many a mealtime contemplating it—the shape, the texture, the moody color changes it sometimes expressed—I was always shocked to see it cuffed to his face. The painful vibrancy it retained; the red-moon geography. New patterns seemed to form from one viewing to the next, spreading and seeping like wine over hard, dry sand. Seeing it a thousand times never spared me a single wince. Ford, on the other hand, wore his scar like a well-thought-out and skillfully designed tattoo. If Ford caught someone staring, which happened with unendurable frequency, he would not blush or turn away. On the contrary, he would call attention to it. "See that?" he'd ask the alarmed stranger as he tapped the tight skin with a dirty fingernail, producing a faint tick, like a beak pecking at a dry bit of gristle. "Got that in Afghanistan," or Iraq or whatever war-torn country came to mind in the moment. Once he got it crashing his helicopter. Once he cut the wrong wire while defusing a bomb. He fought that forest fire out West a few times. If he was tired and less inspired, it was the "god-damn furnace's" fault. Mostly he used it to flirt with the ladies, some of whom he could actually convince to touch it: a trembling finger down the side of his face followed by a nervous giggle, like she had petted a snake. From men he got a salute or appreciative nod for his service, fictitious as it was. But what Ford never got was embar-rassed. When I once heard him invoke 9/11 as the cause, a righteous and moral indignation made me call an end to the charade: "No, you didn't, Ford. Don't lie." I yelped and tripped and fought as he dragged me all the way back to the car. Slammed inside, he pointed a long finger in my face. "Don't you ever bust me out like that again, you hear?" I asked him why he had to make up stories since the truth was just as honorable. "You got the scar trying to save your family, Ford. Just say that." He shook his head. "Trying ain't doing, Dix. Ain't no honor in standing there watching your family burn."

That night I told Aunt Celia what had happened. "Ford wasn't the hero that day, Dixie. Your father was, if you can believe that. I guess people change. Some for the better, some for the worse. I can't figure it, but Ford's never forgiven himself for not being able to save them. It don't matter that he was just a boy and half on fire himself. I guess since your father was just a boy, too, that excuse never sat quite right with Ford." I had been surprised to hear Aunt Celia speak of my father—she rarely did—but when I pushed for more about him, she turned away and told me to go to bed.

I tore my eyes from the scar as Aunt Celia pointed at me to ask Ford, "Do you have any idea what this crazy girl wants to do?"

He glanced at me to shrug. "Buy the old death house on Catharpin Road."

Aunt Celia reared in shock. "You knew about this?"

"No. I can hear every damn word you say in the basement." He shoved me out of the way as he headed to the trash can in the corner. He stepped on the lever, deposited the rat's nest of wire, and stomped it down with his boot. When he stepped out of the can, he had a silver Coffee-mate seal stuck to his toe. "Let her buy it. Who cares?" He shoved me aside as he went for the refrigerator. "Maybe she needs to be there. Might be good for her. Exorcise some of her demons."

I nearly fell out of the way as Ford took my side. He never agreed with me about anything.

"See?" I said. "Ford gets why I want to do this."

"Well, that should be your first clue that you're doing something wrong," Aunt Celia said. For some reason this tickled Ford and he leaned in to get a kiss from her. Aunt Celia smacked him with her dish towel. "If this was the right thing to do, then you would have told Garrett about it."

Ford pulled a face. "Aw, you gotta tell Garrett."

"I'll tell him," I whispered to my shoulder.

Aunt Celia threw her hands in the air to ask "When?" and a drop of dishwater hit my lip. I thought of Leah's death spittle. "Good Lord, Dixie! You close on the house in a few days. You go tell him right this instant!"

"Can't you just agree not to say anything to him about it?" I pleaded.

They said "No" in unison, but Ford prefaced his with a "Fuck."

"Stay out of this, Ford," I said.

"I didn't want to be in it to begin with." He bumped me with his shoulder as he started to walk out, then leaned back to say, "But I'll tell you this much, little girl. That house is gonna eat you up and spit you back out again before it's done with you. Best have Garrett by your side when it does." He let out a laugh as I pushed him away, then pressed close to growl through a green-lipped smile, "I wouldn't keep an axe lying around if I were you."

"Go on, Ford," Aunt Celia said. "You need a shower. And leave those clothes on the bathroom floor. You got grease on the carpet last time and I still can't get it up."

"What Garrett doesn't know can't hurt him," I said once Ford was gone. "And he loves the house, Aunt Celia. You should have seen how excited he was. He'll be so disappointed."

"I don't care. He deserves to know." She rubbed weariness from her forehead with the back of her hand. "I can't believe we're even discussing this. They should have burned that damn place to the ground years ago." She pointed a finger at my face. "That's exactly what you should do. Go to the county and demand its demolition."

"But it's my house," I said softly.

Her eyes were truly sad to learn that I had gone completely insane. She took my dry hands in her damp ones and gave them a solid shake to jar some sense into me.

"Dixie, I know you've struggled with this your whole life. You were too young to know your family. But living in that house is not going to bring you closer to them. It's just going to cause you more pain." She drew me in for a hug. "You don't want to start a new life with Garrett by lying to him. It isn't fair. You have to go and tell him about it right away."

"If Garrett's okay with it, will you be?" I asked.

She held me at arm's length. "He won't be okay with it, Dixie. Nobody would be."

GARRETT AND I were dating almost a year before I came thoroughly clean about my past. A previous boyfriend had suggested that I had a little too much "drama" tucked away in my "baggage" and had broken up with me. True, I had used the death of my family, thus an irrational fear of abandonment, as an excuse for my somewhat overreaction to his ex-girlfriend calling—the remote control missed him by a mile, by the way—but I still was terrified that Garrett might feel the same. Not that he might break up with me, but that he might begin to view me through a different lens. One that had a big crack in it. Garrett knew that my family had died and that my aunt had raised me. That all came out on date one. But he presumed my family had died in some sort of accident, just as I once had. I didn't lie to him about it; I just didn't correct him.

I finally shared my story on a moonlit Virginia beach as we watched for shooting stars, clinging to his sandy hand as though it might slip from mine as surely as the outgoing tide beneath our toes, and upsetting the quiet beauty around us with words like "murder," "severed," and "suicide." When I finished, he grabbed me into his arms and whispered how so very, very sorry he was. With the heat of his breath on my sunburned shoulder, and one of his tears rolling down my back, I blurted out that I loved him. I thought he might leave my sentimentality hanging with the moon, but he screamed that he loved me, too, as he dragged me back from an incoming wave. We fell to the sand laughing. Rolling atop me, he stared deep into my eyes to say that he would never let anyone or anything ever hurt me again. That he would always be there for me. That he wanted to be the family I never had. That I could count on him like no other.

God, I hoped he meant it.

I FOUND GARRETT in the bedroom of our small apartment, crouched on the floor and picking through a box in only his T-shirt and underwear. Three other previously taped boxes were torn open in the middle of the room. "GAR-BDRM" was written on the side of one box, "MISC-CRAP" on another. The one that had been fated for "TRASH" when I left that morning was now piled high with flung clothing. A Sharpie, a roll of packing tape, and a pair of scissors were on the end of the bed. I swept them aside as I sat down.

"Hey, babe," he said, holding up a pair of blue sweatpants like a prize fish. "How come the one thing you want is always at the bottom

of the last box you look in? Have you seen my khakis with the side
pockets? They're not in here."

I shook my head.

"Damn. They were my last clean pair. I might have to wear these
sweatpants to work tomorrow. I'm trying to hold off on laundry until
we get to the new place. I don't want to give that machine downstairs
another quarter. Last time, it only filled up halfway. I still have suds
in my underwear."

I smiled briefly as I wrung my hands in my lap, searching for a way
to tell him the horrible truth about the house while somehow shor-
ing up his excitement about moving into it. Aunt Celia's complete
overreaction to the news had my stomach in a knot. Actually, I had
felt a little off ever since I went to see the house for the first time.
Nauseous, thickheaded, and achy, as though a bad flu was coming on.
Maybe Suanne gave me something. She didn't look sick, but that
didn't mean she wasn't contagious. Maybe some snot-nosed kid had
run around touching doorknobs while his parents viewed the house.
Wherever I'd picked up the germ, this was no time to get sick. I
needed a clear head to handle this conversation with Garrett. One
wrong word could scare him off completely. I couldn't let that happen. Now that I had seen the house, I had to have it. It was mine. The
thought of another family living there, possibly the one with the snot-
nosed kid, gave me a flash of panic. If we didn't buy the house and it
went to another family, I might never get it back. This was my one
chance to live there. I'd tear down anything, or anyone, who tried to
stand in my way. Including Garrett.

I blinked hard to chase the thought away.

Where did that come from?

I could never tear Garrett down to get my way. How could I even
think something like that? Obviously I wasn't thinking clearly. The
stress of moving was getting to me. Getting me sick. Getting my temper up. Muddling my thoughts. I huffed a soft laugh to try and set
myself right again, and Garrett looked up.

"What's so funny?"

"Nothing," I said, then shrugged. "Sudsy underwear, I guess."

"Not so funny when you're the one who has to wear them." He scratched his hip. "I think I got a rash. Did you cancel the cable?"

"No. Sorry. I forgot."

He sighed. "If you don't do it this week, we'll get charged for another month."

"I know. I'll do it."

"Did you make the bank deposit, at least?" When I looked off to think about it, he huffed. "Come on, Dix. I got my hands full with work and everything else. You took off to take care of this stuff for us."

"I'll do it all tomorrow."

He rolled his eyes to begin repacking the box.

"I said I'll do it, Garrett."

He shook his head uncertainly. "I just worry, is all. We're on a tight schedule. I need to be able to count on you with this stuff."

"You can."

The shrug he gave thrashed a strange anger through me. Alien and skittish, like a scorpion. I sat upright as a spiny tail flicked my heart. A sharp breath stung my throat. The voice came like the prickle of tiny feet deep inside my ear: *He's going to say no to the house. He's going to try and stop you.* Though it was hardly a whisper, hoarse and weak, I feared I recognized it. The voice let out a grating laugh that vibrated down my jawline. As I rubbed it away, it slithered through my brain to get to my other ear. *He won't understand. He'll think you're crazy for wanting to live there. Don't tell him.* I shook my head to counter this terrible advice with my own sound instincts: Of course Garrett will understand. He loves me. We're both just stressed out. Just give him a chance. He'll be okay with it. *No, he won't. Don't—*

A hard swallow popped deep in my eardrum, and the voice fell silent.

"I have to tell you something," I said, clearing my throat. "It's about the house."

Garrett looked up from the box. "What? Did the loan fall through? I thought we got the approvals."

"It's not that."

He exhaled a relieved breath as he stepped into his sweatpants. Standing over me to tie his drawstring, he tried: "Termites?"

I shook my head.

"Did the insurance fall through?"

"No."

"Does the roof have a leak?"

"No."

"How many guesses do I get?"

I looked up at him. "You'll never guess it."

He knelt down in front of me to rub my thighs. "What is it? You look upset."

I sighed deeply as I picked a curl of tape from the front of his T-shirt. "Do you know what a stigmatized property is?"

He squinted a confused smile as he looked off to think about it, and then he frowned. "Yeah. I know what it is." He reeled to stand. "Please tell me that isn't your house."

"Well, my family's, yes, but . . ."

"Oh, my god!" He grabbed his head with both hands. "Are you kidding me right now? We're just about to go to settlement. Why the hell didn't you tell me?"

"I really didn't think it was that big of a deal." I followed up the fib with a convincing shrug. "Why, does it bother you?"

"Of course it bothers me, Dixie! Your family was murdered in that house. I think you might have mentioned that to me before you took me to see it."

"I didn't want you to form an opinion about it before you saw it," I said. "I thought once you saw how perfect it was for us, it wouldn't matter that it was my old house."

"You mean you wanted to trick me into buying."

He walked away to brace his hands against the dresser. I couldn't see his expression, but the slow shake of his head in the vanity mirror was furious.

"I'm sorry, Garrett. I should have told you. I didn't mean for this to happen. When I found the house online, I just wanted to go and check it out. I didn't think we were going to buy it or anything. But then when I saw how perfect it was for us . . . I guess I kinda got carried away. And it *is* perfect, Garrett. You said it yourself. It's been totally remodeled. It's like a brand-new house. I bet once we move in, we'll forget all about what happened there."

He turned to level me with a look. "You don't think we're still going to buy it, do you?"

My mouth dropped open, but no response came. I was physically incapable of saying no.

"There's no way I'm living in that house, Dixie."

"Okay." I cringed as the word skipped merrily from my mouth, at how dismissive I sounded, and how strangely excited I was at the prospect of having the house all to myself.

Garrett's hands hit his waist. "I'm serious, Dix."

"I know," I said, swiping a hand to remove any glibness to my tone. "I'm sorry."

"I'll call the agent." He turned in a half circle to look for his phone. "We haven't signed anything yet. We'll probably lose our good-faith money, but we should be able to get out of the contract."

"I don't want to get out of it." I said this softly, but my words knocked him back a step nonetheless.

"What does that mean?" he asked.

I shrugged. "It's my house, Garrett. I don't want to give it up."

"But I don't want to live there, Dixie," he reiterated.

"I know. I heard you. You don't want to live there. But I do, and I'm going to."

His arms fell. "Without me?"

"Well, if you're telling me you won't, then I guess I don't have a choice."

He stared at me in disbelief. "Are you giving me an ultimatum?"

"No . . ."

"It sure sounds like it."

I stood. "Look. I know this is hard for you to understand, but I have to live there, Garrett. I don't know how to explain it, but I feel like this was meant to be. What are the chances that my old house would be for sale at the exact same time I was looking for a new place for us to live? It has to be fate."

"Or a curse."

I crossed my arms. "It's not a curse."

"Feels like one to me. A second ago, we were moving into our dream house and starting a new life together, and now you're giving me ultimatums and threatening to leave. If that's not a curse, I don't know what is."

Told you, the voice said, swishing between my ears like a shark. *I told you he wouldn't fucking understand.*

I took a deep breath to keep the rancor of this thought from heating my voice, but couldn't quite manage to keep my cool. "You're being absolutely ridiculous! If it wasn't my family who died there, you probably wouldn't have a problem with it."

"But it *was* your family, Dixie. That makes a big difference and you know it."

I shook my head to let out a derisive sigh. "You're just looking for a reason to back out." I knew this wasn't true, but if I had any hope of getting to the moral high ground, I had to climb a slippery slope. "You didn't want to buy a house with me in the first place. Admit it!"

"No . . . I don't want to buy *that* house with you." He took my hands in his and pulled me close. "This is our first home together, Dix. I thought we were going to get married and settle down. Start a family. How could we possibly raise children in that house? Why would you even want to?"

"It's just a house, Garrett."

"A murder house," he amended.

I snatched my hands back. "Don't call it that."

"Well, that's what it is." He stepped forward to bear the full weight of his argument down on me. "Your family didn't die from carbon monoxide poisoning, Dixie. They were violently murdered. With an axe. By your father! Why would you want to surround yourself with those kind of memories? Do you want to be miserable? Do you think you owe your family that because you lived and they didn't?"

I turned from him. "Don't analyze me, Garrett."

"Well, it's kind of hard not to," he scoffed. "I can't see any reason for doing this except to torture yourself. Is that it? You want to torture yourself?"

"Of course not."

"Then why do it, Dixie?" His breath was heavy and desperate as he spun me toward him. "Are you really going to break up with me over that stupid house?"

"I'm not breaking up with you, Garrett. I love you. I do. And you love me. My living in that house won't change that." I touched his cheek. "Will it?"

He shook his head. "If you're saying that house is more important to you than I am, and that you'd leave me to have it, then . . . yeah, I think that changes things a little between us."

"That's not what I'm doing," I said. "You mean everything to me. You know that."

"Then prove it. Give up the house and stay with me. We can find another house. One we can both be happy in."

"We will. I promise." I lowered my eyes. "But not right now. I have to do this, Garrett. I knew it the second I found the house online that I had to live there. Something drew me to it. This isn't about you, or us. It's about me and my family. And I have to see it through, no matter how difficult it is. Please try and understand."

"I wish I could." He stepped back to smooth the argument from his shirt. "I would never let something like this come between us. And I can't believe you would, either."

"It can't come between us, Garrett," I said. "Nothing can. I won't let it."

"You already have, Dixie." With that, he turned and left the room. A moment later the front door slammed. I sank to the bed to hold my face and sob. A grating whisper vibrated deep in my ear.

Forget him. Let's go home.

MY UNCLE DAVIS died steadfast in his belief that his brother, my father, was innocent. For this reason, I barely knew the man. Aunt Celia hardly spoke to him or of him. The times she did were usually in a fit of some kind. "Oh, that Davis can drive a dead dog up the wall" was about as much as I knew about my uncle. Aunt Celia kept in touch with Aunt Charlene through Christmas cards and the occasional phone call, but would cut the call short if Uncle Davis came on the line. "I just can't stand to hear his drunken nonsense."

Aunt Celia was the youngest of the three siblings. My father was the oldest, which placed Uncle Davis smack-dab in the middle. From what Aunt Celia has told me, the three were relatively close as children. Their rivalries were of a predictable variety: brains versus brawn versus charm, descending in order of birth. Ford lived just one street over and attended the same elementary school up until the time of the fire. He, my father, and Uncle Davis were thick as thieves. "Running wild and raising hell" was how Aunt Celia described them. After Ford's world burned to the ground, he was sent to live with an uncle several miles away. Because he was no longer within walking distance of the Wheeler home, his friendships with them were relegated to the classroom and after-school sports, except with Aunt Celia. "I just felt so sorry for him." "He had nothing and nobody." "He kissed me when I was eight years old and that was all she wrote." I thought "she" would have done well to edit Ford out of the story well before Leah was born, or to write him in a bit more often once Leah became ill, but such is the essence of a great tragedy. If Uncle Davis believed that my father was innocent, Aunt Celia was equally sure of his guilt. "Davis just can't see the truth," Aunt Celia once said to me. "The police have no doubt about what Billy did, how can he?"

I didn't know. The only conversation I ever had with my uncle Davis was when he made an unwelcome appearance at Leah's funeral. He stayed just long enough to plant a seed of doubt in my susceptible brain, and to raid the buffet table of all its shrimp.

"Your father was a good man, Dixie," he had said, sucking cocktail sauce off the tip of his huge callused thumb. "You know that, right?"

I nodded as I took a bite of cheese that had slid out the side of my roll.

"He didn't do it, you hear? No matter what anyone tells you. Not Celia. Not nobody. Got it?" He wiped his mouth with a crumpled napkin as he looked over his shoulder at the kitchen.

I turned to see Aunt Celia standing with a group of people, her back to us. Ford was standing next to her, hand on her hip. Ford had returned two days after Leah was gone, bitching and moaning that no one had called to say how bad off she was. I'd thought that now the thread that tied them was gone, Aunt Celia would have kicked Ford to the curb, but she had set out an ashtray, stocked the fridge with Bud Light, and bought him a new suit for the funeral.

"He was set up!" Uncle Davis said so sharply in my ear that I dropped my sandwich. As I gathered it from the floor, he bent to say, "I don't know who did it, but I've been working day and night to find out. I owe my brother that. And his only living child. Don't lose faith. Okay, Dixie?"

I nodded as I stared up at his mouth; a celery string was caught between his two front teeth.

"You were too young to know what was happening, but you saw. You saw who really did it. And that bastard's still out there, walking around, living his life, not giving two shits about what he did. It's not fair."

I looked down to consider this and to run my thumbnail between my front teeth to make sure I didn't have any celery stuck.

He knocked the top of my head with his knuckles, and I looked up. "It's in there somewhere. The truth of what happened is in that head of yours. You know what I mean?"

I nodded as I stood.

"You just have to tap into it." He stabbed my head with his thick finger. "I've heard of people doing that. They remember things from when they were too young to remember much of anything. But they do remember, Dixie. You just need to try. Try and remember. Can you do that for me? Can you do that for your father?"

I nodded.

"Good girl." He leaned back to adjust his belt, then quickly leaned forward again. His tie fell across my plate like a tongue. "You know, I've got some of their stuff. You can have anything you want. Just give me a call and we'll work it out. But don't say anything to your aunt about it. Keep this between us, okay? Like a secret. Got it?"

As if sensing an accord was being struck behind her back, Aunt Celia came rushing from the kitchen, politely shooing off condolences as they were tossed her way, Ford fast on her heels.

"What are you filling her head with, Davis?" Aunt Celia demanded.

"Yeah," Ford said, scar blazing up his cheek like a fuse. It always ignited when he got uppity. "She don't need to hear your shit, Davis. Everybody knows you're as crazy as that brother of yours."

"Oh, look who decided to pay his daughter a visit." Davis laughed cruelly. "You're a bit late, aren't you, Ford?"

"Get out of here, Davis," Aunt Celia hissed under her breath, scanning the crowd at the buffet table, who were pretending not to listen. "You're drunk."

Aunt Charlene swooped in to take her husband by his arm. He yanked free and sent her stumbling. Reverend Thomas caught her like she was a dancing girl.

Davis pointed a finger in Ford's face. "You should speak better of the man that saved your life, Ford!"

Though Aunt Charlene couldn't have weighed more than a hundred pounds, she slammed her hands into the side of Uncle Davis with enough force to get the big man walking backward. His finger found me as he leaned over her shoulder. "Remember what I said, Dixie! Don't listen to them! They're all just a bunch of lying ingrates!"

Aunt Celia had refused to take me to Uncle Davis's to look through my family's belongings—much less allow me to bring a single item back to her house if I dared take the bus all the way out to Front Royal, as I had threatened—so it wasn't until I was packing up my meager half of Garrett's apartment that it occurred to me to find out if any of their things had survived my uncle's passing.

Aunt Charlene couldn't have been nicer when I called to inquire, though she did spend the first half of the call saying how truly awful she thought Aunt Celia was for cutting Davis out of her life.

"She's the same way with me," I said. "She won't even talk to me about what happened to my family. She just wants to put it all behind her."

"I never understood Davis's obsession with it, either," Charlene admitted. "He believed your father was innocent until the day he died. Frankly, I think that's what killed him. Cost him his job and all his friends. He got arrested once, you know." I said that I didn't. "Oh, yes. He threatened the detective who had investigated the case originally. Demanded that he find out who really killed your family. He showed up drunk at his house one night and wouldn't leave until he promised to reopen the case. When the detective refused, Davis threw a rock through his window."

"Oh, no."

"He spent all his time out in that damn garage. I'd hear him banging around out there until all hours of the night. I shouldn't tell you this, but once I found him out there wearing some of your father's old clothes and talking to him like he was standing right in front of him. When I asked him who he was talking to, he slammed the door in my face. That was just a few weeks before he died."

"That's so sad, Charlene. I'm so sorry."

"I know." There was a pause, a sniffle. "In the end, I could hardly talk to Davis without him biting my head off. It was like he turned into a completely different man. Turns out, he was doing drugs and all sorts of things I didn't know about. The autopsy found cocaine in his system." She turned "cocaine" into two words: "coke-cane."

I had only met Uncle Davis a couple of times, but I would never have guessed him to be a drug user. Clearly he was an alcoholic, his nose looked like a chunk of red coral, but I couldn't imagine him hunkered down over a mirror—or that his perforated nose could draw any amount of powder through a straw.

"Please don't tell Celia about the drugs, Dixie. I don't want her to think any less of Davis than she already does."

I assured her I wouldn't, then gradually transitioned to the reason for my call. "You didn't happen to keep any of my family's stuff after he died, did you?"

"Oh, yes," she said. "I have all of it. It didn't feel right to throw it away, and I wasn't about to go picking through it."

I sat forward. "Would you mind if I came by and got it?"

"Please do," she said. "I hate having it here. It gives me the creeps. But if you want it all, you're going to need to rent a moving truck. I'll go in half with you. You're doing me a big favor by getting it out of here."

"A moving truck?" I questioned. "How much is there?"

"A whole houseful."

· · ·

SUANNE ARNOLD'S CLAIM that the owners were heartbroken to have to sell their beloved home turned out to have been a sales tactic. In truth, they were desperate to be rid of it. The house had been on the market for over a year and mine was the first offer they had. The upgrades had been performed as a last-ditch effort to sell. When the owners learned that their only interested buyer might have to back out due to financial issues, they offered me a rent-to-buy option. I demanded a month-to-month lease for the first year of occupancy. Though Garrett wasn't happy about the situation, he could live with the idea of our living apart being temporary, and agreed to give me the space and time I needed to . . . do whatever it was I needed to do. All he asked was that I try to accomplish this task as quickly as possible.

The house was mine.

I paid a couple of busboys from work to move my family's possessions from Front Royal to my new/old house in Franconia. Though a lot of the items had mold or rot, rat holes or spider burrows, a surprising amount of it was in good condition. Uncle Davis had taken great care to preserve breakable items in bubble wrap, and plastic tarps had been used to safeguard the furniture. I was over the moon to find my mother's china mostly intact. There were only four teacups to eight saucers, but I didn't figure I would be serving high tea anytime soon, and certainly not to eight people. There were enough pots and pans to cook without doing dishes for weeks on end, and plenty of cutlery, though the butcher knife gave me pause. They must have had more than one. The toaster still glowed red, but the Mr. Coffee needed a few rounds of vinegar before it dribbled clear water.

I meticulously re-created the decor based on the old family photographs Aunt Celia had given me. Grainy snapshots were taped around the house like torn pages from a Martha Stewart catalog. Since furniture had been moved around to accommodate holiday decorations, a lot of the pictures weren't particularly helpful, but I only had to look past three Easter baskets on the coffee table to know that the couch got pushed back against the wall under the staircase when the Christmas tree came down.

I shuffled through the photos until I found one that had the widest view of the living room. The boys were lined up on the staircase, faces still flush from warm beds. Josh and Eddie were hanging over the banister at the waist. Michael was pressed between their knees, peeking through the slats like a prisoner. The camera flashed their wide eyes silver. Their smiles were almost too avaricious to be cute. Overnight, yellow Peeps had laid silver-wrapped chocolates and Jordan almonds. Hand-dyed eggs were nestled in bright green shreds of plastic. Boxed bunnies waited for their heads to be bitten off as my father captured his children's exact moment of Easter euphoria. My mother, stationed at the bottom of the staircase, had her hand pressed against the rush of squealing pajamas about to descend on her. I was in her arms, crying, reaching for the baskets on the table. My gummy grin explained why there were only three, but I did see a stuffed yellow bunny with my name on it lying at my mother's feet. Thrown in protest, would be my guess.

The picture made me like my brother Josh very much. Old enough to be bored sick by these tedious traditions, his smile rejoiced in the joy of his younger brothers. He had Eddie by the hand. Not to hold him back, not to keep him from going headfirst over the railing, but loose and tender, as though it was not uncommon for him to show such affection.

Though I had photographs to reference, they weren't completely necessary. Most of the pieces seemed to remember where they belonged. The sleigh-back rocking chair was at home in the far left corner of the living room before I even found a picture of it—even the green-and-yellow afghan knew it needed to be lazily draped over the back. I slapped a hand over my mouth when one of the guys set a vase in the exact right position on the side table. When I asked him why he had put it there, he shrugged and set a stack of cork coasters next to it. Picture-perfect! The couch was almost too funky to tolerate, but after an entire bottle of Febreze, it freshened up.

Well . . . good enough.

The kitchen table had not been salvaged after the murders, so I bought one at Goodwill that was as close of a match to the original as you could possibly get. Since I couldn't bear to sleep on my parents' old mattress—and the mattresses at Goodwill had not seen much good will in their time—I laid down the cost for a brand-new one. I bought a queen so I could use my parents' headboard with built-in storage nooks. Scotch tape had fused to the enamel over the sliding doors. I skinned off the tawny yellow adhesive with my fingernail to find books and magazines inside—romance novels and *Better Homes and Gardens* magazines on her side, and once-current fiction and *Popular Science* on his. I imagined my parents slipping reading materials over their heads before they clicked off their individual, and currently burned-out, reading lights. Based on its proximity, and a folded corner, I guessed that the last book my father had been reading was John Grisham's *The Firm*. If, after finishing a chapter, he had folded down the corner of the next page, the last sentence my father ever read was: "So long—For now."

THE FIRST NIGHT in the house was scarier than I had expected. Moonlight crept through the venetian blinds like the arms of an albino incubus. Though they were easily vanquished by lamplight, I knew they were still there, seeking out my feet with their cold gasiform feelers. Relocating to the couch downstairs only left the ghoul free to roam the hallway. Back and forth, back and forth, as though it kept forgetting something in the master bedroom. When what could only be knees stumbling to the floor brought me to a stand on the couch, I protected myself with a throw pillow. Though my mouth had run as dry as an oven, I had to swallow every two seconds to keep from choking on a wet lump in my throat.

My eyes followed the dragging sound across the ceiling.

Every urge in my body told me to grab my keys and get the hell out. Jump in my car and drive back to Garrett, beg his forgiveness, kiss my deposit and first and last months' rent good-bye, and crawl under the covers of our bed. Tears filled my eyes as I thought of our old apartment. How safe I felt there. How comfortable it was. All the strange noises had long ago been assigned. You could set the clock by the clang of the radiator. The refrigerator purred like a sleeping cat. The running toilet was my lullaby. One good elbow to the wall could stop scurrying roaches dead in their tracks, and if the mousetrap didn't snap while we were eating dinner, it was a good night.

God, I missed it.

Right now Garrett would be kicked back on the couch watching some documentary that would have bored me to sleep within five minutes. When he couldn't wake me, he'd cover me up with a blanket. I'd shuffle to the bedroom an hour later, annoyed that he'd gone to bed without me. I'd curl up behind him, rub my cold feet on his warm legs. He'd turn and wrap me in his arms, knees fitting behind mine like a twin in the womb. He'd wake first, put coffee on—

Shit! I forgot to buy coffee.

So as to not step off the safety of the couch, I used my big toe to drag my phone across the coffee table. I crouched in a pounce as I cued up Garrett's number, hesitated to press Send, and then closed the screen.

I couldn't give up.

Not yet.

Not after one day.

I looked slowly up as the dragging sound returned in the upstairs hallway: the ghoul pulling itself slowly toward the top of the stairs by handfuls of carpeting.

Thump, thump—swish. Thump, thump—swish. Thump, thump—swish . . .

I sprang off the couch and headed to the kitchen.

I cracked open a beer, shoved my earbuds in as deep as they would go, cued up iTunes, and turned to the boxes that still needed to be unpacked. Of course the first song to shuffle up was "Baby Blue." I skipped to the next. "Hotel California." I don't think so. "Don't Fear the Reaper." Next! "Baby Blue." What the— Next! "Sweet Child o' Mine" wasn't a particularly haunting tune, but I didn't want to hear it. It was one of Garrett's favorites. "Rhiannon" . . . ? Hmm. No. I loved it, and felt myself wanting to sing along, but it reminded me too much of Leah. That, and I couldn't remember ever downloading it. In fact, I was almost positive I hadn't. All my Fleetwood Mac was off the *Rumours* album, which I immediately scrolled to. I worked through the first half of the album until "Baby Blue" somehow shuffled in again. I ripped out my earbuds so fast that it made my ears pop, and grabbed the bottle of Jack Daniel's off the top of the fridge. I looked for a glass for half a second, and then drank straight from the bottle.

Jack at my side, I sat on my heels and ripped the tape off the next box.

Five boxes in, and I had to wonder if my parents actually had lived in the same house as their children. The bulk of their possessions belonged to the boys. The few boxes that contained my parents' things had some sort of toy or piece of sporting equipment mixed in with them. The football helmet was a little tight, but the pink fuzzy slippers fit like a dream. The Slinky I slipped on my wrist was a little warped, but I had found it stuffed inside a blender, so what did I expect?

Clearly, Uncle Davis had bounded between rooms blindfolded. A hair dryer was tangled in a nest of leather belts, bungee cords, and a soft yellow measuring tape; a box of comic books also contained a nose-hair trimmer. I found my mother's jewelry buried under a wad of stiff utility towels.

I turned the jewelry box over in my hands. One of the boys must have made it for her. Her initials were burned so deep into the thin pine lid that you could see straight through in spots. I ran my finger over a tiny black flower that underscored her monogram. Thorns along the delicate stem looked like shark teeth. A wry smiley face sat in the upper-right-hand corner like a postage stamp.

I moved to the kitchen table to pick through the contents. Most of the jewelry was costume: synthetic colored baubles connected by a cheap chain or clear wire. Most of her silver was green. If any one piece cost more than twenty dollars, I would have been surprised. Her engagement ring was up in my own jewelry box—a high school graduation present from Aunt Celia. I always meant to have it re-sized, but never got around to it. I slipped my mother's high school class ring onto my pinkie and held a small, tarnished locket up to the light. Josh and Eddie's school pictures were inside. Josh looked to be in junior high, which would have put Eddie in kindergarten. I wondered why my parents waited so long after their first child to have three more in such quick succession. Josh had been an only child until he was almost nine years old. My parents took a three-year break after Michael before they had me, but not long enough to set me outside his peer group. Maybe Josh had been a mistake. Maybe I was. I closed the locket, wrenched off the football helmet, and slipped the chain over my head.

The next box I opened was fat with coats. Just coats, which seemed unusual until I found a bicycle pump at the bottom.

I tried on my mother's raincoat. A London Fog with a mint in its pocket. I raised the candy to my nose, then bit through the wrapper to draw it into my mouth. The edges were gummy, but the mint was still flavorful. I sucked on it as I donned her scarf and flexed my fingers to stretch the leather of her gloves. The scarf still held a hint of perfume. I wrapped it around my chin and unfolded my father's black wool dress coat. I checked the pockets and found a receipt for a

Chinese restaurant: Peking duck, Mongolian beef, and fried rice. The bottle of Merlot cost $18.50. Only one dessert. Date night. My eyes fell on the date: 10/24/92. A month before the murders. How could it be that just one month before my father planted an axe in my mother's chest, he had taken her on a date? Shared a dessert?

I had never given the time right before the murders a lot of thought. I just assumed that life had been a living hell for the Wheeler family. Aunt Celia once said that up until that day, she thought everything had been normal. She never heard my father so much as raise his voice to my mother, or to the boys. She insisted they were a happy family. Normal. What happened came as a total shock. An "abnormality." I never really believed that. You don't go from zero to axe murder overnight. I thought what Aunt Celia had witnessed was just a brave front the family put on for her benefit, a formal curtain hung over a broken window. My father would have kept his evil under wraps in front of company. Makeup could cover a bruise. The abuse would have occurred behind closed doors, so how could Aunt Celia have known? The boys would have been too scared to talk. I tightened the scarf around my throat and imagined my mother a prisoner in her own home, secluded and afraid. A shadowy face in the crack of a door that always claimed that it was a bad time for a visit. I'd never imagined her slipping a mint into her pocket as she left a restaurant with my father. I got up and spit the mint, suddenly stale, into the trash can.

3

I desperately wanted a hot bath, but couldn't bring myself to take one. Bad things always happened when someone took a bath in a horror movie. And though my tub wasn't one of those old-timey claw-footed thingamajiggies, it would hold enough water to drown me. A shower was no good, either. *Psycho*? Hello? My shower didn't have a curtain I could pull off the rings as bloody water circled the drain, but it did have a drain.

I opted to stay dirty and alive, and brushed my teeth with my back to the mirror, careful not to get a glimpse of my eyes as I turned to spit in the sink. I didn't need to see how scared I was. The squirrelly quality of my heartbeat, the uncontrollable tremble in my knees, and the prick of a million tiny icicle hairs against the back of my shirt were reminder enough. My hands were shaking so bad I could barely get the floss out of the container. I shook my head as I took a seat on the toilet, wiped my brow with toilet paper, and steadied my knees with cold fingertips. Everything would be better in the morning. I just had to get through the night . . . *Live* through the night.

Freddy Krueger ran a knifey finger down my back as I stood to flush.

I checked the time as I got into bed, certain that I only had a few hours until daybreak.

12:50 A.M.

For as tired as I had been, I was wide-awake as soon as my head hit the pillow. I turned on the bedside lamp and began my father's book, grateful that he hadn't been a fan of Stephen King or Clive Barker. Snuggling into the story, I let the fictional realm grow around me like a protective shell. Inside, I was someone else. Someone less alone. Someone with a whole host of other problems to worry about. I wasn't a girl curled up in the bed of her dead parents. I was . . . let's see . . . Mitchell Y. McDeere, an honest lawyer about to be hired by a corrupt law firm and thrown into a world of chaos. Oh, to have such pedestrian concerns. I might have bought into the premise if the book weren't being narrated in my father's voice. I tried to switch it to Matthew McConaughey—who normally read me my bedtime stories—but he barely got through one sentence before my father snatched the book from his hands.

When I was a child, my father sounded like Oscar the Grouch— who scared the bejesus out of me whenever he peeked out from under the lid of his trash can. When I was a teenager, he sounded more like Jack Sparrow, or, more precisely, Oscar the Grouch with a few pints of rum in him. Then one day he cleared his throat and took on what I imagined to be the voice of my father. He didn't really sound like anyone, or anything, except maybe a bloated body calling to you from deep inside a well.

Since my father was sticking to the story, I let him read on. But as the words on the page began to swim in a dark, drowsy fluid, and horrible thoughts permeated the plotline, the fictional world I was immersed in turned into a bloodbath. No matter where the characters went, the walls were splattered with gore. Blood-drenched faces carried on dialogues with people who were way past the point of hearing. What one character said hit a little too close to home: *Hold still, boy! It won't hurt for long. Will you please shut that baby up! I can't hear myself think! Goddamn it, Eddie! Stand still!*

I blinked hard to concentrate and . . .

The tail end of a scream was still fresh in the air as my eyes opened. I looked at the clock: 3:28. I exhaled in frustration and closed the book still open in my hands. A musty scent wafted from the pages as my father exited the bathroom, drying his hands on a towel. It landed on my belly as he slung it at the bed, warm and pink with blood. I flicked it away in disgust.

"Get up, Deb," he said, heading to the dresser and sliding open the top drawer. *"You've got a mess to clean up downstairs."*

"I'm Dixie, Dad," I said. "Mom's dead, remember?"

He looked back at me in surprise. *"Holy shit, you look just like her."* He smiled as he stood over me, began to unbuckle his belt. *"So, you ready?"*

I pressed into my pillow. "Ready for what?"

"Your gift." Black leather slid from his waist and hung between us like an eel.

"What gift?" I asked as he slipped the end of the belt through the buckle.

He frowned like I was being unnecessarily petulant. *"Don't play coy with me, Dixie dear."* He snapped the belt at me like a toothless jaw, smiled when it made me jump. *"Now I'll have to punish you."*

"Punish me." I intended to say this as a question, but repeated it like a chant: "Punish me. Punish me. Punish me." As he tested the strength of the belt, I shook my head to ask, "What did I do?"

He sighed with resigned conviction. *"You kept me waiting here too long, my love."*

My mother's locket grew warm on my chest as he spotted it. The clasp bit into the back of my neck when he snatched it from my throat. The tarnished amulet swung just out of my reach, hypnotic in the moonlight.

"Junk," he declared as he tossed it over his shoulder. *"Now this"*— he snapped the belt again—*"is more your style."* He slipped the loop of leather over my head. Before I could think to object, the buckle was at my throat.

The leash constricted as I turned to get away. Yanked backward, I grabbed at the covers to keep from falling off the bed. They slid in a pile on top of me as I went over the edge. I arched my back to find air, thrashing like a marlin beneath the surface of my cotton sheets. I grabbed for the strap behind my head, stiff as a yardstick. Just as my fingers crawled over his hands, I was lifted off the ground. The strap around my neck burned like acid. The pressure in my head threatened to blow out my eyes in a red throb. I probed the band around my neck to find a hold, but it was slippery with blood. I clawed at my skin around the garrote, not caring if I caused additional pain, desperate to find a way in, around, or under the noose. Taut flesh gave way with a sickening pop. My fingers found muscle, thick and greasy as a slab of uncooked bacon. Pain I never imagined possible filled me like a poisonous gas. Every vein in my body turned to barbed wire that sliced me open from the inside out. Then, suddenly, the pain was gone and I was free. I had the giddy sense of twirling on a swing. The room flew by in a dizzy circle, jarred to a stop, and then spun back the other way, conversely rotating until it slowed to a lazy sway. I looked down upon my father's laughing face as he held up my severed head by the hair.

The sound of my own scream woke me. I was on the floor in a tangle of sheets. I pulled them from my face and looked around the room for my father. My mother's locket was in a puddle on the floor by the bed. I checked the clasp. Broken. Setting it on the nightstand, I glanced out the window and saw that I hadn't quite made it to sunrise. The clock changed to 5:15.

Close enough.

SINCE I DIDN'T have any coffee, I poured Diet Coke into a coffee mug and sat on the couch to await the sun. The room seemed smaller than it had the night before, cramped with yet-to-be-placed furniture and remnants of overturned packing containers.

My eyes fell on a green metal desk near the front window, piled high with broken-down boxes. The desk didn't belong. I couldn't find it in any of the pictures. It wasn't Josh's; his desk had a collage of heavy metal stickers stuck to the top and sides: Metallica, Megadeth, Slayer . . . Eddie and Michael probably didn't have a desk. They would have done their homework at the kitchen table under the eye of my mother, just like Aunt Celia did with me. My mother kept her stationery in a small secretary I had set next to the front door, so the desk wasn't hers, either. The military look of the desk just didn't mesh with a lawless guy like my father. It must have belonged to Uncle Davis. I wondered why Charlene hadn't stopped me from loading it on the truck. She probably didn't want it, either. Drab, sturdy, and impersonal, it was definitely army issue. Khaki-colored metal with three drawers, one in the center and two on the right. Each drawer had its own lock, but I suspected one key would open them all.

I ran my fingers around the inside of the kneehole to see if a key had been taped up there for safekeeping. No luck. Uncle Davis probably had kept the key on a ring with all his others. Discouraged, I sat back to bite a solution from my thumbnail.

Back from the kitchen with a steak knife, I set the mountain of flat cardboard boxes on the floor, pulled up a folding chair, and got to work on the center drawer.

I'd never picked a lock before, and as I suspected, it wasn't easy. Four Band-Aids later, I was pretty sure it couldn't be done. Not on this particular desk, anyway. The military probably built in some sort of tamperproof system to safeguard against counterintelligence. Paranoid motherfuckers. I was just about to give up when the knife sank in with a soft metallic *click*, and the drawer popped open.

I peered into the three-inch opening. A few pencils and pens rode the beveled front tray, along with a smattering of top hat tacks, paper clips, and half a sleeve of staples. A yellow ruler was stationed directly behind the tray. Farther in, just barely visible in the slim opening, was the corner of a thick manila folder.

I scooched back and slowly slid the drawer open with my fingertip.

The file was the official property of the Franconia Police Department. As if it contained intestines that could easily slip out if turned the wrong way, I carefully eased the file out of the drawer, and dropped it flat on the desk. Though the sleeve looked and felt dry, it made a wet splat as it landed.

I knew what it was. What it had to be. But how did Uncle Davis have it?

Maybe he stole it from the detective the night he threw a rock through his window. Charlene didn't say anything about him getting arrested for breaking and entering, but maybe that had been the whole point of the vandalism.

I bent eye level with the file to see if I could see inside without actually touching it. Half an inch thick, it was filled with various colored papers. Most were white or yellow, a few were pink, and one or two were green. Some of the sheets were a lot thicker than the others. Not paper . . .

Photographs.

I stumbled back into the folding chair behind me, landed off center, and jammed my wrist as I hit the floor. I clambered to my feet and ran to the safety of the kitchen. Oddly comforted by the invisible barrier a different room provided, I massaged my wrist as I stared at the file. It seemed to breathe, to pant: quick hiccupping breaths that were in sync with my own heartbeat. A sudden dizziness came over me, hot and hard, and I stumbled around the kitchen table to gag into the basin of the sink.

After splashing cold water on my face, I returned to the side of the desk with a freshly cracked beer. I dragged my finger across the top of the file, then wiped it on the front of my shirt as I backed to the safety of the staircase.

It can't hurt you, I told myself. *Whatever's in there, it can't be worse than the horrors you've imagined.*

I nodded hard to make this true. I had chopped my family into a million pieces over the years, bopped Eddie's head around my mind like a balloon. I had peeled back Josh's scalp to find his thoughts and traced Michael's splintered rib cage to see if it tickled him the same as mine.

But they were only thoughts. Ones I could alter and manipulate as I saw fit. I only visualized what I could tolerate to imagine. I never focused on their faces. They were just screaming blurs, thrashing limbs and wisps of hair being chased around the kitchen. Once the screaming stopped, they were mannequins strewn about the floor, off-center wigs and clean breaks of limbs, dry as snapped chalk. What blood I imagined was thin and diluted, more like watered-down tomato soup. Their skin was way too smooth to be genuine. Those weren't really brains; they were noodles, dyed a pinkish gray to look like brains. My mother's eyes—the only bit of face I allowed myself—were glass. They didn't even look real. You can never get the eyes right.

I flipped the cover open and took a step back. The top page was a tidy police report, nothing gruesome about it.

I took a seat.

Who knew mass murder could be so prosaic. The details included in the police report were professional to the point of banal, almost insensitive. No adjectives, just facts. My family had been dried out, stripped of all humanity, and clipped into uninspired sentences. The "deceased," as they were listed, were like so many items on Craigslist: Deceased Female: approx. 40–45. Deceased Male, Juvenile: approx. 14–16. Deceased Male, Juvenile: approx. 8–10. Deceased Male, Juvenile: approx. 4–6. Their injuries were a sort of nonspecific violence: Trauma to head. Trauma to chest. Trauma to hands. Trauma to neck, to shoulders, to legs, to abdomen . . . Male: approx. 40–45. Trauma to throat. Alive but unresponsive. CPR administered. Dispatched to Franconia County Hospital.

What?

I pulled the file closer, certain I had misread the entry.

I hadn't. The male who was approximately forty to forty-five, and alive when the paramedics arrived, had to be my father.

How could this be?

Did he die at the hospital? In transit? Why didn't Aunt Celia ever tell me? I suppose it didn't really matter if he died on our kitchen floor or later at the hospital, but still, I should have been told. I wanted to flip ahead to see if there was any additional information, but the staple in the top left corner of the police report had me nervous. The crime scene photos were just a few sheets of thin paper beneath my fingertips.

I licked my thumb to ensure a secure grip of a single sheet.

I'm not sure what happened.

I didn't suddenly go crazy and swipe the desk with my hand. I simply, and very cautiously, turned the page. But the next thing I knew, the file was on the floor. Glossy horror fanned out across the carpet like a deck of cards at a blackjack table. A close-up of Eddie's head was at the top of the deck. Of course the most horrific of all would be. Michael's hacked-up back poked out from underneath. The nub of Eddie's spinal cord connected seamlessly to Michael's skinned ribs. Bloody white gristle, both. My mother's scalped forehead was just visible under Josh's parted skull. One of her eyes, green and dead, was staring up at me.

With a whimpering cry, I fell to my knees to gather them up. The glossy paper was slick, and Eddie slipped from my fingers and wafted under the TV stand. I laid my cheek on the floor, but couldn't see into the dark slat. I got to my feet to push the stand aside, but it was stacked high and heavy with odds and ends that hadn't yet found a home. Though most of it was junk, some of the junk was breakable. I ran upstairs to get a wire hanger from my closet. As I entered my bedroom, I tripped over my pillow and landed on all fours. A sharp pain swelled from my wrist. I sat on my heels to work out if it was broken or just sprained, then tossed the pillow back onto the bed with my good hand.

Back in the living room I untwined the hanger to forge a long metal finger. After several failed stabs, I grabbed my phone and downloaded a flashlight app. Cheek to the floor once again, I caught a corner of the picture in a crook of light. Gently, I speared it with the hanger and drew it forward until I could get my fingers on it.

Michael slid into view.

I turned to look at the stack of photos next to the desk.

Eddie was back on top.

THE PICTURES MIGHT have been easier to look at if they weren't so vibrant. All that colorized meat was hard to take now that I knew my family a little better: had played with their stuff, checked their report cards, sucked upon my mother's mint. Blood was an otherworldly shade of red against their alabaster skin, which reminded me of creatures born deep in a fissure of a cave. Generations deprived of light, undeserving of color. Their clothes—warm, rich, fiery colors that put an autumn sunset to shame—seemed a crime against their kind, like a flashy tie around the neck of a toad. My mother's lipstick was a ghastly shade of orange that never should have been in vogue. Was she really wearing cornucopia earrings? Had she bought them special to give her outfit a little Thanksgiving whimsy? Though I hadn't found any in her jewelry box, I suspected she had sets of Christmas tree, Easter egg, and jack-o'-lantern earrings somewhere. I turned her facedown on the kitchen table.

Eighteen photographs were laid out on the floor, countertops, and kitchen table. Eddie's headless body was taped to the dishwasher. I sat in the same spot as my high chair would have been that day, Michael at my feet. I closed my eyes to draw memories on the backs of my eyelids, and could almost feel Uncle Davis rap his knuckles on my head.

It's in there somewhere. The truth of what happened is in that head of yours. You know what I mean?

I knew exactly what he meant. I was there when it happened, sitting in this very spot. Whether I could remember it or not, a memory had been recorded. Everything I witnessed from the time I was born up until that very second had been captured and recorded. From calculus to commercials, good, bad, or otherwise, it was all in my head somewhere. Every millisecond of my life had been chronicled. I just had to access it.

Forget the fact that I couldn't remember where I put my keys half the time, I could remember the first time I saw Garrett's face. His goofy smile as he squinted in the smoky bar. Leah's dead face was as clear to me as if I had just seen it yesterday. I'll never forget Rory's horrified expression as I grabbed his crotch instead of a handful of popcorn. I could clearly remember the face of the girl who punched me in the head in kindergarten, though I couldn't tell you her name. I knew Aunt Celia as a young woman, her face smooth and tan. Leah as a kid, the long ponytail I wished I had twirling between fingers done up with pink nail polish.

I cross-referenced like this back as far as I could remember, back before I could walk, before I could talk. Back to sippy cups and onesie pajamas. Which of the five senses would have been most prevalent to me at that time? Sight, smell, taste, touch . . . ? I couldn't remember what the last sense was—which did not bode well for the exercise—but I had not been quite two years old at the time, so my strongest sense was probably taste. Babies that age put everything in their mouths.

I opened my eyes to search the table for the photograph of my high chair. The Froot Loops on the tray were bloated and gray from sopped-up blood, but a couple in the corners still looked crunchy enough to eat. I didn't have any Froot Loops, but I knew what Froot Loops tasted like. I ran my tongue around my mouth and could only find the faint flavor of mint toothpaste behind a bitter hint of beer.

I smacked my lips disagreeably and pressed my hands to the table to conduct a one-person séance. Closing my eyes, I took a deep breath and rolled my neck to relax. I shifted in my chair, uncrossed my legs, relaxed my shoulders, and took an even deeper breath. Nothing happened. I couldn't get comfortable. Something didn't feel right. Just off by a smidge, but enough to obstruct the process.

I picked up a wide-angle shot of the kitchen to study it.

Something about it, other than violence itself, made me uncomfortable. Maybe that's all there is to the memory of someone so young. Not a memory at all but a feeling. A crawling under your skin. A strange taste in your mouth. An odor you can't quite put your finger on. A sudden sense of danger. I'd had the same sensation when I was in the hallway upstairs earlier, like I had walked through a musty cobweb. And now, like then, I felt a centipede of worry cross my chest.

I stood to stare at the table.

After a quick inventory, I reached out to reposition my mother a fraction of an inch, and accidently nudged her over the edge. As I bent to pick her up from the floor, I noticed something on the back top right corner of the photograph. I walked it to the window and held it under the sunlight. The marking was too small and faint to see clearly, but it definitely had some structure to it. It wasn't a random stain or a blemish. Holding the picture at arm's length like Aunt Celia did to read the instructions on the back of a box, I blinked the number 8 into focus.

I started flipping pictures over.

Right away I noticed that numbers 13 through 16 were missing. The wide-angled shot from the entryway leading into the living room was numbered 28, which meant I was missing a lot more than I'd realized. The last number before that was 21.

I was making a list of each picture as it related to its reference number when a knock at my back jolted me upright. I braced the table for seismic activity as I ran my eyes around the quiet kitchen.

The next knock was followed by a muffled "Hello?"

I glanced back at the kitchen door.

"Anybody home?"

I called for "Just a sec!" as I hurriedly picked pictures off the floor. Turning in a circle, I slung the file into an empty cabinet. I paused to fix my hair and take a breath before I stepped into the alcove. A fair-haired woman was smiling at me through the naked pane. She held up her hand in greeting. I opened the door a crack to tell her it was a bad time for visitors.

"Hi, I'm Vicki." She smiled as she held up a cellophane-wrapped pan. "I wanted to come by and welcome you to the neighborhood."

I nodded to acknowledge that she had spoken, but did not exchange the greeting.

"Are you getting all settled in?" She rose up on her toes to see over my shoulder. "I remember how crazy that can be. I live next door." She nodded left at what I was almost positive was Rory's old house. "My husband, Nick, said I was being pushy coming over like this, but I thought you might like a little pick-me-up." She lifted the pan chin level and took a heavenly sniff. "*Mmm*, nothing like a brownie to get your blood sugar going. I threw in some caramels to make them extra gooey. I bet you could use some power food right about now." She took a step forward in expectation of an invitation, and I tightened to the door.

"Sorry," I said, clearing my throat. "I'm kind of in the middle of things." I looked down and spotted a photo I had neglected to gather with the rest. Eddie's head was poking out from around the corner, watching me with shocked eyes. I did a double take as I thought I saw him blink, then stretched out my leg and kicked him out of sight.

"Oh, sure, I get it," Vicki said with an affable pout. "Can you use a hand? I'm a whiz with a box cutter."

"Thanks, but I'm good."

"Well, just let me know if you need anything. Borrowing a cup of sugar might sound cliché, but ain't it the truth?"

"Thanks," I said.

"Do you have children?" she asked. I shook my head, which prompted, "Married?"

"Nope. It's just me."

"Oh, lucky you!" The sympathetic head tilt she gave eclipsed the candor of her words. "I would love just one day without someone needing their butt or nose wiped. And the kids are no piece of cake, either." She tickled herself with that one and let out a snorting laugh. "Oh, I'm just kidding. Nick's the best. We have three kids. Twin boys and a little girl. The boys just turned eight, and Katie will be two next month." She rolled her eyes. "God, I can't believe she's two already. Feels like yesterday."

"They must keep you busy," I said.

"They keep you on your toes, that's for sure. Nick's a big help. Well . . . most of the time." She frowned, then shook her head to put herself in check. "Anyway. Are you free for dinner tomorrow night? I make a mean lasagna."

"Can I get back to you on that?" I said. "I still have a lot to do."

"Oh, sure. No pressure." She pushed the brownie pan at me. I opened the door just wide enough to take it. "Just give me a call to let me know if you can make it." She took hold of the doorknob. "Here, let me give you my number."

"No," I said, sharper than polite, so I smiled to say, "You know, tomorrow should be fine. What time?"

"Oh, great! We eat at six, but feel free to come whenever you want. I'll get us a bottle of wine. Do you like white or red?"

I didn't like wine but said that either was fine. Nodding good-bye, I stepped back to close the door. She put her hand out to hold it open.

"I'm sorry, but I didn't ask your name." She scrunched her nose when I hesitated to respond.

"Dixie," I said. I held my breath to await her reaction, certain my name was legendary in this neighborhood. But if the name registered with her, her eyes didn't let on. Baby Blue probably would have gotten her there, but I hadn't introduced myself by that name since the first grade. The kids changed it to Baby Boo-Hoo within a minute of my speaking it, and it had taken an entire year to get them to stop.

"Well, it was nice to meet you, Dixie," Vicki said. "See you tomorrow. Super casual, okay?" She gave me a toodle-oo with her fingers as she sashayed around the corner.

I pressed the door closed with my forehead. Why on earth did I agree to dinner? What was I thinking? I can't chitchat about myself over a glass of wine, not to a woman like Vicki. She'd blab about me to all the neighbors. *You know the Wheeler house? Yeah, the one next to mine, where the massacre took place, well, get this . . .* Stupid! I should have made up an excuse. Any excuse. But I couldn't just not go; I'd have to face Vicki again at some point. Our driveways were no more than fifteen yards apart. Maybe I was overreacting. After all, the murders were twenty-five years ago. The neighborhood had to have turned over a few times since then. Anyone who knew my family was long gone. The Wheeler name probably wouldn't even raise an eyebrow anymore.

Feeling less than hopeful about this, I turned with a sigh and set the brownies on the counter. I stared at them for a moment, then ripped off the cellophane and dug out a chunk with my fingers. When I emerged from my trance, half the pan was picked clean. Sickened at the thought of another bite, I wiped my hands on the dish towel hanging from the oven door, picked Eddie up from off the floor, and opened the cabinet to retrieve the file. I was halfway in my turn to the table when I paused. Maybe just one more bite. Vicki was right: Caramel did make them extra chewy. I popped a good-size gob in my mouth and fell sideways into Josh's chair at the head of the table to chew.

I flipped the cover of the file open and tucked Eddie back in with the rest. Maybe I had somehow overlooked the missing pictures when I went through the file originally. Methodically, I reviewed it again, shaking pages to make sure pictures weren't hidden between or stuck to any documents. Frustrated, I sat back to stare at the police report, frowning at a chocolate smudge in the left-hand margin. The name of the detective who worked the case was noted at the top. I leaned forward to tap the name with a sticky finger.

Maybe Detective Stanley R. Cullins knew where the missing pictures were.

DETECTIVE CULLINS HAD retired from the force three years prior. After being told at the district station that someone would be with me shortly, I spent three hours in a common area with a pack of girls who looked to be in high school, but dressed and smelled like hookers after a lucrative night. Finally, I was referred to a detective who couldn't have cared less about a crime that was committed when he was in the eighth grade. No, he didn't have any information about the case. No, he didn't know the current whereabouts of Detective Cullins. Yes, I could use their bathroom.

After a quick search on my phone, I found the addresses for two Stanley R. Cullinses in the area. One lived relatively close to the police station, but proved not to be him, or any relation at all. The other lived in a single-family home in Crestwood, an older neighborhood with gargantuan trees and aboveground pools. Though it was just inside the beltway, it was a good fifty years outside modern civilization. Electrical poles lined the streets like the masts of pirate ships whose crews had been paved over by a wave of black asphalt. Brick and aluminum siding went together like polyester shirts and checkered slacks from the 1970s. I think I passed the Bradys' house on the corner.

I sat low in the front seat of my car to study his house over the nose of my car. The BEWARE OF DOG sign on the back fence and the NO SOLICITING sign on the front door, along with the drawn curtains, made me wonder if Stan Cullins would welcome an unannounced visitor. Before I could convince myself that he absolutely would not, I snatched my keys from the ignition and rushed across the lawn with my fist drawn. I knocked three times in rapid succession.

A dog barked deep inside the house. Small breed. Yippy. Possibly a miniature schnauzer or toy poodle. I smirked at the BEWARE OF DOG sign on the six-foot privacy fence as sharp nails skittered toward the door. The barking stopped to sniff me out from under the jamb. Whatever type of dog it was, it didn't care for the smell of me, and began scratching at the door to satisfy its urge to rip me to shreds.

I knocked again. The dog went totally berserk, but no one came to the door. I stepped to my right to glance through a thin slat in the curtain of the front window. A formal living room that didn't appear to be used with much frequency. A flowered couch sat beyond an antique coffee table that offered the rare guest an empty red glass candy dish.

I turned to look at a white Buick LeSabre parked in the driveway. Someone was home. I spotted a cracked, weathered doorbell sunk into the frame. I pressed it and listened for a chime. If it sounded, I couldn't hear over the incessant yapping. I stabbed the button again and was rewarded with a continuous trilling that carried with it one long, desperate howl.

As the dog and the bell cried out that somebody was at the fucking door, heavy footsteps came at me from inside the house. I put my hands up in surrender as the door flew open and an angry man in a green bathrobe came towering onto the stoop. After looking me up and down to determine if I warranted such alarm, he pushed me aside to address the doorbell with his fingernail.

"Damn!" he yelled. "You got it stuck in there good!"

"I'm sorry!" I said. "I knocked, but you DIDN'T HEAR ME!"

My scream bounded down the quiet street as the dog and doorbell fell silent. The man cinched his robe by its frayed belt. Gray hair rose like smoke above his heated face. "Can I help you, miss?" he asked with affected politeness.

"Oh, um, yes, well, I think," I stammered. "Are you Detective Cullins?"

"No."

I stepped back to check the street number over the door. "Oh, I thought this was his address."

"It's Mr. Cullins," he corrected. "Not 'Detective.' Not anymore."

"Oh, okay, so—"

"What do you want?" he asked brusquely.

"I hoped I could ask you a few questions."

"I don't do interviews."

"No." I shook my head with a reassuring smile. "It's not that. I'm here because I wanted—"

"Not interested." He started back into the house. "And don't ring that bell again."

"Please!" I begged. "I'm Dixie Wheeler!"

He turned back, studied me for less than half a second, and concluded: "The hell you are."

"I am. I swear. Here." I opened my bag and handed him my wallet with my driver's license exposed.

He compared me to the photo with several quick nods and then scratched his head. "Well, whattaya know about that." He handed my wallet back. "Dixie Wheeler, huh?"

I shrugged.

He shook his head. "Well, whattaya know about that."

I shrugged again.

He shook his head once more. "Dixie Wheeler, huh?"

We had reached an impasse.

"Can I talk to you?" I asked.

"Oh, sure, sure." He stepped aside to wave me in.

A small gray-and-white Chihuahua was shivering in the corner of the foyer. When he spotted a stranger entering, he trembled forth a string of ferocious yaps that blasted him off the floor.

"Shut up, Pepper," Mr. Cullins said, bending down to scoop up his attack dog. Pepper's seething growls and bulging eyes advised that I was not welcome in this house, no matter what his servant might have told me. "He's just an old scaredy-cat. Aren't you, boy?" Pepper dropped his tail from his balls to wag it once, then tightened it once again. Mr. Cullins made kissy face with the dog as he said, "She's not going to hurt you, boy. Are you? Oh, no, you're not."

I wasn't sure if he was talking to me or the dog, but I said that I meant Pepper no harm. I offered the dog a whiff of the back of my hand, and got warned off with a snap.

"Sorry. He hasn't been the same since Salt died," Mr. Cullins explained. "He's scared to death of everything now. Aren't you, boy? He didn't used to be like that. Did you, boy?"

"Salt?" I asked.

"His sister. She died last year."

"Salt and Pepper," I said. "Cute."

Mr. Cullins tucked Pepper under his arm like a football. "Salt was the ugliest dog there ever was, but Pepper loved her to bits. Didn't you, boy? Well, come on back." He turned and shuffled down a hall toward the back of the house. "I just put on some coffee, if you're interested."

Mr. Cullins dropped Pepper on a dog bed in the corner of the kitchen on his way to the coffee machine.

"Sorry about your doorbell," I said, glancing around. The decor was way too country clutter for a bachelor. Lots of roosters and dried flowers. It made me wonder if there was a Mrs. Cullins. Based on the amount of loose newspapers and dirty dishes lying about, I sensed both he and Pepper had lost their companions. I looked down at Pepper to sigh, and he turned on his side to raise a paw. The defensive gesture was kind of cute, but his bared teeth weren't even playing.

"No worries," Mr. Cullins said. "It sticks all the time. I heard you knocking, but I was in the can." He shook his head. "I tell you, I can't take a crap without the phone ringing or someone knocking on my door." He opened a cabinet and pulled down two mugs. "I post the times of my daily bowel movements in the paper, but I guess no one checks them anymore." He turned to face me, face straight as a rod.

I shrugged an apologetic grin.

He let out a bark of a laugh, and Pepper backed him up with one of his own. "That's a joke, but you know that might not be a bad idea. Crapuaries . . ." He scratched his head to give the idea due consideration, and then motioned to a counter stool. "Have a seat. You take cream?"

"Please."

"So, Dixie Wheeler," he said, handing me my cup. "Would you look at you?"

I raised my shoulder. "Look at me."

"I never expected to get a visit from you after all this time. What do I owe the pleasure?"

I set my mug down to pull my bag around my shoulder. I wrangled the file from it and set it on the counter.

He picked it up and turned it over in his hand. "Did you get this from Davis?"

I nodded.

He smacked the file on the counter. "I told that idiot not to show it to anyone. And you of all people! I swear, I have half a mind to have him arrested for . . . shit, I don't know, but I'm sure there's a crime here somewhere."

"Well, he's dead, so . . ."

"Oh." Mr. Cullins touched his mouth, chastened. "When?"

"It was a couple years ago," I said. "Maybe three, I'm not exactly sure."

"That long?" He scratched his forehead. "Huh. Well, that explains why he stopped calling all of a sudden. I thought a couple of nights in jail had turned him around."

"I found the file with some stuff he had cleaned out of my family's house. He had been storing it all in his garage. I just found it this morning."

"Well, thanks for returning it." He flipped open the cover and winced at the top photograph. Josh facedown on the table. "Jesus. I hope you didn't look at these."

I nodded that I had.

He rubbed his chin. "Well, this wasn't meant to be seen by you. Davis shouldn't have had it, either. I only gave it to him as a favor. Well, to shut him up about it, if I'm being honest. He was supposed to return it. I kinda forgot he had it. How'd he die? Heart attack? Wouldn't surprise me. The man looked like a walking time bomb. I told him he was going to pop one day if he didn't let it all go."

"I think he OD'd. My aunt was kinda vague about it."

Mr. Cullins's expression found this ludicrous. "Drugs? Davis? No way."

I shrugged. "The autopsy showed that he had cocaine in his system."

Mr. Cullins searched the countertop to make sense of this. "That's hard to believe."

"I know. I couldn't believe it, either." I stirred sugar into my coffee. "I think he was pretty out of control in the end. Everyone thought he was crazy for believing my father was innocent. Even his wife. I guess it finally pushed him over the edge." I shrugged as I tapped my spoon dry on the brim of my cup. "I mean, that's crazy, right? My father couldn't have been innocent."

Mr. Cullins sipped his coffee.

"Well?" I said.

"Well, what?"

"What do you think?" I asked.

"I think it was a long time ago."

"Yeah, but what did you think back when it happened? You were the investigating officer, right?"

He set down his mug. "I thought it was the most tragic thing I'd ever seen. I almost left the force because of it. I handed in my resignation the second I got back to the station." He shook his head. "My blood bucket overflowed that day."

The horrible image of Mr. Cullins on his hands and knees on our kitchen floor, sopping up blood with a sponge and squeezing it into a bucket, flashed before me.

"It's a metaphor," he explained, noticing my expression. "It means how much blood you can see before you've seen too much. A bucketful just might about do it. Before that day, I didn't have more than a few drops in mine, and I'd been on the force for fifteen years. No one should have their bucket filled up in one day. You can't get used to carrying it."

"But you didn't quit."

"No." He sighed pensively. "I got talked out of it by a man who probably had ten buckets full at that point." He pointed to the file. "I'm sorry you had to see those. They're pretty rough."

I nodded. "They weren't as bad as I had imagined."

He scoffed a dour chuckle. "You must have one hell of an imagination."

I shrugged. "I can't explain why, but it helped me to see them."

He took a sip of coffee as he considered this. "So, did you just drop by to return the file?"

"I noticed that some pictures are missing." I flipped the file open and turned Josh over. My mother slid out from underneath to eye me with flat disapproval. I slid her back in with the others, and pointed to the back corner of Josh's picture. "They're numbered. See? I wondered if you had the ones that are missing."

"I gave Davis everything I had. If something's missing, he must have done something with it."

"Would you be able to tell which pictures are missing just by looking at them?"

He held my expectant gaze for a long moment, then set down his coffee and drew the file to him. After retrieving a pair of reading glasses from the pocket of his robe, he bent forward to examine the contents of the file. He moved through it quicker than I thought conscientious, then announced, "The murder weapon."

"What?" I lifted off my chair to get a closer look.

"All the photos with the axe in them are missing," he said. "It was propped in the corner by the refrigerator."

I pulled the file close and searched through the photographs, surprised I hadn't noticed that myself. "You're right. Why would Uncle Davis remove all the pictures of the axe?"

"Got me," Mr. Cullins said. "He also got rid of the witness statements."

"Why would he do that?" I asked, flipping papers over and back.

"I don't know, Dixie. Maybe he stashed them aside hoping I wouldn't notice they were missing when he returned the file."

"You think?"

"I don't know what to think." He turned to refill his coffee. "Davis was obsessed with the axe. Trying to figure out what was written on it. He probably didn't want to give up on it if I asked him for the file back."

"What do you mean, 'written on it'? What was written on it?"

He shrugged. "We could never determine. By the time we found the axe, blood had dripped through whatever it said. Totally ruined it. Our forensic team concluded that it was nothing of significance, just an obscenity, but Davis wasn't convinced."

"What obscenity?"

"The f-word."

"What?" I whispered my guess, "'Fuck'?"

"No, the other f-word," he said. When I searched for it with confused eyes, he said, "Yes, it was 'fuck,' Dixie. What other f-word is there?"

I rolled my eyes. "Why would my father write that word on the axe? I mean, that's a really weird thing to do, isn't it?"

"No weirder than butchering your kids for no good reason." When I looked down, he apologized. "Sorry. I forgot who I was talking to for a second."

I waved off his apology and tidied the papers back into the file, closed the cover, and smoothed it flat. "Can I ask you something else?"

"Sure."

"Do you know if the story about the music playing when they found me was true?"

He nodded. "It's true. I heard it myself."

"Was it the radio or something?" I asked.

"No, it was a cassette. Just that one song over and over again. Filled up the entire ninety-minute tape. Other than that, there was nothing really special about it. The only set of prints on it was your mother's. We figured she must have been playing it that morning during breakfast."

"My mother?" I wondered aloud. I never thought she might have been the one to play that song for me. "Do you still have the tape?"

"I gave it to Davis with the file." His eyes swept a clock over my head. "Shit, I gotta go. Pepper's got a vet appointment."

"What's wrong with him?" I asked.

"It might be faster to tell you what's *not* wrong with him," Mr. Cullins replied. Then he rattled off: "Diabetes, worms, rotten teeth. Hip problems. Stomach problems. Eye problems. He hasn't pooped in three days. I can't get out of the vet's office for under five hundred dollars." He huffed a cynical laugh. "It'd only cost me fifty bucks to put him down."

We looked at Pepper, who was switching his gaze between us.

"Poor thing," I said.

"Yeah. He's nineteen, so he's living on borrowed time as it is."

I collected the file. "Can I keep this?"

He sighed. "I guess at this point it would be harder for me to return it than for you to keep it. But I kinda hoped you wouldn't want to. No good can come from having it around. Just ask your uncle Davis."

4

I wasn't overly sensitive to caffeine, but the coffee I drank at Mr. Cullins's had turned a legion of ants loose under my skin. I slung my bag at the couch and made my way upstairs to change. I was slipping into a pair of sweatpants when I heard the faint jingle of my phone. I turned in a hurry, eyes down on the half-made bow in the drawstring of my pants, and tripped over a soft speed bump in the middle of the floor. I caught my footing just before I hit the dresser face-first. I looked back at my pillow in wonder, trying to remember if I had knocked it off the bed when I sat down to take off my shoes. As the phone rang again, I tossed it back onto the bed and hurried downstairs.

My phone wasn't in its usual pocket. I lifted my bag to dig inside and heard my phone ring farther away than the bottom. I searched the top of the cushions, running my hand between the seams, and then dropped to my knees to look under the couch. The next ring vibrated the center cushion. I flipped it up to find my phone beneath. I gave a quick, confused "Hello" as I knocked up the other cushions to see what else the couch had eaten out of my purse. I found my ChapStick, two nickels, and a red M&M. I hadn't eaten M&M's recently. I scooped the booty into my hand.

"Dix?" Garrett's voice floated up. "You there?"

"Yeah. Hey. Sorry." I reset the cushions to sit down.

"You okay?" he asked.

"Sure. Why?"

"You sounded weird," he said.

Weirder than butchering your kids for no good reason?

"Weird how?" I asked.

"I don't know, just weird," he said. "How's it going?"

I resented his clipped tone, which I knew was deliberate, and gave it right back to him with a terse "Fine."

"How have your first couple nights been?"

"Not bad." I held up one of the nickels to read the date: 1992. The year of the murders. "Just the normal haunted-house stuff: rattling chains and ominous moans. But once I stop moaning and rattling chains, I fall right to sleep." I expected to get a laugh and got a sigh instead.

"Did you get everything moved in?" He sounded breathless and distracted, like he was walking and talking at the same time.

"Yeah, I'm all moved in." The other nickel was my birth year: 1991. "I'm still going through boxes. I can't find my oven mitts anywhere."

"You mean *my* oven mitts," he corrected. "I snatched them out of the box before you left."

"I know. I snatched them back again."

"Well, if you find them, consider them your housewarming gift."

"Oh, gee, thanks."

He laughed, finally. "Everything else okay?"

"Sure." I set the M&M and change on the coffee table. A candy-coated stigmata was left on the palm of my hand. I wiped it off on my kneecap. "Why wouldn't it be?"

"No reason, I guess," he said. The line was quiet for so long I looked at the screen to see if we were still connected. "Okay, then," he said to end the call.

"Wait!" I sat forward. "Will you do something for me?"

He hesitated to ask, "What?"

"Are you busy tomorrow night?"

"Maybe. Why?"

"Do you want to go with me to a dinner thing at my neighbor's?" I closed my eyes to await his answer.

"I can't think of anything I'd rather do less," he said.

"Great. It's at six o'clock."

"That was a no, Dixie," he said sternly, but I could hear a grin lifting a corner of his voice.

"Please, Garrett," I begged. "I need a buffer. I can't be the only thing there is to talk about. Please come with me. Please. Please."

When he was quiet for a long moment, I knew he would say yes.

"Should I bring anything?" he asked.

"Yeah. A hammer. I need to hang up some pictures."

ANNOYED THAT THE "Love ya" I would have normally received at the end of a call with Garrett had been downgraded to a "See ya," I slapped my phone flat on the couch and yelled "What a jerk!" at the ceiling.

I started away, then turned back to see if I could catch a hand slipping up from between the couch cushions to draw the phone down into its lair. When the screen idled to black, I turned for the kitchen. I took another quick look back, just in case the hand was waiting for me to turn my back to make its move. The phone remained unclaimed, but when the screen suddenly winked on, I jumped back with a yelp.

I inched forward slowly, nervous that some portentous text like "IT'S IN THE HOUSE" would be waiting on the screen. The banner said it was my move with Aunt Celia in Words with Friends. I smiled. This was a good sign. It wasn't as promising as a text, but at least she was making an effort. I opened the app to reciprocate with a quick play, and was dismayed to see the word she had played was SELFISH, 58 points. I cross-played HELP, then changed it to HOPE before I passed the game back to her.

I stomped to the kitchen to get a beer, muttering under my breath that *she* was the selfish one. As I turned from the refrigerator, I stumbled into a stack of boxes, knocking the top box off its perch. A spill of paperwork, consisting mostly of old bills, insurance documents,

and report cards, went sailing across the floor along with my un-
opened Miller Lite. After determining the bottle hadn't broken in the
fall, I dropped to my knees to scoop the papers into a pile. I dumped
them back in the box, and turned for the sink to open my upset beer
in a controlled environment.

A lone card had glided under the kitchen table.

A pink kitten in a yellow party hat was being lifted off a small
world by a red balloon. "Look who's 1" was written across the sky in
cumulous clouds.

My stomach gave a queasy flip as I opened the card and found a
long handwritten message from my mother. I sat in her chair to read:

> *My dearest Dixie, my beautiful girl, my joy. Though I know*
> *you are not old enough to read this, one day you will be, so as you*
> *do so now, please know how much you are loved . . .*

I rolled my head back to keep a tear from falling. Of all that I had
found, of all that I had discovered—the house, their belongings, the
graphic pictures of their deaths—this was by far the most painful
discovery. A choke of emotion lodged in my chest like a chunk of ice.
It took three deep breaths to thaw it, and three long pulls off my beer
before I had the nerve to read on.

> *The day I found out that you were to be a girl, my heart sang.*
> *And now, one year later, that song has risen to a chorus. You are*
> *so very special to me, my darling one. I can't wait until you're old*
> *enough for us to have long lunches and to walk side by side. To*
> *talk of life and love and art and music, and to hear that all I have*
> *dreamed for you has come true. What you will become remains a*
> *secret to me today, but I'll let you in on a little secret of my own:*
> *The only thing I ever wanted you to be was my very best friend!*
> *Until then, my sweet Dixie.*
> *Mom*

Though her words stung a gland in my throat I hadn't known was there, I had to wonder why my father hadn't so much as signed the card. I overturned the box and went through it piece by piece. There were many handmade cards from the boys to both of our parents, stick figures under crayon trees, giant orange suns bulging from the corners of hastily shaded skies. Some of the cards were from my mother to the boys, earnest notes that held more worry than hope. There was only one card from my father to anyone. Since it was not personalized, I claimed it as my own. On the cover, Snoopy and Woodstock were sitting on Snoopy's doghouse, peeking inside a box with a single green bow around its center. The voice bubble over Snoopy's head asked, "What could it be?" Woodstock's bubble hoped for "A new birdbath?" Snoopy's: "A dog bone?" Inside: "I hope you get everything you want for your birthday." Below, my father had written just two words: "Love, Dad."

I didn't expect an outpouring of flowery sentiment from a man who would one day murder his own family, but I did expect a little more than an obligatory valediction. I suppose "Love, Dad" was a tad more affectionate than "Best regards, Dad," but not by much.

With my mother's lovely sentiment now spoiled by my father's indifference, I tossed both cards back into the box as I wandered into the living room. I took a seat at Uncle Davis's desk.

I knew the two side drawers would still be locked, but I rattled them anyway. I fingered the steak knife on top of the desk, but I didn't have the patience to pick another two locks. I slid the center drawer out to see what else it held. Once I had found the police file, I hadn't felt the need to look further. I swiped my hand inside and extracted a pad of sticky notes. Uncle Davis had written, but not peeled off, a note on the top sheet:

Call Stan. Convo. P.S. MORE LIES!

I squinted at Uncle Davis's hurried lettering. The pen he had used was on the verge of drying out or hadn't been sufficiently warmed up. Gaps and harder scratches wandered through the gradient message. The period after the *P* could be a disconnected kickstand for the letter *R*. The *5* could be an *S*, though the flat top seemed more characteristic of a number than a letter. But if it was a *5*, what was the *5* in reference to? Or the *P* . . . Maybe it was an *R*. No, definitely a *P*.

I sat back to think.

P.S., P.S., P.S. . . .

As it came to me, I ran to get the file from my bag.

I searched out the number on the back of the photographs. Number *5* was one of Michael underneath the table holding on to my mother's foot. Other than how utterly tragic it was, there wasn't anything remarkable about it. I set the photo and the Post-its aside and searched the drawer for more.

A small, narrow-ruled legal pad was pushed to the back of the drawer. I pulled it forward. Several pages had been flipped over to leave a clean sheet ready. I brought the pages forward one by one. The second page from the top contained a numbered list. Uncle Davis's last question caught my eye first: "No blood on table—was Deb's body moved?"

I sorted through pictures until her green eye caught mine. My mother was slumped forward over the table, cheek resting upon the pillow of her extended arm. The image was a startling contrast of peace and violence, as though she had stretched out for a little nap and erupted in blood. The yellow tablecloth had sopped up most of what had puddled out of Josh, whose damp brown hair was just visible in the photograph to her right, but the area directly below my mother's face was clean, burgeoning with the blue daisy pattern she had chosen for her kitchen. I grabbed my phone to conduct a search. I found one tablecloth that matched well enough on eBay. I almost ordered it, but when I saw that the delivery date was more than three weeks away, I canceled the order entirely. Oddly, I didn't think I would need it by then.

I TOOK A break to use the bathroom and to wash my face in cold water. You could only look at death so long before you needed to cleanse. Retaking my seat at the desk, I flipped the photograph of my mother over and back again like a postcard, hoping more could be learned about the picture on the other side. It didn't make sense that her body had been moved after she was dead, as Uncle Davis's note suggested. But the purity of the tablecloth directly beneath her was curious. Maybe she had sat upright and dead long enough for the blood to congeal before gravity took her down. Maybe the blood had dried by the time it reached the cliff of her profile.

I set the photo aside and started from the beginning of Uncle Davis's list. His first question begged: "How did blood get on back of high chair? Where was Dixie during the murders?"

I started sorting through the photographs until I found a clear shot of the high chair. The back cushion looked like the first color in a Jackson Pollock painting. The blood was smudged, like I had swished back and forth against it, but how did it manage to get behind me in the first place? Had it sprayed up and over my head? Had I ducked out of the way? Had I been lifted out of the chair before the rain of blood began? I shuddered at the image of my father holding me in one arm while he swung the axe with the other.

I read the next question scrawled out in Uncle Davis's longhand: "Why is the faucet running?"

The corresponding photograph was a long shot of the kitchen. Fledgling herbs yawned thin arms from four teacups along the windowsill above the sink—the rest of my mother's set. The camera had flash-frozen water coming from the faucet like an icicle. I didn't think the fact that the water had been left running meant anything, though. My mother could have started the water to do the breakfast dishes.

Maybe my father had been getting some warm, sudsy water going to clean up the mess he made, ascertained the job was too copious for a two-bowl basin, and decided to kill himself instead.

I looked back at Uncle Davis's list. Questions four, five, and six were theories as to who had been killed first. Nothing I hadn't pondered myself. But question number seven was interesting: "Blood on chain. Door locked???"

His curiosity demanded three question marks.

The corresponding photograph offered a dichotomized view of my brother Eddie: his headless body sprawled against the dishwasher two feet away from his bodiless head in the corner. There was a clear shot of the back door around the corner from where his head had come to rest against the bag of—

I rolled my head back to inhale a deep breath of air.

Though I had seen this picture a few times already, it still got to me. More than the rest. Maybe it was how Eddie's left hand seemed to be blindly feeling for his head: *It's gotta be here somewhere.* Or how the sideways glance of his wide eyes seemed a little amused by the irony of the situation: *You need your head to find your head, stupid!*

Fanning a hand at my face, I took a swig of beer. I kept my eyes on the ceiling as I felt around for the bottom edge of the photograph. I slid my hand slowly up the sleek surface until I was sure I had muffled Eddie's scream.

I looked down.

At that time, the kitchen door had a white privacy curtain over the window. Lightweight jackets were hung on an accordion rack on the wall to the right. A couple of pairs of sneakers were shying away from the incoming tide of blood. The slide lock was to the left of the window. Knowing Eddie's open mouth was directly under my hand made my palm itch. I squashed the squirm of his tongue as I bent in for a closer look.

Uncle Davis was right. The head of the chain had tick-tocked thin red streaks upon the white door. Whoever had unlocked it had done so with bloody fingers.

I looked back at the legal pad. Uncle Davis noted that the police were unable to retrieve any viable fingerprints from the small head of the chain, but made no mention of the obvious: If the chain had been set during the murders, how did Rory get in the house? He couldn't have been let in. Anyone who still had a hand left to open the door with was dead. Maybe my father had unlocked the door before he cut his throat to ensure that someone would be able to come to my aid? The police might have reset the lock so no one would walk in on their crime scene investigation.

Reluctantly, I lifted my hand to see the bigger picture.

Several wavy sneaker prints tracked through a guzzle of blood from Eddie's throat. I stared at them for a long, breathless moment, trying to comprehend what I was seeing. They were pointed in the wrong direction.

Going, not coming.

Leaving, not entering.

I started going through the pictures until I found an explanation for the incongruity. It was an overhead view of the kitchen floor. The viewpoint was wide-angled and zoomed out, as if someone had stood on a chair to take the shot with their arm extended like a boom. A communal blood puddle had formed in the center of the room. Dark liquid seeped from the bodies like the arms of their souls and joined together to form a vaguely heart-shaped pool in front of the table. Just to the right, slightly in front of Josh's chair, was a clean spot of linoleum where my father's body must have lain before they carted him off. The thick runoff banked around the ghost of his profile, and was redirected toward the living room entryway. And there, just in front of the gold trim that separated the linoleum from the carpeting—

A blood angel.

The sweep of arms was faint but distinct. Someone had slipped in the blood, and then had swum their arms and legs to get up again. The puddle immediately next to my father's profile was pristine, so he hadn't created the image by flopping around the floor. Eddie might have fluttered around the kitchen floor before he got up—headless!— and fell back against the dishwasher, but I didn't think so. The area was too large to have been made by Michael. And for some nebulous reason, the silhouette just didn't seem female.

The blood angel had to be Rory.

But if it was, that meant that Rory hadn't entered the house through the back door, as I had always believed, that I was almost certain to be a fact. He had entered the kitchen through the living room.

Given our history, Rory and I had only spoken about the day of the murders on one occasion. He, like Aunt Celia, didn't like to talk about that day, especially with me. But unlike Aunt Celia's, Rory's reluctance seemed to stem out of a concern for my tender sensibilities rather than his own. Though I had gleaned very little from his version of events, I did remember him specifically saying that he entered the house through the kitchen: "I opened the back door and almost . . . Eddie was . . . Let's just say it was horrible and leave it at that."

So why had Rory lied? Why not just say he came in the front door if he did? What difference did it make how he entered the house?

I pressed a hand to my mouth as the answer came to me.

Because he didn't enter the house.

He was already inside.

I had just nodded forth the sense of this when I spotted something in the photograph that was more horrible than anything I had seen thus far.

A smiley face on the wall over Eddie's head.

It could have just been a mordantly shaped splash of blood, but somehow it felt . . . deliberate. I tried to imagine my father doodling such an image as I tearfully reached out for my dead mother. Did he draw it for me as a distraction? *Look, sweetie, I drew you a smiley face. See how happy it is? Don't cry, honey. Mr. Smiley Face isn't crying, is he? No, he isn't . . .*

I Frisbeed the picture across the room and slammed the center drawer shut with the butt of my hand. Something ricocheted inside. I slid the drawer open again. The drawer appeared empty, but as I swept my fingers deep into the well, they touched on a rectangular piece of plastic.

I set the cassette on the desk.

My mother's smoky fingerprints were still clinging to the clear plastic edges. A thin yellow label directly above the spindles contained the same case number as the police file, C-32-9049, followed by the number 27, which I supposed made the cassette tape the twenty-seventh item counted into evidence. Below, next to the manufactured stamp for side A—where you'd usually write things like "Mix Tape" or the name of the song, band, or album you had recorded—was a handwritten inscription:

Dixie's Nap Song.

Well, that solved that mystery. I had to admit, I was a little disappointed. I always thought the song played a darker role that day, perhaps even served as some sort of catalyst, the ding that set off the bomb. Nope. Just nap time for Dixie.

But it wasn't nap time.

It was breakfast time. Hadn't I just woken? Why would my mother want me to doze off in the middle of breakfast?

I sat forward as a terrible thought occurred to me.

Was my mother in cahoots with my father? Was her death as much of a suicide as his? Did they agree to kill everyone but me?

Not the baby, Bill, I just couldn't bear the thought of that.

As bright as that idea flashed, I couldn't see it. A mother would not see her children butchered that way. Not when she had two perfectly good tubs to drown them in. Maybe she didn't want to know the specifics, the how of it. Maybe she'd left that pesky little detail up to her husband, who, much to her surprise, jumped out at them with an axe that morning.

I compared my finger to one of my mother's fingerprints. It seemed so small. The dust it was set in felt like talc, velvety, almost wet. I picked up the tape to study it. I didn't own a cassette player. All my music was downloaded on my phone. I looked over my shoulder at a junk pile in the far corner of the room. My parents' old stereo system was half buried under a heap of venetian blinds. The door to a cassette player was just visible between the loose, dusty slats.

I blew off enough dust to see that it was a dual-deck Pioneer with auto-reverse. Unraveling the cord, I stretched it to the outlet and plugged it in. A red power light came on. I popped in the tape, closed the door, and hit Play.

Nothing happened.

I sat back to think of where I might have gone wrong, staring absently at a black rectangular box I was using as a side table for the rocking chair. Its twin was currently employed as a step stool in the kitchen. I rock-walked the speakers to the center of the living room, but could not see a way to connect them to the tape deck. Encased wire was coiled and taped to the back of each of the speakers, but their ends were flayed apart. Stymied, I ran my finger over the tufts of wiry hairs.

I needed Garrett's electronics expertise to do this, but I didn't want to explain what I was doing. Garrett asked a lot of questions. I couldn't just say that I needed to hook up speakers to a tape deck without him asking why, what was I listening to, why didn't I just download the song, what song was it, where'd I get the cassette from, and on and on and on. Reluctantly, I dialed the only other number I had for tech support. Ford's first question was: "You got any banana plugs?"

"Banana what?"

Ten contentious minutes later, Ford determined that the overall problem I was having was most likely due to my lack of a Y chromosome. I thanked him very much for nothing and grabbed my laptop. YouTube had no less than a billion tutorials on how to connect speaker wires. I found one that I could follow without wanting to punch myself in the head—and which also did not require banana plugs—and applied the instructions to a T.

The tape made a strained *whir-thug, whir-thug, whir-thug* as it struggled to make a connection. I popped out the cassette to see if the fingerprint dust was junking up the works. The ribbon was clean and glossy. I checked the deck for any obvious obstructions. A small piece of hard plastic was wedged behind the left spindle. I tweezed it out with my fingernails and set it in the palm of my hand. It looked like a tiny bayonet, one a toy soldier might carry.

Michael!

I set the miniature weapon on the carpet next to me, rotated the spool with my fingernail to make sure the tape was nice and tight, popped the cassette back in, and hit Play.

An airy susurration filled the air, but no music. I cranked the volume up to 70 . . . 80 . . . 90. A waterfall of loud, empty static crashed over me. For a moment I thought the tape was blank. I was just about to eject it when *DUM-DA-DUM-DA-DUM, DAH-DA-DA-DA-DAH, DUM-DA-DUM!* blasted me back onto my rump. The left speaker blew a tortured, high-pitched wail, went dead for a second, and then crackled back at an even higher decibel level. I crawled forward and turned the volume down to 60.

I closed my eyes and traveled back two and a half decades, or twenty-five years ago traveled forward, it was hard to tell, but the haunting sound of "Baby Blue" coming from my family's old stereo system brought me closer to the moment of their deaths than I had ever felt before. The peach-blossom Glade air freshener plugged into the wall socket behind the couch could not mask the iron-rich scent of blood. It ran up my nose and down my throat with a hot metallic sting that caused my eyes to water. The whoosh of the axe was so close that I tucked into a ball to protect myself. The horrible sounds of that day were stamped just below the lyrics. Breathless, discordant screams clawed to the surface in a spike of reverb, and then slid away like a razor blade across a sheet of glass.

The first time I heard the song was when Leah sang it to me as she shaved her armpits in our bedroom. She probably wouldn't have bothered if she'd known in less than six months she would be completely hairless, but at the time, her new bathing suit required a clean shave. I had asked her why they called me Baby Blue as I checked for traces of hair in my own armpit. When I couldn't find any, I tucked one of my pigtails under my arm to make some.

"'Cause of that song, I guess," she said, slathering foam over her thin, sculpted pit. She got a little on her bikini top, but since it was blue with white swirls, she didn't notice.

"What song?" I asked.

She tapped the foam off her razor into a water glass. It stuck to the side, and she ran her finger up to catch it. It plopped on the rug as she pointed her finger at me, and she rubbed it away with her foot. "You know, that song that was playing when they found you."

"Like on the radio?" I asked.

"I guess. They said it was playing really loud, so they started calling you that. You're lucky it was 'Baby Blue' and not 'Hound Dog' or something like that." She snorted a laugh, wincing as she nicked a mole. "Or 'Like a Virgin.'" This made her throw her head back and roar. "Oh"—she turned fast toward me—"'Rhiannon'! That would have been so cool." She wiped the remaining scrapes of foam off with a towel, and hooked her toes on the side of the vanity to check the texture of her right leg. "It's kinda creepy since your name is Dixie, and all. They say your name in the song like a million times. Dixie this, and Dixie that. Like it was meant to be or something." She shimmied off a shiver as it swept through her.

"What song was it?" I asked.

She shot me an exasperated look. "'Baby Blue,' duh. Keep up."

I nodded like I knew what she was talking about, but my roving eyes said maybe not so much.

"Oh, you know that song, don't you?"

When I shook my head, she used her razor as a microphone, and crooned an off-key rendition with such heart that it made me curl my wrists under my chin. When she finished, she clasped her hands to her chest and bowed. I saw the bruise as she turned to set the razor on the vanity. Big as a hand, it wrapped around the back of her thin rib cage, like she had been slow dancing with a large man with greasy fingers.

"Is that song about me?" I asked, confused on several fronts.

"No, it's about some other chick named Dixie and this guy who's all torn up over her. But he's a real jerk. He just took off without even telling her. So she breaks up with him, right? But then he wants her back. So he writes her this song to remind her how in love they were, and how lonely he is, and how she's his Baby Blue 'cause he's so sad, and blah, blah, blah, because she's already over him, right? And he's all like, *You should have known that I loved you and waited for me*." She rolled her eyes. "You know, typical guy stuff. They don't know they want you until they lose you, then they act like they're all broke up about it. So anyway, the guy in the song wants to know what he can do to get her back. Like he's tried everything and she's just being a bitch about it, right? But he knows he screwed up, so he tries to act like he's over her, but you know he's not or he wouldn't have written her a stupid song." She waved her hand glibly. "I don't know, it's something like that. Anyway. It's really sad."

I tried to work it out on the ceiling. "But what's that song got to do with me?"

"Nothing. It's just the song he played for you, I guess."

"Who?" I asked.

"Uncle Billy."

I sat fully upright. "My dad? Did you know him?"

"Oh, sure. I used to hang out at your house all the time. Eddie and I were practically best friends. We played on the same soccer team for like three years in a row. He was so funny. He used to crack me up all the time." She looked off for a wistful sigh. "He tried to kiss me once and I punched him in the stomach. I kinda feel bad about that now. He didn't get mad or anything, but I could tell I hurt his feelings."

"But what about my dad?"

"Oh, yeah. He was kinda tall and skinny. He didn't talk much. But he used to take us for ice cream and go-carts, so I guess he was pretty cool . . . for an axe murderer."

I walked over to Leah's vanity and picked up her razor. "Did he kill a bunch of people or just my family?"

"I don't know." She took the razor from me. "He was probably a serial killer and we didn't even know it. That would be so cool."

"It would?"

"Sure, he could be like Jeffrey Dahmer," she said, shoving me out of her way to grab her beach bag off the end of her bed. "He ate his victims when he was done killing them."

This seemed unnecessarily horrible. "Why would he do that?"

"Because he was crazy. All serial killers are. They kill and eat people all the time. It's disgusting, I know, but they can't help themselves. It's a disease." She turned to look at her back in the mirror. "Oh, man! The bruise is getting bigger. I can't go to the pool like this."

"How'd you get it?"

"I have no idea . . ."

I was whistled back from my daydream by the whirling squeak of a cassette tape rewinding at top speed. Leah was standing outside my front window. A corona of sunlight bounced off her bald head like a spray of water. I blinked tears from my eyes and she sprouted into a lanky flower. Neck broken from a high wind the night before, the stem dropped its head and then fell out of sight.

5

The expression on Garrett's face when I opened the door was obliged impatience. *Here I am, as instructed.* I accepted the hammer he shoved at me and gave him a quick peck on his tight lips. I thought of jamming my tongue in his mouth, like I had done to Rory all those years ago, but he stood back before I had the chance.

I invited him in as I moved through the living room to grab my bag off the table in the kitchen. I called out to ask if he wanted a beer, and then grudgingly returned mine to the fridge when he politely declined. I returned to find him farther outside the doorway than he had been when I left him.

"Come on. It's okay." I patted my thigh like Suanne had the day I came to view the house for the first time, smiling at my private joke.

He left the door open as he stepped inside. "It smells like cigarettes."

"It does?" I lifted my nose to feign curiosity. I had found a pack of Camels in the inside pocket of my father's sports coat. Stale, but still potent. "I think the last owner smoked or something."

Garrett gave me a dubious look.

"What?"

"I thought you quit."

I shrugged. "I only had a couple."

He shook his head as he looked around. "Oh, you gotta be kidding me."

"What?" I asked, following his gaze as it took in the old furniture. The caked-on grime and mildew stains I had selectively decided to overlook now seemed too filthy to ignore. I walked over and switched off the lamp next to the couch.

He circled his finger around the room. "Is this all their old stuff?"

I nodded. "Most of it's in pretty good shape, actually."

"Uh, no, it's not." He rubbed an imagined dirtiness from his hands onto the front of his shirt. "This is so creepy, Dixie. I don't even know what to say."

"I told you I was getting some of their old furniture from my aunt Charlene." I checked my bag for my keys and phone. My phone was upstairs. I decided not to get it. Garrett was the only one who called me anymore.

"Yeah, but I thought it was just going to be a couple of things," he said. "I didn't expect you to set the house up like . . ." He ran a hand over his mouth. "I mean, what the hell?"

"Oh." I dismissed him with a flap of my hand. "I needed furniture, so why not use it? It was just . . . sitting there in my uncle's garage." *Rotting away* had almost slipped out. I cleared my throat. "I can't afford new furniture, Garrett."

"Yeah, but it looks super creepy in here, Dix."

"Will you please stop calling it creepy? It's not helping."

"Sorry, but I don't know another word for it."

"How about . . . 'vintage.'"

"Okay," he said, grinning. "It's vintage creepy. Does that sound better?"

I rolled my eyes. "Well, anyway. Thanks for coming with me tonight. Hopefully, it's not going to be too awful. I want to be in and out of there in less than an hour. So, eat quick. And pass on dessert. Unless she made brownies. You gotta try those. They're amazing."

"So, what are they like? Your neighbors, I mean."

"I only met Vicki." I swiped on some ChapStick. "She seemed nice. Maybe a little too nice, if you know what I mean. She seemed a little desperate for me to like her. Like she's been waiting for her new BFF to move in next door."

"That's great. You could use a friend. Besides me, I mean."

I slung my bag over my shoulder. "I have plenty of friends, for your information. So you better mind yourself, mister. You're not as indispensable as you think."

As he opened his mouth to refute this, a strange sound scuttled over our heads, like a bowling ball scratching down a long gutter.

Garrett clutched his heart as we both looked up. "What the hell was that?"

"I think it's just the heat kicking on," I said, though I had come to imagine Eddie's head rolling across the carpeting in the upstairs hallway. "It's been happening a lot." I pointed at the ceiling as it rolled the other way. "There it goes again."

Before the front door could slam of its own accord and trap him inside forever, Garrett leapt through the threshold and vaulted down the front steps. When I stepped out, he was waiting a safe distance away on the sidewalk. I shook my head to laugh as I turned to lock up. Though I was sure I had pulled the door shut behind me, it was standing halfway open. I pulled it shut with an extra hard slam, and then gave it a firm press to make sure it was closed good and tight. I bent to slip the key in the lock, and it swung inward again. As I fought with the handle to get it to stay closed, Garrett yelled out, "That's not funny, Dix! You're not scaring me, so quit playing around!"

I didn't think it was funny, either. *Forget it*, I thought, *let it stay open*. I gave it one final tug for good measure, and it flew shut with a bang.

Though Vicki thought being neighbors afforded one back-door access, I knocked on the front. Vicki greeted me with an enthusiastic hug, then shook Garrett's hand with polite confusion. She told us to make ourselves comfortable as she scooped and tossed stuffed animals at a playpen on her way to the kitchen.

Their house was mine in exact reverse. The staircase was on the left, as was the entryway to the kitchen. The back door also sat left of their sink. A wide-screen TV was hung over the mantel of a brick fire-place where my side window would have been located. We took a seat on their couch, which was new, overstuffed, and comfortable, and made mine look like it had been made for, and by, a family of hobbits.

Garrett immediately stood again as Nick came down the staircase from the second level. Nick was handsome and fit, and a little too tan for the time of year. Though Vicki had said the dress code was "super casual," I was still surprised to see that Nick had selected jeans and a faded Jimmy Buffett T-shirt as his evening attire. His socks looked new, though.

I apologized for bringing Garrett without asking, but didn't worry for a second if they had enough food. The coffee table was set with enough hors d'oeuvres for a Saturday night at Jay Gatsby's. I stabbed two sausage weenies with one toothpick and dragged them off with my teeth. Next I went for a pastry puff drooling with melted cheese. I chewed for a second before stuffing a potato chip in after it. I wanted to keep my mouth busy so it wouldn't have to make small talk.

"Have you two been dating long?" Vicki asked, hooking a displeased lip at Nick's attire as she poured our wine.

When Garrett failed to answer on our behalf, I covered my mouth to garble "Five years" through a mash of dough and sharp chip fragments.

"Oh, that's sweet," Vicki said. "Nick and I were married with twins on the way by then. Weren't we, honey?" Nick responded by holding his glass out for her to fill. She allotted him half a pour. "So you two aren't even living together yet?"

"No," Garrett said quickly, downing his wine in one long swallow. Nick picked up the bottle and topped them both off.

"That's such a big house for just one person," Vicki said, loading a cocktail napkin with celery sticks filled with some sort of cheese adhesive that kept three black olives from capsizing. "Don't you get scared being there all alone?"

I dragged a knuckle across my greasy lips to say, "Not really."

Vicki handed me a napkin. "You know about the history of your house, don't you? I mean, you know what happened there, right?"

"Here we go," Nick groused as he plucked one of the olives from its canoe and popped it in his mouth.

"What?" Vicki challenged with a toss of her hands. "I just wanted to make sure the real estate agent was up front with her, is all."

"I know all about the house," I said gamely.

"You do?" she asked, touching her chest, seeming a bit annoyed by my lack of concern. "And it doesn't bother you?"

I reached for my wine. "Not really."

"Nor should it," Nick said with a wink.

"Absolutely not," Vicki agreed. She placed a reassuring hand on my knee. "I just didn't want you finding out about it some other way and getting scared off." She released my knee with a firm squeeze and picked up her wine. "That house has sat dark for too long. I was just heartbroken when Jenny and Doug moved. They were the sweetest couple. But they just couldn't stand it any longer. They were totally convinced that house was haunted."

"What the hell, Vic?" Nick exclaimed. He offered me a repentant wince. "Your house isn't haunted, Dixie. Jenny made it out to be a lot worse than it was. Actually, Jenny made a lot of things out to be a lot worse than they were."

"Well, things did happen that were hard to explain, Nick," Vicki said. "You have to admit that."

"A husband should never admit to anything," Nick replied, then laughed as he slapped Garrett on the knee. Garrett jerked as if suddenly woken. "Am I right, Garrett?"

"Uh, sure," Garrett mumbled.

"What kind of strange things happened to Doug and . . . ?"

"Jenny," Vicki finished, eyes teeming with excitement. "Oh, all sorts of stuff. Doors would slam shut all on their own. The lights would flicker on and off. The clocks were never set right. That drove Jenny absolutely nuts. And things kept disappearing and showing up in the strangest places. Jenny once found her toothbrush in the oven!" She laughed with a sort of pleased hysteria that made Nick cringe. "When it first started happening, Doug thought it was mice, you know, dragging things back to their holes, but after a while, even he had to admit that something else might be going on."

"Yeah," Nick muttered, "like a four-year-old little boy."

"That oven door was way too heavy for Brian to open all by himself," Vicki said. "And even if he could, Jenny said he swore he didn't do."

"It must be haunted, then." Nick laughed. "Four-year-olds never lie."

"Well, even if Brian did hide the toothbrush," Vicki said, annoyed but undaunted, "he certainly couldn't have slammed a door when he was fast asleep in his bed, or flicker the light switches. And he didn't even know how to reset the clocks. He was only four years old. No. Something else was going on over there. Something bad."

Nick held out his arms. "What are you trying to do? Scare Dixie so bad that she doesn't want to go home tonight?"

"That's okay," I said. "I don't believe in that sort of thing. People let their imaginations get the better of them. They scare themselves, more than anything."

Nick raised his wineglass to me. "Exactly."

"I heard some strange noises over there tonight," Garrett offered in a thin voice. "I'm sure there's a logical explanation for it, but until you know what it is, I can see how it might freak you out."

"You know," Vicki said, looking off in thought, "something happened to me when I was over there once." She gave a mystified chuckle as she shook her head. "Oh, my god, I forgot all about it. It wasn't anything big. Nothing like what happened to Jenny. But I remember it made me very uncomfortable. Actually, I'm still a little disturbed by it." She sat back to "huh" to herself and wait for someone to drag the details out of her.

As a guest in her home, I felt obliged. "What happened to you, Vicki?"

She waved off my interest. "Nick's right. We shouldn't scare you with all this haunted-house talk."

"You're not scaring me," I reassured. "Go on. I want to hear about it."

"Well, only if you insist." She leaned forward and she lowered her voice, perhaps so ghosts couldn't easily eavesdrop. "I was over there visiting with Jenny one morning, and I was just sitting in the kitchen—that's where it happened, you know. The murders? It was in the kitchen while they were eating breakfast. Anyway, I was just sitting there, waiting for Jenny to come back downstairs, and I felt a hand grab my foot."

Michael.

"I tell you it about scared me half to death!" She leaned over and scrubbed the top of her foot. "I screamed so loud I nearly fell out of my chair. Jenny came running down the stairs so fast she twisted her ankle."

"Ask her how many bottles of wine they'd gone through at that point," Nick said, winking at me again.

"It was ten o'clock in the morning!"

"How many mimosas, then?"

"Oh!" She waved off his impudence, picked up her glass of wine, and aimed the rim at him. "What about you, Nick? You had that thing happen, remember? You didn't think that was so funny. You came running home like the devil was chasing you."

"That's a bit of an exaggeration," Nick qualified. "And I wouldn't exactly call it a 'thing.'"

"Well, you wouldn't go back over there for days. And when you finally did, you made me go with you." She snorted a laugh. "You were hanging on to my arm like a little kid going through a haunted house. Admit it. You were scared to death."

Nick spotted my raised eyebrows. "It was just something weird that happened in the shed."

"There isn't a shed," I said.

"Not anymore. Doug burned it down year before last. He said the lawn mower caught fire, but I think he left a cigarette burning. I mean, lawn mowers don't just catch fire for no reason." He looked around for confirmation, then scooped up some cocktail nuts to shake in his hand as he spoke. "Anyway, I was in the shed helping Doug fix a chair. Its leg got broken when we were playing charades." He shook his head and chuckled. "Now that's a funny story. Talk about drunk. We were—"

"They don't want to hear about the stupid chair, Nick," Vicki reprimanded, then flashed me a tight smile. "Just finish the story."

"Oh. Okay. So, I was out in the shed. Doug had gone back inside to catch the phone or something, so I was out there all by myself. And I was just standing there, holding the leg of the chair in place so the glue would set, and I swear it felt like someone was standing right behind me. I could feel them breathing down my neck." He rubbed the memory out from under his collar. "But when I turned around, nobody was there." He hooked a thumb over his shoulder. "Doug was still in the house, so it couldn't have been him. But I'm sure someone had been standing behind me. I could feel their body heat, like they were right up against me. But when I looked back, no one was there."

"Isn't that creepy?" Vicki asked eagerly.

"It *is* creepy," Garrett said as he turned purposely toward me. "That's a good word for it, isn't it, Dix? There's no other word for it, is there? When something's creepy, it's—just—plain—creepy."

"You're just plain creepy," I whispered behind my wineglass.

"What other creepy things happened, Vicki?" Garrett asked, grin widening as I crinkled my nose at him. Wine seemed to be softening his overall displeasure toward me. He actually giggled as he threw an arm over my shoulders and pulled me in for a swift, good-humored side hug. For a second I wanted to cry.

"Well, that's all that happened to us, I think. But Jenny and Doug had a few other strange things happen to them. One time, Jenny swore she heard that song playing. You know, that song that was playing when they found them? What was it again?"

"'Baby Blue,'" I offered.

"Yes. That's it. Well, Jenny was in the shower, and thought she heard that song playing. But when she went to see where it was coming from, she couldn't hear it anymore." She leaned back with a pleased nod, then sat quickly forward again. "Oh! And another time she thought she heard a little girl crying."

"A little girl?" I asked, confused.

"Yes. It was this loud, horrible mewling. She thought a cat had somehow gotten into the house. She looked all over, but couldn't find what was making that noise. She said it sounded just like a little girl crying her heart out."

"Or a cat meowing," Nick clarified.

"But the little girl didn't die," I reminded her. "So it couldn't have been a ghost."

"Hmm . . . that's true." Vicki touched her chin as she drifted off to explore the veracity of the stories she'd been told. She disregarded any implication of her own gullibility with a wave of her hand. "Maybe I have the story wrong. But it just breaks my heart to think about that little girl. She was just a baby, you know. No older than my Katie. Can you even imagine what she went through?"

I nodded and then shook my head when I realized I had my reactions backward.

"Oh, that poor little thing sat there for the longest time with her family dead all around her. I think she still lives in the area." Vicki looked at me quickly. "You know. I think her name was Dixie, too. Isn't that funny?"

"Hilarious," Garrett whispered.

"What's for dinner?" I said, giving my thighs a hard slap as I stood. Garrett startled his wine onto the front of his shirt.

Vicki jumped from her chair. "I forgot about the rolls. They're probably burned to a crisp," she said and dashed into the kitchen.

VICKI WAS WAVING off a waft of smoke as we entered. She had rescued the rolls one second too late. "The bottoms got a little toasty, but I think they're still good." She pitched one into the sink after inspecting it. "Sit wherever you want. Hope you like lasagna!"

Since there were only four chairs around the oval table—and not a rectangular six-seater like mine—it took me a moment to figure out whose seat it would have been at my house. I supposed it would have been my father's, though it could have been Eddie's or Michael's. The position of a coffee mug before a plate with a half-eaten Pop-Tart in the center had created a level of uncertainty that I hadn't quite resolved.

Garrett nudged me to accept the salad bowl Vicki was handing me.

"Where are your kids, Vicki?" I asked.

"Oh, the baby went down hours ago," she said. "And the boys get to eat pizza in their room tonight." She turned to address Nick. "I haven't heard a peep out of them. Could you go check, please?"

"Isn't not hearing a peep a good thing?" Garrett asked with a confused smile.

"Not with these boys," Nick said. Hitching his belt, he marched from the kitchen as if off to war.

"They can get into a bit of mischief," Vicki explained. She set the lasagna on the table and picked up my plate to dish me out a corner section. "You know, I never asked you your last name, Dixie." She tried to make this sound casual, trailing a string of cheese with the plate, but I knew she was on to me. When she looked up to receive my answer, her smile was gone.

"Wheeler," I said.

"Wheeler?" she questioned, eyes narrowing as they searched my face, perhaps to find the joke in my eyes or a stain of blood on my skin.

I nodded.

She pointed the spatula at me. "You're Dixie Wheeler."

I nodded.

"You're kidding."

I shook my head.

"Dixie Wheeler from . . ." She nodded at my house through the wall.

I nodded again.

"Oh." The sound exhaled from her with such stupefaction that she seemed to lose consciousness for a moment.

Tomato sauce dripped from the spatula as she stared at me. A clock ticked off the duration of awkward silence. I heard Garrett swallow. I turned to look at him, but he had his eyes closed to thwart off the moment. I pried my plate from Vicki's frozen hand.

"Sorry to freak you out," I said.

She recovered with a blink. "Oh, no! I mean, you—"

Nick entered boisterously, headed to the refrigerator: "You know those idiots were using the pizza box as a ramp for their cars! They had it upside down on the floor." He fetched himself a beer and turned toward us to crack it. "They had crusts laid out like little speed bumps." He raised his hands to ask how stupid, or ingenious, this was. "I swear you can't leave them alone for one second." He was halfway through a long slug of beer before he realized that something had happened while he was gone. He swallowed quickly. "What'd I miss?"

Vicki stabbed the spatula at me. "This is Dixie Wheeler."

"I know. We met in the living room." He took the dribbling utensil from her hand. "What's the matter with you? You're getting sauce everywhere."

"No, Nick." Vicki nodded hard toward my house on the other side of their kitchen wall. "This is Dixie *Wheeler* . . . from next *door?*"

"*I know.*" He exaggerated his tone to mock hers. "Are you having a stroke or something?"

Vicki took a deep breath to absorb the true depth of her husband's stupidity. "You're not following. This is—"

I raised my hand to own the moment. "I'm the girl who survived the murders next door." Garrett reached for his wine. "It was my family who died there." Vicki sat down heavily. "I didn't want anyone to know I had moved back in to the house, but I guess it was going to come out eventually."

"Oh, come on." Nick looked to Garrett to let him in on the joke. "She's kidding, right?"

"She's not kidding, Nick," Vicki said, inspecting me with a cock of her head.

"Are you really?" Nick asked.

I nodded.

"What made you want to live there again?" Vicki asked. She picked up Garrett's plate and dished out enough lasagna for four people.

"Well, I saw that the house was for sale, so I went to check it out. I really just wanted to see it. I hadn't been there since . . . Well, never, really. Once I saw it I just felt like I needed to be there."

"Wow," Nick said, taking his seat. "Doesn't it bother you after what happened to your family?"

"Not really," I said. "I was too young to remember anything. It feels like a new home to me."

"Yeah, but it's got to bother you a little, right?" Vicki said, nodding me toward the truth behind my denial.

"The first couple of nights were a little . . . creepy." I looked pointedly at Garrett, who rolled his eyes affably. "But I think that was just nerves."

Vicki pressed her hand to her throat as she looked back on our conversation in the living room. "I am so sorry about what I was saying earlier. I didn't know! I mean, all that talk about . . . Oh, I feel just awful!"

"That's okay. Don't worry about it. I asked you to tell the stories."

"I know, but it's just so . . . I don't even know what to say." She shuddered openly. "I mean, what possessed you to buy that house?"

"Bad choice of words, Vic," Nick said.

Vicki blinked to recall what she had said. "I'm sorry. It's just a shock. I don't know how you can stand to live in that house after what happened. I know I couldn't."

"Well, I'm just renting it for now. But I guess I just needed to . . ." I didn't know how to explain a lifetime of feeling like a hacked-off appendage to people who were wearing the same matching outfits as their kids in a portrait they had hanging on their living room wall. "I mean . . . I don't know . . . um . . . I guess . . ."

Garrett grabbed my knee under the table to say, "She doesn't want anyone to know since it's still a little up in the air, but Dixie's working on writing her memoirs."

Vicki's expression instantly switched from being profoundly disturbed to being thoroughly intrigued. "Oh, that's so exciting. I can't wait to read it. You have to let me see your first copy."

"Ah, sure," I said, taking a burned roll as Vicki tipped the basket to me. I turned a questioning look at Garrett as I reached for the butter, and he whispered, "Just go with it," behind his napkin before he tucked it into his collar. He flashed a smile at Nick, who was watching our exchange, and then nose-dived into his plate of lasagna.

Left on my own, I turned back to address Vicki: "Can you please not tell anybody about me living in my old house again?" I closed my eyes to make sense of my next warning: "Or about the book I'm writing? I want to keep it private for now."

"You hear that, Vic?" Nick cautioned as he picked through the rolls to find the one least burned. "Don't tell anyone about this."

"I wouldn't tell anybody," she snipped.

"Oh, right." He looked at me to shake his head. "Unfortunately, Dixie, you've just told your secret to the neighborhood gossip."

"I am not!"

Nick reached out and patted his wife's hand. "I love you, sweetie, but you know it's true." He rolled his eyes back to me. "You can't sneeze around here without someone calling to say they heard you were sick."

"I won't say a word, Dixie." She gave Nick a hard look. "Nick's just being mean. Your secret is safe with me. I promise. I'm so glad you told me. I think what you're doing is so brave. It takes a lot of courage to face your fears. Especially all by yourself. I mean, when Garrett's not around, of course." She smiled doubtfully as her eyes shifted to Garrett, mindlessly shoveling food in his mouth. "Promise you'll let us know if you need anything."

"Well, if I see any ghosts, I might be banging on your door in the middle of the night." I said this with a laugh, but I wasn't joking.

GARRETT HELD MY hand as he walked me home, but stopped short of taking me up the steps to the front door. I was two stairs up when I felt him hold back. I swallowed my disappointment like an unbuffered pill, grimaced in hopes of a smile, and turned to look at him.

"Aren't you coming in?" I asked lightly. When he shrugged, I stepped down to eye level. "So, I'm writing my memoirs, huh?"

He gave a shy grin. "What, is that not the right word for it?"

"How should I know?"

He shrugged again. "Well, you're the writer."

"Ha-ha, very funny." I swung our linked arms like a jump rope. "So where'd you come up with that one, anyway?"

"That's what I told my sister so she wouldn't think you were crazy for living here."

"She already thought I was crazy for dating you," I teased, pulling on his hand. "Come inside with me."

"Nah." He let go of my hand. "I'm gonna get going."

I sighed, glancing back at the house. I didn't want to sleep in the back seat of my car, but dreaded the thought of tucking into my parents' bed again and waking alone from my nightmares. I could still feel my father's belt tightening around my throat, the cold buckle against my skin, my head ripping away. I touched my neck reflexively, playing the tendons just below my ear like the frets of a guitar, amazed at how vulnerable the human body was. Just four millimeters of flimsy skin stood between major arteries and a world full of sharp objects. Bananas were wrapped in more durable stuff. And even if I did sleep in my car, what's to say that my father wouldn't come along for the ride? And if I tried to stay awake in the house until morning, I could add sleep deprivation to my ever-increasing list of neuroses. It wasn't so much all the unexplainable scary noises that had me spooked; it was all the very *explainable* scary noises: doors slamming, heads rolling, feet dragging, axes swishing . . . It really didn't matter if it was all in my head. Scared is scared. Another night of playing "identify that strange noise" might make me open the silverware drawer and—

"You're afraid to stay here by yourself, aren't you?" Garrett asked smugly.

"I think it was all those ghost stories," I admitted.

"Go pack a bag and come stay with me tonight," he suggested.

I shook my head. "No way. I can't give up that easy."

"There's no shame in being scared, Dixie." He pulled my hand. "Come on. Run screaming into the night with me."

"No. You stay," I urged.

"I don't want to stay."

"Sure you do." I took a step down and wrapped my arms around his waist. "And you've been drinking so you shouldn't drive."

"I only had a couple glasses of wine," he said.

"Tell it to the judge." I laughed, then added, "Why risk it when you could be asleep in bed in less than a minute? Well, you'll be in a bed, at any rate."

He smiled briefly, then got serious. "If I stay, you'll want me to move in."

"So?"

He unwrapped my arms from him. "You know it's not just the house, Dixie. You lied to me. You tried to trick me. I don't like that. I don't want our first home to be built on lies."

"Oh, don't be so dramatic. I only lied to you because I didn't want to tell you the truth." I smiled wide to show him I was joking, and he looked away. "Oh, come on, Garrett. I was going to tell you. I did tell you, remember? Why are you making such a big deal out of this?"

"Because it is a big deal, Dixie. You didn't just lie to me. You moved out on me. You pressed the Pause button on our life together. And for what? What good is coming from doing this? You're miserable. I'm miserable. It's time to come home and put this all behind you."

"I am home, Garrett," I said softly.

He shook his head in weary frustration.

"For now, anyway," I said. "I just need a little more time to work some things out."

"Like what?"

I took a deep breath. "I've found out some information. I don't want to go into a lot of detail about it until I can find out more, but I think I'm on to something."

"On to what?"

"Finding out if my father really killed my family or not."

He took a step back. "What are you talking about?"

"You remember my uncle Davis, right?" He nodded vaguely. "Well, he never believed my father was guilty. I think he might have been right."

"What makes you say that?"

If I told him about the police file, he would want to see it. Pick holes in it. Though I trusted Garrett more than anyone in the world, and never knew him to perform a selfish act, I couldn't say that in his desire to have me home again, he wouldn't say or do anything to get me to give up my quest, especially if that involved him sleeping alone while I investigated a crime that had already been solved a quarter of a century ago.

"Just a bunch of stuff," I said. "But I need to be *here* to figure it out. I don't know why, but I feel like all this is happening for a reason. Like I was drawn to this house for a reason. I can't leave until I know why."

He leaned back to consider my words. "And exactly how long do you think that might take?"

I shrugged. "As long as it takes. But soon . . . I hope."

He nodded. "Yeah, twenty-five-year-old murder cases usually work themselves out pretty quick." I opened my mouth to say something, but before I could, he kissed me on the forehead and left me standing on the stairs.

I SAT OUTSIDE for over an hour after Garrett left, chewing my lip to get up the nerve to unlock the door. Thunder sounded overhead and started a baby crying inside the house. I froze, listening, praying that the cat that had troubled Jenny was still trapped in a closet somewhere. The sound came again. Not a cat. Not a baby. My phone! Stupid Vicki and her stupid stories, I thought as I got up and unlocked the door.

I found my phone on the floor next to the hamper in my room. I was so excited that it might be Garrett calling to say that he changed his mind and was on his way back that it only vaguely occurred to me that I had left my phone sitting on the nightstand. The phone number was unfamiliar, assigned to someone named Unavailable. Probably a telemarketer. It was a 703 area code. Northern Virginia. It could be Garrett's sister's home phone number. He might have decided to stay at her place tonight since it was closer. I didn't know his sister's number off the top of my head, but it had to be hers. I answered with a seductive, albeit condescending, tone:

"Change your mind, lover boy?"

"Dixie?" The voice was male, familiar, but not Garrett.

"Sorry. I thought— Who's this?" I asked, mortified.

"It's Rory."

"Rory?" I sat hard on the edge of the bed. "Oh, my god."

He laughed at my reaction. "I'm good, thanks. How are you?"

"Oh, sorry. It's just— Wow! What a surprise."

"A good one, I hope."

The sound of his voice took me to the front seat of his car. Leather and Drakkar. Steam on the windshield and "Slow Ride" on the radio. The first flakes of snow melting in his hair.

"Yeah, I guess. I mean, of course." The line went silent for a beat. I heard him clear his throat, but he didn't say anything else. "So, what's up?" I asked.

"Nothing," he said. "I've just been thinking about you."

"That's funny, I've been thinking about you, too."

"Oh, yeah? What about?"

"Well, believe it or not, I think I just had dinner at your old house. Did you live to the right or left of our old house on Catharpin?"

"Uh, to the right, facing it."

"Yep. I was just over there."

"What were you doing there?"

I sat forward to untie my shoe. "I had dinner with the people who live there. They're kinda my neighbors. Well, not kind of, they *are* my neighbors. I moved back into our old house."

A moment of silence as he took this in. "When did you do that?"

"Just a couple of days ago, actually."

"You're kidding, right?"

"Why does everybody keep asking me that?" I laughed.

"Because it's—"

"Don't say 'creepy.'"

"Well, I was going to say it was kinda strange, but 'creepy' works." He said this with a note of nonchalance that I was glad to hear. "Aren't you scared living there all by yourself?"

"What makes you think I'm— Wait. Did Aunt Celia call you?"

"She's worried about you, Dixie."

I made a *phish* sound. "I should have known you wouldn't have called me on your own, Rory."

"Actually, I did. I called Celia's to talk to you and she told me about the house. I didn't know you had moved."

Though I doubted this, I let it go. "So, what did you call for?"

"Just to talk," he said. "See how you're doing." When I didn't volunteer my condition, he asked, "So are you okay? Celia told me you had a big fight with your boyfriend."

For as jealous as Aunt Celia could be about her own personal affairs, she was sure generous with mine.

"It wasn't a fight," I said. "Garrett and I are totally cool. I just wanted to do this on my own. That is, if you count living with the ghosts of my dead family on my own." My bubbly tone popped with an anxious sigh.

"Now, *that's* creepy, Dixie," he warned.

"Yeah, I guess it is a little creepy," I admitted. "Especially with the storm."

"Is it raining there?"

"Pouring!" I cringed as a clap of lightning flashed across the room. "And thundering. Talk about the perfect setting for a haunted house. All I need now is for the lights to go off." I silently told the gods that I was not tempting them with this comment.

"Do you want me to come over?" he offered.

I sat perfectly still.

"Dixie?"

"You want to come over?" I crossed to the mirror over the dresser. All things considered, I thought I looked pretty good. The conditioner I had barely rinsed out of my hair had given me an itchy scalp, but it was keeping my split ends in line. My lips could use a little color, but my eye makeup was hanging in there. The zit on my chin felt worse than it looked. I resisted the urge to pick at it and snatched up my hairbrush.

"... I live in Falls Church now, don't know if you knew that," Rory was saying, "but I could be there in half an hour. Forty minutes tops. Do you want me to pick us up some wine?"

"Thanks, but I've had enough wine." I tucked the phone to my shoulder to brush the left side of my head. "You don't have to come over, Rory. I'm fine. Really."

"I want to," he said. "I want to see you."

I stopped mid-brushstroke. "Why?"

He found my confounded tone amusing. "Well, I miss you, for one. But if that's not enough of a reason, then let's just say I'm curious to see the house again. But if *you* don't want to see *me*, then I guess I'll just head home."

"Home?" I tested. "I thought you said you were at home. In Falls Church, remember?"

"I am in Falls Church. I just left a friend's house. They live right around the corner from me."

His use of the word "they" was intentionally vague. Wherever he may have been tonight, I was certain that *she* lived right around the corner.

"It's not that I don't want to see you, Rory," I said, resuming my brushing—short, angry strokes. The issue was that I *did* want to see Rory, more than anything. More than I should, which meant that I probably shouldn't. Rory was like a drug I had given up a long time ago. Inviting him over for a quick visit was like taking one little hit off the pipe; it could only end in misery.

"What is it then?" he asked.

"Well, I guess because the last time I saw you, I was ... um ..."

"Stalking me?" he submitted with a laugh.

"I was going to say 'in a bad place,' but I guess you could call it that. I said some pretty awful things." *I wish you had died that day, too!*

Why don't you just go kill yourself and do us both a favor! I hate you, you Keanu Reeves wannabe motherfucker! Somehow, the last comment had seemed to wound him the most. "I didn't think you ever wanted to see me again."

"I wasn't mad at you or anything. I was just worried that . . . I don't know. It was a long time ago. All I know is that I want to see you now. I think about you all the time."

That Rory had thought of me at all delighted me more than I wanted to admit. Rory was my first love, my first kiss—reciprocated or not. I knew that wasn't how he thought of me, but somewhere in my stomach a butterfly dared to dream. The feeling sank quickly to the pit of my stomach as Garrett came to mind and plucked off its wings.

"Hey," Rory interjected into my silence, "I wanted to tell you: I saw a thing about your family on TV the other day."

"Oh, yeah?" I headed to the bathroom in search of perfume. I hadn't unpacked all my toiletries, and was almost certain my trial-size bottle of Calvin Klein's Obsession was wrapped in a washcloth in one of four boxes that were stacked next to the toilet.

"They were doing a thing on unsolved mysteries and—"

"Unsolved?" I asked, ripping the tape off the top box.

"Well, I guess it was more like unexplained mysteries. Like, why it happened and all. I'll try to find out what show it was. It was pretty interesting. Have you been contacted about doing something for the twenty-five-year anniversary?"

"No. Have you?"

"No. I kinda thought they might ask us to do something. I got a call back at the twentieth. I told them I'd do it if you would, but I never heard back."

"No one cares anymore, Rory," I said, unraveling a washcloth to find one of Garrett's razors inside. Honey-colored whiskers clung to dried foam on the blade. Rather than pining for the man whose DNA

I held in my very hand—the same gene sequence that might one day give our children curly hair and predispose them to peanut allergies—I was disgusted that Garrett would have packed such a filthy, disposable thing.

"I care," Rory said sharply. His tone struck a silent chord between us. And in that stillness, I had an old thought: *Rory's one of my boys.* No matter the rift between us, he was a bridge to my past. Regardless of who the axe hit that day, he had felt its impact. He was the only one who might truly understand why I needed to live in this house again. Though circumstance had led us down separate paths, we had ended up right back where we started: me trapped and alone in this house, surrounded by my dead family, and Rory coming to my rescue.

"So, do you want some company?" he asked.

"Sure," I said, dropping the razor in the box with the rest of Garrett's things. "Just don't call my house creepy when you see it."

6

Rory wasn't as gorgeous as he had been the last time I saw him, which was almost seven years prior; he was twice as. Forty-two by my Josh calculator, he had just a hint of crow's-feet in the corners of his eyes. Flickers of silver along his temples and scruffy beard gave him a woodsy, confident appearance. Though we had shared a few awkward phone conversations over the years, the last time I'd actually laid eyes on Rory was when I bumped into him exiting a movie theater with his date—a waifish strawberry blonde who wasn't at all his type. This was just a few months after I broke into his town house, so I wouldn't say he was particularly happy to see me. In fact, he barely acknowledged me. The cold shoulder hurt, but I didn't blame him. Once a line like that is crossed, you didn't want to step too close to it again.

Having just turned twenty, I had convinced myself that the only reason Rory hadn't made a move on me was because I was Josh's little sister. In his eyes, I was taboo. But taboos could be broken. Luckily, one of his windows was open a crack, so I only had to pop out the screen to gain entry. I followed the snoring to an open door at the end of the upstairs hallway. As I slipped off my jeans, I stared at the lump in the center of the bed. Just one. Thank god. If he'd had a girl in there with him, I would have to do this all over again the next night. It wasn't until my kiss was met with a hard forehead that I realized I might have misplayed my hand, which had a firm grip on him under the covers. Rory flew out of the bed on a scream and head-butted me in the mouth. The blow spun me around, but failed to knock any sense into me. *He doesn't know it's me*, I thought, clutching the sting of panic swelling up in my face. *It's dark. I startled him. He probably thinks some lunatic broke into his home. Once he realizes it's me, he'll sweep me into his arms.* This made so much sense, in fact, that when the overhead light switched on, I truly thought I was golden. Though it's hard to be seductive while checking to see if any of your teeth are missing, I thought I was pulling it off. Licking blood from my fat lip like juice from a ripe berry, I squinted to find him beyond the glare of the light, and patted the mattress for his return. A zipper, or maybe a button, stung my cheek as my discarded clothes were whipped in my face. I cried out that I was sorry as the door slammed. After I dressed, I crept downstairs to sneak out unnoticed. I had almost reached the front door when he called out for a word. Actually, he had quite a few for me.

Though that unfortunate night belonged to a girl I could hardly remember, as I stared up at Rory in my doorway, his build, that grin, those blue eyes, I felt myself slipping through his window all over again. There was just something about him that made me a little crazy.

His flannel shirt was soft and slightly damp as he grabbed me into his arms and swung me into the living room. I stumbled off-balance as he set me down, grabbing hold of the back of the armchair to keep from falling.

"Let me get a look at you," he said, standing back to take me in with a rub of his chin. "Where's the little girl I used to know? You're all grown up. I mean, look at you, Dix. You're a knockout."

"Oh, right," I honked. "I look a mess. But you look great, as always."

He waved off my compliment as he ambled around the room in a slow circle. "What the hell . . ." he wondered, drifting to the couch to look at the seascape painting hung over it. He hooked a thumb over his shoulder as he turned to me. "Is that the same picture?"

I nodded. "Don't touch it. I used a shoe to hammer the nail, so it might not be up there very good." I looked around for Garrett's hammer, but I didn't see it anywhere.

Rory ran a hand through his hair as he took in the room with increasingly wider eyes. "Except for the color of the walls and the carpeting, it's exactly the same as it was." He started the rocking chair with a push of his finger. "I remember this rocking chair. And that lamp. And this coffee table and— Oh, my god! The couch! Holy shit. Josh and I used to hang out on this all the time." He snatched the throw pillow from the corner. "See that hole?"

I walked over to squint at a dime-sized hole on the inside arm of the couch. The edges were melted, singed black. I poked my finger into it.

"It looks like a bullet hole," I said.

"It's from a cigar. Josh and I were smoking one I stole off my father. Man, that was a crazy night. We had just eaten a whole bag of mushrooms right before your mom asked us to watch Eddie and Michael." When my eyes widened, he nodded. "Yeah. Those kinds of mushrooms. We didn't know we'd have to babysit. We thought we were going to the movies. Your mom cut her hand pretty bad, so we had to stick around while your dad took her to get stitches."

"Oh, no." I laughed.

"I know. We were freaking out. But what could we say? 'We can't babysit because we just ate a whole bag of psychedelic mushrooms'?" He looked down at the couch, wagging his head at the memory. "Josh tried to hide the cigar when Eddie came downstairs, and burned a hole right through the cushion. Eddie ratted us out as soon as your parents walked through the door." I liked how he called them "your parents." I rarely got that kind of recognition. "Man, your mom was so pissed. But it kinda worked out. They were so mad about us smoking and burning the couch that they didn't notice we were tripping our asses off." His reflective smile dulled as he turned to give me a muddled look. "How do you still have all this stuff? I thought it would have gotten chucked after the . . ."

Those who knew my history had a hard time saying "murder" in front of me, like it might be a hypnotic trigger word.

I stopped the rocking chair with my foot, and refolded the afghan—which smelled like the wet fur of a dead alpaca that had been spritzed with Febreze as it lay on the floor of a barn—as I re-counted how I came to be living in this slapdash mausoleum. Rory fell back onto the couch to listen. Legs wide and outstretched, mus-cled arms slung across the back of the couch. He shook his head in disbelief when I told him that I had re-created everything from old family photographs, and swallowed hard when I said the kitchen ta-ble was new but the chairs were the originals.

"I don't know what happened to my high chair," I pondered aloud. "I guess it got thrown away after the . . ." I couldn't seem to say it, ei-ther. Not in this house, anyway. I cleared my throat to press on. "They had a few high chairs at Salvation Army that were a pretty good match, but I'm still checking Craigslist for one just like it."

A shadow set on Rory's smile. I gave a quick laugh to lighten the moment, but it came out as a worried screech. I glanced at the paint-ing over Rory's head, half expecting the seagull to have been shot from the sky.

"There's still a bunch of stuff I haven't gone through yet," I said, scratching a phantom itch behind my ear. "Mostly odds and ends that weren't in any of the photographs. Hey, I wanted to ask you"—I pointed at the ceiling—"was Josh's room the first one on the right at the top of the stairs?"

He blinked to refocus. "Uh, yeah."

"Did he share a room with Eddie?" I asked.

"No. Eddie and Michael had the room across the hall."

"Oh," I said, puzzling. "I wonder where I slept."

"I think you were in with your parents. I remember Josh saying he was going to clean out the attic and live up there so you could have his room when you got older."

"I forgot we had an attic." I looked up at the ceiling. "I haven't been up there yet. Do you know how you access it?"

Instead of answering, he asked, "Why are you doing this, Dixie?"

I dropped my eyes to his. "What do you mean?"

"Living here. Getting all their old stuff out of storage. Pretending like it's 1992 again. Why? It can't be good for you."

I shrugged. "I just needed to be here. You get that, right?"

"Yeah, I get it. But doesn't it freak you out?"

I shrugged. "Not really."

He tilted his head.

"Well, maybe a little," I conceded. I took a seat in the armchair. The front leg shuddered to remind me just how truly decrepit everything was. I leaned left to keep pressure off the leg. "Is it really gross?"

His eyes took a nasty lick around the room. "It's more all their old stuff than you actually living here. I think if you bought some new furniture it might help. It smells like grandma's house. And they haven't found grandma's body yet."

"Does it really?" I lifted my nose to catch the odor. "I sprayed air freshener all over."

"That's not helping any." He chuckled grimly. "Is the upstairs the same as it used to be?"

"I think so. But there weren't many pictures of the upstairs. Do you want to see it?"

AS WE ENTERED Josh's room, Rory told me that I had the bed on the wrong wall. "It was over there. And the desk was under the window. And I don't think that was his." He pointed to a skateboard propped in the corner. "That was Eddie's. And there was a Metallica poster over the bed, not the Redskins. That must have been in the boys' room. Josh was a Cowboys fan, all the way. Oh, and he had this funky lamp on his desk. It was this wild Japanese-dragon thing with these crazy eyes and a pink lampshade." It was a Chinese foo dog, and I had accidently dropped it in Uncle Davis's garage. Only the shade survived, which was somewhere. "Man, that thing was ugly, but Josh loved it for some reason. He had a beanbag chair in the corner"—he pointed to where it should have been—"but it had a hole in it, so it probably got trashed. I don't remember that dresser. I'm pretty sure the one he had was white."

"Oh." I gasped as tears rushed in. "I-I tried to g-get it right."

He turned to find me crying and gathered me into a hug. "Oh, don't cry. You did good. Really. You got most of it right. Don't cry. Please. I'm sorry. I was just trying to help."

"I'm so stupid," I sniveled. "Moving here was a huge mistake."

"No." He kissed the top of my head. "You were trying to make yourself feel better. I understand. I don't think you're stupid. A little wacko, maybe . . ."

I snorted a sad laugh into his armpit. "I guess being wacko's better than being stupid."

"Sure it is." He put his arm around my shoulder to guide me out of the room. He stopped us just outside in the hallway. "The attic access is in here." He opened the door to the linen closet and looked up. "Yeah, see there?" I stepped next to him to look up as he pointed at the ceiling. He placed his other hand on my back. "You can get up right through that opening."

There was a small, inserted square in the ceiling. It hardly looked large enough for a body to fit through.

"How was Josh going to get his furniture up there?" I asked as his hand slid down to my waist. A jolt of electricity stiffened my spine. I tucked my hands under my armpits to fake a chill. He gave my back a quick rub to warm me up, and then stepped into the closet.

"He wanted to cut out a bigger hole and build a staircase leading up, but your mom wasn't too keen on the idea." He rolled his head back to look up at the hatch. "Want me to see what's up there?"

I shook my head as I stepped back into the hallway. "Not tonight. I don't want you getting all dirty."

"I'll come back tomorrow," he said. "We can check it out together. Maybe grab a bite to eat, if you want."

My heart gave a happy clap.

We crowded into the narrow hallway as he pulled the door closed behind him. The smoldering heat of his confident stance, stretched tight across the flannel of his broad chest, caught between us and lit a fire in my belly. I melted to the wall as he drew his fingers through my hair, unbearably slow, each strand like an open nerve. "Fuzz," he breathed into my upturned face.

"What?" I asked dizzily.

He held up a gray piece of lint.

"Oh," I said with a quick blink. I snatched the soft nap from his fingers with a mortified groan, and raked my fingers through my hair as I moved down the hall. "I haven't done much in here."

I flicked on the overhead light and stood back as Rory peeked in on a pile of wooden bunk bed slats stacked in the middle of the boys' room like an unlit bonfire. I accepted his offer to assemble the beds for me, but was secretly disappointed that such a wonderfully time-consuming chore had been taken off my schedule. I hopped a safe distance to the right as Rory reentered the hallway.

The master bedroom door was closed, once again. I dismissed it with a flap of my hand as I started back down the hall. "Never mind that room. It's a mess." A soft *click* turned me around. Rory was wandering toward my bed at a slow, engrossed pace. I hurried in after him, snatching panties and socks from the floor as I went.

"Sorry. I didn't think to clean," I said, stuffing dirties into the top drawer of my dresser. "I didn't expect anyone to be in here."

"That's okay," he said. "You should see my room."

I chewed chapped skin off my bottom lip as I watched Rory explore my room like a lion in a new cage. It seemed wrong that a man other than Garrett should be the first to enter my boudoir. But whose fault was that? Garrett could be here right now, if he wanted. I had asked him to stay. Begged him, in fact. That should count for something.

Rory stepped to the window and brushed the curtain aside with

T. Marie Vandelly

the back of his fingers; a lock of hair could not have been moved more seductively from a cheek. My shoulders slumped on an exhale. There was no use fighting it. I would always be hopelessly infatuated with Rory. More than his good looks—though they did play a role, and I can't honestly say how I might have felt toward him if he weren't so handsome—it was the connection we shared that drew my mothy self to his flame, an eternal flame he kept glowing for my family. I saw Josh's smile in his, Eddie's athleticism in his strong arms, Michael's mischievous charm in his eyes. And though Garrett was my future, brighter than any I could have ever hoped for, I couldn't deny my past, and that was Rory.

I set to straightening the bed as he poked his head into the bathroom. My pillow wasn't at the head of the mattress where I'd left it, nor was it mixed in with the blankets. I crouched down to look under the bed.

"Lose something?" Rory asked.

"Yeah. My pillow."

"How do you lose a pillow?"

"I know, right? It keeps falling on the floor." I lifted the drape of the sheet. The only thing under the bed was my father's book, which I was sure I had put back in the cubbyhole that morning.

"Is that it?" Rory said, pointing at my hamper.

"What the hell?" As I picked up the pillow, a strange fragrance came with it. A rotten pork chop marinated in Mentholatum with a hint of sauerkraut. As if my father's aroma and Leah's scent had joined together for a big, stinky hug. "I didn't put this here. I know I put it back on the bed earlier this evening. I haven't been back in the room since."

"*Uh-oh,*" Rory sang in an ominous tone. "You've got ghosts."

"Shit, I guess I do." I tossed the pillow on the bed and fished the book out from under it. "He keeps moving things around."

"Who keeps moving things around?"

I shrugged as I got slowly to my feet. "Mr. Ghost, I guess." Rory held my eyes for a long, gulped moment. He knew who Mr. Ghost was. I tossed the book aside and sat on the edge of the bed to change the subject, though the one I chose was just as disturbing. "Hey, whatever happened to that girlfriend of yours?"

"Which girlfriend?" he asked with a sly smile, hooking his thumbs in his belt loops as he crossed his legs at the ankles to lean against the wall. I wondered if he tried to pose like a Stetson model or if it just happened naturally.

"The last time I talked to you, you were at the hospital," I reminded him. "You said your girlfriend had an accident or something."

I knew that her name was Erin, and that Erin had died from a traumatic brain injury. I read about it in the papers. The police ultimately ruled her spill down the flight of concrete stairs to be an accident, but the wording in the article seemed rather indisposed, as though the decision had been reached with some reluctance. But the stairs at Erin's apartment building were steep, the stairwell poorly lit, so it was easy to imagine how someone could have ended up in a heap at the bottom.

"I've talked to you since then," he said.

"Yeah, but that was the last girlfriend I knew about. Was she okay? Are you still with her?"

"No." He glanced out the window as a flash of lightning x-rayed his face. "She died."

"I'm so sorry! That's so sad. Had you been dating long?" I pulled the pillow onto my lap. This time the whiff was all Leah: Bengay, straight up.

He shrugged imperceptibly. "Just a few months."

I played dumb so I could hear his unadulterated version of the story. "What happened to her?"

"She fell down a flight of stairs. She lived for over a week on life support, but there was nothing they could do for her. She was totally brain-dead. I was there when they unplugged her." He banged his head softly on the wall behind him. "I shouldn't have been in the room for that. I didn't know her that well. I'd never even met her family before. Well, I knew her sister, but that was the first time I had ever met her parents. They kept asking me all these questions. About keeping her on life support and all. Last-wishes type of shit. Like I should have known what she would have wanted. How was I supposed to know? I hardly knew her last name—"

Doyle.

"I mean, we were dating, but it wasn't like we were exclusive or anything."

"Don't minimize it, Rory. That must have been awful for you. Regardless of how long you two were dating. I'm so sorry you had to go through that."

"They thought she was pushed," he said, like I had asked. "Since I was the one that found her, they thought I might have had something to do with it." He swiped his hands to call foul. "Which I did not. They only starting thinking that way after that reporter started filling their heads with a bunch of crap. Calling me the 'Too-Late Hero' and bringing up your family and shit. Like it was my fault I didn't get there in time to save them. Or her." He lowered his eyes to mine. "I mean, why would I want to kill Erin? We weren't in love, but I cared for her. I would never have hurt her."

"Why did they think she was pushed?" I asked.

"I guess because she was in her pajamas when they found her. Her bed was turned down and all the lights were off. The door to her apartment was standing open. They figured she must have been in bed asleep and got up to answer the door, and whoever it was pushed her down the stairs." He nodded to accept this logic. "That makes sense, I guess."

"What made them think someone else was there in the first place?" I asked.

"A neighbor said he heard her arguing with somebody. At first he said that it sounded like two women fighting. Like a catfight. That's exactly how he put it: 'a catfight.'" He held out his hands imploringly. "That's not how you'd describe an argument between a man and woman, is it?" Before I could answer, he rushed on. "It was like a month later when he told that reporter that it might have been a man he heard arguing with Erin. I think she got him to change his story to make me look guilty. In fact, I'm sure of it." He trolled his tongue across the inside of his bottom lip. "Claire Reynolds. What a fucking cunt."

The word landed between us like a hacked-up piece of phlegm that we both wanted to ignore. As I looked away, he cleared his throat.

"Sorry. I know that word's a big no-no with women, but she just pisses me off."

Since I counted myself a woman by anatomy, not sensibility, I shrugged. "Who do you think did it?"

"I don't know. Erin had this new friend she had been hanging out with. I think her name was Donna or Diane or something like that. Debbie, maybe ... I can't remember. I never met her. But Erin told me she was kind of strange. Real possessive and insecure. I told the police about her, but they didn't have much to go on. Erin said she had just moved here from out West. I only saw her once. She was leaving Erin's building just as I pulled up. She was wearing a baseball cap and had on this big coat, so it was hard to tell what she looked like. I only saw her for a second. I didn't really pay her any attention at the time. I wish I had."

He pushed off the wall and punched his palm with his fist. The whap of flesh made me jump. I hugged my pillow as he paced the carpeting just beyond my kneecaps. My father's scent was back.

"I told Erin to stop hanging out with her, but she felt sorry for her. Erin was always taking in strays and giving homeless people money. I don't know why, but I just had a bad feeling about Erin hanging out with this chick. I just know she had something to do with Erin's death." He stopped pacing to rub his face. "I don't know. Maybe she didn't. Who knows what happened. All I know is that I didn't fucking kill her." He started toward the door. "You got any beer?"

I PULLED A couple of Miller Lites from the fridge and sat them on the kitchen table. I took my mother's chair as Rory lingered in the entryway, staring down a memory.

"You haven't been here since that day, have you?" I asked.

He shook his head. "I didn't think I ever would." He took a tentative step forward to test the waters, elbows bent and slightly raised for balance, as if the wood floor might be unreliable.

Looming in the lamplight from the living room, he cast a shadow approximately the same size as the blood angel I had seen in the police photograph. I could tell by his expression that he was reliving that moment: down in a warm pool of blood, panicking to get back on his feet, eyes wide with horror, Badfinger crooning in the background like the soundtrack to some slasher film from the 1970s.

"You lied to the police about that day, didn't you?" I asked.

My question knocked his head upright. I could see a lie working its fingers into his expression, shifting his eyes side to side. He sighed off my question as he shuffled forward and took a seat in what I'd now come to believe was my father's chair. Hard as it was to imagine my father eating a Pop-Tart, neither Eddie nor Michael would have been allowed a cup of coffee, so the seat must have belonged to him.

Rory didn't say anything. He just sat quietly until his stillness became a little intimidating. Only then did it occur to me that I had invited a stranger into my home. I didn't know Rory that well. Not really. Not as an adult, anyway. Most of what I knew of him had been concocted in various adolescent daydreams I had about him. He was kind, because I wanted him to be. He was gentle, because I needed him to take it slow. Neither might be true. I cooled my wrists on the neck of my beer bottle as I awaited his response, wondering if he could knock me unconscious with one punch. I took a quick sip of beer, but couldn't remember how to swallow. I let the foam grow warm and flat on my tongue. It flushed down on a reflex gulp as Rory said, "How did you know?"

"You told the police that you slipped in the blood when you came in the back door. But that was a lie. I saw a photograph of where you fell. You left a shape in the blood." I pointed at the spotless floor behind him. "You fell when you entered the kitchen from the living room. You were in the house that morning, weren't you?" I wondered if I was asking a killer for his confession, and was not at all sure I was prepared to hear it.

He closed his eyes to nod.

A tremor passed from the top of my head to the tips of my toes, raising hairs across my skin as it went. "Tell me, Rory," I said.

He shook his head. I thought he was refusing to answer, but before I could insist, he gasped a deep breath to say, "I'm sorry. I didn't want to, but . . ."

A solid rock of fear splashed hot, soured beer back up my throat as I swallowed. I covered my mouth to ask through trembling fingers, "You didn't want to *what*, Rory?"

"Hide!" He screamed this as though he wanted us to do so now. "You have to believe me, Dixie. I couldn't have done anything to save them. It was too late by the time I knew what was going on."

I held up my hand to pause him, but it really, really wanted to slap him, so I tucked it back into my lap. "Start from the beginning, Rory."

He took a deep, shuddering breath to begin, "When I got here, everything seemed fine. It was Thanksgiving, so the kitchen smelled like turkey, but other than that, it was just like any other day, really. You were in your high chair, and Eddie and Michael were laughing and carrying on. You know, normal kid stuff." His eyes flicked back and forth to navigate the kitchen on that day. He pointed to the chair at the head of the table to his right. "Josh was still eating when I got here, so I asked if I could head up to his room to wait for him." He paused to smile. "We were going to a tag football game up at the school. We didn't play or anything, we just used it as an excuse to hang out under the bleachers and party. You know, make fun of the jocks and watch their girlfriends cheerlead. I remember I wanted to duck out before your mom smelled the bag of dope I had in my pocket. It was seriously skunky. Josh gave me a look, so I knew he could smell it, too. In fact, I think it was his idea for me to wait for him in his room in the first place."

"What were you, a couple of drug addicts?" Though I had done all the drugs he had admitted to and more—pot, magic mushrooms, and few other Schedule I and II narcotics—when partaken in a time of mass murder, I viewed them in a completely different light.

He shrugged. "We were teenagers. I guess we were kind of pot-heads, but weren't into anything heavy. But your mom would have freaked out if she knew we were getting high. And if my dad found out? Forget about it. He would have called the cops on me himself. I already had a DUI. That's why I lied to the police about being in the house. I had stashed the bag of pot in Josh's room. I didn't want any-one figuring out it was mine."

He stopped to twirl his beer and began picking at the label. I watched his hands until he was ready to continue. He looked me in the eye to say, "I swear, I didn't know anything was wrong until I heard them screaming."

"You heard them? Why didn't you do anything?"

"I froze!" He leaned over the table to press the palms of his hands to his eyes. "I was so scared. I didn't know what was happening. One second everything was fine, and then all of the sudden all hell was breaking loose. I started to go down to see what was happening, but . . . the music had gotten turned up really loud. I don't know why that freaked me out so bad. It was just so . . . out of place, you know? Like I knew it meant something really bad was happening." His eyes were wide and pleading as he looked up. "I knew they were being hurt, but I didn't know what to do to stop it. So I hid. I hid in Josh's closet. By the time I got up the nerve to try and help, it was over. I could still hear you crying, but everyone else was . . . dead silent."

Tears dripped onto the table below Rory's hung head. Mine had crystallized to icy flakes in my throat.

"That was the scariest part," he said, "coming down the stairs. I could barely walk. I just knew someone was going to jump out and kill me. That's when I saw the blood." He sucked back a sob. "It was almost pouring out of the kitchen. I wanted to run out the front door and never look back, but you were crying so hard that—I couldn't just leave you there with . . . I didn't know what to do!"

He closed his eyes and took several long breaths, as though he were getting ready to plunge underwater. On his fourth breath, he dove in:

"At first I thought it was a joke, you know? Like they were all playing some sort of trick on me. For a second, I thought, *Oh, right. It's Halloween. They're just fucking with me.* But it wasn't Halloween. It was Thanksgiving. I couldn't figure out why they were trying to scare me like that on Thanksgiving. It didn't make any sense. I know that sounds stupid now, but that's what I was thinking at the time. I guess the shock of seeing something like that had me confused. I just wanted there to be some explanation for it, you know? Something other than what it was. I guess I just couldn't let myself believe that they were dead. I didn't want it to be real. But I knew it was real when I saw—"

My eyes followed his as they abruptly swung toward the other end of the table.

"I didn't see you, at first. I mean, I heard you screaming, yeah, but I didn't know you were there until I saw . . . Anyway, you were reaching out for your mom with your little hand, but she was . . . Ah, god!" He pressed the memory back into his eyes with his fists. "You were all covered in blood. I thought you were hurt, so I ran in to help you, but I slipped, and that's when I saw . . . Eddie was . . . That was the worst! Eddie's body was just . . . I couldn't believe what I was looking at. And Josh! Oh, man! He was my best friend, but I could barely tell it was him. He was all fucked up. I couldn't stand to look at him!" He swallowed to catch his breath. "I almost puked, but I knew I shouldn't, you know? Like I'd mess up the crime scene if I did."

He looked like he might actually puke now, and I leaned a safe distance away.

"Again, I know that sounds stupid," he said through a grim smile, "but I wasn't thinking very clearly." I nodded that I understood, and he looked at the floor between his legs to continue: "Michael was under the table—" Something cold touched my foot. "I swear, it looked like something inside of him had exploded. I couldn't believe the amount of violence. He was just a kid. I don't think he weighed more than fifty pounds. You could have killed him with one punch if you wanted to. He didn't need to be all hacked up like that. That was just . . . cruel."

I reached down and rubbed my foot as he closed his eyes to silently shake his head.

"I didn't even know your father was alive until I heard this gurgling noise beside me. When I turned to see what it was, he was looking right at me. His mouth was hanging open and blood was pouring out. I thought he had his tongue cut out or something." He shook off the image. "Somehow I got to my feet and I just ran for the door. That's when I saw Eddie's head." He glanced into the corner. "I had seen his body, so I knew his head had to be *somewhere*!" The shriek in his voice stabbed through my heart like an ice pick. "When I saw it just lying in the corner . . . staring up at me like that"—he covered his face with trembling hands—"I didn't know what to do. I know I keep saying that, but it's true. I wanted to help. I did. But there was nothing I could do."

Rory hung his head to soundlessly sob.

Oblivious to the emotion of the moment, the ice maker dropped a new batch. Life went on, no matter the circumstances. A faucet ran cold as the blood dried. A dishwasher changed cycles behind the decapitated body of a child. An ice cube was born in a moment of quiet despair. I wished my heart could be so impervious, but at that moment, it was susceptible to his tears, and I turned to catch a distressed gasp with my shoulder.

He looked up. "I'm so sorry, Dixie."

I nodded. "I know. But there was nothing you could have done to stop it, right?"

"I don't think so. But I should have at least tried. But I was too chickenshit scared out of my fucking mind to even go downstairs to see what was happening. I didn't even have the balls to tell anyone that I was in the house, so I made up that I came in after it was over. I was such a fucking coward."

I knew he wanted me to tell him that he wasn't, but instead I said, "You shouldn't have let your pride get in the way of doing the right thing, Rory. You should have told the police the truth. It could have made a difference."

He nodded, taking it like the man he hadn't been twenty-five years ago. When he looked up again, he looked old, older than I had noticed before. A hard frost had spread through his sideburns. The laugh lines around his eyes were much too deep to be untroubled. The web of spider veins around his nose was only slightly less grotesque than the creamy rheum clinging to his left tear duct. I immediately checked mine for eye boogers. Though no face could withstand such close scrutiny, given my blind adoration for Rory, I had thought his might. His beauty seemed to be vanishing before my very eyes.

"I'm sorry, Dixie," he said, wiping the yellow gunk through his lashes with his wrist. I looked away. "I don't know if I could have saved them, but I should have tried."

I waved this away with a napkin as I handed it to him. "You probably would just have gotten yourself killed along with the rest of them."

He shrugged, almost as if to say he wished that had been the case, then wiped his eyes. "That's what I've told myself my whole life. But I don't know if that's true. Maybe I could have done something to stop it."

We listened to the rain in silence until thunder kicked the roof.

"Do you think it was my father who killed them?" I asked.

He slumped back in his chair so hard I heard it crack. "What are you talking about? Of course it was your father."

"But you didn't see him do it," I submitted.

He gave me the standard piteous look that I had come to discount as insularity. "No, I didn't see him do it, Dixie, but it was him. It had to be. Nobody else was in the house but me."

"And you didn't do it, right?" I asked with a sideways look. The roll of his eyes said that he did not take my accusation seriously.

"Look," he said. "If it was somebody else, then your father would have been axed to death, too. Why would the killer drop the axe just to cut your father's throat? That doesn't make any sense." He pointed at the floor where my father's body had been. "He was lying right there, Dixie. I saw him. The knife he used to cut his throat was still in his hand."

I shrugged, unconvinced. "That doesn't prove anything."

"What makes you think it wasn't him?"

"There are a lot of things that don't add up about that day. Just the fact that you were in the house and nobody knew about it tells me that the police missed a few things." I leaned back and folded my arms. "You knew my father, Rory. Was there anything about him that made you think he could do something like that?"

"Not really. He was pretty easygoing, actually. I mean, he had his moments, but so did my dad. Come to think of it, my dad was the one more likely to go off the deep end and kill everybody."

"Where was my father when you got here that day?"

He shook his head. "I don't remember."

"Do you remember seeing him at all?"

He looked back to that day, visualizing it on the label of his beer bottle. "I think I saw him out by the shed. I just saw the back of him, though. He was wearing a blue shirt." He quickly canceled this with a shake of his head. "You know, that might have been a different day altogether. It's hard to remember one morning from another. I was over here a lot."

"Did you see the axe?" I asked. "In the kitchen, I mean. Not in the shed."

"Yeah . . . um . . . It was on the floor, I think."

"You saw it on the floor?" I asked, excited by this new twist in the story. "Not in the corner by the refrigerator? It was on the floor when you saw it? Are you sure?"

He thought for a moment. "Okay, no. That's right. The axe was in the corner next to the fridge. Sorry, I get confused sometimes. The knife was in your father's hand, which was on the floor. The axe was in the corner like you said."

"Did you see what was written on it?"

He looked down. "I don't remember."

"Come on, Rory, think. The killer wrote something in the blood on the blade of the axe. But by the time the police found it, the blood had run through it and they couldn't read what it said. All the pictures of the axe are missing from the file I have. You might be the only one who knows what it said."

"What file?" he asked.

I got up to get the file from my bag in the living room. I set it on the table as I returned. Rory leaned in to see.

"Is this the actual police file?" he asked.

"My uncle Davis got it from the detective who investigated the murders. I found it with all their belongings in his garage." I flipped

the file open and started sorting through the pictures. Since the ones
of Eddie were on the other side of the room from where the axe had
been positioned, I set them aside.

Rory recoiled as though I had tossed Eddie's severed head in his
lap. "Oh, my god!"

"Oh, sorry." I turned the pictures upside down on the table.

"Have you seen these?" he asked.

I nodded absently as I scanned the images for one that might have
captured the axe in a wide view of the kitchen. "Of course I've seen
them." I held up one that included the refrigerator, but it concealed
the corner where the axe would have stood. I thought I could see a
wooden foot poking out near the bottom edge of the wall, but it might
have been a shadow.

"How can you stand to look at them?" Rory asked.

"I can't, but it's the only way I'm going to figure any of this out." I
held up another picture of the refrigerator. The shadow I had seen
was blood, probably dripped from the nose of the axe as it stood in
the corner. "Why hide the axe in the corner, anyway? Why not just
chuck it on the floor? It was going to be found, either way."

"You really don't think your father did it, do you?"

"I don't know." I sighed, laying all the pictures of the kitchen table
on the kitchen table. The paralleled image caused a disorienting moment of vertigo. I braced through the spell, then reached for my
beer. "I always thought he had. But now that I've seen the file, I'm not
so sure."

Rory flipped over the top photograph before him. Josh. He covered his mouth. "I think I'm gonna be sick."

I reached the end of the pile I was holding. "Damn, Mr. Cullins
was right. There isn't one picture that shows the axe. Not even the
handle." I tapped them together to start again. "And you're sure you
don't remember seeing anything written on it?"

His head shook softly as he flipped over another picture, but I
needed a verbal answer to this question.

"Rory?"

"Hmm?"

"Are you sure you didn't see anything written on the axe?"

He nodded, tilting his head at the photograph of my mother. "Pretty sure."

I pulled the picture from under his fingertips and slid it to the back of the pile. I didn't like him seeing my mother that way. It was like showing him nudie pictures of her. They were just too raw.

7

When I came down the next morning, Rory's white-socked feet were hanging off the end of the couch. There was a warm, somnolent maple scent filling the air around him. Garrett smelled like that sometimes, too, as though he had been baking all night in the oven at a low temperature. I watched Rory breathe for a moment, then tapped the top of his head with my finger.

"Hey," he said groggily as he rolled his head back to look up at me. "What time is it?"

"Seven."

He groaned to stretch. "What are you doing up so early? We just went to bed a few hours ago."

"I've got to run out," I said as he swung his feet to the floor. "You can hang out here if you want. I'm out of coffee, but help yourself to whatever's in the fridge."

"Where are you going?" he yawned.

"I have to go see someone." I dug in my bag for my keys, spotted my ChapStick, and swiped on a dose.

He nodded to look around. "How long are you going to be?"

"I don't know," I said, slinging the strap of my bag over my shoulder. "A couple of hours, maybe."

He caught my hand as I turned to leave. "Are we okay?"

I nodded vaguely as I withdrew my fingers, suddenly needing them to scratch the back of my neck. As the night wore on, I had become increasingly pissed that Rory could have saved my family and did not. He didn't even try. Some hero he turned out to be. And though his presence in the house overnight seemed to have kept the creepy noises at bay, now that the sun was up, I wanted him out.

"Lock the door on your way out," I said, adding a sigh as he tickled the air for the return of my hand. The itch on my neck resumed with a vengeance, and now required all ten of my fingers to appease it. He dropped his arm dejectedly, then pressed to a stand to loudly exhale.

"Do you mind if I take a shower?" he asked.

"Sure. I guess."

His shoulders dropped. "If you don't want me to, just—"

"No. Go ahead. I'm totally fine with it."

"You sure?"

"Yes."

"Because you . . ."

"What?"

"Nothing."

As our eyes had the fight our mouths refused to take part in, my stomach let out a fearsome growl. I petted it down with a cross of my arms. Though we had not had sex—and I was pretty sure I could have finally had my way with Rory if I'd wanted—this felt like an awkward exchange at the tail end of a regrettable one-night stand. A beat later, he turned for the staircase as I turned for the door.

"Use the shower in my room," I yelled out as his feet trailed upward. "The one in the hall doesn't have a shower curtain." He grumbled a response that sounded derisive. "And don't use up all my shampoo! I'm almost out!" I yanked the front door open to find a woman about to knock on my face. She looked familiar, but in a famous kind of way, like I had watched her grow up on a sitcom. A tight rim of red hairs framed her ivory face, pulled snug at her temples by a tight ponytail.

Her full, glossed lips revealed a set of clear porcelain teeth when she smiled to say, "Sorry, I was just about to knock." I raised my eyebrows to ask what she wanted. "Are you Dixie Wheeler?" When I looked around to decide, she held out a business card. "I'm a reporter with the *Franconia Dispatch*. I was hoping to ask you a few questions, if you have a minute?" She drew the card back when I made no effort to take it. "You are Dixie Wheeler, aren't you?"

"Sorry, I've gotta go." I reached back to pull the door closed, and she stepped forward to hold me in the threshold.

"Why did you move back into the home where your family was murdered?" Her phone was held in the space between us, screen up. The mic display at the bottom was hot. "What do you hope to gain from living here?"

"Can you turn that off," I said, nodding at the phone. She poked the screen and dropped the phone into her bag. I folded my arms to my chest possessively. "Who told you I was living here?"

She smiled, furtive. "Was it supposed to be a secret?"

"I hoped it would be," I said. "But seriously, how did you find out?"

She shrugged. "I got a tip."

Vicki.

"I interviewed the people who used to live here, a few years back. They claimed that the house was haunted. I'm not sure if I totally believed them, but after what happened here, I guess anything is possible, right?" When I rolled my eyes, she glanced up at the house. "I drive by every once and a while to see if anyone new has moved in." She dropped her eyes to mine. "I feel drawn to it, you know? Like, I just knew a good story would show up eventually. And what do you know? Here you are." She slapped my arm to show she was being blithe. "Actually, I've been dying to meet you for years. Ever since I read about what happened to your family. The story was so intriguing. Really. Just heartbreaking. I couldn't stop thinking about it. In a way, this house has been haunting me, too." She breathed a sad laugh. "Sorry for going on like this, but I'm a bit starstruck. I can't believe I'm actually having a conversation with Dixie Wheeler."

"You're not," I said.

The laugh she gave sounded genuine, snorting and spontaneous, and under different circumstances it might have made me instantly like her, but something about the way her eyes didn't partake in the joke gave me the impression that the laugh, along with her nonthreatening attire, was all an affectation. She probably practiced the laugh in front of a mirror as she tamed her vixen hair into its insipid ponytail. I tightened the fold of my arms.

"Look," she said. "I'm not here to hassle you. Honestly. Even if you don't want to give me an interview—which, I won't lie, I hope you do—I'm just glad I got the chance to meet you. You're like a living, breathing urban legend. I mean, you're *Baby Blue*. To me, that's like meeting . . . freaking Bigfoot or something. Sorry. Bad analogy, but you know what I mean. After the murders, it was like you just up and vanished. I couldn't find one story or picture of you." She shook her head, inordinately mystified.

I rolled my eyes. I didn't grow up in a remote cave in Africa. I just led a very private life in a quiet neighborhood on the other side of the beltway. The few reporters who did come around when I was younger were easily dispatched when Aunt Celia threatened them with a lawsuit. The same news program that contacted me for the fifteenth anniversary had also reached out to me for the twentieth, but things were going really well with Garrett at the time, and I didn't want to introduce a toxic element like Rory—who they said had already agreed—into our relationship, so I told them that I wasn't interested.

"I can't believe that you're standing right in front of me." She pointed a finger at the cement stoop, approximately where my mother had once sat, burping me and waiting for the last picture of her family to be taken. Well, the last one before the crime scene photographer took his. "At the very house where it happened. The courage it must have taken for you to move back here." She let out a whistle. "Not everyone has the strength to do something like that." She swiped away a gush of emotion—nay, a tear—with the back of her hand, and then flapped it at me. "I just think you're remarkable, is all. I write so many stories about female victims, it would be awesome to write one of real female heroism for a change." She poked me in the arm. "What do you say, Dixie? Let's show the world what a badass Baby Blue turned out to be."

"Look." I sighed. "I get that you're just doing your job. I know I'm probably some kind of freak show curiosity. 'Baby Blue Goes Home to Her House of Horrors.'" I framed this over my head. "It's a great headline. I get it. But I'm not going to give you my story."

"Okay, but—"

"Hey, if it wasn't me," I continued, "I'd probably be curious, too. But it is me, and I don't want anyone knowing that I'm living here. So, don't write about me, okay? I don't want to have to sue you. Just go before I call the cops."

"Take my card." She slapped it into my open hand as I motioned her away. "If you change your mind—"

"I won't."

"But if you do, you can call me day or night. Just think about it, okay? If you're worried that I'm not legit, you can talk to my editor. Just call the 800 number on the front of the card. His name is Jerry Ellyn. He'll vouch for who I am. You can also look me up online. Check out some of my stories and see what you think. The Web address is on the card, but it's www dot—"

"Get the fuck out of here, Claire," a voice snarled behind me. *Claire?* I thought, blinking her into a whole new light. Had she withheld her name on purpose so I wouldn't recognize her as the reporter who accused Rory of pushing his girlfriend down a flight of stairs?

I turned to find my face nestled between the swollen pecs of Rory's bare chest. I tried to pull my eyes to his face, but they seemed to want to follow a soft track of hair down to the loose waistband of his jeans. If he'd had on underwear last night, it was gone now. Maybe it's on my bathroom floor, I thought distractedly, as Claire Reynolds, who, up until that point, had not lived up to her "fucking cunt" reputation, let out a garishly gleeful squeal.

"Rory Sellers!" she declared, covering a laugh as I turned back to her. "Oh, this is just too much!"

"Get lost, Claire," he said. "There's no story here."

The laugh she let out transformed her. Back went her shoulders and out came a nice set of tits. In a blink, her hair was down, fingered through, and ravishing. Only a soft crimp was left by the bright green hair band now circling her wrist like a baby snake.

"Oh, I'd say there's a whole *lot* of story here, Rory," she teased. This was a new voice. Throaty porn star. The one she had used on me was still trying to get a date.

Rory draped his arm across my shoulders to nod her away. A tuft of armpit hair tickled my cheek. Claire's eyes flicked between us, held mine for a moment, and then rolled off to pass judgment.

"Dixie doesn't want to talk to you," he said. "Go write your lies about someone else."

"So you *do* read my articles," she said with an incendiary smile. "It's nice to know that you follow me, Rory."

"Not on your life," he said. A smile leaked through his tone, but his jaw had already reset by the time I looked up at him. "This is that reporter I was telling you about. The one who wrote all those lies about me when my girlfriend died."

"They weren't lies," she corrected. "And I gave you every opportunity to tell your side of the story. It's not my fault you came off looking like you had something to hide."

"Oh, right," he scoffed. "You were going to write what you were going to write no matter what I said. You used me."

"*I* used *you*?" she exclaimed. "Oh, please."

"You knew I was in a bad place, and you used it to your advantage." He dropped his arm to step in front of me. "You really hurt Erin's parents, you know. Not that you cared, as long as you got your headline. It was bad enough their daughter was dead, but you had to go and make them think that someone hated her enough to kill her." He tsked distastefully. "I knew you were tough, Claire, but I didn't think you were heartless."

"Oh, my heart's just fine, sweetie," she said.

"Like you have one."

"You should know."

It was hard to tell if their banter was hostile or flirtatious, but the tone was ripe with innuendo. And a little loud. I glanced at Vicki's car in the drive next door. She was home. Hopefully her windows were closed. I touched Rory on the back, hoping he'd move aside and quit blocking me, but he didn't notice. The back of his neck was heated.

"If you were so innocent," Claire went on, "then why did you lie about being at Erin's that day?"

"I didn't lie," he said. "I just forgot."

As I scaled the side of the stoop to get back into the conversation, Claire looked at me to confide, "Isn't that convenient?"

"Shut up, Claire," Rory snapped.

"That's your problem, Rory," she snapped back. "As much as you wanted to, you couldn't shut me up."

I chopped my hand in the air between them. "Both of you shut up." I nudged Rory's warm belly with my arm to get him to take a step back, then turned to Claire. "Look, I don't know what your deal is, but I don't have time for this."

Claire blinked three times to reboot. "You're right. I'm sorry. I wasn't expecting . . ." She glanced over my shoulder at Rory. "I just want a few minutes of your time. Can I come in and—"

"No," I said. Before she could protest, I added, "I was just on my way out when you knocked. I've got your card. I'll call you. We can set something up."

Her eyes flicked to Rory and then back to me. "Okay. But please do call. I promise I won't print anything without your permission."

Rory let out a loud "Ha!" and I elbowed him in the gut.

"I'll call you," I said. "If my story is going to get out, I suppose I'd rather tell it myself than have you put words in my mouth." As she raised a finger to object to my assessment of her journalistic integrity, I turned to Rory. "Go take your shower."

He gave Claire a long, dramatic once-over that made her cock her head defiantly, and then ducked through the doorway and out of sight. I closed the door with a heavy sigh and walked with Claire down the sidewalk to my car. She put her hand on my arm as I went to unlock the door.

"Sorry about all that," she said with a beleaguered grin, gathering her mane back into its ponytail. "Rory and I have a little . . . history. I shouldn't let him get to me like that. Sorry if we made you uncomfortable."

I hated how she made it sound like she knew Rory better than I did.

"Excuse me," I said, nodding her aside so I could open the car door, slamming it extra hard as I got in. I started the car and dropped it into reverse, mumbling to myself that she had some nerve as I slung my arm over the seat to back out of the driveway. When I turned back to shift into drive, Claire was standing exactly where I had left her, staring up at my house. The proximity of her gaze was about equal to the window of my master bathroom. Though I was almost certain you would have to stand on the edge of the tub to be seen from the street, I got the feeling that she was making some sort of connection with Rory through the glass. She turned as my squeaky brake abruptly engaged, gave a cheerful yet startled wave, and then hurriedly crossed the lawn to her car parked at the curb. I waited until she pulled away before I headed out, making a mental note to buy some blinds for my bathroom window on my way home.

I MADE A quick stop for doughnuts and held the bag out to Mr. Cullins as he opened the door. He peeked inside to see if my offering was a suitable cover charge before nodding me in. Without a word between us, I followed him into the kitchen. I got the cream from the fridge and found a plate in the second cabinet I opened. I set the doughnuts out in a nice arrangement as Mr. Cullins poured the coffee. He handed me a mug, the same one as the last time I was there, blue with little white daisies around the rim, and slid the sugar my way. We both grabbed for the chocolate glaze. I let him have it. He broke it in two and set half on a napkin in front of me. I broke off a piece and took a nibble.

"I want you to reopen the case," I said.

He stared at me as he chewed. After a sip of coffee he said, "I'm retired."

"Then you'll have plenty of time to do it."

"Even if I could do it, which I can't, I don't want to do it."

"Rory Sellers was *inside* the house at the time of the murders." I thought this bombshell would rattle him, but he didn't even flinch. "He was hiding in Josh's room the whole time. He told me about it last night."

He nodded. "Did he see it happen?"

"Well . . . no."

"Then what does it change, Dixie?"

"It changes everything. He might know something you haven't thought to ask him about."

He wiped his fingertips on his robe, picked up a powdered jelly doughnut, and tapped half the sugar off into the sink. "If he knew something, he would have said so back when it happened. Memory doesn't improve with time. Believe me, I know."

"Doesn't it bother you that he lied?"

"I knew he was lying back when I first talked to him."

"So you knew he was in the house at the time of the murders?" I said, aghast.

"I suspected as much, but I couldn't prove it." He shrugged. "Not that proving it would have made a difference. It wouldn't have changed the facts."

"Well, Rory seemed to have a lot of information I didn't know about."

"Like what?"

I couldn't think of anything worthy of the contemptuous look Mr. Cullins was giving me, so I shrugged to offer the one little tidbit I had.

"Did you know that he saw my father out at the shed that morning?" This got a rather interested "Huh," which was more than I was expecting. "See? You didn't know about that, did you?"

"What was your father doing?" Mr. Cullins asked.

"I'm not sure. I didn't probe Rory about it. I just wanted to listen. Hear him out, you know? Frankly, I was surprised he told me as much as he did. You might be able to get him to open up more about it. All he told me was he saw the back of my father's blue shirt out by the shed."

"Blue?" Mr. Cullins said. "You sure he said it was a blue shirt he saw?"

I nodded. "Why?"

"Your father wasn't wearing a blue shirt that morning. He was wearing a red T-shirt."

My eyes widened. "See? That's something, right? That's a new clue, isn't it?"

"Maybe."

"What do you mean, maybe? If my father was wearing a red T-shirt, then he couldn't have been the person Rory saw that morning. Someone else must have been in the shed. Like the real killer. In a blue shirt."

"That's a stretch. It was twenty-five years ago. Rory's probably just remembering it wrong. And who knows? Maybe your father changed his shirt."

"My father didn't have time to change his clothes. Rory said he heard screaming almost immediately after he got there. And I don't think he's remembering it wrong, either. Red and blue are two totally different colors. He seemed pretty sure the shirt he saw was blue." Since it didn't serve my argument, I left out that Rory had said he might have had the day wrong entirely. "Come on, Mr. Cullins, this has to be enough to reopen the case."

"I'm not a detective anymore, Dixie. I can't just reopen a murder investigation."

"But you can be a private detective, can't you? I'll hire you. Don't you need a license for that? I wonder how you get one." I pulled my phone from my bag to conduct a search. "You might have to take a test or something. Do you know what kind of license you need?" I scanned the results as they popped up on my screen. "Oh, here! Okay. It's a Class 'C' Private Investigator License. It doesn't say anything about a test, but I bet ex-cops don't have to take one. Oh, wait. That's Florida. It's probably the same everywhere. We can find out, though. Okay. Here's a form for Virginia. Give me a second. It's a PDF."

He raised his hand to slow me down. "I have a license, Dixie. I do some PI work from time to time. But they're mostly insurance fraud and divorce cases. This would be more than I could manage on my own. I wouldn't even know where to start after all this time."

"Start with Rory," I said, tucking my phone away. "Start questioning people who lived in the neighborhood back then. Someone might have seen some guy in a blue shirt hanging around."

"I did talk to neighbors," he said. "Nobody mentioned seeing anyone suspicious hanging around the neighborhood, in a blue shirt or otherwise. I know you think I just wrote up a report and called it a day, but I didn't. I questioned neighbors. I took statements. I ran fingerprints. I did it all, by the book, and at the end of it all there was only one conclusion: William Wheeler murdered his family. Just because Rory Sellers suddenly remembers seeing a blue shirt doesn't mean someone in a blue shirt killed them. And then what did he do? Cut your father's throat to make it look like a suicide attempt?"

"Will you at least talk to Rory? He knows a lot more than he told you back when it happened. He might have a clue that only you would be able to put together. Like the shirt."

His sigh blew a glimmer of hope my way.

"Please?" I begged.

"Okay," he relented. "Give me his number. I'll call him. But I'm not promising anything."

I tried to hide my smile as I dug my phone back out of my bag. "You can talk to him right now. He spent the night at my house. He's probably still there."

"I didn't know you two were that close."

"We're not. I haven't talked to Rory in years, actually. He just stopped by out of the blue."

He raised his eyebrows. "And slept over?"

"He slept on the couch. Jeez, get your mind out of the gutter." I cued up Rory's number from my Recent Calls list. "He just wanted to see the house. I think his being in the house again is what got him to start remembering things."

"Being *where* again?"

I shrugged. "The house on Catharpin Road."

"Wait a second." He set down his mug to shake a startled slosh of coffee from his hand. "You're living in your old house?"

"Don't make a big deal out of it. The house came up for rent, so I rented it. I'm not planning to live there long. I just wanted to check it out."

He snorted derisively and picked up his mug to take a sip.

I rolled my eyes to him. "What?"

"I didn't say anything."

"You think it's weird I'm living there. Go on. Say it."

"Okay," he said. "I think it's weird you're living there."

"No, it's not!" I pulled a pen out of my bag and jotted Rory's number on a napkin. "And I don't need you giving me a hard time about it, either. I get that enough from my aunt Celia. Here's Rory's cell." I waved the napkin at him until he took it. He glanced at it, stuffed it in his robe pocket, and took another bite of his doughnut. "Aren't you going to call him?"

He gaped at me through a mouthful of powdered sugar. "Now?"

"Why not?"

"I'm eating my breakfast." He washed down the rest of his doughnut with a deliberately slow sip of coffee. When he saw that his insouciance was about to make my head explode, he grinned. "I'll call him later," he said. "I want to go through the file before I talk to him. Leave it with me before you go. I promise I'll give it back when I'm done."

I grimaced a hiss through my teeth. "I didn't bring it with me this time. But can I bring it by later. Hey! Why don't I just bring Rory with me?"

"I got a game on at one that I wanna watch."

I frowned at him. "I'll be back in an hour." As I stood to leave, something occurred to me. "Hey, where's Pepper?"

Mr. Cullins sighed. "He's probably sniffing Salt's butt right about now."

I covered a shocked gasp with my hand. "What?"

He nodded solemnly. "I had to put him down last night."

Though Pepper and I'd had an intuitive dislike for each other, the news of his passing brought an unexpected well of tears with it. "I'm so sorry, Mr. Cullins."

He rubbed a mist from his eyes. "Yeah. I miss the little shit already. It's going to get pretty lonely around here without him."

"When did your wife die?" I asked.

"That obvious, huh?"

I shrugged as I ran my eyes around the kitchen: Dried flowers cinched with yellow-and-white-checkered ribbons spotted the country-blue walls; antique cookie jars and porcelain roosters languished in unnoticed dustiness from one countertop to the next. A basket of stitched-eyed bunnies watched our every move from a rosewood accent table in the breakfast nook. "Well, the decor doesn't really seem your style."

He nodded. "I lost Kay three years ago. Cancer."

"Do you have any children?"

He nodded, thoughtful. "A son. Jimmy. He lives in Utah. That's where his wife's from. She turned him into a Mormon." He made it sound like she had turned him into a werewolf. "We don't really see eye to eye anymore."

I shrugged. "Well, I never really saw eye to eye with my father, either."

He nodded forth a weak smile.

"Being alone sucks. My boyfriend, Garrett, and I aren't doing so good right now. I can see him whenever I want, and I still miss him like hell." I glanced at my toes as Mr. Cullins's eyes grew wet, then poked him in the stomach. "But we've got each other now, right? I could use a father figure." I added, "Other than Ford, that is," under my breath.

Mr. Cullins looked up. "Ford still around?"

"How do you know Ford?"

"I talked to him back when it happened." He tapped his cheek. "Memorable guy. He didn't seem too reliable, though."

"That's an understatement," I said. "But he and my aunt are still married. For some unknown reason. I think it's laziness, on both their parts."

He smiled. "Well, if you ever need someone to step in and act all dad-like, I'm your man. Though I've got to warn you, I'm a bit rusty."

"You gotta be better than Ford."

I'D TOLD GARRETT about Rory soon after I revealed myself to him as Baby Blue. Tongue loosened and a little numb from a plate of extra-spicy pad Thai and a few too many cocktails, I rattled off my top ten most mortifying anecdotes like the clock was ticking down on a speed date. From stealing a kiss to my sophomoric stint as a stalker, I left nothing in reserve. Like many foolish couples, we had been testing the resiliency of our newfound love by taunting each other with our tally of lovers, and I felt my list needed a little padding. Since most of the relationships I had had lasted no longer than a good pedicure, and the one that did was no more interesting than that, I felt compelled to come up with a few stories to keep my end of the conversation going. Though Garrett visibly winced as I recounted excerpts of my diary from memory, he had also taken my hand across the table. I loved how he made light of my most embarrassing confessions, making me promise to stalk him if we ever broke up. Later that night, we went to one of the *Saw* movies, and he whispered that I could hold his hand as tight as I wanted but to go easy on his balls. We laughed like hyenas until the people behind us told us to shut the hell up. Though I hadn't spared any of the more shameful details surrounding my exploits with Rory, I had spared Garrett one thing: an adequate description of the man. "He's not even that good-looking," I remember saying. "He's kinda gross, actually. I don't know what I ever saw in him." At the time, I hadn't seen Rory in over a year, and thought I might never see him again, so what harm was there in downplaying his looks. I was trying to seduce Garrett with my borderline psychotic tales, not emasculate him.

So, when I pulled up to my house to find Garrett's snowflake-white Mazda3 hatchback cowering in the driveway next to Rory's big black 4Runner, my thoughts immediately flew back to our date at the Thai restaurant and regurgitated a slightly mai-tai-flavored yelp. My stomach tightened as I pictured Garrett's expression when Mr. Gorgeous answered his knock instead of me. On average, Garrett was not the jealous type. But Rory wasn't your average guy. And I certainly wasn't on the same solid ground with Garrett as I had once been.

As I reached to pull the key from the ignition, the front door opened.

Garrett paused on the stoop when he spotted my car. With a shake of his head, he stomped purposefully down the steps. I quickly unbuckled, jumped out in a run, and fell against the sun-warm door of his car just as he reached for the handle.

He hooked a thumb over his shoulder. "Your boyfriend's waiting for you."

"He just stopped by to see the house," I tried. "Nothing happened. He fell asleep on the couch. I swear!"

"Yeah, I saw all the empty beer bottles. Looks like you two had a pretty good time."

"It wasn't like that, Garrett."

"It's your life, Dix. You can have any guy you want sleep over. Just not me." He gently elbowed my shoulder to encourage me to move. "Please get out of the way."

"No!" I pressed against the car to hold my position. "I'm not going to let you leave until you let me explain."

He stepped back to fold his arms. "Okay. Explain."

I searched his face for something to say that might unclench his jaw, but all that came out was a string of pointless pronouns. "I . . . he . . . we . . . you . . ."

He shook his head. "I've got to get back to work. I'm late for an appointment."

I stepped aside so he could get in his car, and yelled, "I love you!" as he quickly backed out of the drive.

Rory was in the kitchen when I entered. He looked back from the sink when he heard the door slam. I'd hoped he might still be hungover and greasy, but he was freshly scrubbed and glowing, wet hair combed back, like a swashbuckling pirate fresh from a dip in the ocean. I noted with a sigh that his beard was back to being carelessly fetching. The traces of gray that had made him look strung out and haggard last night now made him look seasoned and virile. At least he had put a shirt on.

"Hey, you just missed Garrett," he said brightly.

"Yeah, I know." I sulked to my father's chair and fell onto it. "I saw him outside."

"He didn't seem too happy to find me here," he said with a bashful grin, drying his hands on a towel.

"Nope." I clucked my tongue. "He wasn't too happy about that at all."

He slapped the towel over his shoulder as he leaned against the sink. Mr. November. I palmed my face to shake my head.

"I tried to explain who I was, but he was pretty short with me," he said.

I nodded. "Sorry about that."

He shrugged. "Can't blame him, I guess. I'd be pissed, too." He watched me for a long mopey moment. "I thought I'd stick around and help you take a look in the attic. I haven't been up there yet. I kinda dozed off again after you left. And I ate the rest of your leftover pizza. Hope that's okay."

"That's fine."

He nodded. "So, you want to tackle the attic now?"

"Actually, I want you to come with me."

"Oh, yeah?" He rubbed his hands expectantly. "Where do you want to go? It's beautiful out."

I grimaced to say what I knew would be a disappointing answer. "Just over to Crestwood. Do you remember Detective Cullins?"

His hands fell to his side as his smile disappeared. "Yeah."

"Well, I told him what you told me about being in the house that day, and he wants to talk to you."

"You did what?"

My heart gave an anxious jab as I realized he was cross with me. "Oh. I went to see him. That's where I've been. I wanted to tell him what you told me about being here that day. I think he's going to re-open the case. Isn't that great?"

His expression said this was anything but great. "I can't believe you did that."

"What? Why? I didn't tell him anything bad about you. Just that you were here."

"I told you all that in confidence, *Dixie*." His expostulated tone made my name sound like an expletive. "I didn't think you were going to go tell the cops."

"But I thought you wanted to help me find out what happened to my family," I whined, like he was reneging on a promise to take me to the carnival.

"I do. But I'm not talking to the police." He pushed off toward the living room.

I followed to ask, "Why not?"

He sat down on the couch to put on his shoes. "I'm not comfortable with it. If you would have bothered to ask me first, I would have saved you the trouble of going over there to see him."

"Mr. Cullins isn't really the police," I said. "He's retired. He's just going to look into it for me on the side. As a favor. Nothing's probably going to come from it, anyway."

"I don't care. I'm still not going to talk to him. And I don't want you talking to him about me, either. Or to anyone, for that matter." He shook his head to mutter to himself, "I shoulda kept my mouth shut. This is fucking bullshit."

Stunned silence turned me to stone. I could hardly breathe as I watched him tie his shoelaces.

He stood up and checked his pockets, eyes looking everywhere but at me. "I hope you find the answers you're looking for, Dixie." He took a step forward and planted a dry kiss on my forehead. "I really do. But keep me out of it." He paused in the doorway to throw a "Later" over his shoulder and walked out.

"Yeah! Later!" I punched the door as it closed in my face. "Like in another seven fucking years," I mumbled through tears as I slid down the door, "you Hugh Jackman wannabe motherfucker."

I CALLED MR. Cullins to let him know that I wouldn't be bringing Rory by after all, explaining that he had a prior engagement. Mr. Cullins didn't come out and say that he knew that Rory had refused to talk to him, but his smug tone suggested as much.

I hung up with him and fell face-first onto the bed to cry into my pillow, which wasn't there. I thought of calling Garrett, but I was too tired, and I liked how the bed was lazily spinning along with my hangover. My eyes closed on the inhale of a yawn that sucked me further down than I wanted to go.

By the time I realized that I was being smothered, it was nearly too late. My mind slapped the panic button just as my lungs sounded the alarm that our oxygen level had fallen below the red line. My arms shot out from around the pillow like spring-loaded batons, grabbed handfuls of air that were as plentiful as they were unattainable, and then collapsed back to the bed like evacuated tubes. White spears flew in from a black fringe that was rapidly closing in around me. As my tongue retreated down my throat to cower safely in my stomach, my fingers crawled along my hips and up the side of a frozen rod of skin. Too cold and thin to be human. As the being on top of me leaned in to finish its mission, my fingers probed a thin neck up to a pointed chin . . . a delicate nose . . . a head as sleek and impassive as a Magic 8 Ball.

Leah snatched the pillow back. *"You want me to stop?"*

I responded with a coughing fit that was almost as suffocating as the pillow.

"Okay!" she sang and slammed the pillow back over my face.

Just as darkness crept in to drag me away, the pillow rose. Air shot down my nose like a blast from an air gun, overfilled my lungs, and spun me up and out of my body.

"Oh, I'm sorry. Did you say something?" she asked sweetly. *"Did you want me to stop?"* She pressed her cheek so close to my lips that my next gasp suctioned loose skin into my mouth. The taste of rotting flesh eddied around my tongue like a whirlpool of maggots.

"Please," I begged. The word was barely audible, drowned behind a waterfall of tears.

Her thin lips stretched into a wide, spiteful smile. Loose black teeth clinked like carillons as she let out a gaseous laugh.

"Oh, that's funny, Dixie. You didn't stop when I asked you to. You just kept right on doing it like you didn't hear me. But I know you did. I felt it in your hands. They stopped pressing down. Just for a second, but enough to let me know that you heard exactly what I said."

She fluffed the pillow between her bony fingers. Two broke off under the strain and plopped on my chest like a couple of dry turds.

"Okay, I'll stop," she said. *"But you have to ask me nicely."*

I shook my head to say I could take no more, coughing so deep that a muscle spasm arched my spine and rolled her dismembered fingers into the sweaty pocket of my collarbone. I shook my head again to stop their slow, inching crawl through my hair.

"No?" she inferred by my gesture. *"Okay. But remember . . . You asked for it!"*

The pillow slammed down again, but this time, I grabbed enough air to gather a smidgeon of strength. I worked my fingers between my chin and the tight stretch of cotton, and wiggled out from under the pillow.

"Stop," I begged weakly as I rolled onto my side, hacking hot bile onto the cool sheets. I swept my wrist across my lips as I reached back to keep Leah from coming at me from behind.

There was nothing there.

I flipped over to find that a late-afternoon dusk had fallen across the empty room. Buttery light leached through the closed blinds beside the bed. Though I had napped most of the sun away, I felt even more exhausted. My pillow was teetering on the edge of the bed. I kicked it to the floor, and fell back against the sweat-soaked mattress.

"I'm sorry, Leah," I said in a panting cry. The thin rasp of terror within the quiet bedroom sounded eerily similar to the moment I stood staring down at my cousin's lifeless body. "But you wanted to die, remember? So just leave me the fuck alone!"

I RESOLVED MYSELF to stay in the shower long enough to actually clean myself. A finely mangled rendition of "Baby Blue" began spewing from the exhaust fan just as I lathered up, but slid respectfully aside as I belted out the first line of "My Country, 'Tis of Thee." Not one of my favorite songs, but the only one that came to mind in a moment of panic. I took a breath to sing out the second verse, and "Rhiannon" rang from my mouth like a bell in the night. The a cappella was so clear and so strong that it took me a moment to realize that the angelic sound had come from me. I slapped a lathery hand across my lips.

I sensed that Leah was trying to compensate for smothering me by slipping a song of happier times down my throat. That's how it had been with us: an unexpected compliment after a harsh word, a hug for not ducking in time to miss the shoe thrown at your head. I suppose a palliative earworm was all she could offer me now. I had to admit, the song did have a comforting effect. The tremble in my hands was barely noticeable as I turned my back to the stream to rinse my hair. With "Rhiannon" humming from my chest like some sort of pagan incantation, I closed my eyes and let the water work out a snarl of tense knots across my neck and shoulders.

I had just begun to relax when a guttural moan in the pipes turned the water needling cold. I cried out a curse and blindly fumbled with the knob as shampoo ran into my eyes. When I could neither turn off the water nor adjust the temperature, I danced in a panicky circle to hastily rinse, and then exited the stall in a screaming leap.

Safely on the bath mat, I was able to reach in and turn the water off with one easy turn.

I grabbed a towel to warm my shivers and pat myself dry. Soft cotton absorbed the damp chill from my arms, but flared a sudden sting across my chest. Reluctantly, I turned toward the partially steamed mirror. A score of welts had risen across my neck and chest. I lifted my chin to inspect the damage. They were definitely claw marks. Four enflamed lines traveled from below my left ear to just before my right armpit. I must have scratched myself, I thought. Leah chewed her nails down to the quick. When my reflection didn't reciprocate the nervous laugh I gave it, I dropped the towel to the floor and left the bathroom.

A fist-sized bruise on my left hip ached as I wiggled back into my jeans—which felt one size tighter than when I had taken them off five minutes ago. Pinpoint dots of blood stuck to the front of my T-shirt like tissue. I zipped them out of mind under a hoodie.

In the kitchen, I found a box of my favorite muffins pushed back beside the toaster. A gift from Garrett that Rory had neglected to bring to my attention. I sucked back a well of tears as I unwrapped a double fudge chocolate and scarfed it down over the kitchen sink. The first bite braced itself halfway down my throat, as if it knew I didn't deserve to eat it. I chased it down with half a bottle of warm beer that hadn't made it into the trash can the night before.

How stupid Garrett must have felt holding such a foppish box by its dainty pink string as Rory straddled the doorway like my personal bouncer. He probably cut Garrett down to size with one word: *Yeah?* It broke my heart to think that Garrett might have had to convince Rory that he knew me. That the only reason this wasn't his house, his home, his life, was by choice. I picked up my phone to call him, but I didn't know what to say any more than I had earlier in the driveway. What explanation was there? That Rory meant nothing to me? That he was just a friend? That I actually did consider his Adonis physique and chiseled features to be "kinda gross" in their perfection? Set aside the fact that Garrett knew all too well my history with Rory, the man defied that sort of denigration. No red-blooded woman would want a guy like Rory to be just a friend. Not if they could help it.

A vigorous knock at the front door gave me hope: Garrett back with a clever rejoinder now that Rory's ride was gone from the driveway. I was just about to throw open the door when Claire Reynolds's career-driven face cruised by the window of my thoughts. Claire didn't seem like the type of reporter to give up after one attempt, especially not when another chance encounter with Rory was conceivable. I checked the peephole. Ford was looking around as if he had wandered up to a strange house to ask to use the phone to call for a tow. He pressed his eye to the peephole, then gave a fisted police knock.

I flung the door open. "What are you doing here, Ford?"

"Well, it's nice to see you, too, Dix," he ribbed through a smirk.

"No, seriously," I said, not in the mood for our normal antagonistic banter. "What do you want?"

He held up the shopping bag at his side. "Cel thought you might want some of this."

As I took the bag to peek inside, he slid by me into the living room.

"Would you get a load of this place?" He clapped his hands to throw his head back and laugh. "Holy fucking shit! I knew you had gone off the deep end, girl, but I didn't know you hit your head on the bottom of the pool. No wonder Cel was so worried about you. This is some cuckoo-for-Cocoa-Puffs shit right here."

I bit back the urge to tell him to get the hell out of my perfectly lovely haunted house. I was glad for the company, even if it was Ford. I shut the door and headed back toward the kitchen. The bag contained several Tupperware containers of leftovers. I hoped one of them was her homemade manicotti.

"You're one sick pup, Dixie," Ford shouted from the living room as I loaded the refrigerator. "I'm starting to like you more and more each day. Is this Davis's old desk?"

"Yeah," I said, shuffling a few condiment jars around to make room. Ford muttered a curse as a dim thud came from the living room. "What was that?"

"Uh, nothing," he said, a little winded. "Just knocked something over. I got it."

"Don't break anything," I scolded. "It might be a bunch of crap, but it's all I got. You want a beer?"

He entered the kitchen smiling sheepishly, and snatched the beer from my hand. He twisted off the cap and flicked it at the sink. After chugging half, he burped to say, "Maybe you could drool some ketchup around and get it looking more like the old place again."

"Give me a break, Ford," I said as I slipped into Josh's chair. "I've had a rough day."

He laughed. "I'm just razzing you." He leaned against the thin wall between the entryway and the refrigerator.

I nodded. "Don't tell Aunt Celia about the furniture, okay? She'll never come over if she knows about it."

"Cat's already out of the bag. Cel talked to Charlene last night. That's probably why she made me come over here to check on you." He sighed as I dropped my head into my hands. "She wasn't gonna come around anyway, Dixie. Cel'd rather walk on hot coals than drive past this place in her car. She's scared of it. Shit. I can't blame her. Every time that woman turns around some tragedy's befalling her. I still can't say Leah's name without her bursting into tears."

I rubbed my collarbone as I recalled the caterpillar crawl of Leah's snapped-off fingers. I found it odd that Ford would choose this moment to bring up Leah. In all the time I'd known him, we had never spoken of her. Not once. Not one single reminiscence or remark. I knew he carried a picture of her in his wallet from when I used to

steal singles from him to buy cigarettes, but that was the only indicator I had that he chose to remember his daughter at all.

God, I wish I had a smoke.

As if reading my mind, Ford took a pack of Marlboros from his
pocket. He hopped one from the pack to his lip, then held the pack
out to me. I took one, and then leaned forward to accept a light. Snapping off the flame with a flick of his wrist, he blew smoke at the ceiling
and slipped the lighter into his pocket.

I stared at his blue shirt through a long drag, an empty white
name tag stitched over the pocket. Though a blue shirt was the standard uniform of mechanics, Ford tended to wear his in the off-hours
as well. In fact, that's all he ever wore; only his undershirt changed
color. But a lot of men wore blue shirts. Even Garrett wore one when
he went out on service calls for the water treatment company he
worked for. Besides white, it was probably the most popular color
shirt for men. But not all men who wore blue shirts also knew my
family.

"Where were you that morning, Ford?" I asked, tapping ash in the
cap from my beer bottle like a mini ashtray.

He maintained his smirk. "You accusing me of something, Officer
Dixie?"

"Just answer the question."

He shook his head to laugh. "Put away the cuffs. I was in North
Carolina that day, everyone knows that."

"I didn't know that," I said.

"Well, now ya do." I shook my head in disbelief, not at his alibi—
being gone during a family crisis sounded just like Ford—but at how
uninformed I was about what happened that day. Even small, irrelevant details had been kept from me. "Ask Cel if you don't believe me,"
he said, misreading my incredulity. "I'd been gone over a week. I
didn't get back until midnight. I didn't know shit had happened until
I saw Davis's car in the drive. I thought, *Oh, shit, who died.* But I never

woulda guessed that Billy had gone and chopped his whole damn family up with an axe." He took a slug of beer as I grimaced. "Why you asking, anyway?"

"Rory told me that he saw someone out at the shed that morning, but it wasn't my father. I'm just trying to figure out who it might have been."

"It was probably that neighbor of yours."

"What neighbor?"

He nodded over my head. "House behind you." I turned to look out the window, but could only see Ford's reflection standing behind me. "He used to come by when Billy and me were out there tinkering around. I didn't like him. Talked too much for somebody who didn't know shit-all about anything. Can't recall his name. Old guy. Hell, he's probably dead by now. He only looked half alive to begin with." He crossed to the sink to look out the window. "Shed's gone, huh?"

"Yeah," I said. "It burned down a few years ago."

"Just as well, I guess."

"So you had been in the shed before?" I asked. "Before that day, I mean."

"Sure. I helped Billy build it. It was stocked with half my tools. Didn't get any of them back, though. Davis probably pinched them."

"Do you remember where he kept the axe? Was it close to the front or further in the back?"

He shook his head. "I never saw it before. And believe me, I'd remember an axe like that."

"What do you mean?"

He hooked a thumb over his shoulder as he turned. "Billy didn't use some old wood splitter, Dixie. He went at 'em with a Michigan axe." I looked off in confused disgust. "Two-headed," he explained. "Double-sided. If one gets dull, you just flip it over and keep on going." I cringed out of the way as he swung an imaginary axe in my direction. "That's one serious fucking axe."

"My father wrote something on it in blood, you know." Ford's expression said that this was news to him. "The police couldn't figure out what it said. They think it was just the word 'fuck.' Isn't that weird? I mean, after what he did you'd think he'd write something a little more profound than that."

"Well, 'fuck' about sums it up, I guess." He downed the rest of his beer. "How do ya know about that? About the axe and all?"

"I . . ." I didn't want to tell him about the police file and risk him asking to see it. "I talked to the cop who handled the investigation. I wanted to find out more about what happened that day."

"What else he say about it?"

"Not much." I shrugged. "He thinks I'm crazy for living here. Just like everyone else."

"Being crazy ain't all that bad," Ford said. "Sometimes it gives you an edge."

"So you believe my father did it?" I asked, tipping a drop of beer into my bottle cap and extinguishing my cigarette in it. "I'm kind of taking a poll."

"Well, you can put me down for a big hell-yeah." When I bit my lip despondently, he sighed to roll his eyes. "Look. I know I give you a hard time, but I'm being serious now, okay?" I nodded. "Don't try and make sense out of something you don't understand. You'll just drive yourself crazy. Just like Davis did. I don't want to see that happen to you. Neither does Cel. That's why she's having such a fit about you living here." He took the last drag off his smoke, dropped it in his beer bottle, and pitched it into the trash. "Anyways, I gotta go."

I jumped from my chair. "What? Why? Can't you stay awhile?" I crossed to the refrigerator. "I'll heat up some of Aunt Celia's manicotti." I pulled out a blue tub that contained something smothered in tomato sauce.

"Nah," he said, halfway to the door as I rounded the corner. "I had me some already."

The door slammed as I entered the living room. The seascape painting slipped from its nail and fell behind the couch with a sudden bang
that jolted my nerves. Damn it! Where the hell was that hammer? I was
just about to begin a search when the front door opened again.

"I almost forgot," Ford said, poking his head through the crack.
"Cel said for you to come to Thanksgiving."

I nodded, then yelled "Wait!" as the door started to close.

He jutted his chin around the corner. "What?"

"Can I have your pack of cigarettes?" I said.

He made a not-on-your-life face.

"Please," I begged. "I'll give you money for a new pack. Just let me
get my wallet." I sat the tub of food on the corner of the desk as I
looked around for my bag. I thought I'd left it on the side table next
to the couch. I spotted it on the floor by the stairs. Upside down. A
handful of change, ChapStick, and some loose Advils had spilled out.
I gathered them up and righted the bag to find my wallet.

Ford tossed the pack of smokes at me. "Pay me later."

Before I could thank him, the door slammed once more. As I
stood in the breathless silence, a pattering of feet ran across the upstairs floor.

OPTING FOR NICOTINE over protein, I stuck the manicotti in the
fridge and a cigarette in my mouth. I sat at the kitchen table to reor-
ganize my bag in hopes of finding a lighter or a pack of matches. I was
a little miffed that Ford had knocked over my bag and hadn't bothered to pick it up or point it out to me. As I piled the contents onto the
table, I found that the small, circular wire that held my house key had
worked itself free of the main key ring. As I twisted it back on, I spotted the butt of my purple Bic lighter in a fold of the lining. I lit my
smoke. Puffing hands-free with one eye closed to keep smoke from
getting in my eye, I stuffed everything back into the bag without a
single thought to its organization.

Though the clatter of feet in the upstairs hallway had stopped, I knew it would start again. The silence was just too inviting not to traipse through. Having a sudden desperate need to occupy myself, I went to find my laptop. Taking a seat at Uncle Davis's desk, I started to open Netflix, then clicked on Safari to do a quick search on Claire Reynolds. There were a few Claire Reynoldses on the planet. I narrowed my search by adding "Franconia, VA" to my query, and several links populated my screen. I clicked on the e-edition of the *Franconia Dispatch*, then accessed her archived articles by byline.

Though most of her features were locally driven, homespun, and out for a little fun, Claire did have a flair for the dramatic. Her articles tended to be a little wordy, drawn out in a colorful, almost suspense-thriller style; the original point of the story seemed to get lost along the way. The bake sale she wrote about in her fledgling days led you to believe that the event might end with a dead body being discovered under the cupcake table. The description of a woman who got bit at a dog park was almost too graphic and gruesome to read. I never knew poodles could be so vicious. As Claire's responsibilities at the paper matured—and she had an ever-increasing presence on the crime beat—so did her writing. Several of her first attempts at actual journalism were about the death of Erin Doyle.

As I scanned the first, I realized I had read it before. Actually, I remembered reading a few of her articles. Rory was right; she did make him sound guilty as hell. Stopping just shy of slander, she spoke of Rory in somewhat disturbing, and rather provocative, terms: "Dark, mysterious, secretive . . . *rough.*" He was referenced throughout the piece by his given first name, which I never knew was Gregory. Rory was designated as a middle name to make him sound more serial-killerish: Gregory "Rory" Sellers. She used words like "allegedly" and "apparently" when prefacing any favorable remark about his character or behavior. She definitely had something against him. Was it that she truly believed he had killed an innocent woman, or was it something else? Something personal? From their banter on my front stoop, I definitely sensed that they had been intimate, though that word conjured up a more sophisticated encounter than it probably deserved. Just as I was about to click on an article titled "Ghosts Haunt Wheeler House," my screen froze.

As my router rebooted, I tapped my foot anxiously. Why did it bother me that Rory and Claire might have once slept together? What did I care if they had a "little history"? I hadn't seen Rory in years. Hadn't thought about him in years. Okay, that wasn't completely true, I might have thought of him a few times, but I in no way pined for him. I had Garrett now. I didn't need Rory anymore. I didn't *want* Rory anymore.

I chewed my lip as an old hunger clawed at my gut.

I'd thought I was over this. Over him. It must have been the house. Being here was bringing up feelings that had never been thoroughly sorted out. Rory and that day were knotted together, confused in a tangle of emotions. He was in this house at the exact moment my life changed forever. That meant something, even if he had been hiding in a closet. Rory was all I had left of that day. If I couldn't have my family, I should at least be able to have him. I couldn't just let someone else have him, especially not some redheaded bimbo.

I thought about digging out Claire's business card and calling her, asking her straight out about the true nature of her relationship with Rory. I didn't remember seeing her business card in my bag. I thought I had dropped it inside after she handed it to me. The screen repopulated, and I found the link again. Beneath the photo of Claire was an 800 tip line. Probably the same 800 number as the one on her business card. I reached for my phone.

Thinking the line would roll to voice mail where crackpots could later be weeded out, I tapped my nose to think of a message. A second later Claire Reynolds's breathy voice filled my ear.

"*Franconia Dispatch. This is Claire.*"

"Oh. Um. Hi . . . This is Dixie Wheeler. You stopped by to talk to me and gave me your business card? I'm the one who—"

She laughed. "I know who you are, Dixie. I'm so glad you called."

I stood to pace behind the desk. "So you wanted to ask me some questions?"

"Yes. I do. But I'd prefer to do it in person, if that's okay with you?"

"Uh. Sure. I guess." I glanced down at my screen as a prompt advised me that there was now an overall problem with my computer. I pressed the power button and then clicked Yes to restart. "When do you want to do it?"

She shuffled the phone from ear to ear. "I'd like to meet as soon as possible, but I have a few meetings stacked up this week. I might be able to move things around a bit. What's your schedule like?"

I laughed softly. "I don't really have one. I took off work to move and I'm . . . free. Anytime, really. You can stop by whenever you want. I'll more than likely be here. But Rory won't," I added as she shuffled the phone again.

"What was that?"

"I said if you want to interview Rory, you'll have to arrange that with him."

"No problem."

"Have you spoken to him again?" I asked, watching the slow crawl of a white percentage line across my screen: 49 percent complete. Seemed about right.

"Who, Rory?" She laughed again. "We're not . . . I mean, it's not like that with him and me. We're . . . Well, I wouldn't call us friends, but our relationship is definitely not romantic."

There was a lot of wiggle room between friendship and romance, I thought, but said, "I see. Well, I don't know what you want to know about me." I glanced around the dour living room. "I'm not very interesting."

"Don't worry," she said. "I can make anything seem interesting."

8

I blamed my insomnia on my pillow, which provided all the serenity of a restrained puppy. I rose up on my elbow to punch it into submission, then slammed it flat with the side of my head.

I knew I wouldn't be able to sleep, but I had to make an effort. I had been so worried that a vigorous brush of wintergreen might stimulate me that I hadn't brushed my teeth. Though my body had passed out as soon as I crawled into bed, my mind seemed determined to pull an all-nighter. Segments of dreams I'd had months ago rolled by like commercials to draw me in again. I couldn't let them. Tame as they seemed, I knew as soon as I selected one, the channel would suddenly flip to an all-night creature feature.

I turned over and back again. Kicked my foot out from under the covers. Counted back from a hundred, lost my place at eighty-nine, and started again.

My pillow wiggled uncomfortably.

I truly did believe that alcohol might quell my fidgety mind, but as I sat at the kitchen table with my heels hooked on the edge of my chair so nothing could grab my feet, slamming shots of Jack Daniel's between drags off my cigarette, surrounded by eight-by-ten glossies of the annihilation of my family, I wished I had made myself a nice cup of chamomile tea instead.

The wind picked up as I poured myself another shot. The bottle seemed endless. I wondered if it was still the first bottle I had opened since I moved in. No, it was too full to be the first. It had to be the second. Felt like the tenth. Maybe I should slow down. I pushed the shot glass a good three inches away and looked around.

Even with a light on in every room in the house—more than one, in some—a stark night was pressing in; watery shadows slipped around like silverfish. A large one rushed behind me and turned my head toward the window.

Eddie's head lolled to the side in the corner of my eye, a tongue slipping loosely from a dark hole in his face. I turned quickly back. *It's only a picture*, I reassured myself as I downed the rest of my drink and poured another. A part of me, however—the hysterical part that had driven me to drink to excess in the first place—could have sworn the photograph had curled into a hairy spheroid to stick its tongue out at me.

A wet, uneven thumping started slowly across the floor.

Kah-splunk . . . Kah-splunk . . . Kah-splunk . . .

I held my eyes on the shot glass. My heart was pounding so hard it seemed to make the dark liquid ripple. I reached for the glass to steady us both. Even if Eddie's head had somehow rolled from the picture and onto the kitchen floor, I didn't want to know about it.

. . . Kah-splunk . . . Kah-splunk . . . Kah-splunk . . .

I began to quietly sing "Rhiannon" to myself, hoping it might have the same apotropaic effect it had in the shower, but I couldn't remember the words. "*Rhiannon . . .*" What? What does she do? Rings? Bings? Sings? "Come on, Leah," I whispered, "help me out here. This is your song. Give me the words." I tapped the table to drum up the tune. "*Rhiannon . . . Rhiannon . . . sings . . . because . . . she's so scared she's about to piss her pants and wouldn't you just love to see that.*" I laughed to make the horrible truth of that sentiment funny. "*All your life you've never seen a woman . . . taken by a . . . fucking severed head that's rolling toward her . . . da, da, da . . . Rhiannon, you stupid fucking bitch . . . Why did you move into a house when you knew it was—*"

KAH-DUNK.

The table shimmied as something struck the leg to my left.

I set my feet on the floor to slowly rise in the opposite direction, and then launched onto the safety of the chair as a spidery sensation skittered across my toes. I had just begun to dance off the willies when the world slid out from under me. I had a feathery second to believe that I might still be in bed dreaming before I hit the floor with an all-too-real *thwap*.

I lay there for a long, winded moment, taking inventory of the pain. Everything hurt, but somehow my eyeballs troubled me most. A sharp pulse in my vision had me nearly blind. I was just about to see if I could stand when a wet thudding hurried across the floor to see if I was dead. Icy fingers probed my ankle.

"Stop it!" I cried, curling into a tight ball. "Just leave me alone!"

"I tell you, you kids will be the death of me," a female voice said. *"Everyone sit down and I'll fix us a nice breakfast."* I looked up to see my mother bowed over the utensil drawer. The top of her head flipped forward like an unglued toupee. *"Now where did that knife get to?"*

"Right here, dear!" I flipped onto my back as my father rose from the floor with a butcher knife in his hand. *"But Dixie needs to use it first."* He tapped my arm with his toe. I raised a hand and bared my teeth, much like Pepper had done to advise me to back the fuck off. *"You know what to do with it, don't you, sweetheart? Just slide it across your throat. Like this."* He drew the blade from ear to ear. Something like a tongue, but too black and scaly to be, slipped through the incision he made. *"Shee?"* he gurgled. *"Eeshy."*

"NO!" I skittered backward on the balls of my feet, the pads of my hands, across the floor like a crab. "Stay away from me!" Rolling over onto my knees, I clambered to my feet in midrun. Something grabbed my foot. As I twisted to yank it free, I was wrenched into the air like a carpet being snapped. Rolled out straight, I hit the floor flat on my back. Air exploded from my lungs in the gust of a scream. My family huddled over me, blood dripping off their noses like beads of sweat. Blackness fluttered over me like a dark sheet.

"I think we got her," I heard my father say as I faded away.

"Almost," my mother whispered.

. . .

WHEN I CAME to the next morning, the kitchen was back to normal. The ghosts had slipped back through the cracks from which they entered, and all that remained of their visit was an overturned chair, a half-empty bottle of Jack Daniel's, and an uneasy feeling that my family wasn't done with me yet.

Almost.

I lay on the kitchen floor for a long while, looking out the window over the sink, watching the first glimmers of sunlight baste the remaining leaves of a Douglas pear that stood friendless in the middle of the backyard. I was afraid to get up. Afraid the floor might be the only thing keeping my brain inside my splitting head. But I was thirsty, as thirsty as I'd ever been in my entire life, so with a cry of anticipated agony, I rolled onto my stomach and pushed to a trembling stand.

My stomach pitched up my throat on a wave of sour mash. For a swirling moment, I thought I was headed back down to the floor. I held tight to the back of a chair, and focused on taking long, deep breaths through my nose. I stumbled to the sink and cupped lukewarm handfuls of water into my mouth as fast as I could. Steamy bile rose from the flame in my gut as I braced against the counter, trying not to vomit but knowing I would probably feel a whole lot better if I did.

The events of the night before lingered just beyond a drowsy consciousness. There was a thickness to the air, itchy as wool against my skin. The warm, shadowy scent of my mother swirled in the morning sunlight like smoke. I raised the bottle of dish detergent to see if that was where the scent was coming from. Nope. Too bright. Too clean. I rubbed a lemony zing from my nose with the back of my hand and set the bottle aside. My head was demanding sleep, but I was afraid that if I blinked I might inadvertently summon my family again. I needed to wake up before they took advantage of an accidental daydream.

Upstairs, I let the water in the shower run as hot as my hand would tolerate, and scrubbed myself with a loofah until my skin prickled and stung and my mind abandoned all notion of further rest. Stepping out of the shower and onto the cold tile floor, I frowned at the steamed mirror above the sink. I'd seen enough warnings scratched out by an invisible finger on horror-movie mirrors to have the good sense to pick up the hair dryer and blow away any chance of that happening.

Dressed and feeling as though I had reestablished a connection to the physical world, I was headed back downstairs when the door to the linen closet caught my attention. The floor creaked softly as I stepped inside. Fluorescent light sputtered forth as I ran my fingers over the switch on the interior wall, and turned the veins on the back of my hand into fat purple worms. I rubbed them down as I looked up.

The trapdoor was primed wood, framed in glossy wainscoting that seemed a little too fancy for a closet ceiling. I jumped to try and tap the hatch open with my fingers and missed it by a good foot and a half. Up from a stumble, I laughed at myself for being so stupid even as I found a toehold on the bottom shelf. Just a quick peek to prove to myself that there wasn't anything up there. If I was going to continue to live in the house, I couldn't let it keep secrets from me.

Using my forearm to press open the access, I slid the square of plywood aside and stepped onto the next shelf up. Grabbing hold of the ledge, I did a chin-up to take a quick look around. The air was fusty and cool. Mothballs and mildew vied for the dominant reek. Sunlight sprayed between the slats of a vent high on the back wall, but it was not enough to saturate the dry, dark corners. Using my chin as a bracket, I waved a hand over my head and caught a string. A low-watt bare blub plinked on overhead.

The attic was a much larger space than I had expected, approximately eight feet at its arch, with descending rafters that spanned the second floor of the house. Sheets of plywood served as a rough flooring. Several rolls of carpeting that matched the carpeting in the downstairs living room were pushed under the narrow rafters to my right. The head of an oscillating fan was politely turned away from a naked floor lamp to my left. The skeletal remains of a disassembled bed frame were scattered about the floor in front of me, slung up through the hatch by someone either too lazy or too scared to climb up and position them nicely. Several nondescript cardboard boxes were stacked against the far wall under the air vent. I counted seven—more, if the ones in front concealed some behind.

My arms trembled to hold my weight aloft as I blindly searched for a more secure toehold on the next shelf up. Coarse wood abraded my chin as the step swung out of reach. I kicked my foot to find it, but my fingertips were burning too hot to keep a grip on the splintered wood. After an excruciating moment of trying to hang on by the tip of my nose, I dropped back into the closet.

I was studying the rickety shelving to decide whether it would support a climb all the way up and in, and if the two-foot space between the top shelf and the trapdoor was too precipitous to manage safely, when a knock sounded at the front door.

"Thanks for agreeing to see me," Claire Reynolds said as she took a seat on the couch. Her eyes captured the room in a series of quick blinks. "I thought I might have blown it the last time I was here."

My shrugging eye roll advised that she almost had. "So," I said, smacking a smudge of dust from my pants leg. "What do you want to know? Why I'm living here? How I survived the murders? Am I sleeping with Rory Sellers?"

She smiled, pleased that her fish was baiting its own hook. "Well, now you mention it. Are you sleeping with Rory Sellers?"

"Are you?" I challenged.

Her smile faltered for a second. "Look. Rory already thinks he's God's gift to women. Let's not confirm that by making him the topic of conversation, okay?" I nodded once, and she turned to dig in her bag. "But for the record, he wishes."

She allowed herself a private chuckle as she worked the screen of her phone. The champagne-pink case was more bling than shield, liquid sequins rippled like a frame of rosewater in her hand. The clean, crisp way her French tips tapped across the screen made me hide my chewed-off claws in my lap. After firing off a quick text with a satisfied poke, she set the phone on the coffee table.

"Do you mind if I record this?" she asked as she pressed Record.

"Suit yourself," I said.

She rotated the phone in my direction, then bent forward to speak in a clear, measured voice as she stared at me.

"I'm speaking with Dixie Wheeler, a.k.a. Baby Blue, in the living room of 6211 Catharpin Road in Franconia, Virginia. The site of the Wheeler Massacre. Twenty-five years ago, on November twenty-sixth, Dixie's father brutally murdered her mother and three brothers. Dixie, who was the only survivor, has recently moved back into the house where the murders took place, her childhood home. Thank you for speaking to me today, Dixie." I glanced at the phone, imbibing our conversation with an open red gullet, and nodded. "I have to ask right away about the furniture."

"What about it?"

She glanced around. "It looks . . . Well, I don't mean to be rude, but it looks a little outdated. And the . . ." Her nose crinkled. "There's a mustiness, like something's been in storage for a long time. Are any of these pieces the original furniture from 1992?"

"Some of them are. My uncle kept a few of my family's belongings in his garage. I didn't realize there was an odor." I took a quick sniff to shrug. "I needed furniture, and it was all just sitting there, so I thought I might as well use it." I imagined Claire's home to be as fastidious and clean as she was: white carpeting, crisp chintz pillows, and a fluffy throw blanket, just for show. My afghan was sprawled over the arm of the couch like a dog in need of bathing. I brushed at the dusty smudge on my thigh again. As I crossed my legs to conceal it, I noticed a good-size hole in the mesh toe of my sneaker where my big toenail had sawed through. The last little chip of pink polish glared up at me through the fray. Weighing the unseemly, I uncrossed my legs, hooked my foot behind the leg of my chair, and covered the smudge with my hand. "The couch you're sitting on is an original piece," I said, brushing back a strand of hair as it fell into view. My forehead felt extra greasy.

She took a deep breath to sit up straight, ballooning out her chest, as though she hoped it might levitate her up and off the couch. She set her hand down to scooch forward and immediately snatched it back.

"Why did you move into this house, Dixie?" she asked, shoulders to her ears, a hand to her throat. "It has to hold a lot of bad memories for you."

"Actually, it doesn't," I said. "I don't have a single memory of this house, or what happened. I guess that's why I wanted to live here. To see if it would spark any memories."

"And has it?"

"Not one," I said with a relaxed smile. The armchair wobbled as I recrossed my legs. I jerked to catch myself. The flinch must have seemed contradictory because Claire tightened her eyes to gauge my level of candor.

"What do you hope to learn from being here, Dixie?" she asked.

"I really just wanted to check it out. I think most people would want to live in their childhood home again, if they had the chance. Wouldn't you?" When she nodded, I ran my eyes around the room. The fresh coat of semigloss paint on the walls seemed to accentuate the overall shabbiness of the furnishings. As my eyes swept the entryway to the kitchen, I realized I had left the crime scene photographs lying out on the table, along with a half-drunk bottle of Jack

Daniel's. As I glanced at Claire to see where her eyes were pointed, a shadow scurried out from under the kitchen table in the corner of my eye, fast as a spider but large as a four-year-old boy. In the blink it took me to look back, it disappeared behind the entryway wall. I blamed my sudden jostle on the chair.

"Sorry," I said, adjusting my seat, "the leg on this chair is busted or something. I keep meaning to fix it."

She gave it a dubious glance. "Do you feel more connected to your family now that you're here?"

"No. If anything, I think the reverse has happened. I feel less connected to them than ever before. I wasn't a part of their family. I never knew them. I mean, I know you better than I knew my own mother."

"Have you had any . . . sense of the tragedy that happened here?"

"Are you asking if the house is haunted?"

She shrugged. "Is it?"

"Not that I'm aware," I said, trying my best not to glance at the kitchen. "Just because something bad happened here doesn't make it a bad house. Just because my father went crazy living here doesn't mean I will." A chill ran through me. I laughed it off.

Her phone let out an ethereal tritone—electric wind chimes or maybe a synthesized glockenspiel—that brought me eagerly to stand.

"Go ahead and get that it you want," I said. "I'll be in the kitch—"

"Don't be silly," she said, giving the screen a happy tap to decline the call. "It's just my editor. He calls a hundred times a day."

I lowered back into my seat.

"From what I understand, your aunt took you in to live with her after the murders?"

I nodded. "Yes. My aunt Celia. I lived with her and my cousin, Leah," I said. "Oh, and my aunt's husband, Ford. But he wasn't around much."

"What do they think of you living here?"

I shrugged. "My aunt's not too happy about it. But she's always had a hard time dealing with what happened. Ford seems okay, though. At least he'll come over to see me. My cousin Leah's dead, so . . ." I scratched my ear to offer, "Cancer," and noticed three straight white scars across Claire's left forearm. They were on the top, about three inches below her elbow, so not indicative of a suicide attempt, but their symmetrical structure made me wonder if they were self-inflicted. I squinted to get a better look and she turned her arm.

"Your aunt is your father's sister, right?"

"Yes."

"Do you ever see your father?" she asked.

The question brought me out of my chair. "What the hell? Why would you ask me something like that?"

"I just thought that maybe—"

I held up my hand. "You know, if you are going to ask me stupid questions you can just leave right now."

Her eyes grew anxious. "No. I'm sorry. I didn't mean to—"

"No, I don't see my father," I said, scathingly. "What do you think I am? Some kind of freak or something? Give me a fucking break."

"I'm sorry." She held up a hand to keep my looming temper at bay. "I didn't mean to upset you."

"Yeah, right." I folded my arms to avert my eyes in disgust. The shadow was back, under the kitchen table, curled up like a cat. Knees suddenly weak, I sat heavily to say, "Just ask me another question before I end this interview right now."

She pressed her hands to her lips to pray for a question that wouldn't get her kicked out on her ass. When one came to her, she nodded to give herself the go-ahead. "Previous tenants reported hearing strange noises. Have you experienced any strange activities?"

I shook my head. "You just don't know when to quit, do you?"

She looked taken aback. "I'm sorry, but this is what my readers want to know about. I thought you knew what happened with the previous owners." She glanced in the direction of Vicki's house. "I mean, they were totally convinced the house was haunted. That's why they had to move. Didn't you know?"

"Every house has strange noises you can't figure out," I said dismissively. "That doesn't mean it's haunted."

She leaned forward. "So you *have* heard strange noises."

I was about to downplay the inscrutable sounds as your typical house-settling fare, but as her green eyes flashed with an avariciousness bordering on savagery, I couldn't resist messing with her a little.

"Well . . ." I sat forward to confide. "I didn't want to talk about this because I don't want people thinking I'm weird or anything, but . . ." I waved away the rest of my sentence. "Oh, forget it."

"No," she urged. "Please. Go on."

I motioned her closer, and she slid sideways across the couch.

"The house is haunted," I whispered.

Her eyes brightened. "It is?"

I nodded. "The lights keep flickering on and off, and there all these strange noises. There's like this weird dragging sound and this"—I motioned up a visual from my chest like fumes from a brandy snifter—"guttural kind of crazy laughter. It's hard to describe, but it scares the hell out of me. Let's see . . . Doors slam shut all by themselves and— Oh! Things keep moving around all on their own." When I motioned her closer, her eyes seemed to take a deep inhale. I lowered my whisper to an almost inaudible level to say, "When I came down this morning, all the chairs were stacked on the kitchen table in a pyramid."

A frown pulled her back. "That's from *Poltergeist*."

I laughed. "Oh, my god. You should have seen your face. You were really buying all that crap. I told you the house wasn't haunted, but you didn't want to believe me."

She considered me for a second and then sat back. "Why did you agree to this interview if you weren't going to take it seriously?"

I shrugged. "I was bored. And I didn't want you to keep stopping by. I knew you'd be back if I didn't call you."

"You could have just told me that over the phone and saved me the trouble. I would have respected your wishes."

"And miss your chance to see Rory again? I don't think so."

She raised her eyebrows. "Is that what this is all about? Rory? Oh, please. If I wanted to see Rory again, all I'd have to do is pick up the phone. Honestly, Dixie, my wanting to talk to you had absolutely nothing whatsoever to do with Rory. I'm interested in you. Not him."

"I read your articles about Erin Doyle. You mentioned Rory more times than you mentioned her. It's pretty obvious that you're obsessed with him."

She cocked her head. "Has he ever talked to you about what happened to Erin?"

"Of course." I said. "Rory tells me everything. Clearly Erin's death was an accident, but you turned it into some sort of personal vendetta to make him look guilty."

"How do you know he's not?"

I shrugged. "I just do."

She smiled at my naïveté. "Don't let his looks fool you, Dixie. Rory's not the man you think he is."

"Oh, like you know. Just because you went out on a couple of dates doesn't mean you know him, *Claire*." A speck of spit hissed out with her name, and I wiped it away with the back of my hand. My lips felt numb. The wave of dizziness hit me hard, like my blood sugar level had just plummeted to a dangerous level. Usually, a handful of nuts and a glass of orange juice would set me straight, but this affliction felt way beyond a snack. My next words rolled off a swollen tongue: "I think I know Rory a little better than some chick who thinks she got some sort of insight into his soul by sleeping with him once."

She turned to scoff a laugh into her shoulder, then drew a composed breath to face me again. "Okay, look. I don't want to do this.

Please, let's not do this. I swear my interest in you has nothing to do with Rory. You're making more out of our relationship than there is. I get that you're like his kid sister—"

A sudden cramp in my stomach forced me to bite my lip.

"—and you're protective of him. And I know from conversations we've had that Rory feels the same about you. I can see how my articles about Erin Doyle may have seemed a little . . . unfair toward Rory—"

The sound of her voice was making me sick. Every time she said Rory's name the cramp in my stomach seemed to bore a little deeper.

"—but I won't do that with you. I swear. I won't even mention Rory"—*UGH!*—"in my story, if you don't want me to. I promise. You're the story. You're who I'm interested in. Not Rory Sellers." *FUCK!* "I just want to know more about you. I guess since Rory"—*AH!*—"saved you, I'll have to mention that, but that's all I'll say about him. Or maybe I can take a different angle altogether. Focus on what's happened to you since. Like . . . What motivated you to move back into this house? Why are you here?"

"Because it's our house!" I snapped as the cramp grew teeth and gnashed my bowels.

"'*Our*'?" she repeated, confused. "What do you mean by 'our' house?"

"I mean my family's house." Though I had started us down this path, I felt like I had teased forth something from the darkness that had been pulling at its chain. "Stop putting words in my mouth! You just want to make me look crazy. I mean, that's what sells, right? Crazy!"

My tone triggered an alarm in her eyes. "That not what I meant. I just—"

"This might just be some story to you, but it's my fucking life." Anger tore through me like a dull saw.

"I understand that," she said calmly. "I just wanted to clarify."

Something sleek and hot squiggled through my intestines. I

began to rock, to hum through the pain, biting my lip to draw it up and out of my gut. The chair let out a moan as I bent over my knees.

"Are you okay?" she asked, placing a hand on my shoulder. "Do you need some water?" She started to stand in the direction of the kitchen, and I grabbed her by the hand.

"No," I said, leaning back as the pain subsided. "I'm okay. My stomach's just a little upset. It acts up sometimes." A deep breath wheezed through me like a death rattle. "Go on. Ask me another question."

She blinked. "You want to continue with the interview?"

I rolled my finger for her to carry on.

"Okay. Great. Well . . . why don't we rewind a little and start with some easy background stuff? Like where . . ."

I think she was asking about where I grew up, but I could only pretend to listen as another cramp tunneled through me. I closed my eyes to take a deep, meditative breath. I tried to focus on remaining absolutely calm, but the calm that came over me was as rigid as a seizure. As my jaw locked, so did my teeth, so tight I thought they might shatter. A warm trickle seeped from the corners of my mouth and down my chin. Blood? Drool? Vomit? I wanted to wipe it away to find out which, but my hands were pinned in my lap. I shifted in my chair, uncrossed my legs, and overturned the coffee table. The kick was spastic, the crash terrible, but I couldn't react. I couldn't move, couldn't breathe. Whatever bodily fluid had been trickling from my mouth, it was now a gusher. A warm, wet blanket coursed down the plank of my body. I imagined myself a bloody scalpel slipping from the hand of a weary surgeon. Any second, I was going to slide off the chair into a convulsion on the floor. With what little control I could garner, I pried open one eye to silently beg Claire for help.

Everything was normal.

There was no blood, no drool, no vomit. My hands were folded neatly in my lap. My foot was bobbing, but gently, and well left of the upright coffee table. Claire's lips were moving in easy conversation, but I couldn't hear over the sound of feet pounding down the stair-case behind me. I gave a yelp as I looked for whoever—whatever— was about to materialize on the landing.

"Did you hear that?" I asked.

Claire's eyes followed my gaze. "I didn't hear anything."

Miraculously, my phone rang upstairs.

"Excuse me for a second," I said as I pressed to a stand. "That's my phone."

I started slowly up the staircase on watery knees, holding on to the handrail for dear life. Just as the railing merged with the wall, I glanced down at Claire. She had turned to watch me. The way she was trying to suppress a grin by seeming concerned made me want to launch over the railing at her, rip her open by her rib cage, roll around in her blood, and—I shook off the thought, the unbear-able urge.

"Don't go snooping around," I said. The voice that growled from me was mine, but that was not what I had intended to say. The annoy-ance behind the words didn't feel like mine, either. It belonged to the thing that had been burrowing up from my stomach. Though it had mercifully stopped squirming, it now sat like a cancerous lump in my diaphragm. I cleared my throat to rephrase what I had intended to say a moment before: "I mean, sit tight. I'll be right back."

Claire nodded with obedient confusion.

In my bedroom, I accepted the call but didn't trust myself enough to say hello. When Garrett asked if I was there, I responded with a discordant "Yeah."

"What's the matter?" he asked.

"Nothing."

"You sure? You sounded a little—"

"What do you want, Garrett?" As soon as the words left my mouth, I knew it was the absolute wrong thing to say: the wrong attitude, the wrong insinuation, wrong, wrong, wrong. Garrett didn't have to *want* anything to call me. He could call, and often did, just to hear the sound of my voice. Just to connect with me. Just to let me know he was thinking about me. That I would demand a reason for his call put him in the same class as a telemarketer. Less. I would never speak to a telemarketer in that tone of voice.

He said, "I don't want a fucking thing, Dixie," and then hung up on me.

A rush of frustration threw me back onto the bed. I lay there trying to cry, wanting tears, needing tears, but what spurted from my mouth was a dark giggle. I slapped my hand across my face to silence it before it could rev up to a cackle. I closed my eyes to take stock. Something was going on with me. I had never felt this disjointed, this furious, this . . . completely out of whack in all my life. I counted back to the last day of my period, which was easy to do since it was just last week. This wasn't PMS. This was something else.

Below, a thud was followed by a scuff of soft creaks. There was a clumsy bump, then a stumbling of feet. I sat up to track the movement across creaky floorboards underneath the downstairs carpeting. A set of heels hit the wood floor in the kitchen.

I told that bitch not to go snooping around!

The thing inside me—which, now that I was alone with it, had taken on the voice of my father—pressed against my forehead to look out through my eyes. It tightened its focus by narrowing my expression, adjusting the view like a set of bone-rimmed binoculars. I shook my head to fling it away and slammed it against the back of my skull like a migraine. I pressed my eyes closed, and my father's wretched scent filled my nose.

"LET'S TEACH THAT BITCH A LESSON!"

"Shut up," I cried, gripping my head to squeeze him into submission. "Go away."

"She's in the kitchen, you idiot! Are you just going to let her see us

splattered all over the table? You want Celia to read about that in the morning paper?"

"Shut up," I wheezed through heavy lips, nausea undulating like a clog of snails in my throat.

"I'll shut up as soon as you shut her up. Now get going!"

Suddenly, I was on my feet, but instead of heading to the hallway, I ran for the bathroom. Locking myself inside, I spun for the toilet. Head in the bowl, I tried to purge the sickness from me. It wouldn't come. A finger down my throat only seemed to push it deeper. My reflection rippled like a black eel in the basin. Panting, I closed my eyes against it. The echo of my breath plunged up an evil chuckle. I spit several times, then rolled onto the floor to hold my head in my hands.

Though I had imagined conversations with my father my entire life, this was different. I used to know what he was going to say or, more aptly, what he might say. I just gave the notion voice, like dialogue of a screenplay I might write someday. What I was experiencing was probably nothing more than fatigue, but damn if it didn't feel real. Aunt Celia and Garrett were right: This house was eating away at me, nibbling away at my sanity. Once, I half watched a documentary from the pillow of Garrett's lap where cattle were being devoured by parasites as they stood eating grass. They would just keel over dead, shanks gouged to bone, cud still half chewed in their mouths. That was me. A dumb cow just standing there letting an invisible insect eat away at me. But unlike the cow, I didn't just have to stand there and take it. I had options.

Didn't I?

"Sure you do, honey."

I could just leave.

"If you really want to."

I could drop a match on the floor and walk out the door.

"Let's not be hasty."

A crash rose up through the floor and shoved me to a stand. As I entered the bedroom, the door leading to the hallway clicked shut. I grabbed the knob with both hands and pulled. It wouldn't open. I grabbed my cheeks as another crash rose up through the floor.

"Claire!" I called out. "Are you okay?" I twisted the knob again and again, but it was frozen solid. "Claire! My door's stuck! I can't get out!" I pressed my ear to the door to listen. An indecipherable muffling was followed by a heavy thump. "Claire! Can you hear me? Are you okay?" When no answer came, I pounded on the door with my fists. "CLAIRE! ANSWER ME! CLAIRE! CLAIRE!"

I checked the turn lock on the knob. Flat. The door was unlocked, but my hands were too sweaty to get a grip. I wiped my palms on my shirt and grabbed the knob with both hands. The door flung open and launched me onto my rump. I screamed to Claire that I was coming as I jumped to my feet.

The hallway was an ever-expanding telescope; the harder I ran, the less ground I seemed to cover. Though it felt like I couldn't have traveled slower if I had been moving backward, I hit the staircase at top speed. I grabbed the handrail at the last second. My feet flew out from under me, and I slid to the bottom on my back. The air that was knocked out of me returned with a sudden, extraordinary gasp. I rolled onto my stomach carefully, mindful of my spine. I was just about to push to a stand when a dull clunk raised a tremendous scream in my head. As the blinding white explosion swept me away, then evaporated into darkness, I thought I heard Claire call my name.

I WOKE SENSELESS and thirsty in a darkened house. Crumpled at the bottom of a staircase, I stared blankly at the closed front door. It took a second to understand where I was, and why I had been using the bottom step as a pillow, and why my head hurt so fucking bad. As it came to me, I jolted to a seated position with my fists in the air, ready to fight whatever had been tormenting Claire. Though the sudden movement caused a disorienting bolt of pain through my eyes, I could see that the living room was empty.

"Claire!" I yelled. My brain detonated like a canned bomb. I clutched my head in my hands until the throbbing passed, and then whispered, "Claire," in a kinder voice. The only response was from a dog somewhere off in the distance. As the pain withdrew to an isolated position at the back of my head, I reached around to find a lemon-sized lump behind my left ear. I ran my eyes up the staircase and remembered the fall I took: feet flying out from under me, the impact under my back, a bumpy slide to the bottom. I must have cracked my head on the way down, I thought, but as I ran my hand over the carpeted bottom step, I wondered if maybe I hadn't somehow hit my head on the wooden handrail. Either way, something had knocked me a good one.

I got slowly to my feet and closed my eyes to await another blast of pain. Though my head hurt from the inside out, it seemed to be holding steady at a dull, aching throb. I swallowed back a wave of nausea that I thought might be symptomatic of a concussion, and stepped off the landing.

Turning in a circle, I took in every corner of the living room, half expecting a set of scared eyeballs to peep up at me from behind Uncle Davis's desk or one of the remaining unpacked boxes. I crossed to the window. The only car in the driveway was my silver Nissan Sentra. I crossed to the couch and ran my hand over the cushion. It still felt warm, sort of . . .

The kitchen looked no different. The crime scene photographs were still splayed across the tabletop. Jack Daniel's was standing next to my shot glass, ready for the next round, which I took. Grimacing through the afterburn, I wiped my lips with my forearm and glanced at the clock over the stove. I wasn't exactly sure what time Claire had arrived, but I thought I might have been unconscious for a couple of hours. Prior fatigue might have increased the duration of the blackout. *While she's out,* my weary body probably thought, *might as well catch a few.* My head felt marginally better in a glaze of alcohol, so I took another shot before I headed back into the living room.

I folded my arms to look around. Maybe Claire heard me upstairs, talking to myself in a strange gravelly voice, and decided to exit stage left before I came down in one of my father's suits and showed her how possessed the house truly was.

I lowered myself onto the couch to search the crannies for some sign of her, but couldn't bring myself to slip my hand into the dark space under the cushion. I leaned back to make my aching head think reasonably.

Though hearing me going nuts upstairs might explain Claire's sudden exit from the house, I was almost positive the conversation I'd had with my father had taken place in the soundproof chamber of my mind. But even if it was spoken aloud, Claire didn't seem the type to spook so easily. If anything, she seemed the type to creep upstairs with her phone held out in front of her to record every thrilling moment of my descent into madness. Post it live on her Twitter feed: #babybluefuckingnutballs.

And what about the struggle I'd heard going on down here?

Had I imagined that? Was that also one of my father's little tricks? I was almost positive I'd heard Claire scream my name before I passed out. Had she screamed out of concern for me, or for herself? I replayed her scream in my mind, but could only determine that it sounded frightened, which worked either way. But if her scream was for my benefit, why didn't she stay to help me or call 9-1-1? Had I done something I couldn't remember? Something that freaked her out bad enough to leave me lying unconscious at the bottom of the staircase? I didn't think so. The more I thought about it, the less either conclusion made sense. Claire leaving while I was upstairs was just as unlikely as her leaving after I fell down the stairs. Which left only one other possibility.

Claire had never been here to begin with.

I had dreamed the entire episode.

I sat forward to give this explanation further consideration. The more I thought about it, the more I liked it. Yes, of course. I had fallen on my way down to answer the door. Whoever it had been might not have heard me fall. Or if they did, they might have dismissed the sound for something else, something less alarming. Maybe it had been Claire. Maybe she screamed out when she heard a clamor inside. Not knowing what the sound was, she probably chalked it up to a noisy household chore, like kicking a heavy hamper down the staircase, and left without giving it another thought.

Even as I was convincing myself of this perfectly logical explanation, another elbowed its way to the forefront. Or, rather, Ford's voice shoved it aside: *I knew you had gone off the deep end, girl, but I didn't know you hit your head on the bottom of the pool.*

I rubbed the lump on the back of my head.

Maybe I really had hit rock bottom.

9

From the moment I decided that Claire's visit had been a figment of my imagination, I felt worlds better. Crazy explains a lot of things. All the strange noises and activities in the house didn't seem to bother me anymore. The monotonous sound of Eddie's head bouncing down the staircase was almost heartening in its predictability. Boys will be boys. That my pillow was scampering around the house like a curious puppy no longer upset me. If anything, finding it gave me something to do. Pillows will be pillows. I found that I could drown out the haunting dirge coming from the bathroom fan by cranking up a classical music station on Pandora. They never shuffled in Badfinger. Did my father say something? Nope, that was just crazy old me talking to myself again.

Fuck you, Dixie. No. Fuck you, Dixie.

It was a good three days. I got a lot done. I assembled the bunk beds. They weren't safe to sleep in, but they were erected well enough to hold any weight Eddie and Michael might put on them. I wallpapered the kitchen, not the exact print it had once been, but pretty damn close. I hemmed the lining in one of my mother's dresses, which might fit after I lost ten pounds. I corrected Eddie's math homework. C-minus. I untangled a snared fishing reel and caught a fork in the sink. I even went to Food Lion to buy some coffee and other things that weren't available at the ABC store.

I was on my way home when I decided enough was enough and swung by Garrett's work to make him like me again. He was out on a customer call. Damn. I needed to get my perishables home, but now that I was out in the world, I didn't feel like going back to an empty house. I rolled down my window. The day seemed about as chilly as my refrigerator, so I thought I might risk a quick pop in on Mr. Cullins. He was heading out for a doctor's appointment, so I got no farther than the front door.

"I hope nothing's wrong," I said.

"Nah. Just a checkup. You bring the file with you?"

"No, I was just out running some errands and thought I'd swing by to see how you were doing. I can bring it by tomorrow. Hey, why don't I make you dinner while I'm at it? What kind of food do you like?"

"Anything besides pizza and Chinese takeout sounds pretty good to me."

I reviewed the groceries I had just bought, and promised him spaghetti and meat sauce if he'd pick up a bottle of wine.

He made a face. "I don't like wine. Does beer go with spaghetti?"

I smiled. "Actually, I prefer it. I just said wine so I wouldn't sound like a total redneck loser."

"Don't knock my people."

After leaving Mr. Cullins with a kiss on his cheek, I swung by Garrett's work again, but didn't spot his car in the parking lot. I didn't want to spoil my good mood with another one of Aunt Celia's lectures, but an earful of grief was better than the silence of my kitchen. Lucky for me, she was on the couch with a bad cold and didn't have the strength to climb onto her high horse. She was just glad someone was there to fix her a bowl of soup.

"Where's Ford?" I asked as I set the soup on a TV tray and helped her to a seated position. "Why isn't he here helping you?"

She shrugged as she blew her nose. "Who knows? He got into some bar fight the other night and I haven't seen him since."

"Bar fight?" I questioned. "Where?"

Again she blew her nose. Again she said, "Who knows."

I stuffed a throw pillow behind her back and gave it a hard chop, as I did mine to keep it biddable. "Did he get hurt?" I asked.

"He had a sore jaw and blood all over, but he was all right. It was mostly the other guy's blood. Ford said he barely hit him, but I don't know about that. He changed his clothes and headed back out the door again. I've been waiting for the police to show up ever since. That would be his third strike, you know. He's probably lying low until the heat blows over."

I sat next to her and patted her back through a coughing spell. When I held up a steaming spoonful of soup, she told me to let it cool a bit.

"What was the fight about?" I asked, unfolding a napkin into her lap.

She shrugged. "Probably to find out who the bigger asshole was."

"Ford should have won that argument hands down." I laughed. "Why do you stay with him, Aunt Celia? I mean, he's hardly ever here, and when he is, he causes you nothing but heartache. You're here sick and he's out getting into bar fights. He should be home taking care of you. Don't you ever get tired of his bullshit?"

"Sure I do," she said.

"Then why not have the locks changed and be done with him?"

"You might find this hard to understand, Dixie, but I love Ford. He's the only man I've ever loved. I've been with Ford for . . ." She looked up to calculate. "What, fifty years, now? More, maybe. I can't remember a time Ford wasn't in my life. I guess I don't know any different."

"But that's the point, isn't it? You've wasted so much of your life on him already. Don't let him take any more. You deserve to be happy, Aunt Celia. You've missed out on so much, as it is."

Annoyance filled her sigh. "What have I missed out on, exactly, Dixie?"

"Well, love for one."

"Ford loves me. I know he's no Prince Charming. Hell, isn't even as good as a toad on some days, but he does love me. And I love

him. I've loved Ford since I was a little girl, and that's saying something. He needs me. He's always needed me. He was so burned and
broken after the fire . . . He was the saddest thing you ever saw.
Followed me around like a little puppy dog. I couldn't help but
smother him with love. Eventually, it turned into more. You don't
always get to choose who you love, Dixie. Sometimes, love just happens to you."

"How did the fire start, anyway?" I asked.

"Don't you know?"

"How could I? Neither one of you would ever tell me."

"I don't remember you asking," she said.

"I did ask, and you told me it was none of my business. Just like
everything else I ever asked you about when I was a kid."

"I don't know why you're so curious about the past. Personally, I
don't like to dwell on it, but if you must know, the police thought
Ford's father was smoking in bed."

"Oh, that's terrible."

She nodded. "Ford never believed that, though. In his eyes, that
man could do no wrong. If anyone even mentioned how the fire got
started, Ford would go nuts. Davis made that mistake once, and Ford
busted his nose for it." She shook her head reflectively. "Ford wasn't
always the tough guy he is now, you know. He got picked on a lot for
the way he looked when he was a kid. All through high school, really.
He acts like he doesn't care, but he does. That uncle they sent him to
live with bullied and teased him the most. He was a horrible man.
That was Ford's mother's brother. Oh, and his mother . . . ?" Aunt
Celia shook her head. "Let's just say Ford had it hard before and after
that fire, though he'd never admit it. On the days when he pushes me
to my limit, I try to remember all he's been through, and the sweet
boy I fell in love with."

"I don't think what happened to him when he was a kid should
excuse him for how he treats you now. Taking off all the time and

leaving you alone. Especially when you need him the most. And it certainly doesn't explain how awful he was when Leah was sick."

She appeared shocked. "It explains everything, Dixie. You should understand that better than anyone. Ford stood on that front lawn and watched his entire family burn up in that fire, and he couldn't do a damn thing about it. He couldn't bear to watch Leah die, too. He couldn't stand to see her suffer. He loved her too much. It broke his heart. I think a part of Ford wishes that Billy would have never saved him. That he didn't live only to have to watch his daughter die."

I did understand. I understood with a clarity she didn't fully fathom, or intend. I had moments when I wished that I had been killed with my family. And though I had stood by her bedside, I couldn't stand to watch Leah suffer, either. Ford and I were very much alike in that regard. We just handled our anguish differently. He ran away from it, while I hung back to smother it with a pillow. I cast down my eyes so Aunt Celia couldn't discern the true nature of my shame.

"But you were so angry with him," I said.

"No, Dixie. I took my anger *out* on him. I was angry that Leah was sick. I was angry about what happened to Billy. I was angry that Debbie and the boys were dead. I was angry at Davis for making me think about that day every damn time I spoke to him. I was angry that I couldn't believe in Billy's innocence like he did. I lashed out at Ford because I knew he'd let me do it. He wanted me to do it. Fighting took his mind off his sorrow."

I looked off to consider this and spotted an almost empty NyQuil bottle with a straw in it on the side table. I wondered if this was why Aunt Celia was opening up to me like she never had before. Her inhibitions were down. She was doped up on antihistamines.

"I feel bad about how I treated him, though," she went on, wiping her nose with a tissue. "Ford didn't deserve that. He was doing the best he could. You might not realize it, Dixie, but Ford tries very hard to be a good man." She turned and gave me a soft smile. "I might not understand you living in that house, but Ford's very proud of you for doing what you're doing."

I nodded. "When he stopped by the other night, he was almost nice to me. We actually had a pretty civilized conversation for once."

"He stopped by?" she asked before accepting the spoonful of tomato soup I held to her lips.

"He brought me the leftovers you sent over."

She nearly choked on her swallow. "Is that where all that food got to."

"What, you didn't send it?"

She shook her head, then shrugged. "I told him I was *thinking* about taking you a few things, but I didn't actually send him." She sighed to look at the ceiling, then opened her mouth like a baby bird. I tipped in another serving of soup. "I know he wanted to go see the house again. He probably thought that was a good way to get his foot in the door without coming out and asking."

"So does that mean I'm not invited to Thanksgiving?" I asked. "He said you told him to invite me."

"Well, of course you're invited. You'll come, won't you?"

"Of course I'll come." I handed her the spoon. "I'm not going to miss out on your gravy just because you're mad at me."

"I'm not mad at you, Dixie." She dropped the spoon into the bowl and leaned back to tuck the blanket under her chin. "I just couldn't give you my blessing, is all. Though, being in that house, you probably could use it."

I set the TV tray aside. "It'll probably be just me for Thanksgiving, though. I don't think Garrett will come." I reclined to put my head on her shoulder. "We had it out pretty good about Rory."

"Rory?" she asked in a puzzled voice. "What happened with Rory?"

"He came by to see the house and . . . well . . . Let's just say Garrett wasn't all too happy about it."

"Oh, I'm sorry." She patted my hand. "I didn't know you were speaking to Rory again. I thought you two had a falling-out?"

I sat up to look at her. "Didn't you give him my number? He said he called you and that you gave him my number because you were worried about me."

She shook her head. "Maybe he talked to Ford. See there? Ford's looking out for you. He just goes about it in a strange way. I'm sorry if he caused you and Garrett any troubles, though."

"We're fine. Garrett will come around. Hopefully by Thanksgiving. And I did want to talk to Rory. He's the only one who really understands why I'm doing this."

"So how are you do-do—" I handed her a tissue from the side table as she sneezed. "Thank you—doing over there?"

"It sucks," I admitted.

She patted my knee. "Go home then. Go back to Garrett and work it out."

"I can't. Not yet."

"I don't like you being there all alone. After what happened to that reporter lady, you can't be too careful. Make sure you lock your doors."

I sat up straight. "What reporter lady?"

Her eyes widened. "Haven't you heard? A reporter from the *Franconia Dispatch* was found murdered."

"Claire Reynolds?" I asked through numb lips.

"Yes. That's her. They just found her body in the woods off of Old Keene Mill Road. No more than a mile from your house. Behind that strip mall next to the Best Western. I was going to call you to make sure you were okay, but you showed up before I got the chance. They just found her." She pointed at the TV as though the gruesome discovery had happened simultaneous to her proclamation. The screen showed a car zooming down a windy road. "MUTE" stood in the bottom right corner of the television. "The sheriff's due to give a report any minute now. Oh, I hope it isn't a serial killer. They're just awful. Remember those horrible sniper shooters? That went on for months. That man and that boy?" I stood on phantom legs to float into the kitchen. I leaned my forehead against the refrigerator as she asked from the other room: "What were their names again?" She blew her nose. "Starts with an M. Marco . . . Marvin . . . I tell you, I can't see a white panel van without thinking about it. They still look sinister to me, and that ended up not even being what they were— Dixie! It's not even noon yet!"

I swiped my lips with the back of my hand after a long swig of beer. "I knew her, Aunt Celia."

"Who? You mean . . ." She pointed a finger at the TV. "Oh, no. Was she a friend of yours?"

"Not really. I only met her a couple of times. She wanted to do an interview with me. But I just saw her the other day. I can't believe she's dead."

"Well, that settles it," she said, grabbing for the remote to unmute the TV as a "Special Report" banner flashed across the screen. "You're moving out of that house and that's final. You can live here if you need to."

"Shhh," I said, standing in front of the television as Claire's face filled the screen. Her hair was lighter in the photograph than it had been three days ago. Her red curls were nearly white around her sun-kissed shoulders. Her perfect makeup, hairstyle, and stance all seemed staged, but the beach in the background was absolutely not a studio prop. A rotund boy playing in the sand behind her had a half-moon rising up the back of his swim trunks. Despite the umbrella in the distance sitting atop her head like a pink-and-blue-striped yarmulke, she looked absolutely flawless, unquestionably alive.

"Move, Dixie. I can't see."

"Claire Reynolds's up-and-coming career as a news journalist was cut short after her body was found in the 900 block of Old Keene Mill Road. Though the circumstances surrounding her death remain a mystery, the Franconia sheriff's office has confirmed that her death was no accident, which has the citizens of west Franconia on edge. Local restaurant owner Lou Farris says he was surprised to learn that a murder had taken place just yards from his establishment."

The screen switched from the pretty talking head to a grotesquely hairy blob in a stained white apron. Lou Ferris pivoted his massive body to point at police vehicles haphazardly parked in a field behind his pizzeria. Bright yellow police tape spanned the edge of a wooded area about fifty yards in the distance. A uniformed police officer chased a loose dog across the field and off camera.

"I heard they were looking for a missing woman," Lou said, *"but I had no idea she was lying dead right out my back door."*

"Are you surprised something like this could happen in your quiet community?" a disembodied voice asked before the microphone was thrust back in Lou's face.

Lou scratched a clearing of white scalp in his thinning black hair. *"Well, I got robbed two weeks ago by a couple of punks, so I don't know if it's all that quiet, but yeah. Nothing like this has ever happened. We get kids hanging out back there in the summertime, drinking beer and what-not, but nobody's ever died, far as I know. When I saw all the cops I knew it was going to be bad."* He looked back at the woods again. *"Damn shame. Damn, damn shame . . ."*

I turned to Aunt Celia. "Do they know how she died?"

"They said earlier that she was bludgeoned to death."

"Bludgeoned?" I repeated as Garrett's missing hammer suddenly struck me as a violent repercussion.

"That's what they said."

The station cut back to the studio desk, where the blonde anchor-woman was doing her best to seem concerned while flashing a bright, toothy smile. *"Not since the Wheeler Massacre in 1992 has the*

Franconia area seen such brutal violence. As you may recall, William Wheeler..."

"Why do they have to bring that up?" I snapped as Aunt Celia clicked off the television. "My family has nothing to do with this. That was twenty-five years ago. And it was a totally different situation."

"I guess one dead woman isn't horrible enough." She blew her nose again. "I'm sorry this happened to someone you knew, Dixie. Was she a nice girl?"

"Honestly? Not really."

I DROVE HOME with one eye on the road and one eye on three days ago, frantically pressing buttons to find a radio station that would provide an update on Claire. From what I was able to piece together from teasers leading into commercials and the last few seconds of a "News and Weather on the Eights" report, until the discovery of her body that morning, Claire Reynolds had been missing since the day she vanished off my couch. After checking in at her office that morning, she left to "run down" a story, which meant she probably *had* come to my house that day. She had told a coworker she would be back in time for a staff meeting that afternoon, but was never seen or heard from again. If the timing of her disappearance was accurate and she had already been dead for a few days, I was probably the last person on earth to see Claire Reynolds alive.

I pulled into my driveway five minutes after the top of the hour. I was hunched over, picking crumbs from the plastic casing around my gearshift, listening to commercials, and waiting for the news to start, when a hard knock at my window threw me back in my seat.

Vicki waved at me through the passenger's side window. I gave her a tentative smile as she mouthed something through the glass. I popped the trunk so I could gather my groceries.

"Sorry if I scared you," she said as I got out of the car. "I thought you saw me coming."

"That's okay," I said, rounding the car. "What's up?"

"Just thought I'd say hi," she said, then cocked her head pensively. "You doing okay, sweetie?"

I nodded as I hooked a couple of bags over my wrist. "Sure. Why wouldn't I be?"

"I don't know . . . I just haven't seen you in a couple of days. I thought you might be sick."

"I'm fine. My aunt's sick, though. I was just over there helping her out." As I closed the trunk and moved around the back of the car, I noticed a small boy attached to Vicki's hip. "Hello there," I said. "What's your name?"

The boy looked to his mother for the answer.

Vicki patted the top of his head. "This is Conner."

"Hi, Conner," I said.

"Can we go now?" Conner complained, stretching his neck to elongate his impatience.

"In a minute," Vicki said sternly, then tempered her expression as she looked up at me. "I don't know why he's in such a hurry. He's going to the dentist. Of course the one day I arrange a sitter for Katie so I can get a jump on my Christmas shopping, he wakes up with a toothache."

"Christmas," I repeated in a rather Scroogey way. "Isn't it a little early for Christmas shopping? We haven't even had Thanksgiving yet."

She covered Conner's ears. "Not if Santa wants to find all the best toys, it's not."

Conner wrestled free. "Can I wait in the car?"

"We're going. Now shush." She shook her head at me. "I better get going. But do you want to stop by for a glass of wine when I get back? Nick's out of town and— Oh, hey! How about dinner?"

"Thanks, but I've got someone coming over later," I lied. I'd already told her I wasn't sick, so I couldn't use that as an out. And it was better than saying what I actually planned to do: contemplate my involvement in an open murder investigation. I wasn't sure why I felt guilty. I couldn't possibly have had anything to do with Claire's death. I had been in an unconscious heap at the bottom of the staircase when she vanished . . . Your Honor.

"Bring Garrett if you want," Vicki said. "I've got plenty."

"Thanks, but it's not Garrett."

The way I said this must have told a story because Vicki's face crumpled. "Oh, did you two break up?"

"Sorta. I guess. I don't know. It's complicated."

Vicki cinched her shoulders. "Oo, are you seeing that hunky guy I saw the other day?"

"*Mom!*"

Vicki covered Conner's ears again. "You can definitely bring *him*. He's hot. What's his name?"

"Rory, but he's not the one coming over, either, so . . ."

"Oh, too bad." She sighed. "But that's okay. You can bring whoever you want."

"Oh, no. It's just an old friend of mine. Debbie." My mother's name slipped off my tongue a little too quickly for my liking. "We're just going to hang out and talk about the old days. We'd totally bore you."

I got the feeling Vicki was trying to catch me in a lie. But what she needed to catch was a clue. *I don't want to have dinner with you, Vicki!* Did she really want me to admit that to her face? I should have just said that I was having dinner with Mr. Cullins. Our dinner wasn't until tomorrow, but he probably would have come over tonight if I called him.

"Oh, is she the one I talked to the other day? Red hair? Real cute? Tell her I didn't mean to cut her off like that. I was just in a hurry. Katie was having a fit and I needed to get to the bank before it closed."

I blinked to keep my face stoic. "You talked to her?"

Vicki's eyes switched to find the line she had just crossed. "Oh, not really," she said. "I mean, she just asked me if I knew you. Before

I could even answer, Katie threw her sippy cup and splashed grape juice all over the inside of the car. I kinda just bailed out on her. She probably told you that I was incredibly rude."

I shook my head. Maybe Vicki wasn't the one who told Claire that I was living here. She clearly hadn't recognized her.

Conner began to pull his mother forcibly away by her arm.

"Well, here I go being rude again." She laughed as Conner yanked her out of my driveway and onto the grass easement between our yards. She tossed an apologetic look over her shoulder to say, "Stop by tomorrow, if you want. Nick won't be back until Friday. Okay. See you later." She bent over to give Conner an earful as they moved off toward her car.

I stood frozen until they drove off. Either Vicki hadn't seen the news of Claire's death yet, or she hadn't recognized Claire's picture from the broadcasts. But it would only be a matter of time before she did. I thought back to the first day Claire stopped by. She was on the stoop when I opened the door. As much as I wanted to believe that was the day she and Vicki had interacted, I knew it wasn't. I remembered seeing Vicki's car in their driveway. She hadn't left for the bank. No. Vicki must have spoken to Claire the second time she came by. The day she went missing. A day Vicki could easily pinpoint, if pressed. Her deposit slip from the bank would be time-stamped. And even if she threw the deposit slip away as she left the bank or wrapped a used piece of gum in it, the bank would have a record of her transaction. It could prove that Claire *was* at my house the day she went missing.

She had sat on my couch to interview me.

To record me!

Please, Lord, I thought, adjusting my grocery bags to flip through my keys as I moved up the sidewalk, if my couch never swallowed another thing, please let it have eaten her phone.

And the damn hammer.

. . .

UNLOCKING THE FRONT door, I turned the knob to step inside. The door remained locked. I looked down at the key to wonder why it hadn't worked. I tried it again, turning the key right instead of left. The bolt flipped with a reliable *tink*. The door opened. I stood in the threshold watching the bolt slide in and out as I turned the key several times to see if it would stick. The lock wasn't malfunctioning. I must not have locked it properly when I left. I closed the door, dropped my groceries on the floor, and crossed to the couch.

I shoved the coffee table out of the way and stood back. Bracing myself for any number of awful things hidden beneath—her hand, her ear, her gaudy pink iPhone case—I nodded my head to signal that I was ready, and then flipped up the center cushion like it was covering a basket of snakes.

A silver eye, embedded in the gray lining, blinked up at me. I nearly let out a scream, then picked up the nickel and stuck it in my pocket. I checked under the other two cushions, and then dropped to my knees to peer underneath. Bleakly satisfied that the couch's multichambered digestive system was empty, I replaced the cushions and fell back onto the couch to gather my wits—at least enough of them to think clearly. There had to be a logical explanation for how Claire went from sitting on my couch to being facedown in the woods.

It took a little doing—three beers and some serious self-delusion— but here's what I was able to convince myself of:

After I went upstairs to answer the phone, Claire probably waited all of two seconds before she took the opportunity to snoop around. Hell! I put the idea in her head! First, she peeked around the living room—looked inside a few boxes, sorted through my mail, maybe checked out Uncle Davis's desk. Then, after pausing at the bottom of the staircase to see if I was coming, she clip-clopped into the kitchen. The shock of finding death spread out on the table like Thanksgiving in hell sent her stumbling from the room. As any good reporter would, she ran to get her phone to take a few pictures and, in her haste, knocked over one of the kitchen chairs. She stopped to reset it and knocked it over again. She did this three more times based on the number of clunks and thumps I could recall hearing. Realizing she had made too much noise for me not to address it upon my return, she fled the house—where, much to her surprise, a madman jumped from the bushes, knocked her unconscious, stuffed her in the trunk of her car, and stole away with her. The End.

It could have happened that way.

It's a cruel world. Women get abducted all the time. Just because Claire was visiting a crazy woman at her haunted house on the day she mysteriously vanished didn't mean that said crazy woman had anything to do with her death.

But I wasn't just any crazy woman. I was William Wheeler's daughter, genetically predisposed to violence. I was living in the very house where my family had been butchered. I didn't run from violence; I moved into it. I made merry in it. What if Claire took a selfie with my family at the kitchen table? When her phone was found, the world would know that Baby Blue dined on death. Not to mention the trail of death that followed me here: Leah, Erin . . . and now Claire. A pattern was forming. Any lawyer worth his salt could convince a jury of that.

I could practically read the headlines: "Baby Blue Carries On Father's Legacy."

Dixie Wheeler, she's a keeler, puts your body in the freezer . . .

The kids sang that to me when I was in grade school. I had made the mistake of opting for truth over a dare during recess in the fourth grade. Of course, back then, Billy Wheeler was the keeler who put your body in the freezer—that he didn't put anything in the freezer was secondary to a good rhyme—but it was easy enough to swap his name for mine. Who knows? Maybe he did stick a body part or two in the freezer. I didn't know. When it came right down to it, I didn't know shit.

Aunt Celia never talked about what happened. Leah only had a cursory understanding of the murders, and what she did know was gleaned from newspaper headlines she read when she was nine years old. I spent most of my early childhood completely bewildered, and a little scared. Like Ford, I was picked on a lot. I always felt left out. I stood back while others played. And when I was forced to join in by a well-meaning teacher, it was always my turn in a game I knew little about. I only told the kids who I was and what happened to my family because I wanted them to like me. I didn't know it would make me easy prey for their taunts. I basically invented my father as an imaginary friend to cope. Who knew better how to chop a bully off at the knees?

By the time I became old enough to truly appreciate what hap-pened to my family, I was too busy feeling sorry for myself to delve into details. A butchered family was bloody good fodder for teenage angst, and I bathed in it regularly. I splashed it around at slumber parties. I threw it in my teachers' faces when I didn't complete a homework assignment on time. It worked like a charm every time. It wasn't until after I went through my stalking phase with Rory, which prompted some seriously overdue soul-searching, that I began to wonder what sort of impact the murders had made on my impres-sionable psyche. It took a while—a few sessions at the free clinic with a jaded shrink who always had one eye on a crossword puzzle and insisted I call him "Paul," and some aversion-therapy homework— but by the time I met Garrett, I had put it all behind me. The murders. Leah. Rory. My father. Emotionally, I was in a good place, which Gar-rett only enhanced. Yet there were moments: dark, unexpected flashes of madness that left me wondering if I had come to terms with any of it.

I remembered one movie night with Garrett, leaning forward to slice off a hunk of cheese for my cracker and wondering if I loved him enough not to stick the tiny knife in his eye. It was a fleeting, random thought, one I didn't think I would act on, but I had walked the cheese plate into the kitchen, claiming that I wanted popcorn instead. I dropped the knife in the dishwasher and shut the door, not sure if I could trust myself, not sure if I could stop myself. Had my father had that same inexplicable urge to kill? Had he been unable to stop himself?

Was that what was happening to me now?

Though Ford had once referred to my invisible scars as a "bruised aura"—a poeticism I found wholly unlike Ford, but anyway—I still thought my analogy to a suspect can of fruit was better. Just because my injuries weren't apparent on the outside didn't mean they weren't there, huddled close to the bone, burrowed in soft tissue, warping me on the inside. I was just like that expired can of peaches: You might suspect they're rotten, but until you open the can, you couldn't know for sure. Only then would you discover that the wholesome goodness you'd hoped for had grown vile.

Had Claire inadvertently opened my can that day? Slowly cranking the lever with all her questions? Did she find my sickness inside? Though I couldn't remember hurting her, maybe I had?

I checked the couch for blood, the lamp base for a wad of hair. Everything was fine. I swiped my hands in front of my face to say, *Enough!* I didn't kill Claire. I wouldn't have done something like that. I could never bludgeon anyone to death. And once I found that stupid hammer, I would almost believe it.

"You have it in you," Leah whispered.

"Dixie Wheeler, she's a keeler—"

"Shut up!" The shrill echo of my voice ran up the stairs and slammed a door. I bent over my knees to cry wholeheartedly, and to doubt myself unequivocally.

"Now, now," my father whispered after a moment. *"Don't worry. Daddy took care of it."*

"Took care of what?" I sobbed.

"The evidence."

"What evidence?"

"*The hammer. Her body. Her car . . . There's just one teeny-tiny loose end that still needs tying up.*"

"What loose end?" I asked the quiet room. "What loose end? Dad . . . *DAD!*"

I WAS ALMOST positive my father was full of shit, but until I found out exactly what had happened to Claire, I couldn't be sure. The truth of what happened had to be buried somewhere other than the back of my mind, so after an exhaustive search of the house for the missing hammer, which turned up nothing but a new level to my paranoia, I cracked open my laptop and started digging.

For as popular as I thought she was, and as salacious as her murder seemed, Claire was getting very little media attention. By sundown that evening, the news cycle had rolled on. The shooting of an off-duty police officer in Maryland, a 7.0 earthquake in South America, and the suicide of a former football player I had never heard of were receiving all the coverage. I sat through a grueling amount of commercials to live-stream the eleven o'clock news on WTTG, but the site crashed before it returned to the local news.

It was almost unbearable to think that so soon after Claire's body had been found, she had been discarded again. Of course her employer, the *Franconia Dispatch*, had the most in-depth story on her, but even that was somewhat superfluous: Claire Audrey Reynolds was a local girl. Born and raised in Franconia. Thirty-five, she was divorced with no children and lived with her best friend and stepsister, Kaylee, who declined comment. Claire graduated from George Mason and had been working as a freelance reporter for the *Franconia Dispatch* for eight years. She was an amateur golfer and loved to make people smile.

As the article turned more Tinder profile than journalistic exposé, I scrolled ahead. The article finally circled back to her murder in the last paragraph. The suggestion that the crime had been sexually motivated had me perplexed. Sexual assault didn't match my father's MO. Even if he wasn't working his evil through the puppet strings of his unsuspecting daughter, I didn't think he would go there. Maybe the editor of the *Dispatch* just presumed that a beautiful woman found dead in the woods must have endured some sort of sexual violation. The official police statement only said that her body was found in "disarray." Though that did sound lascivious, it could also mean that torn clothing had left a boob exposed, or that the body had been strewn in some provocative way. You don't end up in the woods without getting a little disarrayed. As of yet, no motive had been ascribed, sexual or otherwise. Her death was still under investigation.

Though Claire's page was private, a public memorial page had already been set up on Facebook. The page was loaded with sad emojis and inspirational quotes centered in various mood-ring colors. Most were too trite to be especially heartfelt, but at least they had made an effort. After checking out a few photos of Claire in happier times, I slipped into a steady stream of comments. Based on the annotations, one might deduce that Claire had gracefully expired on a soft bed of grass as twilight slowly settled over the meadow. There was not one mention of the brutal way she had died. One woman's post worried that a murderer was still at large, but didn't directly link this concern to Claire's death. I was halfway through when I scrolled past a name I recognized.

Rory Sellers . . .

"R.I.P. Claire."

Though others had posted nearly as glib of a sentiment, the impersonal nature of his words caused me an actual chill. The comment felt contemptuous. Mocking. "R.I.P. Claire" sounded very close to "Glad you're dead, bitch." Maybe that was just how I read it, but a comment down, Kaylee Moore wrote: "Sheer poetry, Rory. Sweet. Real sweet."

To which Rory replied: "Nice, Kaylee. Real nice. Leave it to you to pick a fight here." To which Kaylee replied: "Like you care, Rory." Someone named Donna Stringer added: "This space is for friends and family of Claire's to express their grief, all other comments are inappropriate." To which Rory replied: "Whatever, Donna. Go feed your cats."

Damn! Smack talk on a memorial page was like getting into a fist fight at a funeral: undignified, if not downright white trashy. I expanded the comments, but Donna had left Rory's feeble, yet extremely mean, rebuttal at that. Kaylee had added a cryptic apology to the chain twelve minutes later: "Sorry to all. I couldn't help myself. I'm just so upset. Claire would understand."

As I reread the exchange, a thought occurred to me. Did *Rory* kill Claire? Was he the madman who jumped from the bushes? Did he show up while I was upstairs and lure Claire away? Drag Claire away? Why would he? Because she wrote a not-so-nice article about him a few years ago? I thought back to my conversation with him about Erin. *Claire Reynolds. What a fucking cunt.* Okay. So he didn't like her. Perhaps even hated her. But was that reason enough to kill her? As much as I wanted to stamp "SOLVED" on this mystery, I couldn't see Rory as a killer. A coward, yes, but not a killer.

Achy from perching on the edge of a metal folding chair for the last two hours, I reached over my head for a stretch and pulled back a stitch in my side. I closed the screen of my HP, grabbed a beer from the fridge, and took my phone to the couch to continue my search in a prone position. As soon as my head touched the padded armrest, fatigue hit me like a rock over the head. I imagined Claire's last moments as such: desperate to stay conscious; knowing she had to keep fighting to survive, yet too weak to resist the heavenly allure of death. Though I was only fighting off a nightmare, not death—not that I knew of, anyway—that same wisp of terror found a way into my heart.

• • •

I sat up with a jolt.

The finger I had been scrolling with was over my head, sound asleep at the end of my arm. The phone lying on my belly was also asleep. I checked the time as I sat up: 2:59 a.m. I couldn't remember closing my eyes, much less sleeping for three solid hours. Murmuring voices floated out from the kitchen on the faint scent of cigarette smoke.

"Are you crazy?" my father said as I entered. My mother raised her splayed hand to quiet him. He turned to me. *"Talk some sense into this woman, would you?"*

I got a new bottle of Jack Daniel's down off the top of the refrigerator.

"Oh, so now you're giving me the silent treatment, too?"

"I don't even know what you're talking about," I said, taking a seat across from my mother. Her face was a mask of dry, cracked blood, as though she was trying out the latest in facial fad and was ready to wash.

"We gotta go shut up that neighbor of yours before she talks to the cops, and Deb here is taking some sort of moral high ground all of a sudden."

"Because it's a stupid idea," I said. "Killing Vicki's not going to solve anything. It's just going to make things worse."

"Oh, come on! Not you, too. No one will even know. Nick's not home and the kids are probably sound asleep by now. What are we talking? A woman and three little kids? A piece of cake. I could do that with my eyes closed."

"We're not killing anybody, so just shut the fuck up." I took a long shot straight from the bottle.

"So you're just going to let her call the cops? Don't be stupid. Use your head, not your twat, little girl. I thought I raised you better than that. I guess I picked the wrong kid to carry on my legacy."

"Leave her alone, Bill," my mother warned.

The top of her head flapped forward like a beaver tail as she reached across the table for the bottle of Jack Daniel's. She used the wrists of her bisected hands to draw the bottle back, then flipped the flap of scalp back with a snap of her head.

"Oh, okay, Deb," my father gibed. *"We'll just sit here and wait for the police to show up. Great idea."*

My mother gave him a tired look.

Feet slapped across the floor as Michael jumped onto my mother's lap. *"Where's Eddie's head, Mommy?"* he asked, looking up at her with wide, solemn eyes.

"Not where you'd expect to find it," she said, tweaking his nose with her flogged hand. He squirmed off her lap and crawled under the table. *"Get me a glass, would you, Bill?"*

"Women are such pussies," he said as he turned to the cabinets. *"You know she didn't even want to help me make that reporter's death look like a rape, and that was a stroke of genius."* He slammed an old, dirty mason jar on the table in front of my mother. *"A hammer is the perfect multipurpose tool. After you beat her brains in, just flip it over and go to work on her with the handle."*

"That's awful, Bill," my mother said with a low, bawdy laugh as she slowly spun the lid of the mason jar off with her chin. *"How do you come up with these things?"*

"Oh, that's not even the best part." He pretended to hook his thumbs proudly into a set of imaginary suspenders. *"Guess whose fingerprints they'll find on the hammer?"* I shook my head to make what I knew he would say next not so. *"That's right! None other than our favorite not-to-be future son-in-law, Garrett Shiftless."*

"Shifflet," my mother corrected, then tilted her head to give me a viscid wink with her gummy eyelid. *"You have to admit, Dixie, that is pretty smart."*

"Garrett had no reason to kill Claire," I said. "The police will never believe he did it."

My father rolled his eyes irascibly. *"Since when does a man need a reason to rape and kill a beautiful woman?"*

"You never did, dear," my mother said, trying to figure out how to pick up the bottle of Jack Daniel's with her banana-peel hands.

"Goddamn right, I didn't!"

"Garrett didn't rape her!" I shouted as I snatched the bottle from my mother's limp grip. I poured a shot of whiskey into her dirty jelly jar. The white label across the front was framed with a rose vine. "A Fine Pickle—1992" had been handwritten by someone either un-skilled with a pen or who had used their less dominant hand. I shook my head to make myself clear: "A coroner can tell if a woman was raped by a man or a freaking wooden stick. And a man wouldn't have to use a hammer." I slammed the bottle on the table.

My father bit his finger to appear contrite. *"I see what you mean. A man who would do something like that would have to be a real perv."* He clapped his hands to laugh. *"Even better! Or worse, if you're Garrett. Juries just hate that type of gratuitous sodomy."*

My mother raised her drink with flayed fingers. *"Amen to that."*

"GET OUT!"

I screamed so loud I woke myself up.

The kitchen was filling with budding sunlight. I glanced at the clock on the oven, but it didn't matter what time it was, or what room I had woken up in. I had made it through another night. I was just about to stand when I noticed the jar of dill pickles sitting on the table across from me. The lid was off. The juice inside was a murky brown, and more than halfway down the wedge of spears. Or halfway up, if you had a positive outlook, which I did not.

I picked up the jar to take a whiff. The combination of dill and whiskey turned me to the sink with a wretch. Though vomit tasted like a dark sour hell no matter what you ate or drank, I knew the exact flavor of boilermaker that came burning up my throat: Claussen and Old No. 7. I rested my head on the sink to spit and make sense of it.

Had I actually acted out the nightmare? Played all three roles like I was the star of a one-woman show? Had I bounced from chair to chair? Did I pace behind the table when I became my father? Drink pickle juice and whiskey as my mother? Fall gently back into myself when I needed to play yours truly? What other nightmarish deed had

I acted out? What villainous role had I played? A cold breeze found me and I looked up to see that my back door was standing wide-open.

Oh, no.

Had I gone to Vicki's as my father had suggested? Did he decide to take matters into his own hands?

What are we talking? A woman and three little kids? A piece of cake. I could do that with my eyes closed.

I rushed to the door to slam it shut on this ludicrous idea, then stopped to peek my head outside. The backyard looked normal. The neighborhood was quiet. Perhaps a little too quiet. Like all my neighbors were dead quiet. I looked down at my clothes. My jeans weren't bloody in the slightest, but I thought I had put on a pink shirt yesterday, not the green one I was currently wearing. I closed my eyes to think back. Yesterday I went to Aunt Celia's. She was sick. I made her soup. Tomato bisque with oyster crackers. I followed myself through the steps of preparing it, trying to catch a glimpse of my shirt sleeve in the process. As I reached for the milk in the refrigerator I saw that my sleeve was `... pink. Absolutely. No doubt about it. The shirt I was wearing yesterday was green ... I mean pink ... Damn. I couldn't remember. But I think I would remember if I'd snuck away from myself to murder an entire family, wouldn't I?

Sure you would.

The wind must have blown the door open.

Sure it did.

I turned to the table and picked up the jar of pickles. I held the sour stench as far from my nose as humanly possible, stepped on the lever, and dropped them in the trash can. Next to go was the Jack Daniel's—almost a full bottle—down the drain.

10

I washed my face in ice-cold water, brushed my teeth until I spit blood, and then squeezed half a bottle of Visine into my eyes. Redressed in semiclean clothes I dug from my hamper, I started back downstairs to fix myself a bowl of Tums and Pepto-Bismol. I was passing the linen closet when I noticed light seeping out from under the door. The last time I had been in the attic was the day Claire stopped by. Though I couldn't remember clicking off the light as I dropped back into the closet, I thought I would have noticed the light under the doorway before now. I had been up and down the hallway dozens of times since then.

Inside the closet, a shaft of light fell from the trapdoor in the ceiling like the portal of an alien spaceship. I stood in the ray and lifted my face, prepared for it to pull me up like a tractor beam. I gave it a good minute to take hold, then started to climb.

Glancing down to make sure my foot had a secure position on the next shelf up, I clambered to a seated position on the rim of the scuttle door. Before I stood, I looked down at the eight-foot drop, figuring if I fell through the ceiling halfway across, I would most likely land on, or somewhere close to, the bed in the master bedroom. Falling through into the hallway wouldn't be any fun, but it probably wouldn't kill me. Real danger came from landing on the hard edge of the sink in the hallway bathroom, but if I stayed left, I should be able to avoid disaster.

I started a slow, careful crawl toward the boxes against the far back wall, avoiding the bed-frame obstacle course, and wondering if willfully crawling around the attic of a haunted house wasn't the epitome of stupid. But in my current state, I couldn't fathom becoming more frightened than I already was, and pressed on.

I was halfway across when the doorbell *pwing-pwonged*. Instantaneously, the overhead bulb winked out. The electrical system must have a short in it, I thought as I looked back at the dim square in the floor ten feet behind me. Just enough light was leaking into the closet from the hallway to stave off utter blackness. "Hold on!" I called out as the doorbell sounded three impatient but chirpy dings. I retraced my crawl backward until my toe dipped into a puddle of air. I swiveled around, and stuck my head through the opening. I thought of Claire absently opening the front door to let in her would-be killer, and wondered if I should be so careless. I tapped the rim with one fingernail as I contemplated the drop back into the closet, and yelled "COME IN!" as loud as I could.

"Dixie?" The voice that rose from below was male, familiar, but as it traveled up the stairs, down the hallway, and into the closet, it became unrecognizable. I called out for verbal identification. The front door clunked closed without a reply. I held my breath as footsteps rose slowly up the staircase. Two sets? I lowered my head farther into the closet to listen. Josh's door creaked open and shut. A moment later, a shadow passed casually in front of the linen closet on its way down the hall.

"Here," I said, hoping the lumbering shape was Garrett. "I'm in the attic."

The shadow backed up, and Rory leaned in to smile up at me.

"Hey," I said, lying flat on my belly and hanging my chin over the edge. I tried to keep my expression neutral, but my voice had an uncertain quiver I could not contain. "What are you doing here?"

"I thought you wanted me to do that," he said.

"I didn't think you were coming back."

He gave a listless shrug. "Sorry if I freaked out on you. I know you're just trying to find out what happened to your family. You have enough to worry about without me giving you shit. And I'm sorry if I messed things up between you and Garrett." He held up a hand to stop a demurral I wasn't about to give. "Don't worry, I parked way down the street this time, just in case he stops by again."

I grinned dejectedly. "Thanks, but I don't think Garrett's gonna stop by any time soon."

"He will if he's got half a brain in his head." He lifted the corner of a throw blanket on the center shelf, then smoothed it flat. "He wouldn't have gotten so pissed about me being here if he wasn't crazy about you."

"Is somebody with you?" I asked. "I thought I heard someone come up the stairs behind you."

He shrugged. "Just me. It must have been an echo. Or a ghost." My frown made him laugh. "So, did you find anything good up there?"

I glanced over my shoulder. "Um, just some boxes. I'm not sure what's in them."

"You want some help?" he asked.

I nodded, though my gut was telling me to vomit on his head instead. I swallowed hard to say, "Will you run down to the kitchen and get the flashlight that's on top of the fridge? The bulb just went out up here."

He nodded once and disappeared into the hallway.

I lay there wondering if I should have invited a man I loosely suspected of murder to join me in the perfect place to hide a dead body. Regardless of what my father would have me believe, Claire Reynolds's homicide was still an open investigation. Who's to say that Rory didn't kill her? I couldn't, not to any degree of certainty, and I had spent the better part of my life in love with the man. There was so much I didn't know about Rory. His callous comments on Claire's memorial page hit the back of my mind like a barrage of spit-balls: *R.I.P. Claire. Go feed your cats. Nice. Real nice.* Rory had lied about being in the house the day of the murders. What else has he lied about?

I took the flashlight as he entered the closet and held it up to me.

"Move over. Here I come," he said.

As I pushed back onto my knees, my hand fell on a long section of the metal bed frame stretched out on the floor behind me. The scraping sound of metal on metal zinged the fillings in my back teeth.

In two quick moves Rory was sitting on the ledge, facing me. He leaned forward to kiss my cheek, and in a flash, my mind pulled him on top of me and sprawled us onto the plywood floor. I shook my head as I waved a hand to show him around.

"Welcome to my attic," I said.

He pivoted to get a look behind. "Wow. This brings back memories. Josh and I used to come up here and party all the time." He pointed to the back wall. "We'd blow smoke out that vent up there."

The cocoon of a dead insect dropped onto the part in Rory's hair. I looked up at a torn cobweb hanging low over our heads, dotted with tiny cotton candy mummies. That Rory was not aware that he had a dead thing on him made me question his sanity. I once had seen a guy in McDonald's with a dead roach stuck to the back of his shirt and left the restaurant before he could whip a gun from his knapsack and kill everyone in sight.

"I guess you heard about Claire Reynolds?" he said suddenly.

Though I had expected us to get around to Claire in due course, the question caught me off guard.

"What do you mean?" I said.

"She died."

I covered my mouth to appear shocked. "What happened?"

"I'm surprised you didn't hear about it. It's been all over the news."

"I haven't connected my cable yet," I said. "I haven't watched TV since I moved in. Was she in a car accident or something?"

He raised his eyebrows to shake his head, and the fuzzy fibroin sac trundled down his cheek and onto his shoulder. He flicked it away to say, "She was murdered. They found her body in the woods behind Pronto's Pizza off of Old Keene Mill Road. She was beaten to death."

"Oh, my god!" I gasped. "That's awful. Pronto's is only a couple of miles from here."

"Less than that, actually. She'd been missing for a couple of days. They just found her body yesterday."

Though I thought I already knew the answer to this, I had to ask, "When was the last time anybody saw her alive?"

"Monday, I think. She checked in at her office that morning, and then went out to follow up on a story. That's the last time anyone saw her alive. I can't believe it. I mean, Claire and I had our differences, but I always thought she was a good person under that tough-as-nails act she put on. I didn't like some of the stuff she wrote about me, about Erin, but I never wished her any harm. She was actually pretty cool."

For a fucking cunt, I almost added to remind him of what he really thought of Claire Reynolds, but instead said, "I didn't know her well enough to say. Do they know who did it?"

He shook his head. "Just some pervert, I guess."

A man who would do something like that would have to be a real perv.

"That's horrible," I said. "Poor Claire."

"I know. It's hard to believe. We just saw her the other day. Who could have imagined that something like this would have happened to her?"

A long moment passed as we mulled over this rhetorical question.

"So!" He slapped his hands together and I gasped. He laughed and touched my knee. "Sorry. Didn't mean to scare you. Was there something up here you wanted?"

"Oh . . . um . . . I don't know. I haven't had a chance to look around yet." I pointed to the back wall. "You don't think there's a chance that any of those boxes are from when my family lived here, do you?"

He squinted at them. "No way. Not after all this time. The people who lived here before you must have left them behind. Wait here and I'll check them out."

He collided with a rafter as he stood. "Shit! Now I remember why Josh decided against living up here." He gave the girder a punch to show it who was boss, then started off toward the back at a quick pace, hopscotching the bed frame without a single worry that he might fall through the thin flooring. He jumped to slap the highest joist and missed. A wooden plank slammed up a cloud of dust as he landed. I clutched my head to ready myself for him to disappear in a cloud of dust.

"Stop!" I cried. "You're going to fall through!"

"Don't worry." He laughed. "The boards are resting on the ceiling beams. It's strong. But if you step off the side, you might fall through." He pointed to a shore of pink fluff next to the boardwalk. "That's just insulation on top of drywall." He headed farther back. "Man, there's all sorts of stuff back here. I can drag it over if you want to go through it."

As I got to my knees, I glanced through the hatch to consider a last-chance jump to safety. I knew I was being completely irrational. If either one of us was a killer, it was me, but I couldn't shake the doomy chill—chillier than the attic air—that something bad was going to happen if I stayed up here much longer.

"Just stay there," Rory said, sliding the boxes around. "You don't have to come back here if you're scared. It looks like a bunch of crap, anyway."

I got to my feet, clicked on the flashlight, and walked an imaginary tightrope across the attic. Rory looked up from the box he was resetting as I came to his side.

"What's in them?" I asked, smoothing imagined cobwebs from my hair.

"Ah . . . This one feels like a bunch of books."

I pointed the flashlight at the box as he pulled open the quarter fold.

"Are they ours?" I asked, tilting my head to read the titles. "I mean, my family's?"

"Dunno." He wriggled one of the books out and tapped the cover. "Hey, I've read this one. John Grisham, *The Firm*. It's really good."

"What?" I snatched the book from his hands. "I'm reading this exact book right now." I set the flashlight in a V of crossbeams in the wall, and flipped to the page I had left off on to see if it was folded down. It wasn't, but there was a thin crease in the paper from where it once had been. "Wow. That's so weird." My fingers trembled as I set the book on the floor by my feet. "What's in the other boxes?"

Rory opened the next box. It was full of miscellaneous household items: empty picture frames, a handful of chopsticks banded together with a purple hair tie, a can of Off bug spray, an old alarm clock, which, strangely enough, appeared to be right on time. A few small appliances and gadgets—a space heater, a dehumidifier, and a home karaoke machine—were tucked away in their original packaging. The final box was the largest. Lidless, it was stuffed with a navy-blue-and-gray-checked comforter that smelled like it had been packed away wet. The comforter kind of looked like one Garrett had had on his bed when we first started dating.

"Aw, Garrett had a comforter just like this," I said in a misty voice. "I wonder if I can get it clean enough to use again."

Rory kicked the box aside to pull forward the karaoke machine. "Fuck that, let's karaoke!"

"Hold on," I said, stepping around him to lift the corner of the comforter with two fingers. Something clunked to the bottom of the box.

"What was that?" Rory asked.

"I don't know."

As I fingered the comforter aside to get to the bottom of it, the

pink sequins of Claire's iPhone case shimmered up like a hunk of quartz on the side of a cave, then slipped under a fold of darkness. I wanted to reach down and grab it, hold it up to the light and give it a good scream, but I was momentarily paralyzed. *How the hell did Claire's phone get in my attic?* Maybe it wasn't her phone. Maybe it wasn't even *a* phone. I didn't get a good look at it before it fell away. It could be some other type of pink case . . . shaped exactly like an iPhone. As Rory leaned forward, I pressed the comforter down as deep as it would go and nudged the box against the wall.

"What was in there?" he asked.

"Nothing. Let's go," I said, turning away. "I hate it up here."

"Don't you want any of this stuff?" he said.

"Nah. It's just junk. I've got enough of that as it is. I'll throw it away later." I got on my knees to crawl back to the hatch "I'm starving. Let's get some lunch."

"Let's go ahead and bring it down now," Rory said. "I don't want you trying to do it yourself after I leave."

"I won't," I said, sliding the first piece of bed frame out of my way. "I'll call a company to haul it away. Come on. I'll make us some sand-wiches."

"Don't be silly. Why pay someone when I can take care of it right now?"

"Just leave it," I said sharply. I was about to apologize for snapping at him, and to nicely ask him to grab the flashlight, when my tongue froze along with the rest of me.

You know the sound of impending disaster when you hear it: screeching tires, the low growl of a dog, the cock of a shotgun, the rattle of a snake . . . a gasp as the iPhone of a murdered woman is found hidden beneath an old blue comforter in your attic.

RELAXING MY EXPRESSION as best I could while holding my breath, I turned to face up to reality, which, ironically, was the

realization I was completely insane. Rory had Claire's phone pinched between two fingers like a set mousetrap.

"Where did this come from?" he asked.

I shook my head.

He turned the phone over in his hand. "This is Claire's phone."

"It can't be," I said definitively.

He nodded slowly. "Sure it is. I saw her with it the day she was here. What are you doing with it?"

I opened my mouth to begin a lie, but I wasn't exactly sure where the lie began. How far back did I have to go? How much did I have to explain? Which particular lie would justify all the others?

Rory pressed the Home button on the phone. "It's dead," he proclaimed. The spray of light from the flashlight drenched over him like hot wax, glowing yellow and rendering his expression inanimate, but did not reach the hollow of his eyes, the deep crease across his forehead, or the grim line of his lips.

"Did you . . . kill Claire?" he asked.

A breathless whine was all I could summon in my defense.

"Then why is her phone hidden in your attic?"

"I-I don't know how that got there," I stammered. "I swear I don't."

Rory drew a long breath that seemed to double him in size, and slanted an eye toward me. "Claire had her phone with her when she left here that day. She texted me that night, so I know she didn't leave it here by mistake." Understanding came to him in the form of a nod. "You were the story she was following up on the day she went missing. She came back here . . . and you killed her."

"I didn't kill her," I said, backing slowly away as his stare grew hot enough to burn. "You did!"

"What? That's bullshit! I didn't kill Claire."

Something about the way his eyes darted left told me he was lying.

"Yes, you did! And you put her phone in that box. You had time to do it before I crawled across the attic to you."

A fleeting smile gave way to a puzzled look from him. "Why would I do that?"

"To frame me." I pointed a finger at him. "You're the one who hated Claire. Not me. You're the one who lies! You're the one who hides! You're the one nobody trusts!"

He blinked hard and shook his head. "What are you even talking about?"

I wasn't exactly sure, but I had to buy time to think. "You know exactly what I'm talking about, Rory."

He held up a hand. "You know what? I'm not going to play these games with you, Dixie. I'll just give the phone to the police and they can figure out what happened to Claire."

He moved to step around me and I blocked his way.

"I don't think you want to do that," I said, surprised how strong and calm my voice was. "I'll tell the police what you said about her. How you called her a fucking cunt."

"Go ahead. Once they find out who you are, and get a load of this house, they won't believe a fucking word you say." He tried to step around me again and I blocked him.

"Then I'll tell them about Erin."

He stepped back. "Tell them what?"

"That you killed her."

His shocked expression was slightly amused: "Why would they believe you? You didn't even know her."

"Oh, yes, I did." I wasn't sure where I was going with this, and I was too tired to see my next step well enough to know it wouldn't land squarely in my mouth, but I needed to stop him from taking Claire's phone to the police. It proved that Claire was in my house the day she went missing. Who knew what it had recorded while I was unconscious. Just because I woke at the bottom of the staircase didn't mean I hadn't moved a muscle. And let's not forget Garrett's missing hammer. The perfect multipurpose tool. *After you beat her brains in, just flip it over and go to work on her with the handle.* I had neglected the attic when I conducted my search of the house. Since the attic hadn't been cleared, I couldn't definitely say that the phone, and most likely the hammer, hadn't been here prior to Rory's arrival. I hadn't seen the hammer in the box with the phone, but there were other boxes. Until I knew for certain the hammer wasn't in one of them, I couldn't let him go to the police.

Blackmail was my only option.

With what little confidence I had, I jutted out my chin and stepped up on him. "Erin told me all about you, Rory. You weren't very nice to her, were you?" This was a guess, but if his expression was any indicator, it was a good one. "I think the police would be very interested to know that."

His smirk receded under narrowing eyes. "What are you talking about? You never even met Erin."

"Strawberry blonde. Really thin and pretty. She worked at that jewelry store downtown. Silver Thyme. Like the spice."

He snuffed. "You could have read that in the papers."

"I've been to her apartment, Rory." His expression doubted this. "Nine hundred Kenner Avenue? Apartment 3D? Around the back? There was a front entrance, but you couldn't get to her apartment from it. Once they finished remodeling the foyer, they were going to put in an elevator up to her floor, but until then, you had to use the back stairs to get to it. Twenty-three steps. Twenty-four, if you count the top landing."

He searched my face as though it were made of millions of baby spiders, but still his eyes refused to see what lay underneath.

"I'm Debbie, Rory. The mysterious friend Erin told you about? Debbie was my mother's name." I licked off a sneer as the corner of my lip trembled. "I thought you might have figured that one out a long time ago."

The absolute horror in Rory's expression disabused any suspicion

I had that he might have killed Erin. I closed my eyes on a screaming headache, and the night Erin died tumbled down the stairs before me. The spill of flaxen hair and sky blue socks that went on and down for longer than the staircase itself; the sickening *whack* of bone off of every other cement step; the odd twist of limbs that came to rest at the bottom. My wristlet, which I had returned for after forgetting it on her kitchen table earlier that evening, lay on the twelfth step down, zipped open with my driver's license exposed.

Before, the only thing I had ever recalled about that night was regaining consciousness in an alleyway about a block from her apartment building. Curled up next to a dumpster and wondering if I had been mugged. My head felt like it had been bonked with a lead pipe, but all my money and credit cards were safely tucked in my wristlet, which was lying just beyond the reach of my fingers. I convinced myself that I had passed out on my way home. That fourth margarita had been a big mistake. Mortified that I had gotten so drunk that I couldn't remember leaving Erin's apartment, I never called her again. I read about her accident, and her consequent death, in the paper days later, but I never made the connection, or refused to see it, if there was one.

The memory of that night, and what had happened, had been suppressed so deep that when I opened my eyes to look upon Rory's horror-struck expression, I let out a huge sigh of relief. The splinter had finally been extracted.

"You killed Erin." Rory stated this like the answer to a complex mathematical equation he had finally solved. He grabbed a handful of his forehead, seeming to want to rip off his own face. "Why?" he cried. "Because you were jealous of her?!"

"No," I tried. "I didn't mean to. It was an—"

"Are you really that fucking demented?"

"Let me explain. Please!"

"Explain what? That you're a fucking lunatic? That you pretended to be your dead mother to get close to my girlfriend? That you—" He barked a horrified laugh. "I can't even say it!" He covered his mouth to ask: "Did you kill Erin so you could be with me?"

"No!"

He looked right through me to see a memory more clearly. "You were the girl I saw walking away from Erin's building." He held me so tight with his eyes that I could almost feel him tremble. "How did you even meet her? Were you following me? Did you follow me to her apartment so you could kill her?"

"No! It wasn't like that. Erin was my friend."

"*Friend!*" he shrieked. He shook Claire's phone at me. "Were you Claire's friend, too, Dixie? Did you get it in your head that we were dating and kill her, just like you killed Erin?"

"No!" I put up my hands to defuse the accusation. "I didn't kill anyone. I wouldn't do that!"

"Bullshit!" He leaned forward to hack the word in my face. "You killed them both! Stop fucking lying!"

"Why would I kill them, Rory?" I asked with a frank dubiety I couldn't believe I was able to summon with his wet spittle on my cheek.

"Because you're a *Fatal Attraction* bunny-boiling bitch!"

"Don't you mean cunt?"

"You couldn't stand that I didn't want to be with you. You couldn't stand that I was in love with somebody else, so you—"

"YOU DIDN'T LOVE THEM!" I roared. "You don't love anyone but yourself! You hated Claire. If either one of us wanted her dead, it was you! You killed her! Admit it!"

"I didn't kill anyone. I could never do something like that. But you . . . ?" He shook his head to glance down at Claire's phone clutched in his hand, bobbing it gently, as if to weigh its importance. "I didn't want to do this. But now I know what you are. What you're capable of. What you did to Erin. I don't give a fuck what happens to you. I hope you fry in the electric chair."

"What exactly didn't you want to do, Rory? Love me? Help me? Understand me?!" I shoved him in the chest with both hands. He stepped unsteadily back into the boxes, knocking one off its perch. A spill of books tumbled to the floor, but he kept his footing. "You never loved me! You never cared about me!" I shoved him again as I advanced, but he was ready for it this time and held strong. My wrist stung as it collided with a wall of flexed muscle. "You're just a fucking ASSHOLE!"

He bumped hard into my shoulder as he shoved past me. The pain in my wrist shot up my arm and spun me to my knees. Hair hung over my face in a sweaty drape as I watched him float away through a vapor of tears. He skirted the deconstructed bed frame on his way across the attic.

"Fuck you, Rory!" I screamed.

"You know," he said with a nasty lilt as he came to a stop over the lighted portal, "I think I will talk to that cop of yours after all. I bet he'd be very interested to know where I found this." He held up the phone.

"No, wait!" I started forward and tripped back onto my knees. Two lengths of bed frame clapped together. "Please don't!" I cried. "I'm sorry!"

He turned so that he only had to half look at me. "Is that what Erin said before you pushed her down the stairs?"

"I didn't push her! We were arguing and . . ." The entire evening came rushing back. When I knocked on the door to say that I had forgotten my wristlet on her table, Erin held out my driver's license to me. "Forget this, *Debbie*?" An argument ensued. She grabbed me by the arm as I turned to leave, and when I swung around . . . "She fell! It was an accident. I swear!"

With his back to me, he shook his head, staring down into the linen closet through the hatch of light. "How could you just leave her lying there, Dixie? You of all people."

I was about to scream, to tear at my hair, to beat my fists on my chest, anything to stop him from leaving, when the shadows on the attic floor gathered together and rose before me. I stumbled back in horror as the shadow rolled up a head from its thick shoulders and unfurled its long arms in a rousing stretch. I had seen this phenomenon once before: out of the long shadows that fell across Leah's sickbed.

"You're sick, Dixie," he said as the dark shape picked up a length of the scattered bed frame. Though it made a faint *clank*, Rory did not look back. "Sick in the head. Just like . . . your father." The shadowy figure crept forward to line the end of the rod up with Rory's skull. "I knew you had psychological problems, but I didn't get just how sick you were." The rod swung back. "I actually might feel sorry for you, if you weren't so fucking pathet—"

The flat side of the U-shaped steel rod hit Rory just above the back of his right ear. The reverberating crack bounded across the ceiling and down the length of my spine.

For a moment, Rory just stood there, teetering on the rim of the hatch. I thought he might fall headfirst into the closet, but then he gave a series of quick twitches that turned him in a staggering circle. Blinking fast as if to see me through the smoky visage that stood between us, he opened his mouth in a yawning way that might produce a sneeze.

"*Dix-ssiee*," he said in a voice that was unbearably slow and low, "*Whah—?*"

The bed frame struck the side of his face with a stiff *whap!* A mouth-sized flap of skin dropped open just below his left cheekbone. Blood slobbered from the heavy lip as he shook off the wallop. Finally realizing a fight was at hand, Rory dropped Claire's phone and clenched his fists.

The next blow struck Rory across the sweep of his superior jawline. His eyes followed the splash of blood through the air, then

widened to maintain focus as he turned back. The way he was con-
centrating on the tip of his nose suggested that that was the extent
of his vision. With a bullish, defiant snort, he began throwing le-
thargic punches at the air, shadowboxing well short of his opponent.
When his left jab failed to connect, and his uppercut landed in the
air over his head, he reached back for a roundhouse punch. The
swing sent him stumbling to his knees. As if to prove he could hurt
something if just given half a chance, he punched one of the wood
planks that comprised the floor. The solid crack instantly registered
on his face. The cry he let out was so fraught with pain and desperation that my heart crawled off into my stomach to hide.

Moving with the excruciatingly slow determination of someone
stuck in fast-drying cement, he dragged his feet under him to get to a
stand. The next strike was more of a tap than a swing, but it split his
forehead and drove him back to his knees. A crick of blood ran down
his brow, bisecting his face, as if the graze had cut him in two.

I wanted to help him, knew that I must, but I had fallen through
the thin ice of sanity and was being swept away in a current of hope-
lessness. There was nothing left to cling to, no hand to reach out for,
no solid ground to crawl upon; I could only slap my hands against the
inescapable certainty that I was now, and forevermore, lost. I needed
to find a way back. But the hole I had dropped through was too far
behind to ever be found again. I could only watch what was happening up on the surface with wide, horrified eyes as a cold, savage tor-
rent stripped the last ounce of warmth from my heart.

Rory pressed to a shaky stand. He raised his hand to ask for a
time-out, a courtesy nine-count—just a fucking moment, please—
but this was a lawless fight, not gentlemanly at all, and the bladed cleft
of the bed rail came down hard, parting his hair just above his right
ear. A chunk of scalp fell over like the unsnapped flap. Rory took a
weak half punch at the air, staggered forward, and then dropped to
his knees.

The three-inch, steel-footed plate took a chunk from the rafter as the rod reared back for its final blow. As the endcap connected with the top of Rory's head, I screamed, but I was too late: Rory fell forward to the floor with a hard, lifeless *thump*, another stupid cow taken down by a malignant parasite he couldn't see.

"Damn!" my father exclaimed as he chucked the metal rod at the floor, rattling the other pieces of bed frame into a galvanized round of applause. *"That boy just didn't want to go down."*

11

The screaming in my head didn't stop until I fell through the trap-door of the attic and onto my side in the linen closet. I lay there for several minutes, praying that I had broken my neck in the fall, but when I was able to cross my fingers to hope to die, I got up and started screaming for real.

Tripping headlong down the hallway, I slid down the staircase on my belly, then crawled to a stumbling run when I hit the landing. I lapped the coffee table until I got light-headed, then sank down on the couch for half a second before I sprang up the stairs again. I got as far as the linen closet, did an about-face, and slid down the stair-case again. I performed this hysterical, yet somehow oddly comfort-ing, ritual three more times before I landed in the kitchen. I grabbed Jack Daniel's by the throat, but the bottle was dry, so I smashed it into the corner next to the trash can.

"What the hell!" I screamed.

The terror in my voice rebounded off the newly wallpapered kitchen and slapped me across the face like a cold hand. I had to calm down. This was no time to panic. This was time for composed, ratio-nal thought, but all I could think was *what the hell, what the hell, what the hell* and—most helpful of all—*what the fucking hell!*

I couldn't lose control. Not yet. Too many things needed to be done. I had to come up with a way to bring the dead back to life. No. That wouldn't do. Rory wouldn't be right. Not to mention how angry he would be. Reanimating him might create a whole host of other problems. I had to think logically . . . Time travel? That might work. All I had to do was go back in time and not invite Rory into the attic like a complete fucking idiot. There had to be a way to hack into the space-time continuum with the limited household supplies I had on hand. I started opening drawers to take stock: measuring cups, a muffin tin, cheese grater, melon baller, oven mitts. Yay! I slipped them over my hands, sank to the floor, and covered my face to think, think, think . . .

"Dad, you fucking asshole!" I screamed at the ceiling as I threw my head back. "Why did you do that? I didn't need your help! I didn't want you to kill him, you stupid fucking—*AH!* You need to fix this right now!" I stomped the floor three times to summon him. "Where are you? Show yourself, motherfucker!"

When no response came, I ran to the living room, jumped onto the couch, curled my knees to my chin, and did the only thing I could think of to set the world right again: cry myself to sleep. It took a while to relax enough to forget that a man I had once groped in a movie theater had just been beaten to death in the attic of my child-hood home by the ghost of my dead father, but I was too exhausted to remain conscious for long.

The dream tiptoed in like Santa toward a warm plate of cookies. Leah was sitting with my mother and Aunt Celia, chatting and snapping fresh green beans into a bowl in the center of the kitchen table. Leah's long hair was held back in two French braids that met in a loose ponytail at the base of her skull. I flicked one of her braids as I passed, and she called me a brat in a way that made me laugh. I gave my mother a kiss on her cheek and stole her glass of wine. I turned the glass to avoid the burnt-orange lip prints and found them on the other side of the brim as well. I set the glass in the sink next to a ma-son jar. As I started the faucet, laughter floated through the window from the backyard. I caught sight of a red sweater a second before it disappeared up a tree. I could hear Michael counting off the allotted time to hide, but I couldn't see where he was. As it occurred to me that I should not be older than my older brothers, Garrett leaned in to kiss my cheek. He squeezed my shoulders with a promise to be back soon. Though they were not present, I intuitively knew that Rory was still alive somewhere, Ford was long gone after a pack of cigarettes, and my father had committed a solitary suicide before I was born. I didn't miss these gruff men, these harbingers of woe. *"Better off without them,"* my mother mused as I looked back at the table of fine women behind me. They are my strength, my love, what matters, and I am so grateful to have them here to help me prepare for our Thanksgiving feast. The timer on the oven sounded. Time to baste. I slipped on my oven mitts and lowered the oven door. An exhale of heat wafted up a heavenly aroma. The stuffing was golden brown and sumptuous in Eddie's open mouth.

I blinked at the back of the couch as my eyes popped open. Mildew and Febreze. I rubbed a sneeze from my nose. Semicognizant that my pillow had miraculously appeared under my head, but too grateful for the comfort to be altogether concerned about how it got there, I nestled down to sleep some more. I wanted to restart the dream from the beginning. I hadn't seen Leah's face, only the side of her cheek, skin flat where her nose should have been.

"Get up, Dixie."

I shooed away whoever said that with a listless wave of my hand.

"You have to take care of this."

I shook my head.

"Look at me, young lady."

I rolled over with one open eye. My mother's arms were folded against her stomach, mangled fingers hanging limp at her elbows like juicy tentacles.

"You need to bury him," she said, nodding at the ceiling.

"Uh-uh."

"You can't just leave him up there to rot."

"Sure I can."

"He'll start to smell."

"I don't care."

She paced away, then turned back. *"What if Garrett comes over? What then?"*

"I—don't—CARE!"

She tapped her foot. *"We haven't gone through all this just for you to end up in jail. Now get up and get going. Don't make me count to ten."*

"That won't work on me," I said, swinging my feet to the floor. "I'm an adult now."

"Then act like it!"

My phone vibrated the coffee table as it rang. A zing of fear traveled up the length of my spine, flew out my mouth, and scared off my mother. As the phone quivered toward the edge of the table, I bent forward to read the caller ID.

Stanley Cullins.

Shit.

"Hello," I whispered.

"Dixie?"

"Yeah?"

"Is everything okay?" he asked. "Did something happen?"

"What?" I sat up straight. "No. Why would you think something happened?"

"No reason, I guess." He hesitated. "I was just kind of wondering about that dinner you were going to make for me. That was supposed to be tonight, right?"

"Oh, Mr. Cullins! I'm so sorry! Something came up and I totally forgot."

"That's okay," he said. "I just wanted to make sure nothing happened to you."

"No. Nothing happened. I'm fine. I'm just so sorry I forgot."

"Don't worry about it. We can do it another time."

"I'd like that."

"Me, too." Silence intruded upon the conversation until he cleared his throat to say, "Oh, hey, I meant to ask: Did Rory change his mind about talking to me?"

"No!" The exclamation was impulsive. "I mean, no. I haven't seen Rory since . . . I mean . . . You know what, I don't think he's going to change his mind about talking to you, but thanks anyway."

"I can reach out to him myself. Sometimes people just need a nudge to start talking. I won't come down hard on him. I promise."

The bed frame came down hard and . . .

"No, I . . . We worked it out. It was all just a misunderstanding. Sorry. I should have let you know."

"Oh," he said, disappointed. "I was kinda looking forward to wearing my detective's hat again. It's just like the one Sherlock Holmes wears." He paused to share a chuckle that I failed to take part in. "You sure you don't want me to check in with him? I don't mind."

"Yes. I'm sure." I immediately regretted the clipped tone I had used with him, but I needed to end the call before a flood of tears disintegrated the brave face I was putting on. I added a polite "Thank you" as reinforcement, but there was an unsteady shudder to it.

"You okay?" he asked.

"Yes."

"You want to come over? I'm not much of a cook, but I can order a mean pizza. Any kind you want. Just no green peppers."

"Thanks, but can I take a rain check? I'm kind of busy."

"Oh, sure," he said. "Whattaya got going on? Something fun, I hope."

I looked toward the attic as the first teardrops broke through my resolve. I gasped them back to say, "It's just not a good time, Mr. Cullins."

"Did something happen, Dixie? Are you okay?"

"I'm fine. It's just . . . Garrett and I broke up." It was all I could think to say.

"That's your boyfriend, right?"

I squeaked an affirmative.

"Oh, jeez. Well, I guess those things happen, right? I mean . . . Well, shit, Dixie. That sucks."

"Thank you," I sniveled.

"Why don't you come over and watch the game with me? We can drink beers and rag on him. I don't know the guy, but I'm guessing he's a real jerk if he made you cry."

His awkward attempt at sympathy finally broke the dam, and I burst into uncontrollable tears.

"Oh, now," he soothed. I could envision him twisting back and forth in his kitchen, looking for a way out of this conversation, turning from Pepper's empty bed as his eyes fell upon it. The thought of Pepper made me cry harder. "Don't cry, Dixie. Men are assholes. I should know."

"You're not an asshole," I sobbed, wiping snot onto the back of my sleeve. "You're the nicest man I've ever met."

"Well . . . I don't know about that," he stammered. "You sure you don't want to come over?"

"No, thank you," I said. "I'm fine. Really. Don't worry about me. It's nothing I haven't been through before."

"Well, okay, then." His tone seemed unconvinced, but the sigh he let out immediately after was eager to accept my assurances. "I guess I'll let you get back to . . . it . . . whatever . . . Okay, I'll talk to you later."

I hung up and cried myself back into a headachy half sleep. When I woke, Eddie was standing over me, running a matchbox car up the length of his arm. He made a *brrr*-ing motor sound with his lips as he steered the yellow convertible across his chest. When he noticed that I was watching him, he dropped the toy to his side.

"Mom says get up," he said.

"Go away, Eddie." I swiped a hand through his belly and made him disappear for a second. The vibration it caused made my fingers itch. I scrubbed the sensation away on the carpet as my hand fell to the floor.

"You have to. Mom says."

When I hissed to shoo him away, he rolled his eyes impatiently. His right eye took a little longer to reach its mark than his left. For a second he was looking both up and down. I covered my head with my arms to block him out.

"Just leave him," I moaned. "I'll do it later."

"You'll get in troub-bbble." A wet, bloody raspberry blew from a flap of skin under his chin.

"No, I won't."

"Mom says you're a baddy just like Daddy."

Michael skipped through the living room singing, *"Dixie's a baddy, Dixie's a baddy, Dixie's a baddy . . . "*

"No, I'm not!" I screamed. "Go away!"

"They're right, sweetheart," my father said. I peeked under my arm to find him with his hand on Eddie's shoulder. He must have bumped into him, because Eddie's head was slipping slowly across his shoulder like a slug. *"You are just like me. We're cut from the same cloth. It's not our fault it's an old burlap sack covered in shit."* He chuckled as he straightened Eddie's head. *"Now, I admit this has all gotten a wee bit out of hand, but let's not waste time blaming each other. There's work to be done. So, get your ass up and bury that boy."*

"NO!"

"Do it like I told you," Leah said as she appeared at the foot of the couch. The left top side of her bald head had caved in. *"Just play dumb. It worked last time, remember? They didn't know you killed me. They won't know you killed him, either."*

"I didn't kill him!" I screamed as I pushed through my father and Eddie to get off the couch. The sensation was like jumping through a sprinkler of novocaine. I rubbed it from my arms as I entered the kitchen. My mother looked up as I entered. For a second I thought it was Rory sitting on the stove to my right, banging his heels on the small glass oven window. Blood bisected Josh's face in much the same way. He offered me a brain-dead grin and nodded a flap of hair to offer me his seat, which my mother had kicked away from the table with her foot. I ignored them as I turned to the refrigerator. Eddie's screaming head was centered on the shelf. I reached through his open mouth to get a beer out from behind.

"I only did what you wanted me to do," my father said, leaning against the sink. Eddie's headless body stumbled to the floor beside him and stretched out its legs. *"You can't go acting all high and mighty about it now."*

"I didn't want you to kill Rory, you fucking maniac!"

"And what would you have done? Let him go to the police? Let him talk to that detective of yours? Come on, little girl. Use your head, not your twat."

"You already used that line," I reproved. "It wasn't clever or funny then, and it isn't clever or funny now."

"I thought I raised you better than this." He shook his head despondently. *"I guess I picked the wrong kid to carry on my legacy."*

"Leave her alone, Bill," my mother warned.

Wait, I thought, looking around. *This already happened.*

"Oh, okay, Deb," my father said on cue, fluttering his hands. *"We'll just let him rot up there until the health department shows up. Great idea."*

I held my head to steady the dizzying moment of déjà vu. The tired look my mother gave my father was exactly the same as she had given him the night before. I counted down to await Michael's feet slapping across the floor.

Three, two, one—

Michael jumped onto my mother's lap. *"Where's Eddie's head, Mommy?"*

She tweaked his nose with her flayed hand. *"Not where you'd expect to find it."*

This was a dream. I could get out of it if I wanted. All I had to do was—

"GET OUT!" I screamed.

I WOKE, STILL on the couch. Night had fallen. Someone was knocking at the door. Groggily, I got to my feet, praying that it would be Rory and what had happened in the attic had been only a nightmare, just one of many. My heart skipped across my vision as I pressed my eye to the peephole. When I saw who was standing on the other side, I knew I must be dreaming. I opened the door a crack.

"I thought I'd bring the party to you," Mr. Cullins said as he held up a pizza box. "I wasn't sure if you had any beer, so I brought my own." He held up a five-pack.

"What?" I asked, fully expecting something foul to slither from Mr. Cullins's mouth and lick off his face.

"Please tell me you have cable," he said. "I left before my game was over."

"That's very sweet, but you didn't have to come, Mr. Cullins," I said, rubbing dreamy cobwebs from my face as I glanced back at the staircase. My eyes climbed the stairs, scuttled up into the attic, stared worriedly down at Rory's dead body, and then hurried back down to blink anxiously at Mr. Cullins.

"I know, but I thought you could use some company." He held the pizza box out to me. I opened the door wide enough to take it from him. The box was warm and comforting, and for a second, I felt almost normal. I pressed my nose to the box and inhaled deeply. "We weren't shorted," he said. "I ate a slice on my way over." He volleyed a glance over my shoulder when I made no effort to invite him in.

As I stepped aside, he drifted into the living room, sucking in a reverse whistle as he went. Apologizing for shutting the door a little harder than I intended, I balanced the pizza box on my forearm and took the five-pack of beer from his hand. He slipped off his jacket and draped it over the armchair. His chin received a pensive scratch while he pivoted between the crime scene photographs on the coffee table and the kitchen.

"I know. It's creepy. You don't have to say it," I said. I took a quick glance at the staircase and thought I saw a long shadow recede up the interior wall. I took a steadying breath to convince myself it was one of the boys, but there was a sturdiness to the movement that seemed all too real. I listened for footsteps as Mr. Cullins clicked on the table lamp next to the couch.

"You said it, not me," he said, fingering through the photographs. He picked up one of the living room and held it up, angling his body to get the same vantage point. "But I'll say this much: You did a damn good job trying to make it look just that. You got everything right. I feel like I popped back to the nineties."

"Thanks . . . I guess," I said, and headed toward the kitchen. I set the pizza on the stove and opened the fridge to put the beer away. Eddie's head was gone, so there was plenty of shelf space. I clutched one of Mr. Cullins's premium lagers under my arm and got a bottle of Miller Lite from the inside shelf on the door. I pressed the refrigerator closed with my hip and handed Mr. Cullins a beer as he entered.

"I wish you would have told me you were coming," I said. "I was just about to go to bed." I yawned for emphasis. "I'm so tired. I could sleep for days."

My not-so-subtle hint for him to leave went unnoticed as he held up his beer. "You got a bottle opener?"

Since my brand came with a handy twist top, I had to rummage through three drawers to find one: a novelty opener I had stolen from Ford once upon a blue moon. The iron nude held the mouth of the opener over her head. I took Mr. Cullins's beer from him and opened it for him.

"Gracias," he said, clinking my bottle with his.

As Mr. Cullins took a short tour around the kitchen, I slid

sideways into my mother's chair. Out of habit, I peered between my knees to see if Michael was on the floor by my feet. A splash of bright red blood lay across my shirttail and pants leg. My chair gave a distressed screech as I reared from the dreadful sight with an audible gasp. I covered my strange behavior with a hard cough and a quick scoot of my chair nearer to the table. I shot Mr. Cullins a worried look as he turned from the battle he was having with the accordion doors of the pantry. He smiled when he found me watching him.

"The hinges could use some WD-40," he said.

I nodded.

"New floors and counters," he observed, rapping his knuckles on the granite surface. "Nice."

I nodded again.

"What's that about?" he asked with a sideways nod.

I clenched the bloody shirttail between my thighs. "What's what about?"

He pointed at the smashed bottle of Jack Daniel's on the floor next to the trash can.

"Oh, that," I dismissed. "I was pissed it was empty."

"That's not the bottle's fault." He chuckled.

I shrugged us into a long, awkward silence.

"Hey," he said, pulling out the center of his Washington Nationals T-shirt, "bet you thought I didn't have more than a robe in my closet. I've even found some pants." He lifted a leg. "Look! Socks *and* shoes."

I paid his joke the courtesy of a thin smile, and he took a heavy, dejected seat in Josh's chair.

"Look, Dixie," he said. "I probably shouldn't have come over uninvited like this—and if you want me to leave, just say the word—but you sounded pretty upset on the phone. I know I don't have any right to be poking my nose in your business. It's not like I'm family or anything—but hey! You started this. You knocked on my door, remember? And now, like it or not, I'm in your life. And having me in your life means that I'm going to worry about you. Like it or not. It comes with the territory."

I warmed up a smile for him. "I like that you worry about me, Mr. Cullins. But you don't have to. I told you. I'm fine."

"Well, sometimes fine doesn't mean fine. Sometimes fine means you want someone to dig a little deeper to find out what's really going on."

"They teach you that in cop school?" I teased.

"No. My wife taught me that the first day on the job as her husband."

I took a sip of beer, swallowing hard to get it over the lump in my throat. "Well, I really *am* fine. So, please, stop worrying. You're freaking me out with all this sweet-guy stuff."

"I am sweet. And you're not giving me much of a choice." He huffed to pick at the label of his beer. The same way Rory had when Rory was alive. I gasped a small weep that made him grimace. "What the hell did I say?"

I covered my face to suck back the tears, but a loud, bawling moan escaped through my fingers.

"I tell you what's got you so upset," he said. "It's this goddamn house!"

"Oh, don't start, *please*." I fell forward onto the table to pour my grief in the well of my forearms. I was surprised to feel Mr. Cullins tenderly pet my hair. At least, I hoped it was him.

"It's not my place to tell you what to do, Dixie, but I'm making it my place. You need to go pack your bags and leave all this behind. I can see how being here is torturing you. You're shivering all over."

"It's not torturing me," I mumbled into my elbow.

"Bullshit."

I looked up and offered him a miserable smile. "I broke up with my boyfriend, Mr. Cullins. That's why I'm upset. Girls get that way, you know?"

"Having your heart broke is bad enough, but when you're alone in a place like this . . . ?" He looked around with abject disgust. "It can seem downright unbearable. Especially when you're all alone. You need to get out of here, Dixie. Forget about the past. Live your life. Go be with friends."

"I am with a friend," I said.

"Shit, I hope you've got better friends than me." He reached over and squeezed my hand. "This is a bad place, Dixie. I felt it some twenty-odd years ago, and I felt it again as soon as I walked through that door tonight. This house will bring you down. You'll never be happy here. And I'm not sure seeing Rory isn't making things worse."

Upon hearing Rory's name, sorrow flew from me in a gush that made Mr. Cullins rear back.

"Oh, Mr. Cullins!" I cried. "Something . . . I can't!" I pressed my eyes closed. "It's so awful!" Anguish clawed at my face, pulling and twisting at my lips, making it impossible to speak. I laid my head down and cried until my misery turned to soft, sobbing hiccups. Mr. Cullins patted my shoulder, tutting.

"It'll be okay, Dixie," he tried.

"No, it won't," I muttered.

"Sure it will."

"It can't."

"Why not, sweetie?"

With a dramatic head toss, I kicked to a stand and strummed a hand across my bloody shirttail. He kept his eyes on my face. "Look!" I demanded, stretching my shirt out for him to see. "It's blood!"

He nodded composedly. "I saw it as soon as you opened the door."

I sank back onto my chair, stunned. "Why didn't you say anything?"

"You seemed okay. And I knew you'd tell me about it when you were ready." He pointed to my forehead, then tapped his own to mirror where he was gesturing to. "You want to tell me about that?"

I was surprised to feel a patch of tacky blood over my left eyebrow. The cut stung as I explored it. I withdrew my hand to stare at my red-speckled fingertips. I didn't remember hitting my head when I plunged out of the attic, but I must have.

"Garrett do that to you?" he asked.

"What?" I exclaimed. "No! Of course not."

"Rory?" he tried.

I looked over Mr. Cullins's shoulder at my father, who was standing several feet back from the entryway in the living room, signaling for me to keep quiet with giant waves of his hands. I shook my head to answer Mr. Cullins and tell my father to disappear with the same gesture.

"I was up in the attic," I said. "I fell trying to get down. I must have hit my head on something."

"Mm-hmm," Mr. Cullins murmured skeptically. "So, what's so awful, then?"

"What do you mean?"

"You said, 'It's so awful!'" He dramatized this with a protracted, exaggerated frown. "That sounded a lot worse than just falling and hitting your head."

My father ticked a lock and threw the key as far as he could throw it.

"Okay," I said. "I'll tell you. But you have to promise you won't overreact."

Incensed, my father grabbed his hair and spun himself out of sight.

"I never overreact," Mr. Cullins said. "But I promise."

I held Mr. Cullins's impassive stare to say, "Rory killed my family, Mr. Cullins. He confessed. He told me everything. I was trying to get him to turn himself in, but we got into this huge fight. He pushed me down and I hit my head really, really hard." I thought this ploy so clever that I almost giggled. When Rory showed up missing, the police would think he had gone into hiding. Now that was using my twat. "I didn't want to tell you because I hope he'll do the right thing and turn himself in. I know it doesn't make any sense, but I feel sorry for him. Even after everything, I don't want to see him hunted down like a dog."

Mr. Cullins leaned back and folded his arms across his broad chest. He remained unmoved, blinking at me until I wondered if I had actually delivered my ingenious testimony aloud.

"Didn't you hear what I said?" I asked.

"I heard you," he said. "I just don't believe you."

I pointed out the cut on my eyebrow. "I'm bleeding!"

"Oh, I believe you two had a fight. I just don't believe Rory confessed."

"Why not?"

"Because you're only hearing what you want to hear, Dixie."

"What's that supposed to mean?"

"People confess to crimes they didn't commit all the time. They do it for a variety of reasons. Sometimes they do it for fame or to make themselves feel more important than they actually are. But mainly they do it out of guilt. They feel responsible, even if they're not." He shrugged. "And Rory Sellers has a lot to feel guilty about. He blames himself for what happened to your family. He was a coward. And some men would rather be known as a killer than a coward. Personally, I don't get that kind of pride, but I've seen it before." He reached across the table to take my hand. "But no matter what he told you, Dixie—no matter how many details he gave about it—Rory Sellers did not kill your family. Your father did. I'd stake my reputation on it. I wish there was some way to prove that to you, but since—"

"But since my father killed himself, we'll never know what really happened and I need to just let it go. Blah, blah, blah. I know the routine."

Mr. Cullins shook his head. "Dixie . . ."

"I get it, Mr. Cullins. I do. I'm convinced, okay? My father killed my family. Not Rory. Not some mystery man in blue. William Wheeler did it . . . by himself . . . in the kitchen . . . with an axe. Game over. Happy now?" The pitying head shake he gave flung mine back in frustration. "What do you want from me? I said it! My father's guilty and I'm glad he's dead. Isn't that enough?" I stood to rub tension from my face. "Look. I'm not mad or anything, but I would like you to leave now. I have to go to bed. I'm really tired."

Mr. Cullins didn't stand to leave. Instead he leaned back and pressed a fisted knuckle to his lips. I thought he might be on the verge of tears himself, but the look of stunned horror in his eyes told me he was more likely to start screaming bloody murder than to cry. I glanced over my shoulder to see if my dead family had materialized behind me.

My father was standing outside the window.

He nodded down at the utensil drawer.

"Dixie," Mr. Cullins said after a long exhale. "You have to listen to me. Your father—"

"I said I get it, okay!" I threw my hands in the air as I turned fully to the counter. My hand fell on the brass knob of the utensil drawer. "You don't have to keep saying it."

A chair scraped as Mr. Cullins spun me around by my shoulders, ripping my hand from the knob of the drawer. A nest of silver snakes rustled inside.

"Dixie, listen to me," Mr. Cullins said sharply, giving me a hard shake when my eyes refused to meet his. They were locked on my father, who was slowly creeping up from behind. Finger to his lips, he slipped around Mr. Cullins and placed his hand on top of mine. I shook my head to dispel him as he crawled my fingers along the lip of the drawer.

"Dixie, look at me!" Mr. Cullins demanded, giving me another hard shake.

My eyes flicked to his as a murky weight filled me. My fingers wrapped around a long, contoured handle inside the drawer. Though a great darkness was upon me, I fought my way to the surface and found a small opening through my lips. "Get out," I whispered. "I . . . can't . . . stop . . ."

"Listen to me carefully, Dixie." Mr. Cullins clamped down on my shoulders as my father began to pull me back under. "I don't know what you've been told, but your father isn't dead. He's in a mental institution for the criminally insane. I thought you knew."

THE LEVER OF a trapdoor sounded, a hard clank followed by a clap of air that caused a crackle at the base of my eardrums. There was a weightless moment of incomprehension before I plunged feetfirst into a pit of sharp brass tacks. But in that fragile, buoyant moment, clinging to the last wisp of insulated fog, I looked for my father. He was gone. More than gone. He never was. What stood in his place was an unbearable clarity. A truth too zoomed-in to look away from, to ignore, to ever not know again. Like holding a magnifying glass over a freckle to find that it had eight twitching legs, it must be dealt with, but somehow you can't believe that it's . . .

Alive.

"He can't be," I said as Mr. Cullins stroked my arm in a concerned, fatherly way that made me want to rip open the utensil drawer and plunge a corkscrew in his eye. I felt myself succumbing to that same dizzying abandonment as I stepped aside from myself to allow my father control, but this time, nothing happened. This was my horrible urge, not my father's. I was the one who wanted to stab Mr. Cullins until he was an unrecognizable pile of mush on the floor. The seething fury coursing through my veins was not transfused; it was pure and self-produced. I was the evil thing that had ahold of me now.

"Dixie," Mr. Cullins said from somewhere on the moon, "maybe you should sit down. You're as pale as a ghost."

"You don't know the half of it." I chuckled softly as I crossed to the refrigerator and opened the door. "You need another beer?" Before he could answer, I got him out a lager and set it on the table. "The pizza's probably cold." I skirted him to turn the oven on. "What do you think, three fifty or four hundred?" I flipped the dial to broil. "I like the cheese a little burned, don't you?" I went to the sink to wash my hands. "Maybe your game's still on. I don't have cable, but we could try and bounce it through the Apple TV. Oh, wait. Garrett has that. You can watch it on my computer. Just give me a second and I'll bring it up for you."

Mr. Cullins placed his hand on my shoulder. "Dixie . . ."

The water had run hotter than tolerable, but I kept my hands under the faucet. It could never get hot enough to clean what was on my hands. As steam fogged the window above the sink, Mr. Cullins reached around me and turned off the spout. He rotated me by the shoulders to face him.

I looked around the kitchen. Now that I knew it wasn't haunted, it looked so small, so sad . . . so unbearably tragic. The outdated wallpaper I had haphazardly slapped up was lagging in corners and ballooning in spots. The used dining room table the man at the Salvation Army couldn't believe I was eager to buy looked like someone had gone at it with a fork and a box of crayons. The natural-wood finish didn't even match the chairs. Off by a good three shades. The cheap lace-appliqué valance over the kitchen sink was vintage gaudy, yellowing and covered in dust.

I swung my finger around the room. "This is the same wallpaper print my mother had." I let out a hard throaty guffaw that made Mr. Cullins wince.

"This must be a terrible shock for you, Dixie," he said. "I'm so sorry you had to find out this way. I swear, I thought you knew your father was alive."

"Well, you told me he was dead, so I don't know why you would think that." I pushed past him. "What station is your game on?"

"I never said your father was dead," he said, following me into the living room.

I sat at Uncle Davis's desk and flipped open my laptop. "You told me he committed suicide," I said as I tapped in my password.

"I said he *attempted* suicide, Dixie. That one word makes a huge difference."

"I just thought you said that because he didn't die right away. I read in the police report that he was still alive when the paramedics arrived. But I thought he died on the way to the hospital or something. I didn't know everyone was trying to trick me into believing he was dead. Ugh! I have to do an update. This might take a while."

"Dixie, stop it. I don't care about the stupid game. Look at me."

I swung around with an impatient expression. "What?"

"Let's talk about this."

"Talk about what? How I've been lied to my entire life?" I shook my head to give a cynical laugh. "All I heard growing up was that my father killed them all and then cut his own throat. To me, that meant he was dead. In fact, I'm sure my aunt told me he was dead. I know she did. And even if she didn't, I know she never told me he was in a mental institution somewhere. I think I would have remembered that." I slammed the computer lid. "So where is he, anyway?"

"Allied State Hospital."

"Where's that?"

"Richmond."

I grabbed my bag off the armchair and searched for my keys as I walked toward the door.

"Where are you going?" Mr. Cullins asked.

"I'm going to see my father."

He stepped between me and the door as I reached for the knob.

"They won't let you see him, Dixie."

"They have to let me see him," I said. "I'm his daughter."

"It's not the Sunnybrook retirement home. It's a maximum-security hospital for the criminally insane. You'd have a better chance getting into the White House to see the president at this time of night." He pressed all his weight against the door as I tried to sneak around him. "I'll get you an appointment to see him tomorrow. I'll call first thing in the morning. I know the administrator there. He'll work with us on short notice."

I slung my bag at the couch on my way back to the kitchen. The broiler was radiating a hellish heat. I turned it off and fell onto one of the chairs. It didn't matter whose chair it was anymore.

Okay, it was Josh's.

Mr. Cullins entered, saying, "You should call your aunt, Dixie. Let her know what's happened."

"You can go, Mr. Cullins," I said. "I'm okay. Just let me know when I can see my father."

"You're crazy if you think I'm leaving you alone in this house to-night."

"You got the crazy part right."

He leaned against the kitchen counter to regard me. "Pack a bag and come stay with me. It's not the Ritz, but my pull-out couch is pretty comfy."

"No, thank you."

He dropped his folded arms. "Then let me drive you to your aunt's house."

"I don't want to see her. She's been lying to me for as long as I can remember. I don't care if I ever see her again."

"Well, you're not staying here all by yourself. Either you come with me or I'm going to have to sleep on that sorry-ass midget couch you've got out there. I'll probably be in traction for a month, but at least I'll know you're all right."

I opened my mouth to argue, but I could tell by his expression these terms were nonnegotiable. I looked at the ceiling and swore I could see Rory's dead weight bearing down on it. I wasn't sure if his corpse would grow foul overnight, but I couldn't chance waking up to find that it had with Mr. Cullins on my couch.

I stomped out of the room to pack an overnight bag.

12

My nightmares were a tedious brand of terror. A haunted house I had been through a million times before. I could predict what horror would be around the next corner before I even looked. *Duck!* Here comes Eddie's head. *Careful!* Don't slip in the blood. *Watch out!* A skeleton girl's gonna spring out at you. Cue the madman with the axe. *Oo, really scary.* I pressed through the exit door into a blinding light. No ground, of course—I shouldn't have fallen for that one.

The snap of bacon grease brought me awake. I blinked at the ceiling until I realized it wasn't mine. Something was wrong. Different. Not just where I was—which I didn't recognize—but who I was—which I didn't recognize, either. I felt strange, like something had been removed while I was sleeping. *Amputated.* I reached under the blankets and found all my extremities were still present and accounted for, but still, something was missing. I sat up like a bolt as it came to me.

My father!

Alive!

I barely had time to process the significance of this horrible reality before another took its place.

Rory!

Dead!

A toaster popped the ballooning image of Rory's savaged head, and I closed my eyes with a silent weep. A grumble from the kitchen was followed by a slice of toast getting excoriated by a lash of quick, determined scrapes. Though the thought of breakfast being made for me should have greeted me kindly, my stomach raged at the thought of food. Hand over my mouth, I nodded a brusque good morning to Mr. Cullins as I dashed down the hallway to the powder room.

Purged, I washed up and changed into clothes I had hastily stuffed into a recycled shopping bag. None of the four socks matched, and the clean pair of underwear I thought I had tossed in the bag was nowhere to be found. I turned yesterday's panties inside out and slipped on socks that were at least equal in length.

After reverting the bed back into a couch, I took a seat in the kitchen nook, and silently pushed my hungry-man-size breakfast around the plate while Mr. Cullins perused his morning paper. He was dressed in a button-down white shirt and gray slacks. A matching jacket was draped over the back of the chair to his left. Clean-shaven, he had combed his silver hair to his scalp with a musky-scented goo. He downed the rest of his orange juice, righted his newspaper, and whopped it on the table.

"Get dressed," he said.

I looked down at my clothes—which I suppose were not much different than the clothes I had slept in—and asked, "Why?"

"We've got an appointment to see your father at ten."

The sudden screech of a morning bird outside the window startled my mug from my fingers, and toppled it onto the table. "When did you do that?" I asked, plucking a napkin from the holder to pat up the mess. My hand was shaking so badly I couldn't effectively blot. Mr. Cullins threw his newspaper on the puddle before it could spill over the edge.

"While you were sleeping," he said, stepping to the counter to yank a length of paper towels off the spindle. "I've known the administrator over there for years. Dr. Cheatham. I called him at home first thing this morning." He wiped up the coffee, shook his paper dry, and carefully moved to the sink with a mound of dripping towels in his extended hands. "He said you can visit as long as you like, but I told him a couple of hours oughta do."

"Oh," I breathed. "Thanks . . . I guess."

He returned with the carafe and poured me a fresh cup. "What? Did you change your mind about seeing him?"

"No, it's just . . ." I had to get home and check on Rory. Not that he was going anywhere. But it didn't feel right to leave him alone in the attic all day. I glanced out the sliding glass door. Only an hour or so past sunrise, and it looked like high noon already. Though the temperature had been holding steady in the low forties all week, autumn in Virginia was unpredictable. A northeast front could bring snow; a southeast wind might wake the mosquitos. Coats today, shorts tomorrow. It might not get hot enough to wear shorts today, but it could get pretty warm in an attic. Heat rises. Heat swells. Heat expedites the decomposing process. Rory was liable to be a gooey blob by lunch. My only hope was that he might dissolve entirely by the time I got home.

"Just what?" Mr. Cullins asked.

I snapped the front of my Muse T-shirt that was half zipped under my green hoodie. "I can't wear this. Can't we swing by my house on the way so I can change? I didn't even bring any makeup."

"Your house isn't on the way." He frowned at his watch. "And we might hit some traffic getting onto 95." When I slumped my shoulders dejectedly, he shook his head. "They don't have a dress code, Dixie. You're fine in what you have on. And your father won't care what you're wearing, that's for sure."

"What's he like, anyway?" I asked.

Mr. Cullins sighed to retake his seat. "He's basically a vegetable. He hasn't spoken or acknowledged anyone's presence for more than twenty years. He just sits in a chair, staring out a window, drooling. That's probably why your aunt never told you about him. She knew you would want to see him. Why put you through that?"

"So he just sits there?"

"He'll open his mouth if someone pushes food into it, but that's about it. He's pretty good about letting the nurses change his diaper, but—"

"Diaper!" I cried. "Seriously?"

He nodded in earnest. "You need to prepare yourself, Dixie. The man you're going to see is not your father. Not anymore. Hell, he's hardly even a man. He's just a sick, twisted statue that's been locked away in a closet for the last two and a half decades. He may still be breathing, but he's hardly alive. Understand what I'm saying?" He paused long enough for me to say I did, but I kept silent, watching my hand twirl a butter knife like a pencil. "Look, Dixie. I understand why you need to see him. But he's not going to even know who you are."

"Hasn't he ever said anything?"

"No. When he cut his throat, he severed his vocal cords. He lost so much blood his brain shut down. They had to restart his heart three times. I'm not even sure how he survived."

"So he's never tried to communicate, in any form, to anyone, about anything that happened that day?" I felt the need to rephrase my prior question. Subtleties of speech had fooled me once before; I wouldn't be fooled again. If I had just pointedly asked if my father was dead, I might have been given the truth.

"No. They had a few minor breakthroughs with him over the years, but ultimately he regresses back to the way he was. Every time I've seen him he was just sitting there like a rock. Half the time he's too rigid to sit and they have to lie him down and cover him with warm compresses to get him to loosen up. He doesn't even flinch when they give him a shot."

"Is he drugged? Is that why he's so out of it?"

"He's always been like that, Dixie. Ever since they picked him off the floor and carried him out of that house. It's like he died that day, but his heart didn't know it should stop beating. He's living, breathing rigor mortis. I know that sounds callous, and I'm sorry, but I want you to be ready when you see him." He sighed deeply, checking his watch again. "And if you're sure about doing this, then we need to get going."

"Will you go in with me to see him when we get there?" I asked sheepishly.

"I wouldn't have it any other way."

AFTER RECEIVING A perfunctory lecture on the rules and regulations associated with visiting a maximum-security patient by a guard who seemed more interested in the current length of his fingernails than our actual compliance, we were escorted to my father's room by his head physician, the hospital administrator, Dr. Lynd Cheatham—who Mr. Cullins simply referred to as "Ham." Since this was where my father was to be imprisoned for the rest of his natural life, the correct term for the room was probably "cell," but either way, they were pretty nice digs for a 150-year-old mental institution. The room was bright and airy, freshly painted with a gleaming tile floor. A full-length window next to the bed bathed the room in wholesome light. I was surprised to see that the window had no security bars or grille. Save for the red panic button next to the door, and the unfastened restraints dangling from the four corners of a well-tucked hospital bed, you would not have known the room housed a lunatic. I hadn't expected shit to be finger-painted on the walls, but I also didn't expect it to have nicer artwork than I had on mine. The snowy owl in flight was absolutely breathtaking, and the other, an Italian villa at dusk, made me want to sit on a bench to sketch it. A television was suspended from the ceiling in the right corner of the room. I looked up as someone was coming on down on *The Price Is Right*. Dr. Cheatham clicked the TV off via remote and left my wide, anxious face on the screen. I turned away feeling wholly unsettled.

My father was sitting in a wheelchair that was catty-corner to the window at the end of the bed. He was dressed in a blue robe and white scrub pants. A withered foot, rooted to a sweet potato ankle, dangled in a fluffy blue slipper that was a size too big for him. His head was slightly cocked, as though he were trying to identify a curious noise, and offered me a profile of a gaunt stubbled cheek, the tip of a nose, and the fleshy dewlap of a weak chin. His liver-spotted hand, curled inward from his liver-spotted wrist, twitched with the resolve of his damnably strong pulse.

"William," Dr. Cheatham said, bending forward in an attempt to make eye contact with my father. "You have a visitor." With this, Dr. Cheatham turned my father to fully face me. Though my gasp was internalized, Mr. Cullins touched my shoulder reassuringly.

Mr. Cullins had it exactly right: My father was indeed living rigor mortis. This was true not only of his scared-stiff expression, but also in the fossilized quality of his skin and posture, the oculogyric lock of his marbled eyes. The bloodless track of limpid gray veins that ran halfway up his throat was severed by a thick pink garroted scar. His mostly bald head was held slightly aghast, mouth open in a scream of drool and senseless torment. His skin was cured to his face like jerky, and his untenanted gaze hovered just over my left shoulder.

"William, this is your daughter, Dixie." Dr. Cheatham toggled the chair back and forth to adjust the cock of my father's head. He bent forward to see where my father's eyes were sighted, marked my face, and made a subtle adjustment to correct his aim, like he was about to set off a cannon. "As I've explained, William has very little cognizance of the world around him. Please don't be disappointed if he doesn't acknowledge you. That doesn't mean he is not interested in what's happening. He just cannot express himself."

With an experienced, downward kick, Dr. Cheatham set the wheelchair's antiroll lock, and then rounded the human rock formation to stand before us.

"I have an urgent matter to attend to, but I shouldn't be long. There is a guard right outside the door if you should need him. If you wish to leave before I return, he will direct you back to my office." He glanced at my father. "Please take note of any changes you might detect, no matter how subtle they may seem. Even the slightest movement or change in his appearance could be noteworthy. It might not seem so, but this is a very big day for William. He hasn't had a visitor in several weeks. We're very interested to see how he will react to your visit today."

"He's had other visitors besides me?" I asked.

"Not many, unfortunately." He nodded at Mr. Cullins. "Stan's been here several times, of course. And his brother, Davis, used to visit on a regular basis before he died. That was a huge setback for William. We were very close to a breakthrough right before that happened. William had just started to pick out letters on a keyboard using his finger." He sighed heavily. "I regret now telling him that his brother had died, but it didn't seem right to keep it from him. And I didn't want him to think that Davis had just stopped coming to visit."

"Are they the only ones who came to see him?" I asked. "Just Mr. Cullins and my uncle Davis?"

"Well, his . . . I'm not sure the relation . . . but a Mr. Norris came quite frequently in the beginning."

"Ford!" I balked. "You mean Ford Norris? Lanky guy with a scar on the side of his face?"

Dr. Cheatham nodded. "Yes, that's him. He stopped coming as much after Davis died, but he stopped by just a few weeks ago. The nurses don't particularly care for him. He can be a bit gruff, as you probably know. But William really seems to respond to him. More than Davis even. We actually had to ask him to leave once when William became overly excited." He leaned in to confide: "For William that's nothing more than locking up a little tighter than he normally is, but it's almost impossible to get him to unclench when he gets that way. Oh!" He held up a finger. "That reminds me . . ."

I turned to Mr. Cullins as Dr. Cheatham stepped away to make a note in a file hanging at the end of the bed. "Did you know Ford visited my father?"

Mr. Cullins shrugged. "Is that a problem?"

"Well, no . . . I mean, my father did save Ford's life when they were kids, so I guess he might feel some sort of obligation to visit him. I'm just pissed that all this was going on behind my back. I swear, if I hear Aunt Celia ever visited him, I'm going to lose my shit."

"Well, you're in the place for it," Mr. Cullins said.

I rolled my eyes.

"Now then, I must be off," Dr. Cheatham said, stepping to my father and giving him a tender pat on his shoulder. "I'll check back in a little while, William. Enjoy your visit."

After the door shut, I crossed to my father and snapped my fingers in his face. "Hey!" I said. "Hey, you in there, say something!"

"He can't, Dixie." Mr. Cullins sighed.

"Bullshit," I said, snapping my fingers directly in my father's ear. His eyes remained fixed on my left earlobe. "Talk to me, you asshole."

"Come on, Dixie," Mr. Cullins reproved. "Don't do that."

I waved my hand in front of his face. "Do you think he's faking it?"

Mr. Cullins scoffed. "Do you?"

I squatted down to get a view of my father's face from below. The scar strapped around his neck was thick as a rope and serrated. If not for the fact that he was alive, the wound would have appeared fatal.

"Do you think he can hear me?" I asked, poking the tip of his stony knee with my finger.

"I suppose he might be able to. He seems to like music."

"He does?"

"Well, I wouldn't call him a connoisseur or anything, but he seems to relax when certain music is played. He responds best to classical music. He gets agitated when they play polka music or heavy metal, but who doesn't?"

I stood in a turn toward Mr. Cullins. "Can you give us some privacy, please?"

He frowned. "Why?"

"I have a few things I would like to say to my father, and I don't want an audience."

He shook his head. "I don't think you should be alone with him, Dixie."

"Look at him." I waved a hand at my father to laugh sardonically. "He's a statue. I think I can handle whatever he's capable of."

"He's not the one I'm worried about."

I kicked out my hip to resent the implication. "I'm not going to pinch him or anything, if that's what you're worried about."

He looked down at my father for a long moment before he rapped a knuckle on the door behind him. A uniformed officer poked his head in and scanned the room warily.

"Any trouble?" he asked.

"No, we're fine," Mr. Cullins said. "She'd like a moment alone with him, if that's okay."

The guard sized me up with an impartial shrug. "Suppose it's all right. Willy hasn't wiggled a toe in twenty years. I forget he's alive, half the time."

Mr. Cullins pointed his finger at me as he backed into the corridor. "I don't care what they say. If he so much as flinches, I want you to scream for me. Got it?"

I nodded, and he closed the door.

Now that I knew my father was alive, he posed me little threat, but to be on the safe side, I skirted him by a good arm's length as I stepped around the wheelchair to the window.

The late-morning sun pierced the glass like the spine of a wasp. The headache I brought with me to the hospital had developed a clinical intensity since I arrived. It took a few hard blinks until the landscape beyond the window became more than a blurry prism of whites and yellows. The scent of antiseptic was caustic, heavily concentrated by the bed. They kept the facility at a temperature that could be comfortable naked. I unzipped my hoodie to no relief. I thought of Rory roasting in the attic like a turkey about to pop, and sighed as I peered four stories down upon a winding sidewalk. Two doctors in lab coats were strolling in the shade of the building, sharing a bag of potato chips. The young female doctor elbowed her distinguished companion in the side as she tossed her head back for a laugh.

"So," I said, rolling my forehead on the window to glance at the back of my father's walnut skull. The hospital's on-call barber had forgotten to trim the back, or didn't see the point. A dirty doily of long hairs rested on the collar of his blue terry cloth robe. "How've you been, Dad?" I waited the length of my humorless chuckle and returned my nose to the hot glass. "Me? Oh, I'm fine, thanks. Never been better, actually. Thanks for asking. Your concern touches me."

In the second row of the parking lot, a woman with long, straggly blonde hair slapped a man across the face as he tried to gently urge her into the passenger seat of a silver sedan. As he took her by the elbow, she slung him off with a hard twist, grabbed herself by the hair, and flung herself against the hood of the car parked beside them. She clawed weak but desperate fingers at the glass of the window. The man looked embarrassedly around, and then pressed his palms together to implore her to calm down.

"Uh-oh. Looks like someone got released a few days early," I said as the woman took off like a dart across the parking lot, headed for the woods. The man let out a visible exhale, and then started a slow jog after her. "You ever try to escape, Dad?" His stomach responded with a low gurgle. "Yeah, I guess not. You can't even go to the bathroom on your own. Hey, that's kinda funny. The last time you saw me I was in diapers, and now you are." I hoped this would shame him, but somehow I was the one who felt humiliated. "I'm living in our old house, you know? Yep. I set everything up just the way you left it. Uncle Davis had most of our old furniture in his garage. He's dead, in case you forgot. You broke his heart, you know. That's what killed him. A heart attack. I guess you can add his name to your list of victims."

The woman cut around the front of a white Sprinter van as a heavyset woman, walking with her head down and texting on her phone, came around the back side. As they met in the middle, the deranged woman screamed something into the startled woman's face, and took off again. The man chasing after her paused to apologize on her behalf. He held his arms out pleadingly when the heavyset woman clutched her purse to hurry away from him. After consulting the sky for a long moment, he shook his head, and turned to carry on the chase.

"I thought the house was haunted, but now I'm not so sure. I'm not sure of anything, actually. I thought I saw Mom and the boys a few times, but it must have been my imagination. They seemed real." I chuckled blandly. "But then again, you seemed real, too, so . . ."

The man caught up to the woman as she tripped over a curb and landed flat on her face in the grass median. Using her elbows, she army-crawled to a small deciduous tree—possibly a cherry or a dogwood—about ten feet away, snaked under its low branches, and wrapped her arms around the trunk like it was her last best chance to avoid being swept away in a high wind. The man stood over her, shaking his head.

"What else do you want to know?" I asked distractedly, knowing I was probably talking to myself but feeling obliged to carry on the conversation. "Aunt Celia took me in after you killed everybody. She hates you, by the way. Remember her daughter, Leah? Your niece? Really pretty and funny? Yeah, she's dead, too. Cancer. That's not what killed her, though. But I guess you knew that already, seeing as it was you who suffocated her. Oh, right!" I smacked my forehead. "You weren't really there, were you? Sorry. I can't remember what was real anymore."

I chewed a piece of skin off my lip as the man pried the woman's arms from around the trunk, and crawled to a stand with her in his arms. If I had not witnessed the exchange, based on the way her extremities jangled without purpose from the crib of his forearms and the dazed gait of his walk, I would have guessed that he had murdered her.

"Sorry I haven't come to see you before now. I thought you were dead all this time." I pressed my hand to the hot window as the man slammed the woman in the back seat of the car and turned to look in my general direction. "I thought you had been haunting me my whole life. But it wasn't you, was it? It couldn't have been. Living people can't haunt you, can they?" A flash of optimism came with this thought, like finding a pack of cigarettes in an old overcoat. I shook my head to set myself straight. Though telepathic haunting by the living was almost too inspired not to contemplate, I knew it was just a last-ditch effort.

I let this implausible notion drive off with the man and the woman—who was pressed helplessly to the back window, and probably his wife—wondering if he would survive the night. I imagined their children taping a homemade "Welcome Home Mommy" banner over the door and tying a bundle of balloons to the mailbox. A plate of cupcakes would be centered on the dining room table, a handful of spoons nearby, all the forks and knives safely hidden away.

"Why didn't you kill me, Dad?" I asked. "Why was I the one who got to live? Why not Josh or Eddie or Michael? Letting me live was worse than killing me, you know that, right? How could you do that to a little baby? Why did you hate me so much more than the others? Why did you leave me all by myself?"

When I turned to receive whatever bodily function my father would offer in lieu of a spoken answer, the wheelchair had spun completely around. His eyes were still vacuous and rheumy, but they were level and pointed straight at me.

A LONG, STALE wheeze gave sound to the muted scream my father had been letting out since I arrived in his hospital room. Working his jaw slowly to get the hang of it, he yawned wide to get the rigid muscles across his face and neck to loosen their grip. Cupping his chin with the wrists of his gnarled hands, he gave his head a sharp twist to the right and then a sharp twist to the left. The loud zip of vertebrae xylophoning down his spine made me cringe my shoulders to my ears. I clawed my cheeks to await his next move, but his chin simply fell to his chest, his hands to his lap.

As a passing cloud draped the room in an eerie shadow, I reached out with my foot and poked his knee with my toe. His head wobbled as if from a broken spoke. I stood in breathless disbelief. It appeared that in his effort to limber up, my father had accidently snapped his own neck. I was about to fly across the room to slap the panic button when he suddenly tossed himself upright with a shocking cough.

I pushed back against the window, strapping myself to it with wide arms, as he took a dazed look around. His eyes lingered on the ceiling for a moment, then fell to his lap, and then swung toward the bed. He didn't appear to know where he was or what was happening. I thought I might be able to slip around him before he came fully to his senses, but as I shimmied a fraction of an inch to the side, he toed up the metal footplates of the wheelchair and pushed to a trembling stand.

As pigeon-toed slippers stamped toward me at a toddler's pace, my father's eyes brightened on me. I opened my mouth to scream for Mr. Cullins, but could only produce a weak whine around the ball of fear that was lodged in my throat. As gnarled, arthritic fingers reached for me, my father let out a laugh that might have been joyous if it wasn't so monstrously terrifying. He was just about to take another slinging step forward when a derelict equilibrium gave him a panicky jolt. Using his buckled knees as a trestle, he paused to correct, flapping his arms to counterbalance the weight of his head, and then started forward again.

Though I was completely repelled by the sight, I found myself wanting to root for him: *Come on! You can do it! Just one more step!* But as bony fingers clamped into the thin skin over my collarbone, I realized my father's newfound mobility might not be a good thing. Not a good thing at all.

I closed my eyes as his nose searched my braced expression, snuffing and cold, like a bear checking its find for a flavorsome scent. Clenching every muscle in my body in anticipation of a bite, I whimpered as his sticky lips parted on a bone-dry gasp. But when all he seemed inclined to do was to breathe hot, putrid air in my face, I pried open one eye. His smile was ghastly, unbearably ebullient around teeth so corroded with black gunk they seemed to squirm.

"I did want you dead, Dixie dear," he wheezed, finding a blade of voice somewhere between his concave ribs and severed throat. He stroked my cheek with the back of his rawboned fingers. "You don't know the times I tried."

I ONCE DREAMED that I was buried alive. No coffin, just wet, heavy earth shoveled on top of my prone body. Though centipedes were skittering across my arms and belly, and the thrash of earthworms across my lips was enough to drive me insane, I remained perfectly still. I could have dug myself free anytime I wanted; the surface was but a handful of dirt away. But I didn't. I just let the itch take my sanity as I patiently waited to suffocate. Somehow it seemed easier to die than to try. That same feeling came over me as my pathologically catatonic father rammed me against the hot window by my throat.

"Well, look at you." He chuckled darkly. "Ain't you all growed up?"

I turned my head so I wouldn't inhale his foul breath. "Get off me!" I cried.

He threw a worried glance at the door, then lit into me with a grating whisper. "Keep it down, little girl. If that guard hears you, he's gonna run in here and jab me in the neck with a needle. Is that what you want?"

I did very much want that, but couldn't stop my head from shaking.

"You got big problems, little girl, and I ain't there to clean up your messes no more," he said, no longer sounding like the drunken chimera I had conceived in my youth. For some reason, he now sounded very much like Ford: well-oiled honky-tonk. He jabbed my heart with his index finger. "Hear what I'm sayin'?"

I squirmed to find a way out from under the mash of his chest. For a bag of bones, he was unusually squishy, like an octopus, enveloping me, making it hard to find air around him. Everywhere I turned I inhaled a puff of terry cloth or a wattle of loose flesh. My toes grasped for the floor as he lifted me off my feet and jammed me against the window. Though I was sure it was made of an unbreakable there-ain't-no-way-anyone's-throwing-themselves-through-this-shit poly-carbonate, I thought I heard a tiny crack in the glass.

"You gotta think of a way outta this mess, little girl," he growled. "You got a dead man in your attic, and you're here visiting your ol' pappy like you ain't got nothing better to do. You gotta get going. Shake that fucking cop loose, and go fling that rat out by the tail before it stinks up the whole fucking neighborhood."

I closed my eyes to pray, "*Please go away, please go away, please go—*"

"Stop blubbering and listen up." He ground his hip bone into mine as he bore down on me, partly to intimidate me, but mostly to keep from gliding back on the smooth soles of his slippers. "Forget about burying him, if that's what you got in mind. That's a surefire way to get caught. You gotta get rid of the body so no one ever finds it."

"How?" I asked with a panting sob.

"Chop him up," he said. "Stock that new fancy refrigerator freezer you got. He'll keep in there for a while. Once he's good and frozen, you can throw him away piece by piece. Nobody's gonna go looking through your trash. And even if they do, they'll just think he's some meat you never got around to eatin'."

As much as I didn't care to be schooled by the Crypt Keeper, I had to admit that I could use some guidance in the area of corpse removal. And he made some valid points. Burying Rory in the backyard by candlelight could go wrong a million different ways. And trying to stuff him into the freezer whole would be next to impossible. But the thought of laying Rory out on the kitchen table as I cleaved off a leg was just too horrible to consider.

"I can't cut him up!" I cried. "That's disgusting!"

"You want to get caught? Is that what you want? You want to end up in here, like me?"

"No . . ."

"Then do what I say and maybe you won't end up strapped to a wooden table with a rubber ball in your mouth for Thanksgivin' dinner." I nodded and he relaxed his grip just a tad. "Gettin' rid of a body is the easy part. We got another problem we've gotta figure out before Dr. Dumbass and Sergeant Shit-for-Brains get back. I've been thinking about it, and sumpin's not adding up. I know we done some terrible shit, but we didn't kill that reporter lady."

"W-we didn't?" I asked, though I had already concluded to my satisfaction that Rory had killed Claire. Still, it was nice to have my innocence in the matter validated.

He shook his head as he leaned closer to whisper, "But somebody's trying to pin it on us."

"I know. Rory was. But I caught him before he could, so—"

"So why would he? Why frame us? He didn't know nothin' 'bout you bein' there when that girl fell down the steps before you bashed his brains in. Awful risk he took trying to sneak that phone into the house. He could have got caught with it. Why not ditch it? Why risk everything tryin' to frame you?"

"Because he hated me," I sniveled, then threw my head back to cry openly. "Why did he hate me so much? I only ever loved him."

"Oh, for chrissake." He wagged his head despondently. "If I knew how fuckin' stupid you were gonna be, I woulda killed you with the rest of 'em. This ain't about hate, little girl. You got it all wrong." He shoved me against the window again. This time the crack I heard was my skull. "Come on, think! What's his game?"

"I don't know." I tried to twist away, but my elbows were trapped in the hollows of his robe. The hospital gown beneath was gluey damp with sweat. As his slippers fought for purchase on the polished floor, he kneed me in the groin. "I can't think. You're hurting me!"

"You're hurting me, you're hurting me," he teased in a girlish voice that I instantly recognized as my own.

Something clicked.

"This isn't real," I said evenly. His yellow eyes narrowed as I pressed my palm against his chest and glided him back a foot. I could barely feel his weight under my hand. "You're not real."

"Oh, I'm as real as it'll ever get for you, Baby Blue," he cackled. "Take good care, now. Don't do something you might regret."

"See?" I pointed a finger in his face and he gnashed at it. "You saying that, calling me by that name. They're just lines from that stupid song. No one talks like that. This is all in my head!"

He gave me a sheepish grin. "I thought you knew, Baby Blue."

"Stop calling me that!"

He pouted his livery lip. "Oh, why so blue, Baby Blue?"

"Stop it!"

As he reared back to let out a maniacal laugh, I shoved him as hard as I could. The hospital bed threw him back at me as he collided with the safety rail, but I was able to jump into the corner between the bed and the window before his outstretched fingers could grab hold. He hit the window hard with his face and dropped to the floor like a dead bird. The robe, massive around him, swallowed him whole.

I poked the mound with the toe of my shoe, but he made no move to grab me. In fact, it appeared as though he had disappeared altogether. A harder kick proved he was still under there, but produced no reaction. Either he was dead, knocked out cold, or had reverted to his original catatonic state. Any which way, I had some explaining to do.

My eyes flicked to the closed door across the room as voices floated slowly down the hallway. Dr. Dumbass and Sergeant Shit-for-Brains were on their way back.

Crap!

I watched the breathless pile for any sign of life as I skirted carefully around, hugging tight to the bed, hands held up in fists, ready to pummel the heap if it so much as twitched. As I cleared the end of the bed in a turn, icy fingers snatched out and grabbed my ankle.

Falling in a twist onto my hip, I screamed and kicked at a face as it peered out from under a dark fold in the robe. Revealed as the fraud it was, the thing that I thought was my father took its true form. A black bifurcated tongue flicked out from under glinting eyes nestled in a fluffy pelt of blue terry cloth. Four wickedly long fingernails ticked across my sock on their way up my pants leg. Just as the thing began to pull me forward by a grip of skin, my heel connected with a soft crunch, and the hand retreated with a wounded scream.

Scrambling to my feet, I slung the wheelchair out of the way just before I fell into it, and spun myself into the center of the room.

A low whining rose as the robe humped slowly toward me. "Do it like I said," it hissed with an evil laugh. A gray hand slithered out to tap one sharp talon on the tile floor. "Chop, chop, chop, Dixie. Chop, chop, chop! Chop, chop, chop! CHOP, CHOP, CH—!"

A soft knock at the door startled the room silent. I turned as Dr. Cheatham and Mr. Cullins entered, engaged in easy conversation.

"No, that was Stargell," Mr. Cullins was saying. "I think the guy you're talking about was—" He stopped dead when he saw me. "Dixie? What is it? What happened?"

As their eyes flicked past me, my brain searched for a way to explain how my infirm father got overturned in his wheelchair, but all

I could think to do was laugh. I turned a pointed finger his way, as if to say, *A funny thing happened while you were gone*, and found my father back in his chair. Head locked and cocked, hand convulsing, mouth suspended in silent anguish; he looked exactly as he had before they left the room.

"You okay, Dixie?" Mr. Cullins asked.

I shook my head. "He was just . . ."

"Did something happen?" Dr. Cheatham asked, hurrying to my father's side. "Did he move? Did he try to speak?"

I covered my mouth as a fuse of laughter burned a track up the back of my throat.

Mr. Cullins rubbed my arm. "Why are you so upset?"

"I thought that . . ." I began, then rested my head against Mr. Cullins's chest. "I just freaked out. Can we go, please?"

"Where's his slipper?" Dr. Cheatham asked.

I turned to glance down at my father's feet. One foot was bare; long, yellow nails were folded over the tips of his purple toes like corn husks.

"Oh, there it is." Dr. Cheatham bent with a grunt and retrieved the slipper from under the bed. He turned with it in his hands, holding it with delicate caution, as though a mystical property might be released if it weren't handled properly—perhaps reanimating the petrified effigy of a notorious axe murderer, for example. "How did his slipper get under the bed?"

"I don't know," I said with feigned bewilderment. "I must have knocked it off him when I went to look out the window."

Dr. Cheatham shrugged as he stooped to one knee before my father. As the slipper glided over his twisted foot, I half expected a crown to appear on top of my father's head. "We need to get you some new slippers, William," Dr. Cheatham said. "These are much too big for you." He cinched my father's robe across his bony chest and tightened the belt. "I'll get you some socks so you can go outside later."

"Outside!" Mr. Cullins blurted. "You don't really let him outside, do you, Ham?"

Dr. Cheatham turned with a bright expression. "Oh, yes. I prescribe fresh air for all my patients. No better medicine. William gets to sit outside for an hour or so every afternoon, weather permitting." He smiled reassuringly. "He's very well guarded, I assure you." Dr. Cheatham addressed me as I watched a line of clear drool dribble from my father's bottom lip. "So, how was your visit, Ms. Wheeler? Anything to report?"

I stared at him for a long moment, then looked up at Mr. Cullins. "Can we go, please?" I broke for the door before he could answer, not bothering to say good-bye to my father, or even to give him a last look.

"Don't you want to visit some more?" Dr. Cheatham called out. "I've arranged a nice lunch for us in the cafeteria!"

I was halfway down the hall when Mr. Cullins yelled for me to hold up.

13

Against Mr. Cullins's advice, I decided to call Aunt Celia as we crawled up 95 in stop-and-go traffic on our way back from Richmond. As a fat, lazy cloud piddled on the windshield, I dug my phone from my bag between my feet. Wipers chopped the glass at their scheduled preset, a semidry salvo of rubber that swept my nerves of their last bit of patience. The *X-Files* episode with my father had left some seriously mischievous creepy-crawlies under my skin. The Excedrin I had taken only seemed to hasten their intensity. Having made the rash decision to pour all my booze down the drain, I had only a fitful nap to look forward to when I got home, and that was only after I disposed of Rory's body.

Oh, goodie.

Burning down the house with him in it seemed like my only viable option, but I worried that the trees next to my house might hand fire to the trees next to Vicki's house, and so on and so forth down the line. I couldn't risk that. I had enough guilt as it was. Killing myself would make disposing of Rory's body unnecessary, but then Garrett would be left alone, as I had been, to wonder why. Shooting Garrett in the face as I came clean and then turning the gun on myself seemed the more compassionate route to take, if not somewhat romantic. But for all those who had died at my thoughtless hand—Leah, Erin, Rory, and maybe Claire—I wasn't sure I could bring myself to kill the man I loved, even if it was the compassionate thing to do. Besides, I didn't have a gun.

These saturnine contemplations had descended on me between floors eight and LL of the state loony bin as Mr. Cullins hummed softly to elevator Muzak. It sounded like "Baby Blue" to me, but when I asked him if it was, he gave a derisive look to say it was Elvis Presley. When the doors slid open, I made a beeline for the front desk to commit myself. But when the receptionist looked up to ask if I needed assistance, I shook my head and snatched a brochure from the à la carte stand on the counter. *Outpatient Care: The Road to Mental Stability—The First Step Is Yours.* The woman on the front of the brochure looked pretty well-adjusted in her white cotton loungewear and her floppy hat and her stylish beaded footwear. The rock she was sitting on didn't look particularly comfortable, but the ocean was blue and calm—a sunny day on tap. Something about her reminded me of the woman I had seen running through the hospital parking lot: the length of her hair or the slightly crazy way she held on to her knees for dear life. I wondered if she, too, had been sucked in by a promise of a sunny day. I dropped the brochure in the trash receptacle before I pressed through the revolving doors.

As Aunt Celia's number rang in my ear, I glanced into the car next to ours. A mom and one too many kids to count had the windows in a sweaty fog. The mom looked ready to run them all into a tree. The tween in the back seat—based on her braces and dramatic purple eye shadow—stopped running her mouth long enough to roll her eyes as she caught me staring. I gave a friendly, contrary smile to confuse the hell out of her, and she blew me a kiss with her middle finger.

"You'll never guess who I saw today," I said in a snotty tone as Aunt Celia answered the phone.

"I don't know, but did you get my text? The damn washing machine broke and I've got a foot of water in the basement. Can you call Garrett and see if he can—" A loud crash of pans rustled the phone from her ear. "Oh, shoot! Let me call you back."

The line disconnected.

"Shit!" I exclaimed, staring down at my home screen. "She hung up on me." Mr. Cullins snickered. "It's not funny. I was all geared up to tell her off."

"I know," he said. "That's what makes it so funny."

As my phone rang back, I said, "I have half a mind not to answer it."

"Answer it," he instructed.

I put the phone to my ear. "What?"

"Did you call Garrett?" Aunt Celia asked.

"No. We just hung up like two seconds ago."

"All right, call me back when you do."

"Wait!" I exclaimed, sensing she was about to disconnect again. "What?"

"I called you to tell you something and you won't let me talk."

"Well, go on," she said impatiently, which clamped my lips in anger for several heart-pounding beats. "Talk, Dixie! But make it quick. I'm about to drown over here and feel sick as a dog to boot."

"You'll never guess who I saw today," I repeated after a deep breath, determined to play out this conversation my way.

As if to ruin my knock-knock joke by saying, *Come in!* Aunt Celia said, "Just tell me."

"No," I said. "You have to guess."

She sighed wearily. "I don't know . . . The president?"

I rolled my eyes to Mr. Cullins. Eager to play along, he asked who she had said. When I told him, he threw his head back to laugh.

"I know you're upset," he said, "but you gotta admit that's funny."

"Did I get it?" Aunt Celia asked.

"No, you didn't *get* it!" I snapped. "And you'll never *get* it in a million years, seeing that the person I saw today has been dead for TWENTY-FIVE FREAKING YEARS!"

My scream caused Mr. Cullins a pained look as it ricocheted around the warm interior of his Buick. I hoped for an equally distressed expression on Aunt Celia's face across town, but received an exhausted huff instead.

"Don't scream, Dixie. I have an awful headache."

"I just saw my *father*, Aunt Celia!" I said, just this side of a shriek. "And you'll never guess what? *He's alive!*"

"I understand," she said. "Calm down."

"Is that all you have to say to me?" I raged. "Calm down? Aren't you curious how I found out that he was alive? Because that's the funny part about it, Aunt Celia: The person who told me something I should have known my entire life is someone I've barely known a week! You had twenty-five years to tell me the truth. Don't you think you owe me an apology?" I punched myself in the thigh. "No! You know what, forget it. You don't get to be sorry for this. Not after all this time. You don't deserve my forgiveness!"

"Take a breath, Dixie," Aunt Celia said.

I did, but only to build up a head of steam.

"How could you have lied to me for so long, Aunt Celia? I asked you a million times to tell me what happened to my family, and you lied every single freaking time!"

"I don't want to have this conversation over the phone," she said, infuriatingly calm. "Come over and we'll talk about it."

"I don't want to talk about it! I don't want to hear any more of your lies." I looked out the window as tears began to gather. "Now I know my father is alive, I can find the truth from him. He might not be able to talk, but his doctor said that he can pick letters out on a keyboard. It might take some time, but I'll get to the bottom of what happened."

"Can he do that?" she asked, shocked.

"Yes. If you would have listened to Uncle Davis instead of fighting with him all the time, you might have known that. Dad was making progress before Uncle Davis died, Aunt Celia. But now he's got to start all over again. We've wasted so much time. It might be too late now. I know you think you were protecting me, but your lies have made everything so much worse. For everybody! You should be ashamed of yourself, Aunt Celia. But you don't sound ashamed. You don't even sound upset."

"I am upset, Dixie, I'm just not surprised. I knew this day was coming as soon as you told me you were moving back into that house. I told Ford it was just a matter of time before you found out the truth." She paused, sighed. "You may not believe this, Dixie, but I've wanted to tell you about your father for a very long time. I hated having this secret between us. But the longer I waited, the more difficult it became to tell you. After a while, the fact that I hadn't told you seemed worse than you actually finding out." She sighed again. "I hope you find the truth, Dixie. I really do. No matter what it is. But no matter what you think of me, all I ever wanted was for you to have a happy, normal life."

"But I wasn't happy, Aunt Celia. And I was anything but normal." I bit my lip to keep it from trembling. "You made sure of that," I added and hung up on her.

As we turned onto my street, I scanned the cars parked curbside for Rory's black 4Runner. Mr. Cullins tooted his horn as he navigated through the playground my street became every day after school let out. A Frisbee hovered just before our windshield before it drifted under the car. A soft crunch bobbled us as the back tire rolled over it. Mr. Cullins said it served the "little fuckers" right as he tooted the horn at three boys who were standing in front of my driveway. One of the boys was Conner. I waved at him as he stepped aside to allow us to pass. The way he looked away made me wonder if he wasn't under strict orders not to associate with me. Maybe Vicki had finally realized that the woman she had affronted in my driveway was also the dead reporter everyone was talking about.

"You know him?" Mr. Cullins asked as he pulled into my drive.

"Yeah, he's my neighbor's kid."

"No." Mr. Cullins pointed at my house. "Him."

Garrett was sitting on my front stoop.

"Uh, that's Garrett," I said. "What the hell is he doing here? He should be at work."

"You want me to go have a talk with him?" Mr. Cullins asked, shifting the car into park.

"No," I huffed. "You'll just scare him off."

"That's the point."

Though I wanted more than anything to be back in Garrett's good graces, in his arms, snuggled under a blanket and watching an old movie, this was not the time, nor the place, to make up with him. I had to do something with Rory's body, and quick. Buy a baby pool and put him on ice. Drain his blood and stuff him with cotton. The least I could do was roll him up in bubble wrap for the time being. I couldn't manage any of that with Garrett hanging around.

Garrett raised his hand in greeting. Mr. Cullins and I waved slowly back.

"Are you just going to sit there?" Mr. Cullins asked through a plastered smile, continuing to wave as Garrett craned his neck to see through the front windshield.

I leaned over and gave Mr. Cullins a peck on the cheek. "Thank you for taking me today. You're a dear friend. And yes, I'll take all the shit that goes along with that. All I ask is that you call before you stop by next time. I might be in my unmentionables."

"Unmentionables? Who are you, Aunt Bee?"

"Who?"

"*Andy Griffith*?" I shook my head. "*Mayberry R.F.D.*?" I shrugged and he said, "Never mind."

"Well, thanks anyway," I said.

"You sure you don't want me to run him off? No extra charge."

"I'm sure," I said, turning in my seat to unlock my seat belt. "Go home. Retirement awaits."

"Actually, I was thinking about swinging by the pound to see if they got any old, ornery dogs in." He leaned forward to see that the day had turned dusky. "Eh, maybe I should wait. Looks like a storm's coming."

"It's a dog, not the Wicked Witch of the West," I said. "It won't melt."

"Yeah, but I might." He sat back. "You want me to pick you up something while I'm there?"

Do dogs eat people meat? "No, thanks. I can hardly take care of myself."

"Hey," Mr. Cullins said as I reached for the door handle. "I still don't want you staying here alone. At least until you've had a chance to process everything that's happened. Whether you think so or not, you've been through a traumatic event. It might not feel like it now, but you might experience some aftereffects. I'm not sure what the opposite of grieving is, or if there is such a thing, but I bet it's going to be just as hard to deal with. You lost a parent today, Dixie. The father you thought you knew is gone. Don't go trying to act like some tough girl who can handle anything that's thrown at her, okay? If you find yourself alone in that house, I want you to call me. I'll come and get you. You can stay with me as long as you want."

I nodded. "I hadn't thought about it that way. You're a pretty smart guy, you know? You should have been a cop."

He smiled weakly. "No joking around, Dixie. Promise me you'll call."

I crossed my heart and opened the door. Garrett stood as I started up the walk.

"Who's that?" he asked, nodding at Mr. Cullins's car.

"That's my new watchdog," I said, turning to wave Mr. Cullins out of the drive. He tipped a finger in salute, and then looked over his shoulder to back out. "Mr. Cullins. He's the detective I told you about." I looked up at Garrett. "I'm so glad to see you."

"Where have you been? I called you like ten times."

"Sorry, I didn't see you called." I dug for my phone in my bag, incapable of letting a missed call go unnoticed, even if I knew the source. "I had to turn my phone off at the hospital."

"Are you okay?" he said in an alarmed voice as he spotted the scab over my eyebrow. He reached out to touch it. "Jesus. What happened?"

"Oh, that's just a scratch." I caught his fingers in mine to stop them from probing the wound. "I'm fine. I just hit my head on something. It bled more than it hurt."

"Oh," he said, dropping his hand. "Then what were you doing at the hospital?"

"Oh, nothing." I shrugged to draw out the surprise. Garrett gave great reactions if you set your big news up right. "I just went to visit my dear old father."

"Give me a break," he scoffed. "If you don't want to tell me, just don't tell me. You don't have to lie."

"No, seriously," I said. "My father's alive, Garrett. I just saw him. He's in a mental institution. Aunt Celia's been lying to me my whole life. Ever since I was a little girl." I pointed at the driveway, even though Mr. Cullins's car was long gone. "Mr. Cullins told me about him last night. He just dropped it on me like a bomb." I detonated the word in the space between us and blew my hands over my head. "He thought I already knew. Can you believe it? My father's alive, Garrett. Isn't that crazy?"

Garrett waved off the smoke of my revelation. "Wait. How can he be alive? You told me he cut his throat."

"He *did* cut his throat. He just didn't die. Well, not physically, anyway. He's been in a mental institution this entire time. Of course Mr. Cullins thought I knew. Why wouldn't he? I should have known. I mean, he's my father, right?" I shook my head. "I can't believe Aunt Celia was able to keep this from me for so long. And not just her. Everyone had to know he was alive. Uncle Davis did. He used to visit him. Even Ford went to see him a few times. Can you believe that? It's been like some mass conspiracy." I gave him a slanted look. "Did you know? You can tell me, I won't be mad."

"How would I know?" he said. "Before you told me, I had never heard a thing about the murders. Or your father."

"You could have Googled it or something."

"Okay. I did. Once. But it felt wrong. Like I was snooping around or something." He looked up to think, then shook his head. "I don't remember reading anything about your father being alive, though." He cocked his head to consider me. "Why didn't *you* Google it? I mean, I would think you would have."

I shrugged. "Aunt Celia kept a pretty tight rein on my internet usage when I was younger. Now I know why. I thought she was trying to protect me, but she just didn't want her lie exposed. When I got older, I guess I . . ." *was too busy with my obsession with Rory to obsess about anything else; forgot about my family for a spell after I met you; didn't want to hurt Aunt Celia by going against her wishes; worried that I might accidently provoke my father's evil ghost; fell in with a pack of Angry Birds before I got Candy Crushed.* I shook my head. Pathetic as those last two excuses now seemed, they were as good as any. I could hardly admit that to myself, much less Garrett, and hung my head to let out a dejected sigh. Luckily, he took my inability to come up with an acceptable excuse as an excuse in itself, and let it go.

"I'm amazed nobody let it slip," he said. "My family can't keep a secret for five seconds. My sister told my parents about you living here the same day I asked her not to."

I thought back on all the conversations I'd had about my father and could not remember one person actually saying that he was dead. It was heavily implied, though they might have been referring to a passage of time or the schizophrenic change in his personality: *The man I* knew *wouldn't have done something like that . . . He* was *pretty cool, I guess, for an axe murderer . . .* When Claire Reynolds asked me if I ever saw my father, she didn't mean his ghost, as I'd presumed; she meant had I ever visited him in the hospital. Even Mr. Cullins—who was in no way trying to keep the truth from me—had unintentionally misled me: *And then what did he do? Cut your father's throat to make it look like a suicide attempt?*

Attempt.

Maybe I did only hear want I wanted to hear, like Mr. Cullins had suggested. I didn't want to know the truth. The truth had not set me free. If anything, it had bound me to a horrible reality.

A close clap of thunder sent the children in the street squealing for the safety of their homes. An uncaught ball rolled to a stop against Garrett's foot as a downpour closed in around us. Garrett grabbed my hand and pulled us to shelter under the slim egress of my front door.

"Man, that's crazy," he said, staring out at the sheeting rain as I searched my bag for my house key. I wasn't sure which he was talking about, my father or the storm. "So, what happened to Rory?" he asked.

I didn't think I screamed out loud, but Garrett turned to look at me as if I had.

"What do you mean, what happened to him?" My fingers locked on my ChapStick. Suddenly parched, I decided to use it.

"You know . . ." He threw a glance back at the house.

I rolled my eyes up toward the attic as I smooshed my lips together.

"After I left . . ." He nodded me toward understanding. "Did you two . . . Are you two like together now?"

I bumped him hard with my shoulder. "Are you stupid?"

His grin was grudging, at best. "Well, it kinda seemed like you were."

"I love you, Garrett. You're the only one for me. You know that. Or at least I hope you do. Rory and I were—are—just friends." I shook my head, astounded at how easy it was to let on that someone was either alive or dead. "Not even, really. He's a jerk. He got all bent out of shape because I wanted him to talk to Mr. Cullins." I rolled my fluttering eyes in exasperation. "That's a whole other story. I'll tell you about it later. But Rory left right after you did. I haven't seen him since. I probably won't see him for another five years."

"Oh," he said, confused. "I thought I saw him drive by last night. He's got that black 4Runner, right?"

"Last night?" I grabbed Garrett's arm. "When? What time? Are you sure it was him?"

"I thought you didn't care if you ever saw him again?"

"I don't," I said with a quick flinch. "I'm just surprised. Mr. Cullins came by and brought me some pizza. I stayed at his house so we could leave for the hospital first thing this morning. We didn't leave here until after ten o'clock. What time did you see him?"

"It was late. Probably two or three in the morning." He grimaced as he scraped his hair from his forehead. "I feel stupid now, knowing you were with Mr. Cullins and all, but I didn't just stop by. I've kinda been here all night. I was waiting for you to come home. I thought that . . . I didn't know if . . . Forget it. It doesn't matter."

I blinked his disheveled appearance into focus. I was so preoccupied with the revelation that my father was alive, Aunt Celia's lifelong betrayal, and how to go about the problem of disposing of Rory's body that I hadn't noticed Garrett looked like hell on laundry day.

"You've been sitting on my stoop all night?" I asked.

He nodded with a grimace. "Can I use your bathroom?"

I TOOK A giant sniff of air as I opened the door. It was hard to tell the root of the scent, or where it was originating from, but something was certainly rotten in Denmark. Garrett seemed unfazed by the stench, which made me wonder if my house normally smelled like a decomposing body.

Glossy chunks of bloody flesh were splashed across the coffee table. I hurried over to clean up the crime scene photographs as Garrett slipped into the powder room. It wasn't so much that I cared if Garrett knew I had the pictures; I just didn't want to explain why they were laid out on my coffee table like a scrapbook project. I held them to my chest as I turned for Uncle Davis's desk and tripped over the leg of the armchair. The pictures went flying. As I crawled around to gather them up, I noticed that I was two short: Eddie was gone. Top and bottom.

"What do you have there?" Garrett asked, exiting the bathroom.

"Oh, just some bills I was going through," I said, circling the desk in a half stumble, holding tight to the pictures so they wouldn't slip from my abdomen like entrails. As I stuffed them inside the top drawer, something heavy scratched across the metal bottom and jammed the drawer open. After a brief but frantic battle to close it, I slammed it shut with a tremendous bang. I smiled nonchalantly as Garrett shot me a startled look, then frowned as another waft of moldering putrescence touched my nose.

"What's that smell?" I said, nosing the felonious odor out into the open before he could. "I think a mouse died in here or something. Do you smell it?"

"It's probably me." Garrett chuckled grimly, pulling his shirt over his head and holding it to his nose as he took the stairs. "I haven't showered in two days. I can hardly stand myself."

"Where are you going?" I asked in a worried voice.

"I'm going to take a shower," he said, flinging me a baffled look before he disappeared behind the dividing wall. "You just said I stunk."

I hurried up after him, talking a mile a minute to distract him, as though the ears and nose might somehow be connected. Maybe if I spoke loud enough, his olfactory system would shut down. *Hear what I'm smelling*? Didn't we used to say that as kids? Was there any medical verity to it? Most childhood tropes had a little truth to them. I was almost positive that whoever smelt it dealt it.

"You should have seen my father, Garrett," I said in a rush. "It was like someone made a statue of a crazy guy and stuck it in a wheelchair. No kidding. He's frozen solid."

I bypassed him to take the lead as we reached the top of the stairs, walking sideways with inverted hands to demonstrate my father's rigid countenance. Though I didn't stop speaking long enough to get a good whiff, I didn't detect the same level of foulness I had in the living room. The odor was still there but less pungent, which was odd. The scent should have grown stronger as we approached ground zero. Maybe the heat pump was sucking all the foul air downstairs to be reconditioned.

"He can't even talk," I went on, walking backward as Garrett plodded toward me. The linen closet door was fast approaching. I could almost feel its cold breath at my back. "He cut his vocal cords when he cut his throat. He's got this huge scar all the way across his neck."

I dragged a finger under my chin as we arrived at the linen closet. I didn't want to draw attention to it, risk Garrett flinging it open to see what it contained, but I couldn't help giving it a quick, worried glance. Rather than coming off as casual, I openly gasped as my eyes did a double take. The door was ajar. I could have sworn it had been closed just a moment before. I inhaled a wisp of air as I pressed the door shut with my palm. Fabric softener and maybe just a hint of—

"I really gave him a piece of my mind," I said as Garrett skirted me to take the lead. "I don't know if he could hear me or not, but it made me feel better to get it off my chest, you know what I mean?"

Garrett muttered "Uh-huh" as we entered the bedroom. He slung his pants and underwear to the floor, and kicked them into the corner, just like he used to do at our old apartment. A sudden pang of homesickness took my breath away. I covered my mouth to stop the all-out sob that constantly seemed to be on the verge of erupting. My mind flashed to the previous winter. The power had been out for two days. We made love by candlelight, dozens of them, every candle we could find, and then sat on the bed to share a cold can of ravioli and a warm beer. Thinking back on it now, that night seemed like a scene from a movie Garrett and I had watched a long time ago, curled up and wishing we were like that couple, obliviously in love, too young and stupid to realize that making love by candlelight was nothing more than a fire hazard.

Garrett grabbed my arm and pulled me against his naked body. "I'm so sorry, Dixie," he said, stooping to burrow his nose in the nape of my neck.

"It's okay," I said, patting his back like it might be blistered. "Seeing my father didn't bother me as much as I thought it would."

"No. Well, I'm sorry about that, too, but I'm sorry for how I behaved about Rory. I should have trusted you. You've never given me a reason to doubt you." He held me tighter. "I don't want to lose you."

"You haven't lost me, Garrett," I said, not returning the full force of his hug. "And I'm not mad. I'm just glad you're here."

He broke away and took my hand, pulling me toward the bathroom. "Shower with me."

I snatched my hand back. "I showered this morning," I lied, turning him around to give him a relatively forceful shove toward the bathroom. "I don't want to get my hair wet." He slumped off through the doorway. "Don't use all my shampoo. I'm almost out. And don't use my razor! There's a box of your stuff in that top box next to the toilet. You've got a razor in there. There's a fresh towel under the sink, so don't go looking for one in the linen closet in the hall." If Garrett thought my warning strange, he didn't say anything. "I might be out of shower gel. There's a bar of soap next to the sink if you need it."

"Hey, I've been looking for this stuff," he called out as a box rustled. "I think you took a few of my boxes by accident. I kept meaning to ask you about them. My alarm clock was in there, you know? That old wind-up one I got after we lost power that time?"

I thought of the alarm clock I saw in one of the boxes in the attic . . . the comforter. Could those possibly be Garrett's boxes? If so, how did they get up there? Had the guys who helped me move carried them up without me noticing? Wouldn't they have asked me first? I pictured the bed frame strewn in front of them. Didn't one just like it come with my new mattress? Was I the one who had slung it up there? And if I had, why couldn't I remember?

Suddenly dizzy, I held my head in both hands to say in a strong voice I hoped wasn't shrill with panic, "I was just thinking about that night! I haven't seen your clock, though!" I started to back out of the bedroom and into the hallway. "I'll go look for it down—"

"That was a good night!" he hollered as the shower turned on. "I hope this storm knocks out the power again so we can snuggle up all night like we did before."

"Don't say that!" I called out. "This is a haunted house, remember? We don't want the lights going out." Or the central air, I thought, glancing at the ceiling.

"Oh, yeah." He laughed. "Scratch that. We can just light some candles and pretend like the power's out."

"Sounds good!" I backed fully into the hallway and pulled the door gently shut. I had just started to turn for the linen closet when I heard the water cut off.

"Dix!"

I stepped back into the room, rolling my eyes as I took a breath to keep my tone level. "Yeah?"

"I love you."

"I love you, too, sweetie."

"Do you want to get some lunch after I shower?" The water started again. "I'm starving!"

"Sounds good!" I yelled.

I stood quietly watching the ceiling until I heard Garrett's body part the steady stream of water, and then loped down the hallway on my tiptoes.

THE HATCH LEADING up to the attic yawned an inscrutable blackness. The stench I'd prepared myself for failed to impress as I unplugged my nose. The closet did smell a little musky, even a little pissy, like a litter box had once been kept here—or a feral cat had secreted itself among the eiderdowns—but there was no hint of a body in decay. I could smell that Garrett was using up all my shampoo, and he was behind two and a half closed doors at the end of the hallway, but I couldn't smell Rory's deadness just a few feet over my head? After almost twenty-four hours, he should have been as ripe as a jockstrap in a gym locker.

Holding on to my B-cup breasts like they might inexplicably burst, I made several chubby-white-girl jumps to determine if I could see anything in the attic without actually going into the attic itself. I could instantly tell that I was out of shape, but that was all I could discern. A quick look-see at Rory couldn't be had from the safe vantage point of the closet. I would have to scale the mountain to see what lay on the other side.

I took three preparative breaths, got a handhold on the uppermost shelf, and began to climb. My right foot hesitated to take a step, and then stepped back down to the floor altogether.

Just looking at Rory's dead body wouldn't accomplish anything. It would only make me more anxious. There was no telling how long Garrett planned to stay. It being Friday, he might stay the entire weekend. That was too long to wait. Though I couldn't smell anything now—and was starting to believe that what I had smelled earlier had probably been Garrett—Rory was going to turn sooner or later. There was no time to get him into a deep freeze, even if I had the means to do so, but I had to trap the scent of his rotting corpse somehow . . .

As an internal clock ticked the time Garrett needed to shower, dry, and dress—something I knew with instinctive accuracy from the years I had spent waiting for him to get ready in the morning so I could use the bathroom—panic started a swinging climb up my spine. I rifled through the shelves of the linen closet for something to wrap Rory in. My blankets, towels, and sheets were all too porous; he'd stink right through them. I found an electric blanket stuffed inside a plastic drawstring bag. That might fit over his head, but what would I do with the rest of him? I needed something big. Like a—

I ran downstairs to the living room.

The three clear plastic tarpaulins from Uncle Davis's garage were folded in the corner next to the stereo. They were decades old and pitted with holes, but they might do the trick. I dashed back up the stairs with them battened to my chest. After slinging them up, I climbed up and took a seated position on the rim of the hatch. With a finger on my wrist to persuade my pulse to bring it down a notch, I peered into the gloaming expanse of the attic.

Though the thunderstorm was enjoying a momentary reprieve, even in its malaise, the late-afternoon sun was no match for the wall of gray clouds it was hidden behind. The iota of sunlight coming through the vent on the far wall was just enough to make the dark shadows on the floor even darker. I waved my hand for the string, but no light followed the clink this time. The tarps were in a frothy jumble before me, obstructing my view. I smacked them aside, angry now, just wanting this to be over. Though I knew Rory's cadaver was halfway between the hatch and the back wall, I couldn't see it. I got to my knees and started forward. My hand stuck to something sticky on the plywood floor. I didn't need to see it to know what it was. Wet, dry, or tacky, blood had a singular feel all to itself. Like the scent of urine, there was no mistaking it, or trying to convince yourself that it might be something else.

I wiped my palm on dry wood to my side and continued to inch forward. A section of the bed frame clanked as my knee came down on a sharp endcap. Wincing, I waved my hand closer to the floor, moving rods aside as I came to them. A few feet past the bed frame, my fingertips brushed something firm and soft. A cry escaped me as I snatched my hand back. Focusing all my might on my vision, I saw what I had touched.

A box.

I had made it all the way across the attic.

I turned and looked back the way I had come. Steamy light rose from the hatch and seeped across the attic floor. I could see everything clearly now: the tarps, the bed frame, the plywood floor, the shiny puddles of blood . . . Everything was here.

Except for Rory.

"Dixie!" Garrett's muffled voice called out from below.

Oh, shit.

"Hey, Dix?" he yelled again. Closer. In the hall.

"Yeah!" I shouted at the attic floor. "Be there in a second!"

"You up there?" In the linen closet.

"Coming!"

I started a mad scramble back to the hatch as Garrett's head popped up through the opening like a whack-a-mole. A terrified laugh burst out of me as my hand fell upon a shaft of metal bed frame.

"What are you doing?" he asked, looking around. "I thought we were going to lunch?"

"Yeah, okay," I said, sweeping the attic with my eyes in case Rory had managed to crawl half dead into a corner and I just hadn't seen him yet. He wasn't visible, but he had to be up here somewhere. I crawled to the pink insulation that ran along the side of the plywood walkway and patted it with my hand to see if he had buried himself inside.

"What the hell are you doing?" Garrett asked.

I sat back on my heels, scratching my head to think. I thought people only scratched their head thoughtfully in movies, but it somehow seemed to help, so I scratched harder, frantic to make sense of this unlikely development. I scanned the other side of the attic. The insulation looked pristine.

Where the hell was he?

"Did you lose something?" Garrett asked.

"What? No. I was just checking it out," I said, crawling forward. My hand skidded out from under me as it found a thicker patch of blood.

"This is a pretty big space. You could turn it into an office, if you wanted," Garrett said, looking around.

As I reached the hatch, I pressed Garrett down by the top of his head. As tall as Garrett was, he stepped easily down to the floor below. "Move over so I can get down," I said. As I glanced through the opening to make sure Garrett was out of my way, I noticed a glistening splotch of red in his wet hair. I withdrew back into the attic and looked down at my palm. It was thick with blood.

"Come on," Garrett said from below. "I'll help you down."

"Hold on. I . . . um . . . I think I cut myself."

"Oh, shit!" Garrett exclaimed. "Are you okay?"

I said I was fine as I looked around for something sharp. The bed frame had loose screws in the slots, but finding one sharp enough to cut myself with would take too long. As I looked up in thought, I spotted a nail protruding from one of the wood rafters. Gritting my teeth, I dragged my palm across it, slicing my hand from thumb to pinkie. I contained the pain with my good hand as I rocked back and forth to silently cry out. Careful not to use my injured palm to brace myself, I spun awkwardly on my elbow and stuck my feet through the access. Garrett took hold of my waist and guided me gently to the floor.

"Let me see?" he said. I held out my hand to him. "How'd you do that?"

"On a nail."

"*Sssss*, it's really bleeding." He grimaced. "We should get it looked at. You might need stitches."

I snatched my hand back. "I'm fine."

"It's bleeding like crazy, Dix. You need to go to the hospital."

I walked out of the linen closet and into the boys' bathroom. I flicked on the overhead light and turned on the sink. I ran my hand under the cold water. The scratch wasn't that bad, in fact, for as much as it stung, my hand was hardly cut at all.

Garrett peered over my shoulder. "When was the last time you had a tetanus shot?"

"You get tetanus from dirt, Garrett. Not rust."

"I don't think that's right," he said skeptically.

"Well, I had a shot not too long ago," I lied, "so I should be okay. They're good for ten years, right?"

He scrutinized me in the mirror. "I don't remember you getting a tetanus shot."

"It was before I met you." I counted off years with tips of my head. "Yeah. It was about two years before that. They're good for ten years, right?" He nodded. "Then I shouldn't need another one for three more years, at least." I smiled at him in the mirror. "Thank goodness. I hate getting shots."

His frown saw right through me. "What did you get one for?"

I shook my head to comprehend the idiocy of the question. "Uh . . . because I cut myself. Why else would you get a tetanus shot?"

"Yeah, but how did you cut yourself?"

"I don't know. Mud-wrestling a wild boar." I wrapped a hand towel around my barely scratched hand like a hemophiliac. "Stop grilling me. I'm hurt."

"You're a terrible liar, Dixie." I looked sideways to hold my breath. "There aren't any wild boars in Virginia." When I rewarded his wit with a pretentious laugh, he folded his arms. "So what were you doing in the attic, anyway?"

"I just wanted to check it out. Come on. Let's go get something to eat. I'm starving." I turned out of the bathroom and down the hall toward the stairs. I was about to take them when I realized Garrett wasn't behind me. I turned back just as he was entering the linen closet. I rushed back, saying, "What are you doing?" His feet were disappearing through the hatch as I made it to the door. "Garrett!"

"I'm just *checking it out!*" he sang sarcastically. There were some rummaging sounds, some creaking wood, the scuff of feet, then *twhink*. Light fell into the linen closet from above. *Oh, sure, now the light works*, I thought as Garrett cried out, "Oh, my god!"

I stepped inside to look up. "What?"

"There's blood everywhere!"

"Well, yeah. I just cut myself, remember?" I unraveled the towel from my hand. The scratch was fiery red, but it was no longer bleeding. I pressed it to my mouth to chew open the wound.

I dropped my hand as Garrett shrieked, "It's everywhere!" The bed frame clanked. "This can't be from your hand, Dixie. There's too much of it."

Now if this had been yesterday, and my father was still dead enough to haunt me, he would have known just what to do. There'd be a second after Garrett dropped back into the closet when he would be slightly off-balance and unprepared. The dusty fire extinguisher in the corner was solid enough to lay him out flat. But my father wasn't dead anymore, and Garrett wasn't just anyone.

I stood back as Garrett peered down at me from above. "What the hell's going on, Dixie? Where did all this blood come from?"

I opened my mouth to speak, then turned and walked out of the closet.

Mr. Cullins's lager tasted like flat, buttery tar, but it was the only alcohol left in the house. I was just finishing my first bottle when Garrett entered the kitchen.

"Dixie!" he said sharply, a million accusations contained in that single word.

I pressed my scraped palm at him and continued to drink.

"What happened?" he demanded.

When the bottle offered no more than a mouthful of bitter foam, I reached into the open fridge and replaced it with a fresh one.

Garrett snatched it from my hand and held it behind his back. "What's going on? Whose blood is that?"

"It's Rory's," I said, walking to the pantry. I found a bottle of pinot grigio behind a bag of flour. I'd bought it in case Aunt Celia ever decided to stop by, which seemed less likely now. I started rooting through drawers for a corkscrew. Ford's bottle opener was strictly a beer gal.

"Goddamn it, Dixie, tell me what happened!"

I yanked the next drawer too hard, and it smashed to the floor. I dropped to my knees to clean up the mess. Garrett stooped down and put his hand against my cheek. I didn't know I was crying until I felt his damp fingers against my skin. I covered my face to weep. I couldn't tell if I was feeling relief that I hadn't actually killed Rory or fear that I hadn't actually killed Rory.

Garrett pulled me into his arms.

"It's okay," he reassured. "I just want to know what happened. Whatever it is, you can tell me."

"I thought he was dead," I sobbed, clinging to him.

He spoke through a kiss to the top of my head. "Why? What happened?"

"He attacked me!" I cried. "I tried to get away, but he came after me. That's how I cut my head. I was so scared I just hit him with that bed thingamajiggy." I swiped my hair off my face to really pour it on. "He went crazy, Garrett! I thought he was going to kill me! I had to stop him!"

"Why would Rory attack you?" Concern filled his eyes as he searched my face, but doubt creased his brow. I lowered my head to give it a hard shake. "Tell me."

"I can't."

"Why not?" When I did not respond, he filled in the blank: "Were you sleeping with him?"

The accusation pitched my chin indignantly upright. "What? No. Of course not. Why would you ask me something like that?"

"Well, that's the only thing I can think of that you wouldn't want to tell me about."

"I wasn't sleeping with Rory, Garrett. God, I wish it was something that . . . simple." My head fell forward on a heavy sigh. "It's so much worse than that. I think . . . I'm not positive, but . . . I think Rory might have murdered that reporter."

"What?" he exclaimed. "You mean, the one they just found down the road from here?"

I nodded as I looked up. "Her name was Claire Reynolds. She thought Rory had something to do with the death of an old girlfriend of his. The police ruled her death an accident, but Claire believed Rory may have killed her. She wrote a bunch of articles about it. She wanted to write a story about me. About my family. She came by the other day when Rory was here. When Rory saw me talking to her, he got really mad. I think he thought she was trying to pin my family's murder on him, too." My eyes widened with this thought. "Maybe he *did* kill them. He lied about being in the house the day of the murders." *What's his game, little girl?* I grabbed Garrett by the front of his shirt. "Maybe Rory thought Claire was getting too close to the truth of what really happened to my family and he killed her to keep her quiet."

Garrett glanced around for something to say, then settled on: "Jesus."

"When I confronted Rory about Claire, he attacked me. I didn't know what to do. I just picked up the closest thing I could find and hit him with it."

"When was this?"

"Last night. I thought he was still up there. I don't know what happened to him."

He looked at the ceiling in disbelief. "You just left him lying up there bleeding? What the hell, Dixie?"

"I thought he was dead, Garrett. Mr. Cullins showed up right after it happened. I was freaking out. I didn't want to leave him like that, but . . . I guess I thought it could wait. I mean, if he was dead, then there wasn't any hurry."

"You thought *what* could wait?" Disgust twisted his expression. "Getting rid of his body? Is that what you mean? What were you planning to do? Bury him in the backyard or something?"

Chop, chop, chop, Dixie. Chop, chop, chop.

I stood to take a step back. "I needed time to think, okay? I thought I had just murdered a man. I didn't know what I was going to do."

"What was Rory doing here, anyway?" His tone contained an accusation. "Had he been here all week?"

"No!" I turned to the sink to wash my hands. The self-inflicted nail wound was like a flame across my palm. The cold water felt boiling. "He just stopped by yesterday. I hadn't seen him since the day you were here. I was in the attic, and he just let himself in and came up. I was shocked to see him. He was acting really strange. He had dead bugs in his hair and shit. Like he'd gone crazy! For all I know, he came here to kill me, too."

I glanced up as Garrett's reflection stood in the window over the sink. He rubbed his face with both hands and then set them on my shoulders.

"We have to call the police." As I shook my head, he said, "Or at least Mr. Cullins. If Rory killed that reporter, and you even suspect that he may have murdered your family, then we're talking about a very disturbed man. You could be in danger."

I turned to look at him. "I don't think we have to worry about that. If Rory's alive, he's not in any shape to come after me. I hit him so hard, Garrett. You saw all the blood. He was out cold. I really thought he was dead. If we go to the police, they might arrest me. I don't have any proof that he killed Claire or my family, just theories. It'll just be Rory's word against mine. And he's the one who got the shit beat out of him."

"They'll understand. You were defending yourself. Just because he got the worse end of the deal doesn't mean he's innocent."

I shook my head. "I have to find out what happened to him first. He might have had the strength to walk out of here, somehow, but that doesn't mean he's not dead, or lying in a coma somewhere. Just let me call him first, find out what's going on. Make sure he's okay. If he's dead, that changes everything. The police will never believe my story."

Garrett shook his head disagreeably, but said, "Okay. One call. Then we go to the police."

14

Garrett frowned as I went to light a cigarette. I had bought the pack when Mr. Cullins stopped for gas, and was eager to get started on it. Sighing, I slipped the cigarette back into the pack and shoved it across the table. I picked up my phone and then set it down to pick up my glass of wine. I was anxious about making the call, especially with Garrett sitting within earshot, and especially without a smoke.

I couldn't believe Rory had walked away from the walloping he received. I closed my eyes and saw the river of blood that had run down the center of his forehead. The light in his eyes had winked out as surely as the attic lightbulb. I could still feel the concussion of his body as it shook the floorboards. Deadweight. In my panic, I hadn't stopped to take his pulse, but there had been no need to confirm what I knew to be true: He was dead. I was certain of it.

"Are you gonna call him?" Garrett asked impatiently.

"Give me a minute." After a deep breath, I picked up the phone. Rory's phone number was cued up and ready to go. "What am I going to say to him, Garrett? 'Hey, Rory, I just want to see if you were alive. Oh, you are? That's great! Okay, thanks. Talk to you later.'"

"Just find out what's going on. If he sounds okay, then we can go to the police and tell them what you suspect about him killing that reporter. I wouldn't bring up anything about your family, though. Not yet. It'll just cloud the issue and make you sound crazy." I looked off uncertainly, and he reached over to touch my hand. "I'm not saying you *are* crazy, it just might sound crazy if you start accusing Rory of murdering your family out of the blue. And it's better if you talk to the

police before he does. If Rory gets to them first and claims you as-
saulted him, then everything you say after that is going to sound like
a deflection. You want it to be your word against his, not the other way
around. Unless he's dead . . ." When my eyes widened with alarm, he
shook his head to negate the concern. "Let's not worry about that until we know for sure. But no matter what, we handle it. Okay?"

"We?" I asked.

He gave my hand a hard squeeze. "Of course. We're in this together. But we can't make a plan until we know what's going on with
him. And we won't know that until you call him."

I closed my eyes to take a deep breath through my nose and
pressed Send. It rang five times before the line connected. A dark
voice grunted something in the vicinity of "Yeah?"

"Rory?" I asked, too startled to breathe. No matter what had become of his body, no matter how it got out of the attic, no matter
where it had ended up, I knew in my heart that Rory was dead. I had
to be talking to a ghost. Not my first, but this time it felt different.

"Yeah?" he said again, casual, like he didn't know exactly who I
was or why I was calling.

Suddenly pissed, I stood to yell, "What the fuck, Rory? Where the
hell are you?"

"*Dixie?*" he asked in a thick, unintelligible voice. He sounded like
he had just woken up.

"Yes, it's Dixie, you asshole!" Garrett made a hang-up gesture, and
I turned away. "Where are you?"

He exhaled a one-syllable word that I couldn't understand.

"Where?" I demanded.

He tried to enunciate by breaking the word into two distinct syl-
lables, which made it all the more unclear. I was about to ask him to
repeat himself again when I realized he was trying to say that he was
at *home*. He must have brain damage, I thought as I reached for my
nonexistent cigarette in the ashtray. I clenched the jonesy feeling in
my fist.

"Are you . . . okay?" I asked.

"Yeah."

"Are you hurt?"

"No."

"Bullshit! Yes, you are! Why are you doing this?"

The line went dead.

"Ugh!" I screamed. "He hung up!" I rehit Send.

"Don't call him back," Garrett said as the phone rang in my ear. "Obviously he's not dead. That's all we wanted to know. You're just going to antagonize him."

I patted Garrett's concern down as the line connected. I opened my mouth to scream when a happy voice said, *"Hey, this is Rory, leave me a message . . . Beep!"*

"Rory! What the fuck is going on? Call me back right fucking now, you fucking jerk!" I disconnected and slammed the phone against the table.

Garrett picked up the phone and looked at it as if I had been texting the conversation. "What did he say the first time you called?"

"Yeah, what, huh," I mimicked in a grunting voice. I grabbed my bag and slung it over my shoulder. Garrett stood to block me.

"Where are you going?"

"I'm going over to Rory's," I said as I moved around him.

He stepped in front of me. "No, you're not. You're going to the police like you promised."

"Not yet. Something strange is going on." I started around him again, and he put his hands on my shoulders to hold me stationary.

"We have to let the police handle this, Dix. You don't need to see Rory again. Why would you even want to? He's dangerous. He's obviously not hurt that bad. If he was, he would have called an ambulance and he'd be in the hospital already. That's all we wanted to find out. Now we know he's okay, we can go to the police."

"We're still in the same boat, Garrett. I don't have any evidence that Rory killed Claire. If I go to the police, I'll have to tell them everything. I don't think they're going just to let slide that I hit Rory ten times with a metal rod and left him to die in my attic. That's assault with a deadly weapon."

"Ten times?"

"Yes! I freaked out, Garrett. See what I'm saying? If they don't believe me about Claire, then what? Rory might press charges against me in retaliation or to make it look like I—" My phone rang. I turned and snatched it off the table. I gave a distraught sigh as I read the caller's name. "It's Mr. Cullins." Garrett mouthed *Tell him* as I shook my head and said, "Hello?"

"How ya doing, kid?" Mr. Cullins asked.

"I'm okay," I said.

"You still with Garrett?" he asked.

I looked up at Garrett, who was snapping his fingers open and shut like an apoplectic duck. I grabbed his hand to silence it. "Yes," I said calmly into the phone. "Did you get a dog?"

"As a matter of fact, I did," he said as a dog barked in the background. "They had this really old, ugly-as-crap English bulldog. He looks like he's trying to eat his own face. His name is Dingle."

"He sounds perfect for you."

Garrett shook his head in defeat and walked out of the kitchen.

"This is just a visit to see if we're a match. I think they only let me take him because I'm an ex-cop, and because they're full up. I was lucky to get out of there with just one dog. I have to go back and sign the final paperwork. I guess we're getting along. He's made himself right at home. Pissed on the couch as soon as he got here." I laughed in a phony way that made him ask, "What's wrong?"

"Nothing," I said, sinking onto my mother's chair—no, Josh's—whatever.

"Hey, have you gotten a call from Allied Hospital?" he said.

"No. Why?" I swatted a hand at Garrett as he walked back in with a finger in the air. He turned and stomped away as I said, "Did something happen to my father?"

"I don't know. Ham—uh, Dr. Cheatham—left me a message. He didn't leave any details, but said it was urgent. I tried to call him back, but I got his voice mail. The front desk wouldn't give me any information. I thought they might have called you since you were just there."

"No one's called me," I said. "What do you think happened?"

"I don't know. I'll try to find out when I get back. I have to run back out and get a leash. Dingle chewed through his on the way home."

"Let me know when you hear something," I said.

"Will do. Okay, talk to you late—*Dingle!*" he screamed as he disconnected the line.

I turned to find Garrett standing behind me. The iron head of a wooden-handled hammer bowed from his hand like a guilty vulture. Three long strands of red hair dangled from a splat of blood on its blunt face.

I stood slowly with my hands in the air, ready to pat out the fire that was burning bright in Garrett's eyes.

"I thought you said you hit Rory with the bed frame?" he said in a thick voice. He toyed the ends of the hair with the tip of his finger. "And I don't remember Rory having long red hair."

"Where'd you get that?" I asked.

"It was in the top drawer of the desk. I also found these." He held up a rumpled grab of crime scene photographs. "I was looking for a pen. I wanted to write you a note about what you should say to Mr. Cullins."

I knew I should say something, but all I could do was blink.

"Jesus, Dixie. What have you done?"

WHEN SOMEONE WOULD ask me how many siblings I had, I always said three. It didn't feel right to say none, and anything otherwise required a complex explanation. One of the first questions Garrett asked was if my family lived in the area. Thinking of the cemetery across town where my mother and brothers were buried—I presumed my father had been cremated when I couldn't find his grave along with the others at Leah's funeral, and Aunt Celia hadn't corrected me—I almost said yes. But when I saw that his interest might be more than just idle chat, I said, "I lost them." He had looked around the crowded bar as if that was where I had lost them, nodding like he might be able to help me find them, and for a moment, I believed he could. "My parents and three brothers died a long time ago," I amended, looking at my feet, feeling more orphaned than ever. "All of them?" he asked. I downed the rest of my drink to prepare myself to tell him how they died, exactly, but he didn't inquire. Instead he said, "Well, that sucks," and bought me another whiskey sour. That he could take the death of an entire family in such unquestioning stride told me he might be the man for me. Even when I finally told him that they had been hacked to death with an axe, he didn't freak out. He wasn't even that shocked to hear I had nearly beaten Rory to death. But as I looked up at the blank horror in his expression, I realized that his tolerance for my ghastly enterprises had reached its limit. Garrett's blood bucket was but a wee little thing.

"Put down the hammer, Garrett," I said.

He glanced up, rather surprised to find the hammer raised over his shoulder, and dropped it on the table. When I asked him to sit down, he obediently pulled out a chair. He lowered himself onto it steadily enough, but the crime scene photographs drifted dazedly to the floor at his side. I knelt down to gather them.

"Is that the hammer I gave you?" he said, like I had hocked a piece of jewelry he had given me to buy drugs.

I set the photographs facedown on the counter and took a seat across from him. "I think so. Yes."

He closed his eyes and kneaded desperation from his brow before it could fully harden into rage. "Whose hair is that?" When I didn't answer, his eyes flicked up to mine. "Is it that reporter's? The one you *claimed* Rory killed?"

I gave a soft shrug to shake my head.

"Was she murdered with *my* hammer?"

He seemed more fixated on the hammer part of it than the murder part of it. I sighed "Apparently" with just enough tedium to draw his brows to a sharp point.

"Don't say it like I asked a stupid question, Dixie. I'm just trying to figure out what the fuck is going on."

"I know. I'm sorry."

I stared at the hammer for a long moment. The three strands lying on the table were just those that had fallen loose; quite a few curls were tangled around the neck and claw, matted to the face in what looked to be a slice of paper-thin scalp. I was relieved to see that the handle was shellacked with wood varnish and nothing else. It had not been used to violate Claire, as my father had boasted.

Garrett prompted me to continue with a clear of his throat.

"I think that's her hair," I said. "It looks like it."

"You think?" he challenged.

I shrugged. "I don't know any more about it than you do, Garrett."

He chided me with a hoarse laugh. "I don't think that's possible."

I pointed at the hammer. "I haven't seen that since the night you lent it to me. I didn't know what happened to it. It just vanished."

"Then how did it get in your desk?"

"It's not my desk, it's my uncle's."

He shook his head wearily as I slammed back the rest of my wine. I reached for my cigarettes, which were lying in the clawed nook of the hammer, and withdrew my hand. "The only thing I can think is that Rory used it to kill Claire and then planted it in the desk to frame me. Just like he tried to plant the phone."

"What phone?"

"I caught Rory trying to slip Claire's phone into a box in the attic. That's what we were fighting about."

"Why didn't you tell me that before?"

I shook my head. "I forgot."

"That's a big detail to forget." He shoved the hammer toward me with his knuckle. Like his fingerprints weren't already all over it. "Tell me everything. And no more lying or selectively forgetting."

"I'm not lying, Garrett." I pushed the hammer back at him with the tip of my finger. The handle spun three times and landed on me like I was "it" in a game of spin the bottle. As the cigarettes twirled clear, I snatched up the pack and lit one. I took a long drag before saying, "When Rory came over yesterday, I was up in the attic. He went to the back of the attic to look through some boxes that were up there. When I came over to see what was in them, I found the phone. Claire Reynolds's phone. I accused Rory of killing her. He attacked me. And I hit him with the bed frame. That's it. That's all I know. He must have slipped the hammer into the desk before he came upstairs."

"Why would he try to frame you for murder? I thought you were friends."

"I've been trying to figure that out myself. I guess that after he killed her he got scared. I guess he thought I was a good person to try and pin it on."

"Why would you be?"

"He probably thought that because I moved back to this house people would believe I went crazy and just started killing people." The sharp laugh I gave was too manic to be merely incredulous. I took a drag off my cigarette. "I mean, everyone thought I was crazy for moving back in here. You did, so did Aunt Celia."

"That might have been a crazy thing to do, but that's a far cry from murder, Dixie. That woman was beaten to death and dumped in the woods." He cocked his head at the ceiling. "Sounds a little familiar, doesn't it?"

"What's that mean?"

He shrugged. "Pronto's is right down the road from here. Is that where you were planning to dump Rory's body, too?"

"What? No!" I slapped the table so hard the hammer flipped over, like a fish giving one last thrash after you thought it was long dead. "I didn't kill Claire, Garrett. Jesus! What do you think I am, some kind of monster?"

"I don't know. I mean . . ." He rubbed a plaintive chuckle from his mouth. "You have to admit this all looks pretty bad, Dixie."

"I know! That's why I can't go to the police." I stood in a turn toward the sink to run water over the tip of my cigarette. I dropped it into the open mouth of the disposal and I stared out the window. No sign of Eddie. "I know how bad this all looks, Garrett. And after telling you what I did to Rory, I can see how you might think . . ." I shook my head. "But truthfully, I don't think I had anything to do with Claire Reynolds's murder. I really don't."

In the quiet, I heard him swallow. "Don't you know?"

My phone rang. I turned and glanced at the screen. Mr. Cullins. I pressed Ignore as I retook my seat.

"I haven't been honest with you about some things, Garrett. I have these . . . I don't know . . . blackouts, I guess. I've had them ever since I was little. I never told you about them because they had stopped. I hadn't had one in years. Not since I met you, in fact." I smiled my appreciation, and he rolled me on with his eyes. "Anyway. They just started up again. When I moved into this house, actually. I guess you were right. Moving in here was a big mistake."

"Blackouts," he said. "What, like you wake up someplace and don't know how you got there?"

I nodded. "Or what happened. But that's not all." I lowered my head to pick at a fingernail. "When I have them, it's like . . . my father kinda takes over. Like I'm possessed by him or something."

"Your father?" he breathed. "Dixie, that's—"

"Crazy? I know! That's what I'm trying to tell you, Garrett. I'm crazy. And now that I know my father's alive, I'm even crazier than I thought. I know this is hard for you to understand, and this isn't an excuse, but the truth is: I don't know exactly what happens when I black out. I just know that I go away and . . . and then he's there."

"He's where?"

"Around me. In me." I set my face in my hands. "I don't know. I can't explain it."

"Up until recently—until you decided to blame Rory for it, all of a sudden—you believed your father was an axe murderer. Is that what you're trying to say? That, what? He murders people through you or something? Is that what you're trying to fucking tell me?"

Garrett's harsh tone sat me back. This wasn't going at all as I intended. What was I thinking telling Garrett about my father? I wasn't ready to come clean like this, and he was definitely not ready to understand. Not with his bloody hammer lying between us. I opened my mouth to retract my incredibly rash, and thoroughly incriminating, statement altogether. Play it down. Call it a joke. But all I could do was offer a dull, shameful nod.

"Oh, my god, Dixie," he breathed.

Though I knew I had made a terrible miscalculation in telling Garrett about my father—one that I hoped we would both live to regret—to say my darkest fears aloud was like shedding skin that was too tight for me. I could finally breathe, and words escaped in a rush:

"I thought my father was haunting me, Garrett. I really did. I know that sounds crazy, but I really believed that he was a ghost. I've been seeing him ever since I was a little girl. But he wasn't dead, so he couldn't have been a ghost. I guess that means I really *am* crazy. But the thing of it is, I don't think I am. Not completely, anyway. I know I was the one who hit Rory with that bed frame now. I *was* terrified of him, Garrett. That part is true. Only . . . when it was happening, I did black out. Or pretended to black out so my father could come through. I'm not sure which. I guess I just didn't want to believe I could do something like that, so . . . I made my father do it for me instead."

I shook my head, hearing how truly absurd that sounded. I looked up to gauge Garrett's reaction, but he just blinked at me through a stoic expression.

"I don't blame you for not understanding. I don't understand, either. But the truth is"—I pointed at the hammer on the table—"I don't know how that hammer got Claire's blood and hair on it. Or how it got in the desk drawer. Or where it's been for the last few days. Until you found it, I had no idea what had happened to it. I thought it was lost. I guess with these blackouts, I can't rule out my having something to do with it, but I'm pretty sure that Claire wasn't one of the people my father . . . I mean, I . . . killed."

"One of the people," Garrett said through his fingers as he covered his mouth. "Who else have you killed, Dixie?"

I bobbed my head indecisively. "Well, I thought I had killed Rory, and then there was . . ." I looked down to take a breath. "Leah."

"Leah?" Garrett looked for the name in the corner of his eye. "You mean your cousin? I thought you said she died of cancer."

I shook my head as I lowered my eyes. I had never told anyone about Leah. It felt as though I was about to break a promise to her.

"Leah did have cancer. Stage four. She was so sick, Garrett. You know when you hear someone is being eaten away by cancer? Well, that was Leah, through and through. She was nothing but skin and bone. She was in such pain. Unimaginable pain. I don't know which was worse on her, the cancer or the cancer treatments. Both were eating her alive. She couldn't take the pain anymore." I closed my eyes to finally tell what I'd sworn I never would: "Leah asked me to kill her. She asked me to smother her with a pillow. She begged me to do it. She told me exactly what to do, step by awful step." I looked up with bright, tear-filled eyes. "But I couldn't. I couldn't do it, so . . . my father did it. He took the pillow from me and . . . and then everything went black. When I opened my eyes, Leah was dead."

"Oh, Dix . . ."

I waved off his sympathy as my phone rang again. I clicked the side button to send Mr. Cullins to voice mail.

"I have to own that I killed Leah. And I have to own that I tried to kill Rory. Blackouts or not. Senseless as I might have been at the time, I still had good reasons to want both of them dead. One asked me to do it, and one was asking for it. But I didn't have a reason to kill Claire, Garrett. Rory's the one who hated her. Then I find out Rory had lied to me about being in the house the day my family was murdered. He always said that he came in after the murders, but he lied. He told me he was hiding in my brother Josh's room the whole time. Rory had access to the hammer, both to take it and to put it back. I really think he killed Claire, Garrett." I shook my head as tears rolled slowly down my cheeks. "I don't know. Maybe I did kill her and just can't remember. Maybe I am just like my father. Maybe I just needed to believe that Rory killed her, just like I needed to believe that my father killed Leah. But he didn't kill Leah. I did! I'm the killer!"

Garrett came around the table to kneel beside me as I burst into tears.

"Just because you helped your dying cousin commit suicide when you were a little girl doesn't make you a killer, Dixie. And that's exactly what it was, okay? Suicide. You didn't murder her. You were trying to help her. She had no right to ask you to do something like that. You were just a kid. How were you supposed to deal with something like that? No wonder you pretended that your father did it. You invented him to help you cope. I understand. You can't blame yourself anymore. It wasn't your fault."

"But it was my fault, Garrett. I was the one who held the pillow over her face, whether I remember doing it or not. Who knows what else I've done during these stupid blackouts? Claire Reynolds was in this house the day she went missing." I pointed at the living room. "She was sitting right on that couch. I went upstairs to get my phone when you called, and when I came back down she was gone. That was the last time anyone ever saw her alive. I must have killed her, but I just don't remember doing it. Just like I don't remember killing Leah."

"Yeah, but it's just like you said. You had a reason to kill Leah. You were trying to end her suffering. And you had every reason to knock the snot out of Rory with that bed frame. You thought he was trying to frame you for murder. Shit. I would have done it, and I wouldn't feel the least bit sorry about it, either. Like you said, he was the one who hated Claire, not you. You had no reason to kill her. You hardly knew her, right? Why kill her?"

I gave a hopeless chuckle. "I guess I just thought that my father was on a murderous rampage again."

"But now you know better, right?" I nodded and he squeezed my knee. "So, if you think about it, you really haven't killed anyone. Leah . . . whatever. You did what she asked you to do. And we know Rory's alive, so you didn't kill him, right?"

I nodded. I couldn't tell Garrett about Erin. That was just one too many dead bodies to justify.

Garrett nodded at the hammer. "Is that the only thing that connects you to Claire Reynolds's murder? Just the hammer? Nothing else?"

I nodded before I remembered: "Oh! And her business card and phone."

"Where are they now?"

"I don't know where her business card is, but her phone is"—I looked at the ceiling to cringe—"in the attic."

ONCE I KNEW where the hammer had been hiding, I found Claire's business card easily enough. But after searching the attic three times over, her phone was nowhere to be found. Garrett did, however, find his alarm clock boxed up with some of his other possessions. His slanted glance questioned my lack of knowledge as to how his boxes came to be in my attic, but happy to have his clock back, he let it go.

"Maybe Rory took the phone with him," I said. "I remember him dropping it before . . ." I shook off an image of the phone slipping from his hand with a hard shudder. "But he could have picked it up before he left." I looked around the floor. The dried blood looked black in the long shadows. There wasn't as much of it as I had feared, or to merit Garrett's shrieking exclamation, but still I dreaded the thought of cleaning it up. Nailing the hatch to the attic shut and forgetting about it seemed like a good solution.

Garrett nodded. "He must have taken it. If it was up here some-where and it was still on, the police would have traced it, and you'd be in jail by now."

"Well," I said, turning to leave, "if Rory took it with him, I'm toast."

"Why?"

"Because Claire taped our conversation the day she was here. That proves she was in my house the day she went missing. If Rory gives it to the police, they'll never believe I had nothing to do with her death."

I lowered myself carefully to a seated position on the rim of the hatch and dangled my legs through the opening.

"Why didn't he use it to call 9-1-1?" Garrett asked. I looked back at him. "If he was that injured, and thought you had just tried to kill him, why not call the police? Or at least ask for an ambulance to take him to the hospital."

"I don't know. I can't picture him driving himself home in his con-dition. And he would have had to walk a ways to get to his car," I added. "Rory told me that he parked way down the street so you wouldn't freak out if you stopped by while he was here."

"That was nice of him," Garrett said sarcastically.

"I don't remember seeing any blood in the closet or the hallway, did you?" I pointed at the dark puddle at Garrett's feet. "Rory must have been bleeding all over the place. He should have left a trail of blood, right?"

Garrett shrugged. "Not necessarily. He might have found some-thing to wrap his head in. Or maybe it stopped bleeding by the time he left."

"Are you sure it was Rory's SUV you saw drive by last night?"

He looked off to picture it. "Not really. I dozed off for a minute. I woke up just as it raced by. I can't even say for sure that it was black. It was a big SUV, though." He shrugged. "It looked like his."

I thought for a moment. "I didn't see it when Mr. Cullins drove me home today, but I was so upset after talking to Aunt Celia that I—" I covered my mouth to gasp.

"What?"

"I called Rory on his cell phone."

"Yeah, so?"

"I just assumed he was at home, but he could have been any-where."

I turned onto my belly and started to climb down. The bunk bed ladder Garrett had brought in from the boys' room was a little short, but was tall enough for me to reach without hanging by my chin. As I hit the floor, I looked up at Garrett, who was looking down at me through the hatch.

"Come on. Let's go see if Rory's 4Runner is still parked down the street." I left the closet saying, "Shit, he might be sitting in it, for all we know."

15

The black SUV was parked on the corner of a cul-de-sac no more than an eighth of a mile down the road from my house. I slapped the window of Garrett's Mazda just as he reached a top cruising speed of ten miles per hour.

"There it is!" I thought of the movie *Fargo* and added, "Tan Sierra! Tan Sierra!"

"Okay, Margie," Garrett said in an upper Midwest accent as he pulled to the side of the road.

That was what I loved most about Garrett: He always got me. A sudden wave of emotion came over me or, more accurately, departed from me. For a second I didn't recognize what I was feeling. The dark shadow of dread that I had been living under was being slowly eclipsed by a glimmer of hope. I wasn't completely in the clear, but a ray of light had begun to crest the moonless horizon. And that was because of Garrett. The ease I felt with him next to me, and the gratitude I had for this, leaned me over to give him a long kiss.

He smiled as I sat back. "What was that for?"

"For sticking with me. I know this hasn't been easy on you. Any of it. My moving out and living in this house. Lying to you about it. All the stuff with Rory. All the stuff about my father. What I told you about Leah. Finding the hammer and . . . Claire." I shook my head. "And to top it all off, I've been a complete bitch about everything. Most guys wouldn't have hung around for half the shit I've put you through. I just want you to know how much I appreciate all you're doing for me. Your being here means the world to me. It's been so lonely. I've been so scared. But now you're here, I feel like everything might actually be okay." I took his hand in mine. "I've missed you so much. I love you more than anything, Garrett." I went in for another kiss, and he caught my face in his hands.

"I love you, too. Believe me, I'd like nothing more than to sit here and watch you grovel. And I promise I'll come up with some creative ways for you to make it up to me later. But right now, we need to focus." He kissed my nose. "Okay?"

I nodded.

"Could you tell if Rory was sitting in his truck?" he asked.

"No. I only saw the back of it. It's parked on the corner." I reached for the door handle.

"Hold on," he said, unbuckling. "You wait here."

"Why?"

"Because we don't know what Rory's deal is."

"If he's in there, he's probably passed out or seriously incapacitated. If he was in good enough shape to drive, he would have been gone by now."

Garrett tilted the mirror to get a rear view. "Still, we need to be careful." When the mirror failed to provide him a visual advantage, he turned to look over his shoulder. "Just stay here while I go and—"

I was halfway around the car before he finished the sentence. Eyes locked on the back of Rory's black SUV, I squatted low as I slowly approached the tailgate, hand outstretched so as not to scare it away. I pressed my ear to its back to locate a heartbeat within. And though I knew it could not be so, I thought I detected a breath of Drakkar emanating from the tailpipe. The slam of a car door spun my back to the bumper. Garrett was coming at me low and fast, crawling like a pissed-off daddy longlegs.

"Goddamn it, Dixie," he whispered as he turned to squeeze in beside to me. "Stop fucking around."

"Shhh," I said, then craned my neck to look down the long driver's side of the truck. The door was closed. I glanced in the side-view mirror, but could only see a banner of glossy black paint under a darkening sky. I looked up as it started to drizzle. "I can't see anything," I said. I turned to tell Garrett that I was going for the door, but he was gone. I crawled to the other side of the SUV and saw Garrett rising to a half squat to peek in the passenger's side window. As I hurried up behind him, he thrust out a hand to hold me back.

"What do you see?" I whispered as he peered in the window over my head.

"Nothing," he said, straightening fully. "It's empty."

I stood and wiped condensation from the window with the sleeve of my jacket. "Shit. I really thought he'd be in there." As I reached for the door handle, Garrett stopped me. "Don't touch it with your hands. We don't want to leave fingerprints."

"What does that matter?"

"I just want us to be careful. A woman was murdered, after all. If Rory did it, then his car could be impounded. Let's not leave any evidence behind that could implicate us."

"Good thinking." I used the front pocket of my jacket like a glove to try the door handle. "Locked," I announced.

Garrett used the tail of his shirt to try the tailgate, smiling as it lifted with a soft hydraulic swish.

I stood next to him to stare inside. Golf clubs and a gym bag were set neatly to either side of a pristine cargo area. I yanked the canvas gym bag forward. I pinched the zipper between my knuckles to open it.

"What are you doing?"

"Just looking," I said as I flung a jockstrap aside.

"For what?"

"Maybe Rory stuck Claire's phone in here or something."

Besides the jock, the bag contained gym clothes, a towel, a plastic water bottle, a can of rubber balls, terry wristbands, a small tennis racket, and four PowerBars. I was about to zip it back up when I noticed some papers poking out from an inside side pocket. I un-folded the first one. A receipt for a smoothie shop called the Frosty Organic. Three more receipts proved that Rory really dug their mango-kale energy boosts. I almost discarded the last folded piece of paper as another smoothie receipt, then opened it on a whim. The receipt was for an oil change and tire rotation from Denny's Auto Works.

"What the hell," I said.

Garrett peeked over my shoulder. "What?"

"This receipt is from the garage Ford works at—when he's home, anyway."

Garrett took the receipt from me to examine it. I tapped the name of the establishment with my finger. "See? It's from Denny's. Look at the date." Garrett squinted at it. "That's the day I moved into this house."

Garrett handed back the receipt with a shrug. "That's probably just a coincidence."

"Denny's is in Warrenton, Garrett." I shook the receipt at him. "Rory lives all the way out in Falls Church. This receipt is for an oil change and a tire rotation. Would you drive half an hour down 66 at—" I glanced at the time stamp on the receipt. "What's 1800 in hours?"

"That *is* hours."

I gave him an exasperated look. "You know what I mean. 1800 is at night, right?"

Garrett nodded. "Six o'clock P.M. You subtract twelve hours to get—"

"Whatever. Point is: Would Rory drive all that way in rush-hour traffic just to get his oil changed?"

Garrett shrugged. "I wouldn't, but he might."

"Ford and Rory hate each other," I stated. "I don't think they've ever spoken more than two words to each other in all the time I've known them. Ford wouldn't give Rory a deal on a broken watch, much less hook him up for a free oil change."

"Free?"

I turned the receipt to him. "Zero point zero zero. And he only charged him ten bucks for a tire rotation. I'm sure that costs more than that."

"Ford never gave me a free oil change."

"And Ford likes you," I professed.

"I wouldn't go that far. I don't think Ford likes anybody, really." Garrett shrugged. "Okay. I agree, that's a little strange, but who cares? What's that got to do with anything?"

I sighed. "I don't know. I just think it's weird."

The sound of car brakes screeching to a stop turned our heads. A white sedan was at the curb in front of my house. The driver's side door swung open, and a rather rotund bulldog hopped ungracefully out, shoulder-rolled onto his side, then got to his feet in a loping run.

"What's Mr. Cullins doing here?" I said as he chased the dog across my lawn.

I hurried down the street as Garrett ran to get his car. As I got to the sidewalk in front of my house, I saw Mr. Cullins standing in my flower bed to peer in the front window through his cupped hands. I shouted "Hey!" and the pudgy bulldog stopped peeing on the corner of my stoop to bark at me.

Mr. Cullins yelled something that sounded like a question wrapped in a curse as he turned in the soft mulch and tripped over his feet. I stepped forward to help him, but the dog thought it best if I stayed right where I was. Paws planted firmly, he howled a warning that was half terrifying, half adorable. I stepped carefully forward as Mr. Cullins came at me full steam. He yelled at Dingle to stay, which to Dingle meant: *Get to her before I do.* The dog reached my feet just as Mr. Cullins pulled to a slipping stop in the wet grass in front of me.

"I've been calling you for two hours!" he yelled over Dingle's frothing yowls.

I pointed over my shoulder at Rory's SUV. "Sorry, I was—"

"Didn't you get my messages?"

"No," I said, holding the back of my hand out to the dog. Dingle swallowed his last bark to sniff it. I looked up to smile, but quickly frowned when I saw how red in the face Mr. Cullins was. He looked ready to pop. "What's wrong?"

"It's your father," he gasped. "He's missing. They think he might have escaped."

DINGLE WATCHED US from his semisleeping guard position by the front door. Each time a car drove down the street, he would raise his head, give a bark, look at me like I had somehow let him down, sneeze distastefully, and then settle back into his puddle of drool. Though this exact scene had played out more than thirty times in the last two hours, I rose to look out the window at my driveway.

"Mr. Cullins should have called by now," I said, retaking my seat on the couch next to Garrett. "He knows we're waiting to hear from him."

Dr. Cheatham had asked Mr. Cullins to come to the hospital to assist with the search for my father, and to liaise with the police while he met with Allied's attorneys to draft an official response to the media. Searchlights at a mental hospital for the criminally insane tend to draw attention, and a convoy of news vans had descended on the old grounds in a matter of minutes.

I checked my phone to see if I had missed a text from him, vaguely wondering if a man of his age would text even if it occurred to him to do so. Only a weather update sat on my screen. Light rain was due to begin in the next hour, dropping temperatures into the low forties overnight. I wondered if it was raining in Richmond, and if Dr. Cheatham had gotten my father some slippers that fit. Not that they would help much against the cold, damp night to come; he probably wasn't wearing more than a threadbare robe and a thin pair of cotton scrubs. "I can't believe my father escaped," I said as I closed my phone.

Garrett, refusing to participate in the same conversation once more, indulged me with an apathetic nod.

"I mean, it's impossible. He couldn't even walk. How the hell did he get away from a maximum-security facility? And why would he? What is he planning to do?" I glanced at Garrett, whose eyes had closed. I elbowed him. "I can't believe you can sleep at a time like this."

He rubbed his face to sit up. "I'm not."

"We still have Rory to worry about, you know."

"I know."

"I've been thinking about it, and there's no way Rory would have left his car behind. Not if he could have helped it. He couldn't have walked all the way home. It's too far. So what did he do? Call for an Uber? Catch a bus? No way. Not the way he looked." I shook my head querulously. "Something else is going on. I don't know what, but he's up to something. I can just feel it."

"Hey!" Garrett said with a sudden, revived gasp that startled me. "What if Rory helped your father escape?"

I scrunched my forehead. "Why would he do that?"

"I don't know." He shrugged. "To mess with your head, I guess."

"Well, that would certainly do it," I said through a nervous laugh. "But how did he pull it off without the 4Runner? What did he do, give my father a piggyback ride?"

"Yeah, I guess not." He sighed back into his malaise. After a long, infectious yawn that spread to both Dingle and me, he said, "Maybe Rory called someone to come and take him to the hospital."

"And bust my father out of an insane asylum?" I balked. "No one is that good of a friend. I wouldn't even ask you to help me do something like that."

"No. To take Rory to a hospital to get his head looked at. I take back the whole Rory-helping-your-father-escape idea. That was stupid."

"Maybe it's not. I don't think it's any coincidence that my father and Rory are both missing under unusual circumstances. If you think about it, neither of them were in any condition to launch an escape on their own. Rory from my attic, and my father from the hospital . . . They feel connected, don't they?"

Garrett nodded as he patted his leg to get Dingle's attention. The dog opened one eye, and then closed it. "I still think you should have told Mr. Cullins that you suspect Rory killed your family. I get why you didn't want to tell him about Claire, we have to be careful about how we handle that, but you should have at least given him a heads-up that you think your father may be innocent. The Richmond police are on a manhunt for a crazed axe murderer. They might shoot first and ask questions later. That would suck if your father didn't do it."

"I *did* tell Mr. Cullins that I suspected Rory of killing my family and he didn't believe me!" I dropped my head into my hands. "And honestly, Garrett, I'm not sure who killed who anymore. I'm so freaking tired, I don't think I can trust my instincts about anything. I need sleep and time to think before I say anything to Mr. Cullins. And don't you say anything to him, either."

"He might be able to help."

"Yeah. Help arrest me. I'm linked to every bad thing that's happened." I sat up to tick them off on my fingers. "Claire goes missing the same day she interviews me. Her phone and murder weapon are planted in my house. I nearly beat Rory to death in my attic. And the day I visit my father for the first time is the day he decides to escape." I spread my hands in exasperation. "If I wasn't a baby when my family died, I'd probably be a suspect in those murders, too. No one is going to believe I'm being framed. I hardly believe it myself. I don't have one plausible reason for why Rory would want to frame me in the first place. None of it makes any sense." I shook my head. "I just have this horrible feeling that if I told Mr. Cullins about any of it, it would all backfire in my face."

"You're lucky Mr. Cullins didn't see the hammer when he was here before. It was lying right on the kitchen table."

I threw my head back. "Oh, shit! I forgot all about it! Do you think he saw it?"

"Relax," Garrett said. "I stuck it in a drawer when I went to get Dingle a bowl of water. Mr. Cullins had his back to me the whole time. There's no way he saw it. I was just pointing out that we're being a little careless."

I deflated into the couch. "Oh, thank goodness."

"Look, until we can prove that Rory killed that reporter, we have to start covering our asses. That hammer is evidence. My prints are on it. Your prints are on it. Every second it's in this house we run the risk that someone might find it. We need to get rid of it immediately."

"I love how you keep saying we, Garrett, but maybe you shouldn't get involved. I'd never forgive myself if you got into trouble because of me. Go home and play dumb. I can handle it from here."

He raised his eyebrows to hook a thumb at the door. "Really? I can go? You sure you don't mind?"

When I nodded in disbelief, he shook his head.

"Don't be stupid," he said. "I'm not going anywhere." He shrugged a heavy sigh. "What difference would it make, anyway? I'm probably already an accessory. I've been aiding and abetting you all day long."

I gave him a smile. "Okay, you can stay and be my accessory, if you really want to be." Dingle's head appeared between my knees as I tried to stand. He took the light tap I gave his nose as an invitation to climb onto my lap. "You're right. Our first order of business should be getting rid of the hammer." I ducked back as Dingle came in for a kiss. "Why don't we give it to Dingle to bury?" Dingle snuffed that this proposition was fine by him. "Maybe he'll just eat it whole. His mouth's certainly big enough."

"I've got a better idea," Garrett said. He returned from the kitchen with the bloody hammer wrapped in one of my mother's tea towels. "Let's go turn the tables on Rory."

AFTER PLANTING THE hammer in Rory's gym bag, we returned to the house to pat ourselves on the back, and to await Mr. Cullins's return. The plan was to casually mention that we had seen a vehicle that looked like Rory's 4Runner when we let Dingle out for a pee. When Mr. Cullins went to check it out, he would find Rory's abandoned SUV, thus the bloody hammer, and Rory would be in jail by morning. After that, it wouldn't matter what Rory told the police. Trouble was, Mr. Cullins never returned to set our plan into motion, nor was he answering his phone.

I picked up my phone to dial.

"You're not calling Mr. Cullins again, are you?"

"No. I'm calling Aunt Celia. I should have called her right away. She needs to know that my father's escaped in case . . ." I shook the horrible thought from my head before it could fully form. "She's all by herself, Garrett. When I went to see her she told me that Ford hasn't been home in days. Who knows what's going on with my father? She could be in danger. I'm going to tell her to come over here, whether she wants to or not."

As the line connected, I was greeted by a stark grunt that mimicked Rory's brain-dead speech pattern to a T. I glanced at the phone to make sure I hadn't accidently redialed Rory's cell phone number. "ICE" was written across the top of the screen. Aunt Celia was my In Case of Emergency contact. I put the phone back to my ear to ask, "Who is this?"

"Who wants to know?" The underlying sneer in his voice was all the clarification I needed.

"What are you doing there, Ford?" I demanded. "I thought you took off."

"Off and back again," he said. "What's up?"

"Let me talk to Aunt Celia."

"She's asleep." I told him to wake her up. "Can't. She took a couple of sleeping pills. She's dead to the world."

"She's been sick, Ford. She was sipping NyQuil through a straw like it was a juice box. She shouldn't be taking sleeping pills. Don't let her do that."

"I ain't her doctor. Cel knows what's best for her."

I huffed my displeasure. "Did you hear about my father?"

"What's to hear?" His laugh was dry. "He's dead, ain't he?"

"You know he's not," I said. "You can stop lying now. I know everything. I went to see him today."

"I heard all about it. Cel's been in a state ever since you called. I told her sumpin like this was gonna happen. You were bound to find out eventually. I predicted this from the very start. Damn, I shoulda placed a bet."

"Well, did you know he escaped?" I taunted.

"Bullshit," Ford said.

"I'm serious."

He fell silent for a moment. "When?"

I was a little surprised that Ford's first question was when and not how. "What do you know about this, Ford?"

"I don't know shit about shit, Dixie. Last I heard, Billy couldn't scratch his own balls, much less take 'em on the lam. How'd he escape anyway? Pretend to be dead so he could just walk out of the morgue without anybody watchin'?"

That was actually a very plausible idea. "I don't know how he did it. I'm waiting to hear."

"I'd lock my doors if I were you. Maybe he's lookin' to finish what he started twenty-five years ago. Clip that loose end he left hanging around."

I ignored him to ask, "Have you seen Rory?"

Garrett lifted his head and I shrugged. The question had come spontaneously.

Ford snuffed. "Where would I have seen Rory?"

"Well, you're his good buddy, arncha?" I said in a snottier tone than I intended. Something about Ford brought the brat out in me.

"I don't know if I'm his, but he sure as hell ain't mine."

"I saw the receipt, Ford. Free oil changes? That seems pretty buddy-buddy to me."

"What the fuck you talkin' about, Dixie?"

"Nothing, I was just—"

A soft chime sounded in the background. Tritone. It struck a chord with me.

"Whose phone is that?" I asked.

"That's my cell. Hold on." His voice faded as the phone dropped away from his ear. "I gotta take this. You want me to have Cel call you when she wakes up?"

"Yes," I said. "And tell her about my father. I wasn't bullshitting, Ford. He really did escape. Or he's missing, at least. I'm not sure what's going on. But you guys need to be careful until they find him, okay? Don't leave Aunt Celia alone."

"I won't." The way he said this led me to believe he might. The phone in the background let out a celestial ringtone again, and he hung up on me.

"Huh," I said as I set the phone down.

"What?" Garrett asked.

"Ford's ringtone."

"What about it?"

"It kinda sounded like Claire's."

"Like a song or something?" Garrett asked.

"No. It's just a standard ringtone, but it's one of those weird ones nobody uses, like Moonbeam or Stargaze or something like that. It's just a strange one for Ford to use."

"Do you think it was Claire's phone you heard?" Garrett asked. "Why would Ford have it? What's he got to do with any of this?"

"Maybe Rory asked Ford to hide it for him. Keep it safe until he could figure out what to do with it. If they are friends, he might have. Do you have Ford's cell phone number set up in your phone?"

"Yeah. Why?"

"I want you to call him."

Garrett dug his phone from the front pocket of his jeans. "What do you want me to say?"

I cued up Aunt Celia's home number again. "I'm going to call Ford back. I want you to call him so I can hear what his phone sounds like when it rings."

I grabbed my heart when it was my phone that suddenly rang. Full volume. It was Mr. Cullins.

"Where have you been?" I demanded. "I've been worried sick!"

"Is Garrett there?" he said.

"Yeah, why?"

"Let me talk to him, please."

His tone told me that he wanted to tell Garrett something that he couldn't bring himself to tell me.

"Say it," I insisted.

He let out a heavy sigh. "I think they found your father."

MY FATHER'S BODY was found in an alleyway on Richmond's lower west side, about three miles from Allied State Hospital. The area was primarily known for its many street-corner vocations, homeless population, and high crime statistics. The man who notified a passing patrol car of a bloody carcass attracting rats at the far end of the alley—possibly a dog or small child, though he admitted he only said that it might be a child to entice them to investigate—had not witnessed the attack. He thought he may have heard a scuffle as he cowered under the lean-to of his cardboard hovel, but had not heard anyone scream for help.

Anyone with a functioning larynx would have screamed. My father had been so severely beaten that they needed three bags to put
him in. One body bag and two Ziploc baggies: one for his left hand
and the other for the right side of his face, both of which had been
hacked off during the attack. The tag in the collar of the blue terry
cloth robe proclaimed the wearer to be the property of Allied State
Hospital. That was good enough for me, I told Mr. Cullins as we sat
in a narrow waiting room outside the coroner's office.

"He needs to be properly identified, Dixie."

"Then you do it," I said.

"I think it needs to be a relative," he said. "Why don't you call Ford
and see if he'll come down? He and your aunt need to know about
this, anyway."

An elevator dinged at the other end of the hallway. Dr. Cheatham
rounded the corner, headed our way at a brisk walk. As he came to a
breathless stop before us, Mr. Cullins stood to greet him.

"Are they positive it's him?" Dr. Cheatham asked. "Are they sure
it's William?"

"They're pretty sure, but his—" Mr. Cullins glanced down at me,
then pulled Dr. Cheatham to the side. After a few murmurs, Dr.
Cheatham covered his mouth to solemnly nod, then vanished
through the swinging doors behind them.

"Ham's going to identify him," Mr. Cullins said as he retook his
seat. "Since your father was in his custody, he's the one who needs to
do it."

I nodded. After a moment of listening to Mr. Cullins tap his foot,
I asked, "Who would have done this to him?"

"Probably just some asshole getting his jollies off of killing homeless people. They've had some trouble down there before. One guy
got lit on fire a while back."

I let this horrible image stop, drop, and roll through my mind before asking, "How did my father end up in that alley?"

"It's not far from the hospital. A lot of the homeless who end up there are former patients of Allied. If no one picks them up when they get released, they just follow the road until they find it. Or smell the soup kitchen. It's right around the corner."

"That's so sad."

Mr. Cullins nodded. "I guess your father just wandered off in that direction. Ham's a good friend of mine, so I shouldn't say this, but you have a pretty solid lawsuit if you want to pursue this legally. Allied had more than a few breaches in their security today. The guard who was supposed to be guarding your father?" I nodded. "He was on a date with a nurse in a broom closet. Then the guard at the front security gate fell suddenly ill. They found him passed out in a puddle of his own puke inside his booth. No one knew he was down until they discovered him during the search for your father. Ham said it was food poisoning. Bad tuna salad or something. Then there's the guard who mans the monitors for the grounds. He was playing some kind of game on his phone. Didn't see a thing, even when Ham was waving at the camera for him to sound the alarm."

I thought of the woman I had seen running through the parking lot, and how her husband had looked to the building, as though he was certain a guard would be watching.

Mr. Cullins shook his head. "Sometimes you gotta wonder if forces aren't aligning to carry out some sort of master plan."

I squinted at him. "You don't seem like the type to believe in that kind of thing."

He shrugged. "After today, I'm starting to. A whole lot of things had to go wrong at the same time for something like this to happen. This was Allied's first escape in thirty years. If you can even call it an escape. It's more like your father just bungled his way out of there while no one was looking."

"Yeah, but how did he even do that? He couldn't walk."

He glanced down the hall. "It's possible Ham hasn't been completely up front about your father's progress. Maybe he was capable of a lot more than we knew about. I'm not saying that Ham necessarily knew your father's vegetable routine was all an act, but as his doctor, he must have suspected something. Ham could have been covering for him."

"Why would he do that?"

"There's no statute of limitations for murder, Dixie. If your father were to regain his faculties, he would have to stand trial. That's four murder counts. He'd most likely get a death sentence. Maybe Ham didn't want to see that happen. He's become very protective of your father. You saw how he was with him. Fussing over him and worrying about his stupid slippers, letting him out to get some fresh air. It wasn't always like that. That nice room he was in is an upgrade. He used to have just a cot in a windowless room in the basement. He got moved to that new room after Davis and Ham got all chummy. I think Davis convinced Ham of your father's innocence and he's been protecting him ever since."

The door to the coroner's lab opened and spit out Dr. Cheatham, who appeared to have been accidently embalmed while he was in there. Pale, stooped, and marginally thinner than when he entered, he looked as though the whitish sheen of sweat covering his face had been topically applied rather than secreted. He took a giant drag of stale corridor air and exhaled it like smoke from a long-awaited cigarette.

"Is it him?" Mr. Cullins asked.

Dr. Cheatham rolled his head in a way that could have either meant yes or no or that he was about to throw up. "I think so," he said, taking a kerchief from the breast pocket of his jacket to blot his upper lip. "But . . ." He glanced at me, then nodded Mr. Cullins to the side.

"I want to know," I said, holding Mr. Cullins back by his sleeve. "Finish your sentence, Dr. Cheatham. But what? His face is too messed up to tell if it's him or not?"

Dr. Cheatham looked at Mr. Cullins, then sighed and nodded.

"Politely put, the body cannot be identified by any sort of facial rec-ognition. But based on his height and weight and overall physical condition, I'm almost a hundred percent positive it's William. His identification bracelet was . . . lost during the attack, but the robe and pajamas were the ones we assigned him. The robes we distribute have a reference number sewn into their tag so laundry doesn't get them confused. The number starts with the patient's initials. This robe's ID number started with 'WW.' I'm having William's records sent over so they can compare fingerprints, but I consider that to be a formality." He glanced at Mr. Cullins before addressing me. "They want to know if you have any preference in regards to his remains, Miss Wheeler."

"What?" I asked, trying to process the news that my father had come back to life only to pass away in the same twenty-four-hour span. I didn't know how to feel: relieved, dejected, indifferent . . . Frankly, I felt a little annoyed, like this had all been one big cosmic psych-out.

"They want to know if you want him buried or cremated," Mr. Cullins explained.

"Oh." I shook my head. "I don't know. Up until yesterday, I kinda thought that he had been cremated already, so . . . let's go with that. Burn the son of a bitch." Both men grimaced . "Or bury him. I don't care."

"Does she have to decide this right now, Ham?" Mr. Cullins said, placing a hand on my shoulder. "It's been a long day."

GARRETT AND I crawled onto the bed with our clothes on, just a little nap before we got up to brush our teeth and went to bed for real. The Xanax Dr. Cheatham insisted on prescribing when he spotted me bowed over and hyperventilating next to the watercooler had anesthetized my tongue, among other things, but was doing nothing to slow the spiral of anxiety I was currently caught in. My pulse was kicking in my throat like I had eaten a half-dead rodent, and the shiver running through me was set on a thirty-second timer. I wanted so badly to sleep, but there was too much to think about. Only I couldn't do that, either. Each thought I held up for consideration slipped from my grasp and shattered into a million others, sharp little worries that were as impossible to understand as they were to collect.

I turned restlessly away from Garrett to stare at the ceiling.

Though the house was ghostly quiet, no ghosts came. I thought my father might, now that he was really dead, truly dead, certifiably dead, but he was as gone from this place as the rest. The house was clean, as the eccentric medium in *Poltergeist* would have put it. More than clean. The house seemed to have completely lost its spirit. It was so ... peaceful. I should have been grateful for this development, but I knew I would not stay. First thing in the morning, I'd start packing.

I had decided on the ride home, and Garrett agreed, that I would tell Mr. Cullins everything. About Rory, and what I had done to him. About Claire, and what little I knew about the day she disappeared. We'd leave the hammer where it was, we weren't complete idiots, but we'd forgo the ruse and tell Mr. Cullins where the SUV was parked and how long it had been there.

With any luck, Rory was still very much alive and just lying low at an unsuspecting girlfriend's house—a dumb one who might believe that he had been jumped by a gang of pipe-wielding hooligans in the quiet Northern Virginia suburb she had picked him up in—revising whatever diabolical scheme I had temporarily upset while he recuperated in comfort. Garrett added that after getting more than he bargained for when he decided to fuck with me, Rory might not try to seek retribution. I wasn't convinced. Whatever game Rory was playing, it wasn't over yet. I just hoped the police would find him before he was able to make his next move, or that another bed frame would be close at hand if he found me first.

With such possible turmoil ahead, I needed a good night's sleep, and I nestled under the blankets to try. The dark, putrid, bedridden scent had at last aired from my pillow, which was exceptionally docile, and with Garrett snoring beside me, I believed I might get a solid eight hours of rest. The faint creak of a floorboard in the hallway tried to pry one of my eyes open. I wouldn't let it. Probably just a mouse, I thought with an indifference I hadn't known since I arrived. A soft, contented smile touched my lips as sleep slammed a heavy door in my face.

A GASP OF sleep apnea woke me. My heart, just then realizing it needed to go to work again, stomped the pedal three times to get some gas in the line. Winded from the physical exertion of waking, and moderately blind from chronic dry-eye syndrome, I blinked at the clock on the nightstand, wondering if it was 8:20 A.M. or 8:20 P.M.; closed blinds on a cloudy day had the bedroom cloaked in an eerie twilight.

I slapped a hand at Garrett's side of the bed and found it empty. I had a vague memory of him kissing my cheek, a whisper that he was leaving, but I couldn't remember exactly where he said he was going. I curled back under the covers to hide from the day. I wasn't ready for it to begin. I had to go to Aunt Celia's to tell her that her "let's pretend he's dead" brother was now actually dead, and then head over to the funeral home to decide between a casket and an urn. I didn't want to do any of it, and what's more, I didn't feel obligated. I didn't owe Aunt Celia any consideration, and that went double for my father. I had just decided to give exactly zero shits about any of it when my phone rang. I slipped my fingers out from under the warm blanket and grabbed my phone from the nightstand. I pressed Accept and tucked the phone between the pillow and my ear. Sleep returned in the click of airspace between me and whoever was on the other end of the line.

"Mmm," I breathed.

"Dingle ate an entire bag of Bacon Ranch Doritos," Mr. Cullins said. "Do you think it will hurt him?"

"No more than you, I guess," I yawned, curling into a ball to rub my cold feet together. "Why did you give him Doritos?"

"I didn't *give* them to him. I turned my back for a second and they were gone. I also think he ate a tube of Neosporin. I can't find it anywhere. Needless to say, I'm not looking forward to our walk."

"What time is it?" I asked.

"Eight thirty."

"A.M. or P.M.?"

There was a censorious pause before he informed me that it was morning.

"Ah, god." I yawned again. "How can you eat Doritos for breakfast?"

"They were a snack," he said brusquely. "I had breakfast hours ago." He softened his tone to say, "So, how ya doing, kid? You get any sleep?"

"I was trying to before the phone rang." I rolled out of the bed and padded to the bathroom. "Why are you calling so early? Is my father alive again or something?"

"Not that I know of," he said with a surly chuckle.

"Did they find out who killed him?"

"That's what I was calling about."

"Really?" I said, wincing at my reflection in the mirror. I stuck out my tongue to find that it was not the fuzzy caterpillar I thought it would be. "That was fast."

"No. They haven't found the person who killed him yet, but they did find something very interesting."

"Oh, yeah?" I unscrewed my mouthwash, took a sip, and gurgled, "Whah?"

"They found Rory Sellers's SUV about a block from where your father's body was found."

I swallowed half the mouthwash before I was able to spit it out.

"We're still trying to confirm, but they found one of your father's slippers in the rear compartment. I'm pretty sure it's the same one he had on at the hospital. Looks just like it. Did Rory have any reason to want to kill your father?"

"Are you sure it was Rory's SUV?"

"Registration was in the glove box. I'm not sure why he abandoned it. Maybe he got spooked and took off on foot. The police are out looking from him."

"That's not possible."

"I know this must be a shock," he said, misconstruing the context of my disbelief. Mr. Cullins credited me for having had more than my fair share of shocks as I hurried to my bedroom window. Even if a tree weren't blocking my view, I wouldn't have been able to see the corner of the cul-de-sac from there.

"What else did they find in his SUV?" I asked.

"Besides the slipper? Just some personal items. Nothing of value to the investigation."

"What about the—" I almost said *hammer*. "I mean, did they search it? Really search it?"

"Yes. I was standing right there when they went through it. They pulled it apart. Processed everything by the book." He paused. "Why, what did you expect them to find?"

"Ah, nothing," I said as I sat on the corner of my bed to slip on my sneaker. "I just wondered if they found the weapon that was used to kill my father."

"Not yet. But they're still going through the alley. That's going to take a while. Believe it or not, one of the homeless guys put up a stink about the police needing a warrant to search the dumpster he's been living in. He said that as the occupant, he had rights." He chuckled. "He's got a point. I think they're trying to obtain one so they don't run into any issues in court."

"Anything else?" I said to conclude the call. I wanted to get down the street to see if the SUV we planted the hammer in was still there. Maybe it just looked like Rory's 4Runner. One that just coincidently got its oil changed at Denny's Auto Parts. I checked the label on the bottle of Xanax sitting on my nightstand. 0.25 mg. Refills: 0. Damn. Maybe Dr. Cheatham would call in a refill if I asked him. He did say to let him know if I needed anything else . . . I shook out one of the three remaining pills and dry-swallowed it. I gave it half a second to work, and then took another.

"Yeah, there is something else." He exhaled a pensive breath. "Did Rory get injured the night you two had that fight?"

"Why?" I smacked myself in the head as the word flew defensively from my mouth. Guilty people ask why. Innocent people say no. Though I had planned on coming semiclean with Mr. Cullins about the fight I'd had with Rory, I needed time to think. Rory's connection with my father's death might change things in ways I couldn't antic-ipate. I wasn't thinking clearly enough to come up with some quick answers on the fly. I needed to be sensible, run the situation by Gar-rett, and make sure we had all the bases covered.

"Just answer the question," Mr. Cullins said.

"What does it matter? Who cares about the stupid fight I had with Rory? Obviously I had every reason to fear him."

"There was a lot of blood in his SUV, Dixie. It was all over the headrest and driver's seat. Enough to make us believe that Rory might have been seriously wounded. Hell, there was enough blood to make us think he might be seriously dead. I just need to know what we're dealing with here."

I didn't remember seeing any blood when I looked in the win-dow of what I'd thought was Rory's SUV. And since I couldn't fathom how his SUV ended up in Richmond, I thought "I really don't know" seemed the most prudent response, not to mention the most truthful.

"Is Garrett still with you?" Mr. Cullins asked.

I stood up too fast and felt the room tilt. Taking a double dose of sedatives on a sleepy, empty stomach was probably not a good idea. Breathing deep, I closed my eyes before the stars could form a supernova.

"Dixie?"

"What?"

"Is Garrett there?"

"No. He left before I got up," I held my phone out to check the time. The screen was too blurry to read. "I think he went home to change. He should be back soon. I know he wanted to go with me to the funeral home." I fell against the dresser as I tried to hook on my other sneaker. I needed some food ASAP. I lowered my head and aimed it at the doorway.

"Okay. I want you to lock all the doors until he gets there, okay? Until we find Rory, I want you to be extra careful. I'm going to head back down to Richmond and check in on the investigation. I'll stop by on my way back." He paused to sigh. "I don't like you being all alone. Or Dingle. Shit. I guess I'll have to take him with me. Hey, you wanna come with us?"

"I can't. I've gotta go talk to Aunt Celia. She doesn't even know what happened yet." The warm scent of bacon wrapped its arms around me as I entered the hallway. "And Garrett's back. He's downstairs making breakfast. Thank god, I'm starving. I don't remember the last time I ate."

"Tell him I said not to leave you alone. That's an order."

"I will. Call me when—"

The phone slipped from my fingers as Eddie stepped from the wall and into the hallway in front of me. His head lay sideways between his shoulders, blindly smooshed into the pulpy fissure of his collarbone, like a hard-boiled egg served on a wilting bed of red cabbage.

Mr. Cullins's voice rose up from the carpeting. "Dixie? You okay?"

Keeping my eyes firmly locked on Eddie, I squatted down to speak at the phone: "Yes. Sorry. I dropped my phone. Thanks for calling and updating me on everything, Mr. Cullins. I really appreciate it. I'll talk to you later, okay, bye." I pressed Disconnect and cut Mr. Cullins off midsentence:

"Okay, but I—"

A horrible chortle frothed up from Eddie's throat as his head slipped off its perch and plopped between my knees. I scrambled back with a kicking motion and sent his head bouncing down the staircase. Squealing laughter bounded up on its way down. Eddie ran off after his ball.

"Josh!" my mother's voice called from below. *"Breakfast!"*

"Coming!" Josh said as he turned out of his room. He stopped to look down at me. *"You coming?"*

I pressed against the wall to shake my head.

"You sure?" He stuck his hand out to help me to my feet. *"He has a big surprise for us. You don't want to miss it."*

"It's not a good surprise," I said, curling my hands under my chin so he couldn't touch them. "Don't go down there, Josh."

He gave me a playful frown, and then turned down the staircase. He slapped Rory a high five as he passed him on his way up.

"Hey, Dix," Rory said as he turned into Josh's room and immediately vanished. He was much less visible than Josh or Eddie. A mist of water catching the light.

With a sudden blast, music filled the house, so loud it jarred my head into the wall.

DUM-DA-DUM-DA-DUM! DAH-DA-DA-DA-DAH! DUM-DA-DUM—!

"NO!" my mother screamed. *"JOSH! OH, GOD! JOSH! NO! EDDIE, RUN!"*

"DADDY! HELP ME!" Eddie screamed. *"NO, DON'T! DON'T—"*

The sound of their suffering bled through the music and dripped into my ears like acid. The whack of the axe striking wood, bone, Formica, was like a strap across my skin. My own screams were being ripped from my throat on a strand of barbed wire. I covered my mouth as a rush of sick bounded up on a hacking retch.

A baby cried out.

The cry was so desperate, so afraid and helpless, that I ripped at my hair to add pain to the sound.

I had to stop the massacre from happening, but my legs refused to champion me. I fell back into the wall to cover my ears. I told myself that it didn't matter what I did now: My family was already dead. Twenty-five years dead. To have grown up loved by a healthy, living family would have changed everything. I might have never met Garrett if my family hadn't died. I would have traveled a completely different road, one that might not have led to him. I certainly wouldn't have known Mr. Cullins. My family needed to have died for me to be who I am. Where I am. Why I am. It was time to accept the hand I had been dealt.

Haunt me all you want, you dead things, you worn-out old nightmares, you childish monstrosities, I thought as I took a calming breath. *I can no longer be scared by the likes of you.* I had just begun to warm to this toasty conviction when it was dowsed in the icy cries of my mother.

"STOP! PLEASE, STOP! I'LL DO ANYTHING! JUST STOP! NO! AHHH—AH—AH—"

I covered my ears as her screams were hacked into silence.

"Come here, you little bastard!" a man's voice said, so thick and rough with exertion it was hard to recognize.

CHUNK CHUNK CHUNK!

Based on the sequence of bloodcurdling events, I knew this sound was the sharp end of the axe going after little Michael as he tried to crawl away.

CHUNK CHUNK CHUNK!

As their screams died off, the music restarted. Heavy footsteps made their way from the kitchen into the living room. They started a slow climb up the stairs. I pressed my eyes closed, tucked my head between my knees, and awaited my turn.

Finally. My turn.

16

Fear rose incrementally up the staircase. One slow step after another, stomping hard to make sure I was good and scared when my time came. I had no urge to fight. I let my hands go limp at my sides as I stretched out my legs in front of me. My toes tapped in time with the music, the percussive drumbeat of feet up the flight of stairs.

Whoever it was—the ghost of my father, a brain-dead Rory, or a demon I had yet to meet—seemed to be caught halfway up, stomping but not ascending. If it was meant as a scare tactic, it was working. Thorny tears blossomed in my eyes, took root in my chest, and coiled around my bladder. Though it was my life that hung in the balance, it was Leah I thought of. How strong she had been when her time came. How elegant. I wanted to do her proud. I wouldn't cry or beg to live. I'd just let death come. A dark pillow over my face. I'd do it like she said, though I did allow myself a single whimper in the fading moments when the track of music dimmed, the house grew quiet, and the stomping intensified.

THUMP THUMP THUMP.

Thump thump thump.

Thump, thump.

I unclenched one eye. The door to Josh's room was open. Unless he was in the closet, there was no sign of Rory. The music began again in earnest, but it sounded different now. It wasn't playing through some sort of haunted time warp, a twenty-five-year-old echo. And it wasn't in my head. It was live on the stereo downstairs. The wavering crackle in the left speaker was a dead giveaway. It had blown when

I cranked the volume up to ninety the first time I turned it on. And those weren't feet thudding up the staircase. Someone was knocking on the door.

"Garrett!" I cried, getting to my feet. As I stumbled down the steps, the music became insufferably loud. I ran to the stereo and spun the dial from ninety-nine to zero. The knocking came again, a bit more urgent than it had been. I ran to the front door, fumbling with the dead bolt as I stuck my eye to the peephole. No one was on my stoop. The knocking came again. From behind. The back door!

"Coming!" I yelled.

I threw the latch to relock the door, and a baby let out an angry squeal that turned the hairs on my arms to ice pellets. Whipping around, I fell back against the door, blinking fast at the unbelievable sight in my kitchen.

My father—my real father, not some ghost or delusionary fiend but the warped, gnarled scrap of a father I had visited in the hospital— was sitting at the head of the table. His walnut head was bowed, and his hands were hidden in his lap beneath the loose folds of a filthy flannel shirt. Three inches of what I was sure would lead to an even longer wooden handle and, ultimately, the head of an axe, jutted over his bare, bony thigh.

Vicki was seated to his right, eyes bulging and frantic. The duct tape across her mouth strained to release a muffled scream. One of her boys, I supposed, the fair-haired one I had not met, was seated across from her, to the left of my father. The boy's hands were tied with rope to the slat of the chair behind his back. The entryway wall blocked the rest of the kitchen from view, but based on the various octaves of crying murmurs floating from the room, I knew we had a full table for breakfast.

"What's this?" I asked breathlessly as I dragged my toes across the living room carpet, feeling overly sedated and in no hurry to attend what looked to be the worst surprise party ever thrown. As

I slowly approached the kitchen, the rest of our guests came into view.

Beside Vicki sat Ford. Across from him was Conner, seated next to his brother. At the other end of the table, across from my father, was Rory, head down and looking quite dead. Beside him in a high chair, which was far nicer than the one I had intended to buy at the Salvation Army, was Vicki's baby girl, Katie.

No one was eating the breakfast that had been set out on the table before them. The eggs, served in the same frying pan that they had been scrambled in, were glued to the sides by a gelatin of barely cooked whites. Bacon strips were aligned on an open napkin directly on the tabletop, burned to a black crisp on one end and flaccidly raw at the other. Butter lay melting on toast done to a golden perfection, but there were only two slices for the entire table.

Even if our guests were inclined to eat, they couldn't; their mouths had been taped shut. Ford was working his like an itch that couldn't be scratched. The thumping I earlier thought was some variety of demon climbing the stairs, then discerned to be someone knocking at the front door, was actually the legs of the kitchen chairs striking the floor as their captives struggled to free themselves. The baby, who was the only alert hostage not muzzled, was rearing in her high chair and furious; thin eyebrows were as white as snow against her outraged brow. She clutched her hands for me as I came into view, and I placed a finger to my lips.

"Dad," I said, staring at his profile as I took a tentative step forward. His expression was the same as it had been in the hospital: slightly tilted as if to extrapolate a curious noise from the air. "What are you doing?"

Vicki shook her head violently, tears pouring from her wide-open eyes. The boys whipped their heads around to see who had spoken. Unintelligible words were screamed at me through the tape over their mouths. Flapping their jutted elbows, they pecked their noses to spell out an obscure message in the air before them.

"Dad," I said again, dropping to one knee to look up at him. "Give me the axe."

Vicki went wild, thumping in her chair, bucking back and forth, riotously whipping her head and shoulders, stabbing her eyes at my father and then at Rory and then at Ford. As a member of the bound-and-gagged club, Ford seemed to understand this form of communication and nodded at her as he began to thrash anew. His knees struck the bottom of the table. All but one glass of orange juice toppled over. Conner was blinking like an electric current was coursing through the duct tape across his mouth.

I reached out and grabbed a handful of napkins from the holder in the center of the table.

"It's okay," I said. "I got it."

Vicki and Ford rocked to a stop, breathing hard through their noses as I calmly tamped the table dry. I pitched the wad of wet napkins at the waste bin and wiped my hands on the back of my pants. I regarded my father with a soft smile, touching a thicket of sharp gray whiskers that were mottled with drops of dried blood on his hollowed cheek.

"You look so tired, Dad," I said. "You don't have to do this. You don't have to hurt anyone else." I ran my fingers over the top of his lumpy head as I placed a kiss on his brow. "It's okay. Give me the axe."

THE HANDLE OF the axe was silky smooth and warm as summer skin in the palm of my hand. My fingers wrapped around the slender hilt like the wrist of a disobedient child. I held my breath to bolster my confidence and gave the handle a firm tug.

My father's shoulders waggled passively, but he did not let go.

"It's okay," I said in a playful, upbeat tone, as if coaxing a dog who had one of my shoes clamped in his teeth. "Give it to me."

I pulled at the axe handle again, watching my father's vacant eyes for any sign of life, fully expecting him to yank the axe from my hand and bring it down upon my upturned face. His expression remained impassive, wholly ambivalent. I gave the handle a firm twist to un-screw it from his clenched fingers.

The warm bead of drool that fell from his lip onto the back of my hand unlocked a frustrated grunt that had been waiting patiently at the back of my throat. With fear rapidly becoming the lesser of my emotions, I yanked and twisted the handle in one forceful move. My father's withered head bobbled as though it might topple off, but the axe remained inexorably pinned to his lap.

Careful, as careful as I would have been taking a snake by the back of its neck, I reached out to pry the damn thing from my father's fin-gers. As I eased my hand into the nook between his lap and the table, the cuff of his shirt drooped lazily aside and exposed a liver-spotted hand. His fingers were an angry, constricted purple, swollen and rigid, and extended well past the handle of the axe. A silver manacle was clamped around his wrist just above a blue-and-white hospital ID bracelet: "WHEELER, WILLIAM. DOB: 8/07/52. ADM: 12/23/92." A series of encrypted edicts were listed below: "RA, ARMD, GERD, UC, A+ . . ." The wood handle of the axe was jammed through the underside of the silver band around his wrist. He wasn't holding the axe at all; it was duct-taped to him.

"What the hell," I whispered.

Just as my mind began to process what this meant, a low mewling began to rise. It was quickly joined by a galvanic hum that seemed to recharge with every beat of my heart. Chairs stamped the floor in a sort of primitive war rally. I turned slowly. All eyes were on the other end of the table. As Rory lifted his head fully, my hand released the axe to cover a gasp.

Though a part of me was relieved to see Rory had indeed survived the beating I had given him, another part of me wished I had finished the job. His once beautiful face had become a fractured mask of bruised flesh and split skin. Pinkish-yellow snot dripped from the crust around his nostrils. The tight slit between his bulging forehead and swollen left cheek offered no sign of the eyeball within, and only made the right, desperately alert and quite normal, all the more unsettling in contrast. Since his head had been down, I hadn't noticed that his mouth had not been duct-taped into silence like the rest, though that might not have been necessary; his lips looked far too fat and tight and purple to form a sound. But just as this thought occurred to me, they did:

"*SOR-RAY!*" he cried. The sudden explosion caused his right eye to flutter and roll white. "*Eh mah . . .*" he tried, then shook his head, as if confused as to why his mouth wasn't working as it should. He licked his engorged lips to feel his way around the obstacle. "*Eh . . . may-ah . . . eh . . . dah . . . hit!*"

I shook my head. "I don't under—"

"*MAH . . . ME!*" he screamed. A teardrop squirted from the butt of skin around his left eye as he tossed back his head to draw a long, shuddering breath. He raged a few grunting slurs at the ceiling, and then dropped his head to let the words drip out with a bloody thread of drool. "*Ee . . . made . . . me.*" The full body spasm that followed seemed to do him in, and he fell silent.

"Who, Rory? Who made you? My father?"

He lifted his head a notch, and then dropped it once more.

"Come on, Rory! Stay with me. Who made you do what? What are you talking about?"

Rory flung his head back with a desperate cry, "*FOR-DAH!*"

In a flash of silver, blood sprayed across the breakfast table. It happened so fast that for a moment, I thought the weight of his head being tossed back had ripped his throat open. Choking gurgles erupted from Rory as the font spurted twice more, and then subsided into a steady stream down his chest.

Ford yanked the strip of tape from his own mouth and let out a whooping laugh.

"Oh, man, that felt good!"

There was a startled pause just before Vicki blew a scream through her gag and started her boys stomping in their chairs again. The baby let out an ear-piercing shriek that managed to rouse my father's head from its stooped position. Confused beyond all thought or action, I could only stare blankly at Ford as Rory slowly fell forward and cracked a plate in two with his forehead.

Ford brought the knife down on Rory's back again and again. The blade *whished* in and out of his crisply pressed oxford like he was a bag of sand. When the blade lodged too deep to continue to plunge with any momentum, Ford wrenched it free with a sickening crack of bone.

"Fuck you, Rory, you dumbass motherfucker!" Ford spat. He wiped the back of his mouth with the wrist of his clean hand. "Do what I tell ya next time, *asshole.*"

A COLLECTIVE GASP traveled around the room as wide, terrified eyes tossed around a single question: *Who would be next?* Ford just stood there, breathing off the physical effort of stabbing Rory, and then clanged the bloody knife into the sink. Vicki let out a loud whimper and then closed her eyes, as though she had just lost at Flinch. Her eyes popped open as Ford knocked over a plastic cup grabbing a dish towel off the rack. His eyes fell on me as he cleaned his hands.

"I can't believe you fell for that, Dixie." He nodded over my head as he swabbed his fingers. "I thought for sure you saw me scratch my nose right before you came in." He dropped the towel to his side to chuckle. "Funny how your nose never itches until you can't scratch it."

I ran my eyes around the kitchen, waiting for the nightmare to make itself apparent: a clock melting on the wall, piranhas jumping from the cool depths of the bamboo flooring, my own scared face peering in at me through the window over the sink. Except for the nightmarish laughter coming from Ford, the catatonic look of horror in Vicki's eyes, and the low, dreamy vibration of Xanax coursing through my veins, I was dreadfully awake.

The only word I knew that might sum together and convey the million chaotic thoughts scrabbling around my brain was "What?"

"*Wh-wh-what?*" Ford simpered, teasing me with the sound of my own gullibility. He laughed as he nudged Vicki in the side of her head with his elbow. Her cheeks puffed out as she bellowed a startled scream through the duct tape. He rested his chin on the top of her head to say, "I don't think she gets it."

"What is this?" I said, staring at my father. "I don't understand."

"You never did, Dixie," Ford said dourly. "Look at you with your mouth hung open and your eyes all bugged out. You look as brain-dead as ol' Billy boy there."

My mouth snapped shut, but I couldn't seem to blink my eyes. They were drawn to the corner of the room, riveted on my mother as she slipped through the wall behind the high chair to sneak a quick peek at the baby. Her hands, no longer flayed, were clamped to her heart. Her eyes brightened as the baby turned to smile up at her. Same age, same hair color, same chubby cheeks—she was me when my mother knew me last. The sudden, heartbreaking confusion in my mother's eyes brought forth a single memory of our brief time to-gether. There wasn't enough detail to actually call it a recollection; it was only a sensation: a jerking upward motion, the graze of sharp plastic across my thighs, a darkness folding over me, the loopy sensa-tion of a slow fall. She had tried to protect me. She had grabbed me out of the high chair. She had fallen to the floor with me in her arms. She had curled around me. Her damaged hands held on as best they could until she was dragged away.

My mother retreated back through the wall as Ford grabbed Vicki by her hair and wrenched her head backward.

"What do you think, sweetheart?" he said.

Vicki mumbled an angry, unintelligible sentence at him, but Ford nodded as though she had answered reasonably.

"Yeah, I'm a little disappointed, too." He gave her head a hard shove as he tossed his hands in the air. "I mean, come on, Dixie! It's been staring you right in the face the whole damn time. I practically confessed to you the other day, and you still couldn't figure it out. How'd I know what kind of axe Billy used? The papers withheld that information."

The insanity Ford had been concealing all these years burst forth with the brilliance of an atomic explosion. And in a flash, the dark cloud I had been floating through life in was obliterated, a lifetime of sickness made unendurably well in one sterilizing instant.

I might be crazy, but Ford was a true maniac.

I must have blinked my thoughts through some sort of paroxysmal Morse code because Ford said, "Oh, I know I'm crazy." The laugh he let out this time had a forced diabolicalness to it. "Not that I'm bragging or anything, but it takes a certain type of crazy to do what I did. I've thought about that a lot over the years. It's not your run-of-the-mill sling-your-shit-at-the-wall type of crazy. It's way more refined than that. All your best serial killers have it. It's in the eyes. Bundy had it. Gacy, Dahmer, Son of Sam . . ." He patted his stomach to proudly include himself. "You can't hack up a bunch of people clearheaded. You'd lose your nerve. It takes a whole lot of crazy to stay that cool. Know what I'm sayin'?"

And though I did, in fact, know what he was sayin', I still needed verbal confirmation: "So . . . *you* killed my family?"

He pointed at me. "And set it up to make it look like Billy had done it. Don't forget that. That's the best part."

"Why?" I shook my head to make sense of it. "I thought he saved your life. He pulled you from that fire."

Ford sighed wearily. "I told you I owed him for that. Killing his family was my payback."

"You paid him back for saving your life by killing his family?" I scoffed. "That's doesn't make any sense."

He pulled a face, as though I were the one being absurd. "No. I was paying him back for *killing* my family."

"Your family died in a house fire," I said. "You told me about it. It had nothing to do with my father."

"I told you *some* of it. I left out how the fire got started." He paused to massage the molten scar on the side of his face. "That's a horrible way to die, ain't it? Getting burned alive. Can you even imagine what that's like? Flames all around you, smoke burning your lungs and eyes, skin melting off your bones." Vicki whimpered as he drummed his fingers on her head. "There really isn't a more horrible way to die, is there?"

"Your father caused the fire, Ford," I said. "Aunt Celia told me. He fell asleep smoking."

"Uh-uh-uh," he sang, toggling one of his long fingers. "That's not true. That's a fucking lie." He glanced at my father, who hadn't shown any reaction since Ford began his revelation. "Your daddy was a pyro back in the day. He was always making fires. The second I smelled smoke, I knew who done it."

"Then it was an accident," I said. "He didn't mean to do it."

"Oh, he knew exactly what he was doing."

"But he was just a kid. Even if he was playing with matches or something, he couldn't have known the fire would get out of control and end up killing your family."

"Yes—he—did," Ford seethed.

I glanced at my father, ashamed that in some dark, distorted, selfish way, I still needed him to be a murderer. I shook my head. "But why would he do something like that?"

"Because he was a little fuckin' prick! He used to do things all the time just to hurt me. Make me cry in front of everybody. He thought that was *reeeal* funny. I woulda liked him better if he woulda just beat me up and been done with it. But he was a sneaky little shit. Laughing at me behind my back and making up stories about me. Telling everyone I skinned a cat and stomped on that shitty little bird of his."

"Well, did you?" I asked.

Ford grabbed a juice glass off the table and whipped it at my head. I fell to my side and it shattered against the refrigerator. "THE CAT WAS ALREADY FUCKING DEAD!" I covered my head as another glass smashed, then another, and another. "I DIDN'T KNOW"—*smash!*—"I STEPPED ON HIS"—*smash!*—"STUPID"—*smash!*—"FUCKING BIRD!"

When I lifted my head, his calm expression had been restored, and the floor was littered with glass.

"I shoulda known you'd take his side. Everybody did. Nobody believed me when I told them that Billy burned down the house. *Sweet little Billy wouldn't do something like that.* Bullshit. He did it. Little fuckin' pyro. I saw him with the matches just a couple days before."

"Then why were you friends with him?" I said. "He was sleeping over the night your family died, right?"

"He wasn't my friend! I didn't want a piece of shit like him sleeping at my fucking house. Someone was sick or dead and his parents had to go out of town. Billy couldn't go for some reason, a science fair or something, so my parents offered to let him stay with us until they got back." He laughed harshly. "And look what they got for their kindness." He shook his head. "Not only did this fucker"—he kicked my father in the leg—"burn the house down, he wouldn't even let me save my little sister. She was only five years old! She was the sweetest little thing you ever saw. Hearing her scream for me like that . . ." He rubbed his forehead, and then bent over to stare into my father's face. "You remember that, Billy? You remember Bonnie screaming?!" He spit in his face, then turned to look at me. "Oh, I wanted to kill him so bad. I laid in the hospital bed for weeks just dreaming about doing it. I wanted to burn his house down, too, but everyone woulda known I done it. Besides," he said, standing, "I didn't want to see Cel and Davis burn up like Bonnie did. They were the only real friends I had. So, I pretended it was all okay. I knew someday I'd get my chance."

"Why did you let me live?" I asked.

He smiled. "Somebody had to live to wish they were dead, just like me. And when I saw your eyes glowing like they did that day, I knew it had to be you." He pivoted the point of his finger from me to the baby. "Just like it has to be her. Isn't that right, pumpkin?" Katie threw her head back to laugh. "Now!" He slapped his hands together. "We better get started. This might take a little while."

"No, wait!" I held out my hand as he started around the table. "Tell me about the day you killed my family. You owe me that, at least."

HE GLANCED AT the clock over the stove. "Okay. But only 'cause it's a doozy.

"That day was pure luck," Ford began. "I'd been out of town. I got a lady friend down in Raleigh I see from time to time. She don't know about Cel, and Cel don't know about her, but I guess that don't matter none now."

The way he smiled privately to himself made me wonder if the affair didn't matter anymore because Aunt Celia was already dead, or because once he killed us he planned to leave town for good. It was hard to hope for the latter, so I had to believe the former was true. Oh, my god. Poor Aunt Celia.

"Anyway," he went on, "I was on my way back for Thanksgiving. The fire had been on my mind all day. My cheek was really burning. It does that sometimes when I think about it too much. Well, I was just driving along, and my car runs out of gas right at your exit. I knew I needed gas before I left, but for some reason I just kept on driving, like something wanted me to run out of gas right there." He shook his head, marveling. "I had a gas can in my trunk, but it was empty, so I got it out and started walking. I didn't get more than ten feet when this guy pulls over to see if I need help. He takes one look at me and one look at the gas can and says to me, 'Don't burn yourself.' But he says it really shitty, you know, like he was laughing at me. Then he says—and I'll never forget it—he says, 'Make 'em pay.' Then he just drove off. I thought maybe I heard him wrong, but the more I thought about it, the more I knew that's what he said. 'Make 'em pay.'" Ford pulled his eyes from that day to look at me. "I don't know if him saying that put the idea in my head or if it was in there already, but that's pretty fucked up, right?"

I nodded to validate how truly fucked up I thought everything was.

"When I got here, I spotted Billy heading around the back of the house, and I followed him out to the shed." Ford chewed the inside of his lip to look off. "Something just came over me when I saw that axe sitting there. Like everything suddenly made sense. I'd never seen it before. It was this monster thing. The head was gleaming like it was plugged in or something. Billy said Josh had picked it up at a yard sale to use as part of his Halloween costume that year. Well, I guess your mom didn't think that was too good an idea, so Billy locked it in the shed for safekeeping. He told me I could have it if I wanted it. As soon as I picked it up, I knew I had found what I had been looking for." He smiled wistfully. "It was my fire, my burning house, right there in my hands. You shoulda seen it, Dixie. That thing was a beast. Sharp as hell and evil as all get-out. I could feel the power in it. Shit. I was a little scared of it. Holding a weapon like that is like holding death itself in your hands."

As he gripped the memory in his fists, I glanced at the axe in my father's lap. That it looked to be just a regular axe didn't make me feel any better about it.

"I told myself no. That Deb and the boys didn't deserve to die that way. They were innocent. But then I thought of my sister. My sweet little Bonnie. She didn't deserve to be burned to death. She didn't deserve to die. She was innocent, too." He leaned his head back to close his eyes. "I could hear her screaming for me. 'Help me, Ford! Please! Help! It hurts!' I was thinking of her right when Billy turned around. The axe was at his throat before I knew what was happening. Like it knew what needed to be done, and it wasn't about to let me chicken out. At first Billy thought I was just playing around. He even laughed." Ford looked at my father. "Ain't that right, Billy?"

My father rustled slightly at that sound of his name. The wag of his head seemed to disagree.

"Well, he did," Ford corrected. "But when he saw the look in my eye, he knew I meant business. I told him it could go down one of two ways. I could either kill him right there and then—and still go inside and kill everybody else—or I could kill him later, after he watched them die." Ford shrugged. "Tough call, right? On the one hand, you're dead and don't know no better. But on the other hand, you're thinking that if you wait, you might be able to stop it from happening somehow." Ford snuffed a laugh as he looked at my father. "He started crying and begging me not to kill 'em. Shit, if I were him?" He touched his chest. "I woulda bum-rushed me so fast, I woulda had that axe before he knew what was going on. But Billy? Pure chicken-shit. He didn't even try to make a grab for the axe. He just stood there cryin'. I made him tie his hands with one of those long zip ties and pull it tight with his teeth. But not too tight, I didn't want it leaving any marks.

"When we came in the kitchen, it was like a dream. I thought that, you know? That I must be dreamin'." He closed his eyes again, and I saw Conner nod at his brother, who promptly shook his head. "Music was playin'," Ford said in a dreamy voice, "and there was this strange light that I'd never seen before. Everything looked pink." He opened his eyes to point at the baby, who was playing with a loose strap in her high chair. "Your mom was feeding you over there."

He dipped his finger to Conner and his brother, who were now as rigid and still as target props in a shooting gallery. In a blink, they became my brothers. An overlap of time and circumstance. Michael was hovering in Conner's lap, Eddie a mist over his twin brother. They were laughing and playing . . .

"Eddie and Michael were playing thumb war," Ford said.

Eddie pinned Michael's thumb as they disappeared.

"Nobody even looked up to see what was going on," Ford said. "Billy did just like I told him to and sat in the corner like a good little boy. Your mom told him to go get your blanket from upstairs, but she didn't even look back to see if he would. Eddie was the first to see me. I tell ya, that kid screamed so loud I almost dropped the axe and ran out. But then Josh turned around and looked at me. Real slow, like he was expecting me to be standing there or something. He wasn't scared at all. Not even a little. He just stared at me." Ford ran a hand across his mouth. "Man! The look on his face. It was like he was try-ing to melt me with his eyes. They didn't even look real. They were glowing red like some science fiction character." He dropped his eyes to me. "That's when I knew I didn't have a choice. I had to do it. They all started coming at me with those red eyes. Like zombies! I had to kill them before they killed me."

Ford cleared the terror from his expression with a long swipe of his hand.

"The axe just came up and—" He drew his hand over his head and brought it down on Vicki's skull. "*WHAM!*" Vicki let out a startled hum as Ford karate-chopped her. "That axe hit him so hard I thought I'd slit him right down the center."

His story—even if I bought the whole zombie-apocalypse rationale—didn't match up with the crime scene photographs. Josh had been blindsided. Hit from behind while he sat in his chair. The wound was to the back of his head, not the front. He had fallen forward onto the table.

"They all started screaming in this weird high-pitched way," Ford said. "It reminded me of those cicada things we get in the summer sometimes. I couldn't think! It was like they were trying to fry my brain from the inside. Eddie was the loudest, so I took care of him real fast. But even without a head, he wouldn't stop making that fucking noise! I was just about to kick it out the door when the music got turned up really loud and drowned them all out." He pointed at the living room. "Rory was standing right there. Just staring at me. I thought I'd have to kill him, too, but then he just turned around and floated up the stairs like a ghost."

I shot Rory a scolding look, but his face was down in a puddle of blood.

"I liked that song that was playing." Ford hummed a bar. *"Hmm, hmm, hmm . . . what I deserve . . . na, na, na . . . kept you waiting there . . . do, do, do . . . my baby blue . . ."*

Katie let out a happy squeal to clap along, and Vicki shot her a look similar to the one I had just given Rory.

"Then everything went black," Ford continued. "Like someone shut off all the light in the world. But I could still see their red eyes glowing. That's how I could find them in the dark." His shoulders slumped as he let out a glum sigh. "I wish I could remember doing it. I shoulda taken my time, enjoyed it a little, but when I could finally see again, they were all dead. 'Cept you and Billy boy, of course. You were crying and carrying on, but . . . your eyes, Dixie." He stared at me as though I had just appeared. "Your eyes weren't like the others. Your eyes were crystal blue. Glowing like a lightning bolt. They shot out at me!" He ducked to avoid the memory. "And that song . . ." He pointed to the living room again. "It was singing about you. Baby Blue. And you were. Swear to god! You were like that song had come to life."

"It wasn't real, Ford," I said as he stared at me, awestruck. "I was just a normal baby. They weren't zombies. They were just scared. My father didn't mean to kill your family. It was just an accident. Don't you see? You've got it all mixed up in your head."

His eyes narrowed shrewdly. "If it ain't real, then why does that baby over there have the same glowing blue eyes you did?"

I glanced at Katie, who did, in fact, have unusually big blue eyes, and shook my head.

"She's just a baby, Ford."

He smiled. "I can tell you're lying, Dixie." He pushed off the counter. "Your eyes are all red."

FORD CAME AROUND the table and leaned his elbow on my father's head like it was a newel post. I scuttled back through shards of juice glass to cower against the refrigerator. Movement under the table caught my eye. Michael was lying flat on his stomach, a finger pressed to his lips. Beyond him or, more precisely, visible through him, was a body heaped in the corner next to the rubber-footed high chair. Mouth taped shut, blood slashed across his nose and chin, his shaggy hair hung loosely over his closed eyes.

"Garrett!" I screamed.

Ford leaned back to peer into the corner over Vicki's head. "Oh, yeah," he said. "Almost forget about him." He waved a dismissive hand. "Ah, he's fine. I was careful not to kill him. We're gonna need him later."

"Why are you doing this?" I demanded as I swung my legs around to get on my knees.

My question left him genuinely perplexed. "I'm doing this 'cause of you, Dixie."

"Me?" I grabbed my head to make sense of it, but there wasn't any sense to be had, so I screamed, "You're crazy!"

"Well, yeah," he conceded, turning to retrieve something off the counter. Vicki shrank into herself as he reached behind her. "But that ain't why this is happening now. I didn't think all this up until yesterday. 'Fore that, I was just trying to get you to kill yourself, or at least make everyone think you had. But when Cel told me about you going to see Billy, and how he was trying to pick out letters on a keyboard again, I knew I had to kick the game into overdrive."

"This isn't a game, Ford!"

"Sure it is." He laughed. "And I'm just gettin' to the fun part."

He held up the crime scene photographs. Excitement cinched his shoulders to his ears as he picked out one and held it over Vicki's head for me to see. It was an aerial view of Josh with his forehead planted on the table, the back of his head split open like a baked potato. He set the photograph on the plate in front of Vicki and made a yummy sound. Vicki turned her head as tears rolled down her cheeks.

"Yeah," Ford said, craning his neck to see over her head, "that one's pretty gross." He patted Vicki reassuringly on her shoulder. "But that one's not for you." He sorted through the pictures, then set another on her plate without showing it to me first. "This one is."

Her scream tore the corner of the tape free. High-pitched air blew out the side of the flap like a punctured life raft. Ford bent over to reseal her tape, excruciatingly gentle, like he was reapplying a Band-Aid. He kissed her cheek when he was done. Vicki grimaced as she slid sideways in her chair.

"You might not survive as long as Dixie's dear mother did, but that's okay. If you need to die right away, that's perfectly fine with me. I can do most of it without your help. But I'm gonna have to start with your hands, so . . ." Ford sucked air through his teeth. "That's gonna hurt."

Vicki's eyes rolled white as she passed out. The legs of her chair lifted as she slumped forward onto the table. Ford slammed her chair to the floor with the heel of his hand. Vicki's eyes flew open as her head jarred back. She looked wildly around, like she was surprised to find that she was not home in her own bed and that the nightmare was still in progress.

The gunshot sound of the chair striking the floor frightened a flock of fluttering cries from the baby. Ford stuck his thumbs in his ears to make moose antlers as he waggled his tongue at her. Instantly, Katie's hitching whimpers turned to spitting laughter. Unfamiliar with this game, she attempted to mimic him by sticking her thumbs up her nose. Ford leaned his head back for a gleeful laugh.

This cutesy moment between her little girl and a ghoulish madman made Vicki scream in angry protest. Unable to either expel or take air through her gag, she began to panic, then to choke. Her eyes flared with terror as her chest lurched with a cough. Spit bubbles leached out of the compromised corner of the tape. Her cheeks drew so gaunt they nearly touched, and then puffed so full they threatened to burst. Desperate to free her hands, she rocked her chair side to side. When that didn't work, she slammed her head forward, striking the table sharply with her face. The breakfast plate cracked in two. She must have thought she was onto something with this maneuver because she did it again, thrashing her face in the broken shards. She threw herself upright with a frustrated cry, and I could see that she had succeeded in ripping small fissures across her cheeks and forehead, but the tape across her mouth remained obdurately intact. Out of options, she seemed to try to draw air in through her eye sockets.

Ford patted her back as if a sip of water had gone down the wrong pipe.

"She's choking, you idiot!" I screamed. "She going to suffocate! Take off the tape so she can breathe, for chrissake!"

He looked at Vicki as though he hadn't realized the extent of her emergency, but rather than removing the tape, he bent forward to closely examine her blanching face.

"You know," he said, tapping her nose, "I bet Blondie here would rather suffocate than exsanguinate. Wouldn't you, sweetheart?"

Such fancy words wrapped in a bumpkin accent were like caviar served in a hotdog bun, and it took Vicki a moment to comprehend the decision being offered her. Ford dragged his finger across his throat to make one of her options horrifyingly clear. She took quick, panicky puffs of air through her nose to nod. *No worries here. All good, thanks.*

Ford patted her on the head, and then slung another photo across the table. It skidded to a stop in front of Conner.

Up until now, the boys had been on their best behavior, little angels letting the adults conduct their adult business, but as Conner looked down upon his fate, he began to weep and buck in his chair. I didn't have to see the picture to know that it was one of two: Eddie's headless body banked against the dishwasher, or Eddie's bodiless head banked against the potatoes. Both were equally horrendous.

"Now, I don't know you boys," Ford said in a fatherly voice as he picked my box of Honey Nut Cheerios from the table and shook a few rings out onto the tray of the high chair. Katie smacked them with her hand, then brought her chubby palm to her face to inspect the destruction. "But you seem like fine young men to me. I can tell your daddy raised you better than ol' Billy boy here raised his boys. They didn't have an ounce of respect between the three of 'em."

Michael appeared under the table, pressed his finger to his lips, and then vanished. He reappeared in the middle of the table, stomped it once, and was gone. As the plates and silverware rattled to a stop, Ford glanced under the table at Conner's and his brother's feet, which were planted squarely on the floor. He shrugged to continue, pointing a long finger at the boys.

"But let me tell you what I do know. You don't—and I repeat, do not—want to live through this day. Do they, Dixie?"

17

Ford hummed/sang "Baby Blue" as he retrieved the butcher knife from the sink. Holding it up to the light, he shook his head, turned on the water, and rinsed it clean of Rory's blood. After drying it, he checked the sharpness with his finger, pausing to stare at his reflection in the glimmering blade. He shook his head as if he'd seen something he didn't like, and then wiped the flat of the knife across Vicki's back. Vicki smiled at her boys with her eyes, nodding that everything was going to be all right, and then grimaced a moan as Ford brought the knife to her throat.

"Now, if I'm gonna get away with something like this twice in one lifetime," he said, looking at me, "it needs to look like you done it. Like you wanted to re-create that day. Living in this house finally got to you, and you just snapped." He glanced around the room. "I'd really like to use the axe again, but I don't think a woman would use an axe. It's too heavy. Too messy. But a woman might use this." He held up the butcher knife. Vicki slumped in relief as the blade left her throat. "And you'd need to tie everybody up nice and tight so they'd sit still while you did it." He waved a hand to show that he had taken care of this detail. "Now all you gotta do is walk around and cut their throats."

"I'm not killing anyone," I swore through gritted teeth.

He rolled his eyes. "It's just gotta *look* like you done it. I'm gonna kill 'em for you. My pleasure." He bowed theatrically to accept my unspoken appreciation.

He stayed stooped at the waist so long that Vicki and I shared a confused glance. I could hear him mumbling in a strange, strangled voice as he swung from side to side, scraping the knife across the floor. Vicki nodded at me to do something. I shrugged to ask what. She pointed out the axe in my father's lap with her eyes. I nodded and began to inch forward, one eye on Ford, one eye on my father's lap. My hand was just reaching for the handle when Ford suddenly straightened.

Vicki closed her eyes in frustration as I sat back on my heels.

"Now, if I was you, I think I might like to take my time and have a little fun with this SOB." He performed an absurd, off-balance pirouette, and then lunged forward to stab my father in the arm. My father gave no reaction to the pain this must have caused him, but I felt it. A stab of panic that time was up.

"Your plan won't work, Ford," I tried. "I was here with Garrett when my father went missing. Mr. Cullins knows that. He won't believe I had anything to do with his escape, or any of this."

Ford grinned coyly. "That's why ya had Rory break him out for ya. See, Dixie?" He tapped his temple with the tip of the knife. "I thought of everything. I know that hospital like the back of my hand. I know when Billy gets rolled out and how nobody watches him. I know where all the cameras are and when the guards take a break. I wore a hat and Rory's coat just in case someone spotted me, but I wasn't too worried about it. But I tell ya, it was a stroke of luck that I spotted Rory's 4Runner when I did. That might have ruined my whole plan. I ditched it down in Richmond and took the bus back. I had Rory sign a confession sayin' that he broke your father out and killed that bum so the police would think he was dead." Ford pouted his lip. "He felt so guilty for not savin' your family he'd do just about anything to make it up to you."

"Why bring my father all the way back here?" I asked in a rush. Though I couldn't stand to hear another word out of Ford's mouth, I had to keep him talking. "Why not just kill him? That was a big risk. Someone could have seen you."

"And deny you the pleasure of killing him yourself?" Ford said, stabbing my father in the cheek. I clutched my face in a wince, but my father remained as inanimate as a slab of marble. "I don't think so. But you're gonna have to do a better job cuttin' his throat than he did. He did try, I'll give him that. I thought he'd just cut himself a little bit to make a show of it, but he damn near cut his own head off."

I shook my head, confused. "Wait. I thought you cut his throat to make it look like a suicide."

"Nope. Billy did that to himself. That was the deal. You or him. He could either cut his throat or watch me cut yours."

I looked at my father, blood dripping off his chin and onto the bib of some bum's stiff flannel shirt—the bum Ford killed because he was just as emaciated as my father; the faceless bum Dr. Cheatham identified because he was wearing my father's scrubs and robe—and felt a profound shame. I had spent my life believing that my father had let me live to punish me, when in actuality he had sacrificed his own life to save mine. I couldn't bear to think of what he went through that day: watching as a maniac butchered his family as some sort of misguided retribution for saving his life. That in order to save me he had to kill himself. My father didn't hate me. He loved me more than anything in the world. I wanted to run to him and hold him, tell him how so very sorry I was, but it was too late. He'd die never knowing how much I appreciated his sacrifice, or how I had squandered my humanity as a result.

"Oh, don't look so scared," Ford said, misinterpreting the tear running down my cheek. "I don't expect you to cut your own throat. But you will have to kill someone. That's only fair. I'll let you decide between these two." He waggled the bloody tip of the knife between Garrett and my father.

"NEVER!" I screamed.

Vicki shook her head at me, flicking her eyes between her

children, pleading with me to do whatever this maniac asked me to in order to save her babies. I looked away as Ford laughed.

"You think you got a choice, Dixie?" he said. "I've been manipulating you from the very start. I've been watching since you moved in here. I almost passed you in the hall one night. 'Bout shit my pants." The horrified gasp I emitted must have sounded disbelieving because he felt the need to say, "It's true! Rory snatched your house key the night he stayed here. I made a copy so I could come and go without jimmying the door every time. I'm pretty good at it, but it still takes a while. I didn't want one of your neighbors to spot me and call the cops." He hooked a thumb at the end of the table. "Dumbshit over there was supposed to sneak the key back into your purse the next day, but he never showed up to get it back from me. I had to come over here and do it myself."

I thought about the night Ford brought me the sack of leftovers from Aunt Celia, and how he had knocked my bag to the floor. I'd discovered the house key off its ring when I was searching for a lighter, but didn't for one second think it had been removed. I cursed myself for being too drunk or too tired to see things for what they were.

"I've been sneaking in and moving your shit around for days," Ford went on, "trying to make you think the place was haunted. I only wanted to get you a little off-balance so everyone would believe you went crazy. I didn't think I would drive you completely over the edge." He pointed at the ceiling. "I was hiding in Josh's old room the day you bashed Rory's brains in. I couldn't hear very well, but it sounded like the devil himself was up there doing it. Shit, it scared me, and I don't scare easy. It took me a minute to figure out it was you making that weird voice." He cocked his head to squint at me. "You really went to town on him with that bed frame. What'd he do to piss you off like that?"

I glanced at Rory. "I caught him trying to frame me for murdering that reporter they found down the road from here. He was planting her phone in my attic. I didn't mean to hurt him like that. I just wanted to stop him and . . . it kinda got out of hand."

Ford laughed. "Man, you still don't get it, do ya, Dixie?" My head gave a quick, involuntary tremor. "I killed that reporter! It was all me. Rory didn't do shit."

I shook my head, confused. "Why would you kill Claire? You didn't even know her."

"I thought Rory might be trying to pull a fast one. I saw a text he sent to her, saying how he needed to talk to her right way, and how he had some information he thought she might be interested in. I knew he was talking about me. I wasn't sure if he had talked to her yet, so I thought, why not kill two birds with one stone. If he had talked to her already, then killing her solved that problem, and if he hadn't, I could use her murder to keep him in line. I planted the hammer and her phone in his house. Guess I didn't hide them good enough, huh?" He placed an innocent hand on his chest. "I didn't know he was gonna turn around and try to frame you. I have to admit, for a dumbass that was pretty smart."

"Why me? Why not frame you?" I asked. "That would be easy to do since you were the one who actually killed her."

Ford shrugged. "You'd hafta ask him, but I don't think he's talking much anymore." He scratched his chin with the tip of the knife. "He probably pussied out. I don't know why I was worried about him ratting me out to that reporter in the first place. He'd never go through with it. When push came to shove, Rory was pure chickenshit, just like your daddy here." He sighed as he looked between them. "I shoulda killed Rory that day with everybody else. If I knew he was going to go moving shit around after I left, like you and your momma, I would have. I told him to just leave you on the floor. You were happy as a pig in shit when I left. I didn't know what he'd done until Davis showed me those pictures. When I confronted Rory, he said that he put you back in your chair so you wouldn't roll around in the blood.

Then he had to move Deb closer to you since you were screaming and crying for her." He shook his head. "I told him not to touch anything and to wait ten minutes after I left before he called the cops, and he couldn't even fucking do that."

I glanced at Rory to shake my head. Those must have been the longest ten minutes of his life. I pictured him doodling a bloody smiley face on the wall to keep me entertained while he counted off six hundred Mississippis. *Don't cry. Mr. Smiley Face isn't crying, is he?* The thought broke my heart and I covered my mouth to keep from weeping.

"Don't go feeling sorry for him, Dixie," Ford said. "He's the whole reason Davis is dead. I'm still pissed about that."

"What are you talking about?" I asked.

"Davis might not have started asking all those questions if Rory woulda done like I said. Him moving y'all around was what got Davis suspicious. How'd blood get on the chair cushion behind Dixie? Why wasn't there any blood on the table under Deb? Why was the faucet left running in the sink?" Ford pointed at Rory. "'Cause dumbass over there had to clean himself up after touching everything, that's why. Then he forgets to turn the water off and slips and slides all the way out the door." He paused to laugh. "The water being on didn't mean nothin', but Davis thought it did, and I couldn't exactly tell him it was just a stupid-ass mistake."

"Why was Uncle Davis so convinced that my father was innocent in the first place?"

He shrugged. "He couldn't believe his brother would do something like that. In the beginning, everyone thought he was crazy for thinking Billy was innocent. Nobody took him seriously, 'cept maybe Charlene. And once he started drinking for a living, even she stopped paying him any mind. Davis let it go for a good long while. Years, in fact. Maybe a decade or more. I thought he'd finally come to terms with it. Or was too drunk to care anymore. But then he got his hands on that police file a few years back, and it all started up again. I told him to let it go, but he wouldn't listen. Shit. I didn't want to haveta kill Davis. He was my oldest friend, but—"

"Wait!" I grabbed the top of my head. "You killed Uncle Davis?"

"Well, I was back home asleep in bed when he dropped dead, but it was me who put the cocaine in his bottle of Wild Turkey." He waved off my horror. "His heart was about to give out anyways. I probably didn't speed it up more than a day or two, at most. I had to do it. He figured out what numbnuts over there wrote on the axe."

I thought back to what Mr. Cullins had told me about the missing pictures of the axe, and how an obscenity had been written across the blade in blood. A four-letter word that starts with *F. Yes, it was "fuck," Dixie. What other f-word is there?* But there was another four-letter obscenity that started with *F: Ford.*

"Davis wasn't a hundred percent sure what it said," Ford went on, "but all the sudden he wanted to show me the pictures. Like he wanted to gauge my reaction when I saw them. I tried to play it cool, but I couldn't keep my eyes from bugging out when I saw my name on that axe. It was clear as day to me, but I guess you had to know what it said to see it. Davis tried to play it cool, too, sayin' he was sorry if the pictures shocked me and all, but I knew he knew. I could see it in his eyes. I was about to go for him right then and there, but Charlene came out to the garage with our beers. I didn't wanna haveta kill her, too, that woulda been a fuckin' mess, so I snuck back later and spiked his whiskey."

My cell phone rang in the upstairs hallway.

"Oops!" Ford said, rolling his head to the ceiling. "Sorry, kids. Story time's over. We better get a move on."

FORD GAVE MY father's head a hard rap with the butt of the butcher knife as he skirted around him and crossed into the living room. I thought he was going upstairs to retrieve my phone, and nearly made

a grab for the axe across my father's lap, but shook my head in response to Vicki's encouraging nod as the music started up again in
the living room. Ford reentered the kitchen, dancing. Katie shrieked
with joy and began to bounce in her seat.

Ford tapped the flat of the blade on the palm of his hand to pon-
der, "Who should we kill first?" In a disturbing game of duck-duck-
goose, he tapped both of the boys on the top of their heads with the
knife as he circled the table. The baby turned to watched him pass
behind her, then cried out when he didn't include her in his game. He
pivoted back to give the top of her head a light tap, and then turned a
wickedly bright smile at me.

"Oh, I don't think I can wait," he said. "Let's kill Garrett."

"NO!" I screamed, getting to my knees. "Please!"

"Okay," Ford said with a shrug. "Blondie it is!" In one quick move,
Ford grabbed Vicki by the hair, yanked back her head, and stabbed
her in the stomach.

The boys went berserk, shouting incoherently as they stomped the
legs of their chairs against the floor.

"Are you two twins?" Ford asked conversationally, pointing the
knife between them as the blood of their mother dripped from the tip
of the blade. "I know you're not identical, but you look the same age
to me." The thumping of their chairs was joined by a high-pitched
mewling from the baby. "*WELL, ARE YOU?*" Ford screamed.

The sharp report of his voice was like a gunshot through the trees,
and the children fell silent as startled birds. Hitched cries caught in
the boys' throats as they nodded. The baby blinked her wide eyes
between Ford and her mother lying facedown on the table. She
sucked in an angry face, and then coughed it out in a harrowing
scream. She had had enough.

Ford pointed the knife at her. "Shut up!"

Katie threw her head back to avoid his command, then pressed to
a wobbling stand in her seat. For a horrible moment it looked as

though she was going to dive over the side. I was just about to shoot myself under the table to try and catch her when she turned and crawled across her tray. The legs of the high chair slammed back as she scuttled onto the table toward her lifeless mother.

Ford circled back, grabbed the baby by her britches, and walked her to the pantry like she was a stinky diaper. Her screams only became marginally less strident as he closed her inside. Ford gave a satisfied nod as he turned his attention, and the point of the knife, back to the boys.

"All right," he asked. "Who wants to be Eddie?"

"Don't hurt them!" I screamed, scrambling to my feet. Before I could launch myself fully, Ford turned and shoved me to the floor. My hand skidded through shards of broken glass as I slid into the refrigerator. A second later, Ford's boot drove into my stomach, and then into my throat. I only had a second to gasp before the flashlight—which I had retrieved from the attic and returned to its customary position back on top of the refrigerator—cracked me in the skull.

"Do that one more time, Dixie," Ford warned, kicking me in the shoulder twice more as I curled into a ball, "and everyone gets to be Eddie. Got it?"

I cradled my head in my hands to nod, wheezing for a sliver of air as a fire ignited in my belly.

Ford kicked the fair-haired boy's chair to turn him away from the table. The boy went wild, screaming so wide and loud that I thought his skin would rip from the duct tape. Lashing at Ford with the only weapon he had at his disposal, the boy reared back his head and threw all its weight forward. Ford saw it coming, and stepped quickly out of the way. Panic flashed across the boy's fierce expression as the chair began to overturn. He jarred his body to the side to avoid landing on his face, but smacked the floor mightily with his cheek, all the same.

"Now look what you did," Ford said. He lifted the boy by the wings of his elbows and sat him upright again. He grabbed the boy by his cheeks to stop his head from thrashing. "Calm down, kid! You'll be dead before you know it."

As Ford drew back the knife, the boy threw himself sideways and slammed back to the floor on his shoulder. Using his feet to kick in a circle, he spun his head around and scooched himself under the table.

"Come back here, you little shit!" Ford exclaimed.

As Ford bent to yank the boy out from under the table, I turned my head so I wouldn't have to watch him die, and my eyes landed on a far more disturbing sight.

My father's warped, atrophied body was quivering to a stand.

In a move I would have thought him incapable of, my skeleton of a father deadlifted the axe over his head. The duct tape strained to hold the instrument aloft by his twiggy wrists, but if anything were to tear free, it would be his hands. Teeth clenched with gritty pain, he glanced up as the axe handle vibrated over his head like an exposed electrical wire. Bolt after bolt coursed down the length of his body like a kite string. Agony tugged at his jaw. Neck tendons stood as rigid as drawn arrows. The old flannel shirt he was wearing rose up over a set of walking sticks that shot into the ten-gallon-hat holes of his not-so-tighty whities.

He swung a foot out by the ankle to take a wobbly step forward. He gave it a second, eyes flicking to see if a fall might follow, and then took another. Called to stand for the first time in over two decades, his legs bowed out at the knees like a wishbone about to snap. His hollowed eyes shifted to me for an instant, expressed a sort of profound adoration that took my breath away, and then pointed a fierce, blank hate at the hunched back of his brother-in-law, who was still trying to drag the boy out from under the table. Twisting slightly to take sidelong aim, my father inhaled a fortifying breath that filled his eyes with glee, and then swung the axe downward.

. . .

THE SHARP CHIN of the axe blade clipped Ford just above the waist-band of his Levi's. Ford threw his head back to yowl. The sound was wholly animalistic, wounded and savage. Though the force he was struck with was agonizingly weak and maddeningly slow, Ford dropped like a tranquilized bear. The chair the boy was tied to held for a second, and then smashed to the floor like a squashed spider.

With a second baleful cry—a tad more sanguine than the last—my father hoisted the axe to take another swing. If a determined look were enough to power your muscles, he might have been able to do it, but sadly, it wasn't. His body sputtered out the last of its gas as the handle of the axe cleared his shoulders. As the weight of the iron head began to take him in a slow cartwheel to the right, he wrenched his body left, overcompensated, and slammed sideward to the floor. The axe landed on its knob like a small-footed, large-billed bird that had been carrying my scarecrow father around as it searched for a place to alight. It swiveled its steely beak side to side as my father, suspended in a side plank, struggled to hold it vertical. But the head of the axe outweighed him, and began a slow plummet forward. I saw the target of the axe's bill a second too late. The sharp corner pecked the side of my ankle. White-hot pain shot through my body and out of the top of my head like a bottle rocket.

For as slow motion as my father's sprawl to the floor had seemed, it had occurred within the breath of Ford's initial shriek, and our wails joined in agonizing duet as I grabbed hold of my wounded an-kle. My father, capsized on the floor at my feet, let out a frustrated groan as he struggled to flip himself over.

"Billy boy!" Ford screamed with a laughing cry as he rolled off the crumpled boy beneath him and onto his back. "Oh, shit!" He reached his hand behind him and pulled back a handful of blood. "Fuck, that hurt!"

With his would-be executioner momentarily disabled, and his

twin brother crushed flat on the floor beneath him, Conner seized the opportunity and threw himself sideways at Ford. There was a dense, organic thud as their heads collided, and Ford went limp. Conner lifted his head to take another shot, but the second blow was not nearly as powerful, and only seemed to set Ford straight again. He let out a rejuvenated roar as he reached over his shoulder, grabbed Conner by the hair, and slammed his face into the floor. Blood spilled out from under Conner's nose like a stomped ketchup packet.

Ford let out a painful yowl to push to a stand, but quickly collapsed. "Goddamn it, Billy! I think you cut my fucking spinal cord." This seemed to tickle him more than worry him, because he laughed as he elbow-dragged his way to my father.

Pinned facedown to the floor by the scaffold of the axe, my father was helpless to fight off an attack, and simply lay there as Ford crawled onto his back. Setting the butcher knife on the back of my father's neck for safekeeping, Ford began to peel the tape away from his wrists. "Shit, I was just going to slit your throat again, but after that I think I'm going to have to chop you into little fucking pieces."

My father lay motionless, staring at me with one dazed eye as a bloody pool of drool formed under his open mouth.

I kicked at Ford with my foot. I tried to scream "Leave him alone!" but my crushed throat closed around the searing whisper as it burned up my esophagus. I scooched closer to give another kick, and connected with my heel.

Ford shook off the blow to his forehead and picked up the knife to point it at me. "The more pissed off I get, the worse he's gonna get it, got it?"

I looked down at my father, who blinked rapidly at me to cool it. I nodded as I slunk back, and Ford went back to working on the tape.

"I'm sorry, Dad," I said with a helpless cough. The kick I had taken to the throat was making speech an excruciating challenge. Each intake of breath came on a shard of pure agony, plunged deep into what

I was sure was a punctured lung, and then exhaled in a spray of fire. As I braced for my torturous next breath, trying to keep it as shallow as possible to prevent it from expanding my lungs, my father pulled his lips into an unreassuring half grin over a mouth full of bloody teeth. I could barely breathe, much less talk, but I needed to make sure my father knew that "I thought . . . you were dead."

"He will be in a second." Ford laughed.

"Fuck you, Ford!" I cried out reflexively, then grabbed my throat as it flared to a new height of pain.

"Maybe," Ford said. "We'll see how it goes."

THE KITCHEN SWEPT into a dreamy, tear-filled tidal wave of crashing panic that would soon drown all hope. If there was a way to stop Ford from killing us all, I couldn't see it, much less execute it to any degree of success. Any strength I had left was circling the drain; soon I wouldn't be able to do more than lie on my back to await my turn to die. But I couldn't just let Ford kill us all without a fight, no matter how much it hurt.

I ran my eyes around the room for some sort of weapon. All the knives were in drawers too far away. I might have been able to writhe across the floor to get to the cupboard that held my cast-iron skillet, but the weight of it might only anchor me farther away from Ford than I was now. As the baby screamed and rattled the pantry door, I turned to see that the flashlight lay just a few feet away. It was made of light, cheap plastic, but it was filled with two heavy D batteries. Slowly, I wiggled sideways, trying to seem as though I was just repositioning myself to get comfortable. Ford glanced up, but looked away as I moaned to settle back. I walked my fingers out blindly, feeling my way over an obstacle course of broken glass. I wanted to look to see if my hand was anywhere close to the flashlight, but I had to keep my eyes on Ford. Finally, my knuckles brushed against the smooth tube. In one amazingly quiet, and surprisingly quick, grab, I had it.

Glass fragments dug deep into my palm as I gripped the chute like a baton. Rearing back, I lunged forward to knock Ford into next Sunday, but didn't even come close. The swing was high and short, and whiffed right over his head. As I readjusted my grip to get a better swing, the flashlight slipped from my bleeding hand and fell to the floor.

Ford looked up at the sound, but when he saw my hands palms up at my sides, he went back to work on the tape, which really seemed to have him vexed and now required the use of his teeth.

With my one and only plan dashed, and all my energy expended, I laid my head back to cry. I couldn't stop what was happening any more than my father could stop it twenty-five years earlier. For being such a loser in life, when it came to death, Ford was the conquering hero.

I listened to the music drifting in from the other room, recognizing bits of lyric just before they were ground into static.

"... deserve ... long ... love ... time ..."

Eddie swam in from the depths of my tears and floated to a stop just a few feet behind Ford. Though his skin was frighteningly pale, almost translucent against the red of his sweater, his eyes were strong and clear and blue. Bluer than mine had been, I suppose, the day they freaked Ford into letting me live. Eddie's shoulders slumped as he dropped his head, which was squarely attached to his neck, to get a better look at his father on the floor at his feet. He bit his lip as if he were undecided, and then squatted down to place a hand over the old man's bony fingers. My father's eyes opened with a start. Straining to see as far left as his pinned neck would allow, he flexed his fingers in a desperate attempt to grasp for whatever was there. Giving them a gentle squeeze that went all the way through my father's liver-spotted skin, Eddie leaned over and kissed the top of his bald head. Tears stood bright in my father's eyes as his son withdrew his hand and stood. Eddie sighed and gave me a sweet grin, and then snapped his fingers.

At this inaudible beckon, not one that I could hear, at any rate, Michael crawled out from under the table to take Eddie's outstretched hand. Dishes vibrated as my mother traveled through the table to stand between her two youngest boys. Josh, entering from the living room, circled my father to stand shoulder to shoulder with them.

For a while they just stood there, staring down at Ford with a strange look on their faces. Too enlightened to be overtly hostile, they showed the malevolence they felt for the man who murdered them only in their tightly pressed lips.

"Help me," I pleaded, searching their blank expressions. "Please. He's going to kill us all."

Ford whipped around with the knife outstretched and stabbed Eddie right in the belly. Eddie made a grab for the blade as Ford swung the tip from Vicki's slumped body over the table to her sons lying in a haphazard pile on the floor and then back to me. "Who you talkin' to?"

I shook my head as Michael ineffectively slapped and kicked at Ford's back. A small fist burst through Ford's mouth as he said, "Stop fucking around!" He glanced nervously over his shoulder before dropping his head back to his work.

Eddie bolted around Ford and came to my side. He nodded at the flashlight. I shook my head to say I didn't have the strength, or the nerve, to hit Ford with it. As I blinked to tread consciousness, he took my hand and placed it over the stalk of the flashlight. A strange kinetic energy traveled up my arm. I clenched my fingers as they began to tingle. The muscles in my hand convulsed with a tremor that ached all the way up and into my armpit, deep in the tissue, as though an intravenous tube of adrenaline had been rammed under my skin and set off like a sprinkler. The rest of me still felt on the brink of death, but my hand felt freaking amazing. I almost let out a giddy laugh as I gripped the flashlight with my newly acquired strength.

I looked up at Eddie, who was grinning ear to ear. In hope that whatever power he had given me might take over the rest of my body in short order, I tried to pull my feet under me to stand. No doing. I could barely wiggle my toes, much less move both my legs. I shook my head at Eddie to say it wasn't working, just as Josh hurried to my side to take my left arm. A shock traveled through it, a revitalization, but it wasn't nearly as strong as the zap Eddie had laid on me.

Slipping under each of my arms for support, my two brothers began to lift me from the floor. Every part of me began to tremble, a zing of energy that nearly made me squeal with delight, but my legs still felt numb, and I feared I might fall if they were to let go. My sudden doubt seemed to cause their power to withdraw, and little by little, I began to sink slowly back to the floor. Josh and Eddie made sweeping grabs to keep me suspended. The jarring sensation of their hands passing through me, through bones and muscles and tendons, started a cramp in both my arms, and I felt the flashlight starting to slip from the stiff hook of my fingers. Glass chewed hungrily at palm as I readjusted my grip. I pressed my lips together to keep from screaming as the spasm converged on my chest. I couldn't take any more. I rolled my head to silently plead with Josh to put me down. For a second, he looked just as alarmed as I was, and then he smiled to nod my attention forward.

Quick as a flash, Michael leapfrogged over Ford and grabbed me by my right foot. A jolt of euphoric pain ran up my body and flashed through my head like a bolt of lightning. Ford looked up at the sound of my head colliding with the refrigerator, grabbing up the knife as he did.

"I told you to cut it—"

The toe of my shoe caught Ford under the chin as Michael bent my leg at the knee and slung my foot upward.

Ford tumbled off my father and onto his back. The butcher knife flew from his fingers and cut a trilling path across the floor. The tip of the blade came to a stop under Conner's cheek, a fraction of an inch from his eye.

Groaning in pain, Ford rolled onto his stomach, turned around, and crawled back onto my father's back. Using both hands, he yanked back on the axe handle to strip it from the scant pieces of tape still clinging to my father's wrists.

Eddie turned and grabbed my arm to swing the flashlight at Ford's head, but as it came forward, it went flying across the room and smashed into the dry rack next to the sink.

Ford ducked as a fork flipped up and bounced off his shoulder, then let out an elated yip as the left end of the axe handle sprang free. Spider quick, his fingers scurried down the stalk of wood to get busy on freeing the business end of the axe. With one of his hands now unimpeded, my father grabbed Ford by the wrist and pulled his hand toward his gnashing teeth. He got in one good bite before an elbow to the head knocked him out cold.

In a flash, my mother had me by the waist, and together with her sons, they flung me across the floor like a human sled. Conner's eyes grew wide as I barreled at him at breakneck speed. A head-on collision might do just that, I thought, and with not a second to spare, I slammed the rubber toes of my sneakers into the floor. I came to a shuddering stop an inch from Conner's grimacing face. He opened his eyes to glance nervously down as I eased the knife out from under his cheek.

Not wanting a repeat of the flashlight, I gripped the hilt of the butcher knife as tight as I could and prepared myself to be spun and flung in the other direction.

Nothing happened.

For a second, I thought that that was it. My family had either left me to see this through on my own or had done all they could. As I glanced over my shoulder to see if they were still with me, something caught my eye under the far side of the table. Garrett! Hands taped behind his back, he was on his knees with his butt in the air, writhing like crazy to pick himself off the floor. Our eyes met for a second just before he launched himself upward. But as his head lifted out of my field of vision, I saw panic pull his eyes wide. I instantly saw the problem. His ankles were also bound together with tape. As he lunged forward to hop his feet under him, he faltered headfirst into the wall and smacked to the floor on his chin.

The sound of Garrett's sprawling collapse turned Ford's head, but he saw me coming out of the corner of his eye. With half the axe still taped down, Ford grabbed my father by the few hairs he had left on the back of his head, and wrenched his scrawny neck back. He got a cupped hand under my father's chin just as my mother got the butcher knife in my hand to his throat.

"Let him go," I whispered through a cough, wishing the power my family had given me extended to my voice.

"I'll snap his neck, Dixie! Swear to god, I will!"

"Do it and I'll cut your throat," I rasped.

Ford glanced down at the knife vibrating in my hand like the blade of a friction saw and held his up in surrender. "Okay. Take it easy. You win."

"*Take it easy?*" I scarcely screamed as fire lit up my throat. My mother urged my hand forward, forcing the blade steady as it creased his skin, firm and sure, but careful not to draw blood. I glanced up at her and she smiled weakly, beginning to flicker in and out of focus. This was our moment, but I was the one who needed to speak for us, to reclaim our destiny. It hurt so badly to talk, but I pressed on to have my say . . . our say: "You don't deserve to get off easy. We're going to fucking kill you, you fucking psycho."

"We?" Ford chuckled, relaxing somewhat as my lip quivered up a steady stream of tears. "Who? You and your weak-ass daddy here?" He glanced down. "I don't think Billy's in any condition to help you, Dixie, but okay. Go ahead." He lifted his chin. "Cut my throat." As he closed his eyes to goad me, my mother released my hand. I instantly felt weakened, and the blade lagged slightly away. Ford opened one eye to peek down. "Go on. Do it!"

My mother stepped behind Ford to shake her head. I wasn't sure if she was telling me not to kill him or saying that this was my decision to make and she couldn't offer an opinion in the matter.

I bit my lip, unsure what to do. Anything I did required me to breathe, which seemed next to impossible. I hiccupped a few small breaths, just enough to keep me from passing out, and a barrage of tiny bullets hit my lungs.

"What are you waiting for?" Ford sneered. "KILL ME!"

As an urgent pounding came from the front door, my family began to vanish. Eddie took Michael by the hand and walked him out of the kitchen through the dishwasher. Josh winked out after a quick wave. The last to remain was my mother, flickering and lovely. She forced a gentle smile through a look of unbearable sadness, then blew me a kiss as she swirled away.

Mr. Cullins's voice cut through an eerie silence as the music in the living room abruptly stopped. "Dixie! Dixie!"

The doors to the pantry rattled a new level of frustration from the baby trapped inside.

Dingle let out a sharp bark.

"Might as well go let him in," Ford jeered nastily. "You're not gonna kill me and you know it."

I flinched as Mr. Cullins threw his weight against the front door. My fingers were numb under the sting of glass in my palm. Blood dripped down my wrist in a maddening tickle. I relaxed my grip to get a new one, but I couldn't bear the pain it caused. Without the strength of Eddie or my mother to guide it, my hand had reverted back to its formerly weakened state, and began to shake.

Ford's laugh was victorious. "You can't do it! You don't have what it takes to cut a man's throat, little girl. It's not as easy as you think.

You have to put some effort into it. You gotta cut through all those tendons and cartilage and shit. It's not like slicing up a tomato. My skin's tough!"

I glanced down at the back of my father's drooping head, the long gray hairs sweated to his frail neck, the small beetle crawling out from under the dirty collar of a dead bum's flannel shirt, and felt a debilitating sadness come over me. He was my father. But I didn't know him. He hadn't raised me. He hadn't taken me to school, or taught me how to tie my shoes, or helped me with my math home-work. Ford had done all those things. Not well, and not without some yelling, but he had done them. Ford was more father to me than Wil-liam Wheeler ever was. Despite all the fighting and insults, the mul-titude of disappointments, a part of me had once cared for Ford. Like a junkyard dog that didn't know any better, Ford made you love him even after he nipped your hand and ran away for the umpteenth time. But now, as I stared at the smug look on his grotesquely charred face, the mood of his scar currently as black as his soul, I hated him with every drop of blood in my body.

But could I kill him?

As the front door started to splinter under Mr. Cullins's shoulder, fear and indecision wavered through my hand and agitated the knife. A trickle of blood trolled across the edge of the blade and down Ford's neck.

"Uh-oh!" He laughed, glancing down. "Careful now. I think you cut me."

"Shut up," I growled through a stream of tears.

With the sound of his rescue ripping its way into the house, Ford's laughter gained confidence.

"You want to do it so bad, doncha, Dix?" he jeered. "You got that same look in your eye as your momma had. She had her chance, you know. She got a knife, too. But she hesitated, and I chopped it right out of her hands!" He pressed his face close to mine, digging the blade into the stubbled skin of his throat. "You might think you want to kill me, Dixie. Hell, you might even be mad or scared enough to try. But until you look someone in the eye, you can't know what it feels like to end a life. Murder takes a kind of evil you don't have in you . . . *Baby Blue*."

He was right. I didn't have that kind of evil in me. That part of me was gone. But I didn't need to be evil to make Ford pay for what he did to my family. In fact, evil wouldn't do at all. This required something far more powerful than mindless, dispassionate evil. The strength I required had to come from the heart. What I needed was . . . *rage*. Heated and focused, and just a little insane. And as Ford taunted me with his jutting throat, daring me to take from him what he so needlessly had taken from my family, I felt it rise up in me. I didn't even have to step aside to allow it to take me over. It was already there. I had it in me.

Ford's eyes widened as my quivering lip steadied, my breathing slowed, and my tears turned to an ice-cold stare. The blade of the knife joggled as he took a nervous swallow.

"Oh, I have it in me," I said, relishing the pain as I tightened my grip around the knife. "This is for my family, you fucking asshole."

The smile that cut across my face felt almost as deliciously deep as the cut I made across his throat.

EPILOGUE

I have never been able to serve breakfast to my children at the table in our kitchen. I'm not worried that I might rummage through the utensil drawer for a knife to cut their throats with, or break a bottle of orange juice to work its jagged bottom into their big, beautiful eyes; I just don't like that those ideas always seem to spring to mind as I stir the oatmeal to keep it from lumping.

Garrett doesn't mind eating off a TV tray in the living room, and the boys—*my* boys, William and Davis, four and almost three, respectively—love to eat cereal sitting on the floor before their morning cartoons. I will have to use the high chair again when the little bundle of joy in my stomach becomes a cordless baby, but once Garrett wheels it into the living room, it won't bother me as much.

Once I killed the monster that killed my family, I wasn't afraid to start one of my own. Though bad things happen to children all the time, and you can't always keep them safe, I thought I might have a keener eye for danger than most, and decided to chance it. Turns out, I wanted a family more than anything. Not to replace the one I lost, but to express all the love I never got to share: lavishing them with kisses, taking pride in their accomplishments, rejoicing as they grow to men. Though I think our next child might be a girl. Leah. Garrett thinks it's too soon to consider the sex of our next little darling, but I've heard him whisper that name to my stomach as he rests an ear upon it.

We have all new furniture now, though I did keep the bunk beds and the rocking chair. The seascape painting still hangs over the couch—mostly because I had done such a fine job of nailing it back to the wall, it would take a demolition team to remove it—and there are a few other odds and ends that I couldn't bear to part with. It broke my heart to throw most of their stuff away, but vanquishing the funky odor took a process of elimination. Many a suspect thing had to go. The scent sometimes resurfaces on rainy days. Maybe the afghan . . .

We didn't move from my childhood home for several reasons: I got pregnant—not that that meant we couldn't move; I just had such terrible morning sickness I didn't want to be more than five feet from my bathroom, which was attached to the house. And since the property had been further stigmatized by two more dead bodies—one of whom was an axe-murdering son of a bitch and would most likely be an even more vicious ghost—we figured no one besides us would ever want to live there. Besides, we like the neighborhood—even if Vicki feels she can walk in my back door without knocking anytime she wants.

I thoroughly expected Vicki to hold nearly getting stabbed to death in my kitchen against me, but it didn't seem to upset our friendship in the least. Nearly dying might leave a horrible scar, but it also leaves you with a really good story to tell, which Vicki does with great enthusiasm at neighborhood dinner parties. Nick will roll his eyes good-naturedly when he hears her opening segue, "Talk about [fill in the blank: stubbing your toe, morning traffic, fly-fishing . . .], did I ever tell you about . . . ," but I can sense the unease as he turns from being reminded, once again, of how painfully close he came to losing his wife and children.

He and Garrett are in the midst of building us a new shed. Not one big enough for Garrett's longed-for boat, but that might come in time. Our boys absolutely adore Katie—who tolerates them well enough for a seven-year-old—and make a huge stink when I tell them she isn't old enough to babysit yet. Conner and Liam, Vicki and Nick's fair-headed son, used to drag their friends by to show off the kitchen where it "went down" and to point out "the lady" who cut that "dude's throat." "She had to do it," they had told the police. "He was about to chop that old guy's head off."

Though I thought we had said our final good-byes that day, I saw Eddie dashing through the backyard not one week later. I was just home from the hospital and thought he might have been a Percocet-induced delusion, but when I found my mother sitting at the table when I came down to get a drink of water, I knew they had never really left me. One more reason not to move. If we did, they might not be able to come along. This house was our connection, and I was as bound to it as they were.

Oddly, my mother came less frequently once I had a baby of my own to care for. Maybe she didn't want to intrude, or have me think she doubted my ability by looking over my shoulder. Either way, I haven't seen her in almost four years, though I sometimes get a whiff of her perfume as I bandage a scraped knee or take a temperature in the wee hours of the morning.

Michael and Eddie are a regular presence, though. They just love to chase the boys around the backyard. I sometimes have to knock on the window to stop Michael from spinning out of control. What's the fun of tag if you can never tag anyone? William and Davis will stop playing to look confusedly at me through the window, but once I wave, they'll run off, perhaps in search of the boy in the red sweater scampering about the woods. Man, that kid's fast.

And though this Thanksgiving is also the thirtieth anniversary of my family's murder, we are all in good spirits. Aunt Celia and Mr. Cullins are coming over later for Thanksgiving dinner. Married three years now, they still act like they're on their honeymoon. I've already set a dish of water on the back patio for Dingle.

Aunt Celia was almost dead when we found her. Ford might have been a whiz with an axe, but he wasn't as proficient with a hammer— yes, *the* hammer, much to Garrett's dismay—and the whack he gave Aunt Celia as she crept into the basement to find my father tied to a support beam knocked her the rest of the way down the stairs and broke her left leg in two places, but failed to kill her. We figured that since she had chased a couple of sleeping pills with close to a pint of NyQuil, if Ford had checked her for a pulse, it would have been too woozy to detect. She spent a week in the hospital, and three more home in bed. And though she may always walk with a limp, that's okay; she has Mr. Cullins to lean on now.

I came clean about beating Rory to a pulp in my attic, but served no jail time. Since Vicki had witnessed Ford cut Rory's throat and stab him multiple times in the back, his prior injuries seemed less dire and somewhat irrelevant, or so the judge who adjudicated my case concluded. At the advice of my lawyer, another friend of Mr. Cullins, I waived my right to trial and pled guilty to second-degree assault. I think the judge, also a friend of Mr. Cullins, couldn't bring himself to send Baby Blue to prison, though the crowd outside the courthouse, with their WE LOVE YOU BABY BLUE and LET DIXIE GO signs, probably had some influence over his decision. It seemed I had suffered enough.

Since Ford had confessed to the murder of Claire Reynolds, I cleared myself of any involvement in her disappearance and subsequent death. Though the mystery of how she went from sitting on my couch to lying in disarray in the woods died with Ford, I did find her phone. It was buttoned down in the front pocket of the bum's flannel shirt my father was wearing. I spotted it as I rolled him over to tend to his injuries while Mr. Cullins was calling for emergency assistance. Whether or not it was Claire's phone I heard in the background when I was speaking to Ford, it was as dead as he was when I slipped it from the back pocket of my jeans in the bathroom of my hospital room the next day. Once I recharged it, I deleted the recording of my interview, reset it to the original factory settings, wiped off my fingerprints, and chucked it into the woods after I stopped off for a slice of Pronto's Pizza. As far as I know, it has never been found.

Even though Erin's accidental death was entirely my fault, I let the newspapers call it murder and lay it six feet under at Rory's feet. I wrote several anonymous letters to her mother, though, all of which contained my sincerest apologies and most heartfelt remorse for my involvement in her daughter's death, and all of which I promptly deleted from my laptop upon completion. What would be the point of confessing? It wouldn't bring Erin back. And the next judge I faced might not be a friend of Mr. Cullins, or be inclined to let Baby Blue go, even if she was an expectant mother. And since Erin's family now had Rory to level their pain and anger at, I thought it rather cruel to take that from them. And really, taking the blame was the least Rory could do for me. After everything he did—allowing Ford to get away with killing my family, standing by while my father took the rap, helping Ford in his scheme to drive me to suicide, and trying to frame me for Claire's murder—I was pretty sure he deserved it. Though sometimes, when I'm in the linen closet, I'll stop what I'm doing to look up, take a moment to remember the man I once idolized. Every so often I'll hear laughing whispers floating around the attic, shushing a private joke as it drifts like smoke out the vent on the back wall. Josh is such a forgiving spirit, a friend for life and far beyond. Maybe in time I will be able to forgive Rory, too. After all, he was one of us, a victim of Ford's, as mortally betrayed as anyone.

It has taken a while, but I have forgiven that girl in a Happy Bunny T-shirt who didn't quite comprehend the enduring pain of her actions, though I sometimes wonder if she hadn't known better. If killing Leah was so merciful, then why did I conjure up an evil spirit to do my dirty work? Just because Leah wanted to die, and was destined to die no matter how events unfolded, doesn't excuse what happened. I should have seen that she wasn't in her right mind that day. That pain had pushed her, and pulled me, into doing something we both regretted the minute it was over. I trust that Garrett will never tell Aunt Celia that I had been Leah's angel of mercy, though I one day plan to tell her myself. Just not when she seems so happy, which I hope will never end. I look forward to Leah's rebirth every spring, a flower outside the window to everyone's eyes but my own.

My father, cleared of any and all wrongdoing, is no longer remanded to Allied Stare Hospital, but decided to stay on as a voluntary patient. I was a little disappointed; I'd wanted him to live with us. But the level of care he requires is way beyond our abilities. Maybe in time. I visit him twice a week, and take the boys to see him every other weekend. He will never be able to speak, but physical therapy has unclenched his hand well enough to hold a pen. He's learning to write again, hard slashing letters that take a while to decipher, but little by little, he's making progress. He surprised me with a handwritten note the last time I visited: "I love you!!!"

Three exclamation points!!!

I no longer think of myself as Baby Blue. She was a desolate child, ruled by the anger and pain of a catastrophe that was beyond her understanding, the insurmountable reach of her high chair tray. I tucked her away with the rest of the horrible pictures of that day. Her haunting tune calls to me no more. I deleted the song from my playlist, and change the station if it comes on the radio, which is rare. It's time to choose my own theme music, a song that can define my life, and what I have gone through, and the woman I have become. But I haven't gotten here alone. Others paved the way. Thin bodies lie in the dirt behind me, propelling me along like railway ties. They gave their lives, their happily-ever-afters, so I could have that and so much more. Since I cannot speak for them, or even of them, in some cases, the song needs to pay them homage, let their silenced voices sing, if only to my ears alone. I think they would want me to live well in their stead, let my hair down and dance until I can dance no more, especially Leah.

So far, nothing I've downloaded strikes the right chord with me. They're either way too hokey or a little frantic, excruciatingly long or impossible to sing to. I don't necessarily have to love it, but it can't be just any old song, either. The lyrics have to stand the test of time. Today through the hereafter, the melody must pick me up when I'm feeling down, bring on the tears when I need a good cry, lull me to sleep when my mind thinks otherwise, and somehow get me through one more load of laundry. Naturally, it has to be somewhat haunting, and just a little bit wicked. Oh—"Rhiannon"!

That would be so cool.

Acknowledgments

My love of books was a gift to me from my parents. From an early age, my mother instilled in me the desire to read, reading aloud to me until I could read quietly to myself. Then, through his own aspirations, my father imparted the desire to create and write stories of my own. Though my father is no longer with us, I know that he would be extremely gratified to learn that our dreams have come true. My mother, who reads a book a day, has been my greatest champion. Without her generosity and unflinching support, I would still be waiting for someday to come. I am so grateful to have been raised in a home where the bookshelves were always full and our minds were always off on an adventure.

Thank you to my wonderful agent, Zoe Sandler at ICM, for taking a chance on me. Her unfailing enthusiasm and tireless efforts to find my story a home kept me driven and positive in the face of rejection.

Thank you to my brilliant editor, Stephanie Kelly at Dutton, for her passion, spot-on insights, and dedication. Her ability to understand the storyline and characters as well as, if not better than, myself was truly astonishing.

Thank you to Kris Spisak for her astute critique and perceptive questions while editing the first draft of my manuscript, they sent me down all the right roads.

A special thanks to my husband, James Vandelly, for his insightful suggestions and for being the best spellchecker a girl could ever have. Also, thanks to my sister, Celine Thompson, for her help with proofreading and for being the first person to call me her "favorite author."

Thanks to Beth Girone for all her support and for taking the one truly great picture of me.

Thank you to all my friends and family who have supported, encouraged, and cheered me on throughout this process. When I told you I was going to cash it all in and be an unemployed writer for the time being, you didn't even flinch.

About the Author

T. Marie Vandelly has wanted to write her entire life but due to a career change has only recently been granted the freedom to pursue her dream full-time. She lives on Gwynn's Island, off the Chesapeake Bay, with her husband and their two dogs. *Theme Music* is her first novel.